"YOU'RE SAYING I'M USING YOU?"

"That's exactly what I'm saying. You want me to fill you in on everyone's background, reveal their secrets if I know any. You want to pry into everyone's personal life, to get at *the truth*. Then you file your little report, you'll pack your bags and leave us. If some of us are shattered by your probing, well, it's all in a day's work."

Ben's eyes were a stormy gray. "That's a damn lie. I don't deliberately hurt people. And I can do my job just fine alone. I have for years."

The parking lot was nearly deserted, and the darkening sky hinted at a summer storm brewing. For some utterly stupid reason, Maggie wanted to believe him. "If that's so, if you work best alone, then why did you invite me to tag along? I know I asked to go, but you could have easily refused."

"I could have, yeah." He stepped closer, backing her up against his Jeep. "Maybe I have another reason, a personal one." With that, he lowered his head and took her mouth in a kiss . . .

Please turn the page for critical praise of Pat Warren . . .

Praise for Pat Warren and Her Award-winning Novels

"From page one, drama and mystery hang over your head, pressing you onward. *Beholden*'s superb visual intensity also helps make this a 'frightfully good' read."
—Affaire de Coeur

"Pat Warren is in top form with this fast-paced and exhilarating novel. *Beholden* is great entertainment."
—Romantic Times

"[A] moving novel featuring timely plotting, timeless romance, well-realized characters, and plenty of suspense."
—The Paperback Forum on *Forbidden*

"[A] well-written and emotionally fulfilling story that will warm your heart."
—Rendezvous on *Forbidden*

"Captures the drama, action, and passion that one has come to associate with the Montana Maverick series."
—Affaire de Coeur on *Outlaw Lovers*

"Ms. Warren melds chilling suspense and passionate romance into a marvelous amalgam of reading pleasure."
—Romantic Times on *Till Death Do Us Part*

No Regrets

Also by Pat Warren

Forbidden

Beholden

Published by
WARNER BOOKS

PAT WARREN

NO REGRETS

WARNER BOOKS

A Time Warner Company

WARNER BOOKS EDITION

Copyright © 1997 by Pat Warren
All rights reserved.

Cover design by Diane Luger

Warner Books, Inc.
1271 Avenue of the Americas
New York, NY 10020

Visit our Web site at
http://warnerbooks.com

Ⓦ A Time Warner Company

Printed in the United States of America

First Printing: October, 1997

10 9 8 7 6 5 4 3 2 1

This book is dedicated with warm affection to
Louise Lee for years of friendship—and for being
my strength and salvation in Jamaica in May, 1965.

ACKNOWLEDGMENTS

My sincere thanks to William Crook, retired law enforcement officer and currently Investigative Claims Officer for Metropolitan Insurance, whose advice on internal insurance procedures and on methods of insurance investigation were invaluable.

I'd also like to thank Joe Peres, a young man I've known since he was born, whose knowledge of Michigan's Upper Peninsula filled in the gaps where my memory failed.

Again, I need to thank Mark Ruffennach, Community Affairs Unit, Scottsdale Police Department, for answering my many questions on police procedure and protocol.

And finally, my heartfelt thanks to Ray Geiger, retired from Metropolitan Life Insurance, for patiently walking me through the complex world of insurance, and for reading all my books!

In all cases, I followed their recommendations as closely as fiction would allow. If there are errors, they are mine.

Prologue

The house was the last one on a dead-end street that backed up to a wooded section. A cold March wind whipped at Reed Lang's carefully dyed black hair as he fumbled in his pocket for the key. Vacant homes were always such a pain to show. He especially hated going out on a Friday evening with a light snow falling. Still, business was slow in the winter and he couldn't afford to pass up a possible sale.

Inside, it was eerily silent and dark, but fairly warm. The Miller place had been empty since before Christmas, but he'd made sure the furnace was left on so the pipes wouldn't freeze and burst. Stuffing his gloves into his coat pocket, Reed walked around turning on lamps. He'd also advised the owners to leave some furniture until a sale was completed. Empty places didn't look inviting. People had no imagination. Reed ought to know; he'd been dealing with buyers and sellers for twenty-five years.

Stroking his mustache, he checked all the rooms, then returned to the front, satisfied that he'd done all he could until the prospect arrived.

If the prospect arrived. No-shows were a fact of life for realtors. The voice on the phone asking to see the house just as he'd been about to lock up and leave his office had been raspy but impatient, so maybe he'd luck out. Jay Marsh, or perhaps J. Marsh, the caller had said. Reed had never heard the name before.

He didn't list many homes in Gwinn, some twenty miles north of the small town of Riverview in Michigan's Upper Peninsula where he'd lived and worked most of his life. The Millers were friends, which was why he'd agreed to help them sell. Peering out the front window, he wished Marsh would hurry.

The heat came on and the house moaned and creaked like Reed's knees as he bent to pick up a flyer he'd overlooked that someone had shoved through the mail slot. Fifty-four wasn't all that old, he maintained, straightening. He was in pretty decent shape and could still get into his college gym shorts, which was more than he could say for some of the friends with whom he'd gone to Northern Michigan University. Maybe because he'd never married and most of them had. Women and home cooking made a man soft.

He'd thought about marriage last year, had even looked at rings. Nancy had made him feel handsome, virile. But his friend, Jack Spencer, had quietly looked into her background. The things he'd discovered had changed Reed's mind.

The sound of a car approaching had him hurrying to open the door. A dark sedan stopped in front instead of pulling behind Reed's Buick parked in the driveway. He stood watching as the driver, wearing a long, hooded coat, got out of the car and started toward the house. The snow was coming down harder now.

Reed's face registered his best salesman's smile. "You must be Jay Marsh. I wasn't sure you'd find the place. Kind of off the beaten path." He held out his hand. "Reed Lang."

Silently, the prospect offered a gloved hand for a quick shake, then stepped inside past Reed.

Always a pro, Reed handed over an information flyer on the house and began his pitch as he led the way from room to room, pointing out the virtues and advantages of the house. "The appliances all remain," he said as they came to the kitchen. "The roof's new and so's the furnace." In the over-head light, he peered at Marsh, trying to see past the folds of the hood at the face oddly averted. "Are you from around here?"

The prospect ignored the question. "I'd like to see the basement." The voice was low, raspy.

"Sure." As a realtor, Reed had run across a lot of strange ducks over the years. This was just another one to contend with. If the buyer's money was green, why should he care? He opened the basement door and flipped on the light switch. "Follow me and hold on. The stairs are kind of steep."

Reed was on the third step when he felt a thick gloved hand at his back. He turned, but not quickly enough. A hard shove followed and suddenly, he lost his footing. One hand groped blindly for the railing that was just out of reach, the other flailing helplessly as he fell. The scream from his throat echoed in the dank, empty basement, then died out as Reed Lang landed headfirst on the solid cement floor.

The prospect carefully climbed down the steps, removing one glove. Two fingers pressed to Reed's throat confirmed that he was dead. It took a moment longer to find the note in his coat pocket, the one that read: J. Marsh, Miller house, 7:00 P.M.

The smile was slow in coming. "Chalk up one more."

Heavy footsteps trudged back upstairs while the glove was replaced. It took only a minute or two to turn off all the lights. The lock clicked as the front door closed. The snow was coming down heavily now, covering up the footsteps.

The house was once more silent.

Chapter One

It was too nice a day for a funeral, Maggie Spencer thought. The sky was an incredible blue with a smattering of white puffy clouds. Bluejays and wrens and a few cardinals chirped and chattered in the nearby trees and a freshwater stream propelled by a distant waterfall raced over sandstone rocks just yards away. A warm breeze caressed her cheeks. It wasn't right. Burials should be under gloomy skies with thunder drowning out the sounds of weeping and rain drenching the mourners.

And there were plenty of mourners standing on Spencer's hill this first day of June. Father Arthur Crispin stood at the head of the closed casket bearing the remains of her father, his solemn voice informing them that Jack Spencer was now in a far better place. Maggie could almost hear what Dad would say to that. Hogwash!

To her father, no place in heaven or on earth was better than his home, the acreage he'd bought and the house he'd built for his high school sweetheart who'd become his bride. That was why Maggie had insisted he be buried right here on the land he loved. The priest had tried to persuade her otherwise, tried to shift her attention to the small Catholic cemetery. But Maggie wouldn't budge. After all, no one knew her father better than she.

Dad hadn't been much of a churchgoer, but he'd loved people. He'd be pleased at the turnout today, she mused. Neighbors and friends would soon mingle in the house after the service, eating the casseroles and cakes people had contributed, and the other dishes Fiona Tracy had prepared. The tall Irish woman who'd kept house for the Spencers for nearly thirty years took comfort in rituals such as feeding the mourners. Personally, Maggie thought she'd rather have a root canal than spend the next few hours listening to "Jack stories." But there was nowhere to hide.

There'd be endless tears and toasting and reminiscing. She badly wanted everyone to go home so she could be alone with this brand new sorrow. But Dad would have wanted her to be hospitable. Jack Spencer had always loved a good party. A sob caught in Maggie's throat as she realized she'd never again see her father hold up a frosty mug of beer, give her a smile and a wink, then slowly drain the pint.

Standing next to her, Fiona slipped an arm across Maggie's slender shoulders. "There, there, dear. Jack would hate to see you carrying on, and that's a fact. He's with God and the angels now." She gave Maggie's arm a squeeze before turning back toward the priest. Fiona's own grief was just as real, just as strong as his daughter's, for she'd loved the man they were burying today. Loved him in her silent heart, a love she deeply regretted not revealing to Jack. She'd put off telling him, waiting for just the right moment. Suddenly now, they'd run out of time.

Maggie brushed back strands of blond hair shifting in the summer wind. She didn't want her father to be with the angels just yet. Dear Lord, he was only fifty-four with so much living ahead. How had this happened?

Who would give her away should she ever walk down that center aisle? Who would spoil the children she might one day have? Who would take her snowmobiling when she came to visit in the winter or coax her to play tennis on her summer trips? Who would phone her at her New York apartment and say, 'Aren't you tired of the Big Apple yet, Maggie, my girl? Come on home where you belong.'

A forsythia along the fence line was a riot of yellow near the spot Maggie had picked out for her father's final resting place, and opposite a deep purple lilac bush was budding. A robin cocked its head from a branch of the old maple where the weathered swing Jack had put up years ago still hung. Memories dating back to her childhood crowded in on her and she blinked back a fresh rush of tears.

If only she'd done as Dad had asked months ago when he'd started calling more frequently, urging her to return if only for a short visit. But her own problems had weighed heavily on her, so she'd put him off. Maggie swallowed around a lump of regret. She couldn't have prevented the accident that had killed Jack Spencer, but she could have spent some time with him before he was taken from her so unexpectedly, so violently. Selfish. Why had she been so selfish?

As Father Crispin's voice droned on, she gazed out at the land Dad had loved too much to ever leave. A silverfish jumped high above the clear creek, then dove back under. Upstream, the splash of the waterfall could be heard. The tall white pines, the cedar and birch along the perimeter of Spencer land, most planted by Jack himself, formed a natural fence. In the distance a loon sang out its mournful tune.

She'd looked out on the scene countless times, yet saw it all again now, through her father's eyes. 'I just think it's so beautiful up here, honey,' Dad used to say, 'or is it because I'm a Michiganer? I'd sooner die than leave here.' And, except for a stint in the navy, he never had left the Upper

Peninsula of the state he loved, not even once to visit her in New York.

As Jack had loved Riverview, so the town loved him. Most anyone who could walk or crawl was here, standing on Spencer's hill, eyes damp and hearts heavy. Her father had known every one of them, gone to school with many, attended their weddings, held their babies, and built most of their homes over the years.

Because her mother had died young and they'd had no family to speak of, Dad's boyhood friends had become like family. Behind dark sunglasses, Maggie's blue eyes moved through the crowd, seeking comfort in familiar faces. They'd changed, of course, as had she. Although she'd visited as often as her work permitted, six years had passed since she'd left.

It seemed a lifetime ago.

Mr. McCauley from the mortuary instructed his men to remove and fold the flag draped over the coffin. Maggie had arrived the day before yesterday on an early-morning flight from New York, and been faced with the necessity of picking out clothes and a casket for her father's burial. How ironic, Maggie thought. It had taken a personal crisis of her own for her to decide to visit Dad. He'd been so elated when she'd called to tell him she was coming. Then, the night she was packing, the phone had rung just as she'd snapped shut her suitcase. Fiona's voice had trembled with tears as she'd told Maggie about Jack's accident. The shock had sent her reeling. She still hadn't recovered.

Since her mother's death when she'd been twelve, she and Jack, who'd never remarried, had been very close. Nearly a thousand miles of distance hadn't weakened their strong bond. She loved him dearly. And now, she'd never again be able to tell him. As Mr. McCauley handed the tri-folded flag to Maggie, she found she was unable to speak, could only nod. She was grateful for Fiona's steady arm.

Maggie felt dozens of eyes on her and prayed she could stay in control until she got back to the house, back to her old room and eventually some privacy.

He stood by a split birch, quietly observing the proceedings. He'd been in Riverview only two days, yet already he knew most of the players by name, the rest by sight. But he stayed in the background, for he knew he was a stranger, and outsiders in small towns were usually regarded with distrust and curiosity.

Ben Whalen was used to being a stranger in a new town. Insurance investigators traveled to many cities, stayed only long enough to get some answers, then moved on. Some visits lasted a few days, the occasional one several weeks. Most investigators hated life on the road, never being able to stay in one place for the time it took to make permanent friends or put down roots. Ben liked it just fine.

A tall man with wide shoulders and coal-black hair that just brushed the collar of his white shirt, Ben had the rugged looks of an outdoorsman, a choice he much preferred over desk duty. He carried a small scar in his left eyebrow, a reminder of his days as an undercover cop and the young punk who'd come close to blinding him. Too damn close. Beneath somewhat shaggy brows, he had watchful gray eyes that missed very little. Right now, they settled on the heir apparent, Maggie Spencer, Jack's daughter.

At Rosie's Diner where he'd had breakfast the last two mornings, much of the talk swirled around the builder's terrible accident, and the rest involved Maggie. Maggie who'd been the apple of her father's eye, the high school homecoming queen and valedictorian of her Northern Michigan University graduating class. To a person, the locals he'd overheard liked and admired Maggie, but wished she hadn't chosen to leave Riverview and move away. Jack hadn't been the same since, they all agreed.

Why had she left? Ben wondered, noticing the erect way she held herself, the way she chose to hide behind those oversize sunglasses. Had it been a broken love affair, a quarrel with Daddy dearest, or just a bit of the wanderlust? Riverview seemed like a nice enough town, as small places went. But it hadn't taken him long to discover that, other than working for her father's construction company or any one of a dozen other small businesses, a young college graduate didn't have many career options here.

Or maybe Maggie Spencer had realized she didn't belong here. She looked way too sophisticated for Riverview in her smart black suit, the white silk blouse, the expensive cut of all that lush blond hair just brushing her shoulders. She looked exactly like what the report he'd read on her said she was: a New Yorker with a high-profile job with Innovations, a big PR firm. All that aside, she seemed to be genuinely grieving, gripping the arm of the older woman beside her, her slender hands shaking slightly.

What she didn't seem like was a young woman who'd hire someone to push her daddy off the second-story framework of a house he'd been inspecting at dusk with not another soul around. Had Jack gotten careless or become dizzy and fallen? Or had someone helped him along to his great reward? It was Ben's job to find out and primary beneficiaries were always suspect, even if they weren't in town at the actual moment of death. In his line of work he'd run across stranger things than a daughter arranging "an accident" in order to become very wealthy. Some of them had appeared grief-stricken, too.

Ben stepped away from the birch tree and swung his gaze to some of Jack's neighbors and friends. More possible suspects, some who might have motive, means, and opportunity. He spotted the butcher, the baker, the florist, the banker. And then there was Wilbur Oakley who ran the local insurance agency, a man who wasn't thrilled that the Home Office had

sent Ben to Riverview. With around thirty years' insurance
experience, Oakley should realize that the head honchos get
mighty upset when two men from the same small town die
within a couple of months of each other, both insured by National Fidelity for tons of money. Yet Wilbur seemed to take
his visit as a personal affront. Annoying.

A short distance away, watching everyone with as much
interest as he, was Grady Denton, the local sheriff. Ben had
seen him arrive, dressed in full uniform, accompanied by a
tall brunette wearing a dress that clung to her curves and was
as red as her lipstick. On stiletto heels, she moved to flank
Maggie's other side, giving her a long hug. The two seemed
like old friends, Ben noted.

Before this was over, he'd know that and much more
about both women.

At last, Jack had been eulogized by several boyhood
friends, prayed over yet again, and "Taps" had been played
for the fallen soldier. The ceremony ended and Ben studied
the folks who wandered over to speak to Maggie, and those
who didn't. His shrewd gaze took in several people whose
names he didn't know yet. But he would. Little by little, he'd
question and poke and prod and pick away at all the secrets
this little town held. Eventually, the truth would surface.

Maybe Jack Spencer had died accidentally. But maybe
not.

Standing with his hands in his pants pockets, Ben shifted
his gaze back to Maggie. Most everyone had gone down the
hill and still she stood alone, staring down at her father's casket. Her lips moved, but Ben couldn't make out what she
said. At last, she placed a single red rose on the silver lid,
drew in a deep breath and turned, showing a flash of leg he
couldn't help admiring.

Slowly, she turned and looked his way. She seemed startled at the sight of him. He could almost feel her trying to

place him. Appearing shaken, she removed her sunglasses, studying him intently.

Maggie got her racing heart under control, but just barely. At first glance, she'd thought she was hallucinating. Chet Garrett here, in this small town? Impossible. He hated suburbia and ridiculed it with regularity.

However, without her shades, she saw that the stranger was slightly taller and built more muscular. His hair was casually cut and windblown, whereas Chet had a careful trim every week. And this man's eyes had a silver cast where Chet's were a cold ocean blue. No, whoever he was, he wasn't Chet. Thank God.

Ben stood his ground, silent and unmoving, watching conflicting emotions come and go on her expressive face.

Finally, Maggie became aware of the housekeeper who'd come back for her, and let the woman lead her down the hill.

Ben stared after them until they'd disappeared inside the big Colonial. He wished he could have spoken with Maggie Spencer while looking into her eyes. Then maybe he could have determined whether or not she already knew she was about to inherit a small fortune.

A big man, Jack had built himself a big house with spacious rooms and high ceilings, then filled it with generous, masculine furniture. Ben strolled the rooms, sipping coffee, and decided he admired Spencer's taste. Leather and oak were Spencer's choices, blues and browns his colors, warm paneling and wide windows his preference. If there'd ever been a woman's touch in this house, it had been long removed or minimal at best, noticeable only in a few toss pillows and some fresh flowers, probably sent by friends and neighbors for today's reception. He knew that Jack had been a widower for years and wondered how much decorating input Maggie had had. Perhaps her old bedroom was a feminine oasis.

Then again, studying her as she hugged Ed Kowalski, the

stout man Ben had been told was the town butcher, her slender hands clasping his chubby fingers, he didn't think Maggie was the sort who'd sleep with lace curtains billowing on the windows nor would she choose a girlish canopied bed. Her taste would run to more classic lines, he decided, as he watched her accept the older man's condolences. Her choices would include pastel percale sheets, scented candles, soft music. He had no trouble picturing her there, wearing something long and sleek, satin maybe, and . . .

"Don't look now, but you appear to be drooling, Mr. Whalen," a voice alongside him said. "I take it you approve of our hostess, Miss Spencer."

Caught in the act, Ben cleared his throat and turned to gaze into the disapproving eyes of Wilbur Oakley who was looking at him as if he were something Wilbur should scrape off the sole of his shoe. Of slight build with a receding hairline and no chin, Oakley was the only man present wearing a suit with a vest. Conferring with the owner of the local two-person agency over the last two days, enduring his veiled jibes in the interest of company harmony, Ben had grit his teeth and hoped the officious little man would be put out to pasture soon.

"Sorry if that disturbs you, Wilbur," Ben said, taking a step back, away from the lingering smell of the man's overpowering aftershave. "It's part of my job, to study everyone, to check out the deceased's relatives, friends, and neighbors. And the name's Ben."

Oakley's lips thinned distastefully. "You could have waited. Everyone here is in mourning. Your timing needs work."

Battle lines drawn, Ben thought. I don't like you, either, pal. He'd been patient, but it was clearly time to set a few ground rules. Apparently Wilbur felt that lifelong residency in Riverview gave him the right to criticize the behavior of newcomers. "Yeah, well, the sooner we get started, the quicker I'll be out of your hair. The Home Office told me you'd be happy to cooperate. Were they wrong, Wilbur?"

Bristling inwardly at the reminder, Oakley removed his frown, but was loath to let it go. It was demeaning, he thought, having to take orders from a man who'd scarcely been born when Wilbur began his career. Whalen looked more like a battered football player than a reputable insurance investigator. And his outfit—a khaki sportcoat over a wrinkled white shirt open at the throat with no tie, and, of all things, jeans—was extremely inappropriate. "What exactly do you need from me?"

Ben allowed himself a small smile. "I'll let you know as we go along. For now, who's that distinguished-looking, gray-haired man talking with Maggie Spencer?"

Oakley's pale blue eyes swung over and back. "Judge Fulton, an old friend of Jack's. He's widowed and retired, lives just off Main Street on Crandall. The judge is erudite, intelligent, a chess player and a gentleman."

"Trying to say I'm not, Wilbur? Don't bother. I never tried to be."

It was all Wilbur could do not to ball his hands into fists. "I believe I gave you the names of all of Jack's close friends when we met yesterday. They're all here—the Beckers, the Kowalskis, George Cannata, and the sheriff. Perhaps you can arrange to talk with them, at a more suitable time." Oakley hoped the lunkhead would get the message. He'd never been particularly fond of Jack Spencer and his cronies, thinking them to be a snobbish, tight-knit group who'd never invited him to their Friday night poker games. But he had no intention of telling that to this upstart. "I'll be in my office in the morning. Now, if you'll excuse me . . ."

"Hold on." Ben nodded toward the tall brunette in the red dress who was walking up to Maggie, the one who'd hugged her at graveside. "Who's that? I don't believe she was on your list."

If possible, Wilbur's face looked even more critical. "The sheriff's daughter, Carrie, by his first wife. She's as wild as they come, married some vagabond several years ago and left Riverview. She recently returned without him and opened a boutique, which is probably where she got that outlandish outfit she's wearing. Rumor has it she's filed for divorce and her husband is in prison."

Ben's lips twitched. "I take it you don't like red, Wilbur."

"It's shocking, to wear that to a funeral."

Ben noticed Maggie's face relax considerably as the two women talked, the affection between them seemingly genuine. "Carrie's a good friend of Maggie's?"

"They grew up together, both of them raised by a single father."

"Is that a fact?" Old chums always knew a lot of buried secrets. "Did Carrie's mother die, too?"

Wilbur fussed with the perfect knot of his tie. "No. Camilla left Grady and ran off with a summer visitor." How had he gotten involved in this gossipy conversation? Still, he couldn't chance this arrogant fool reporting his unfriendly attitude to the Home Office. He had something important brewing and he didn't want anyone messing up his plans before he was ready to make his move.

Ben smiled. "Small towns are fascinating, aren't they?" He glanced through the archway at the sheriff who was handing a glass of wine to a not-so-young redhead wearing a ton of fake jewelry and some gauzy dress. "So, is that wifey number two with the sheriff?"

"Yes. Her name's Opal. She operates the local beauty shop. Couldn't you tell?" He wondered if Ben caught his facetious remark. "I'm afraid when it comes to women, the sheriff's brains slip below his belt." Appalled at his brash statement, Wilbur glanced up and noticed the amused look on Whalen's face. "I have to leave. My wife's at home and she's not well." Without another word, he turned and made his way to the front door.

Well, well, Ben thought. So the sheriff's drawn to brassy women and his daughter's ex is in prison. Interesting.

Turning toward the dining room, he saw a plump woman wearing a purple number dotted with tiny white flowers, the kind his mother used to call "a house dress," her white hair looking freshly permed, her sensible oxfords spreading to D-width. She headed straight for him. Unlike Wilbur's, her blue eyes behind wire-rimmed bifocals were smiling.

"I don't believe I know you, young man." She held out her hand. "I'm Lucy Hanover."

"Ben Whalen, ma'am." He took her small round hand in both of his because she looked like everyone's idea of a grandmother. "You must be a family friend."

"Yes, indeed. I remember when Jack Spencer was born." She shook her head sadly. "Isn't it a shame, his terrible accident? I still can't believe he's gone."

The afternoon was improving. A chatty woman could spill a lot of town secrets. "I've heard that Jack Spencer was a very careful man. Hard to believe someone who's been in construction for nearly thirty years would suddenly get careless."

"We all have our careless moments, Mr. Whalen." Lucy peered up at him through her glasses. "Are you a friend of Maggie's?"

"No, ma'am. I'm an insurance investigator for National Fidelity, the company that insured Mr. Spencer."

"Oh, I see." But she didn't and Lucy frowned. "Do they usually send someone to investigate an accidental death?"

"Very often." When the dollar count is there, especially. "What did you think of Jack?"

Her smile warmed. "He was a wonderful man. My house was one of the first he built right after he and Noreen married and started the business. She worked in the office and was sweet as could be. They were always helping folks."

Ben shifted his stance so he could see Maggie over Lucy's shoulder. "And how about their daughter?"

Lucy turned to follow his gaze. "She's lovely, isn't she? I think she's outgrown us all, though, after moving away. Her daddy worried about that. Whenever she called to say she was coming to visit, that man could talk of nothing else."

"Why'd she move away, do you think?"

Lucy swung back to face him. "Young people seem to want more from life these days. You see Carrie over there, Grady's daughter? She left about the same time as Maggie, married and divorced and now she's back, too. Still, I wonder if she's happy." Her eyes checked out his left hand, saw no ring but decided to dig a little. "Is your wife with you, Ben?"

"No, ma'am. I came alone." Which, he reminded himself, was exactly the way he wanted it.

"I've buried two husbands myself. Gets lonely at times." She glanced back to Maggie. "That poor girl's had a hard time of it, although Jack was glad when things didn't work out with that New York fella. They were never formally engaged, but after her Christmas visit, Jack was down in the dumps thinking she might marry and stay there. But quite recently, he mentioned that they'd broken up. You see, he never lost hope she'd move back for good one day."

Ben watched Maggie talking with Carrie and rubbing at a spot above her left eye as if she had a headache. "Maybe now she will."

"Oh, I doubt it. Of course, Maggie's never been as restless as Carrie, so I suppose it's possible. But you know what they say about how hard it is to keep a young one down on the farm once they've seen the big city." Lucy chuckled at her own joke as she eyed the buffet table. "I believe I'll go over and taste the goodies. Nice talking with you, young man."

"Same here." Peripherally, he saw her head for the dining room, but his eyes again were on Maggie Spencer.

He hadn't seen her cry, though her hands weren't steady and she was very pale. From across the room, she reminded him of Michelle Pfeiffer at her most vulnerable. Her face was calm, almost stoic. He wondered if she was in shock and just going through the motions. Her fingers threaded her hair back off her face as she shook her head at something Carrie said. Then he saw her full lower lip tremble. Her control seemed fragile, as if she were hanging on by a thin thread.

Glancing around, Ben spotted the priest sitting by himself with a cup of coffee. Maybe their clergyman could enlighten him a little about the Spencers. In investigating a death, you could never learn too much.

"How are you holding up, girlfriend?" Carrie Denton Edwards asked her old friend as she moved with Maggie to a thankfully deserted corner of the room.

"Managing, Carrie, but that's about all." Determined not to cry, Maggie took a step back and glanced at her friend's outfit. "Pretty snazzy duds." Carrie had often dressed somewhat flamboyantly, more in defiance than because she had bad taste. The shocking red dress was gorgeous on her curvaceous figure, even though Maggie probably wouldn't have worn it to a funeral.

"You know what we should do, girlfriend?" Carrie asked, again using her old nickname for Maggie. "We ought to jump into my brand new convertible after this wingding and head on out of here. See where the wind takes us. I think we could both use a change of scene."

There was some appeal to the invitation. Maggie longed for a time when she could leave her worries behind and be carefree again, like when she and Carrie were teenagers. But the reality was that her life was riddled with turmoil right now and a trip seemed like a faraway dream. "Maybe another time, Carrie. I can't right now." To let her know her refusal wasn't personal, she slipped an arm around her friend's waist. "It's so good to see you. I missed you at Christmas." Christmas. It seemed a lifetime ago.

"Me, too." Yanking off an earring that was too tight, Carrie glanced over her shoulder to make sure no one had sidled up. "I moved back in January after Gramps's estate was settled finally. He left me some money, you know."

"Dad told me about his accident. I'm really sorry. I always liked him." Carrie's grandfather, Henry Denton, had been Grady's father and also the sheriff years ago. He'd died in an accidental fall while hiking last September. "Was the money what finally made you decide to leave Wayne?"

Carrie had been reckless and somewhat frenzied in college, dating twice as often as any two other girls. It had been a surprise to everyone when she'd eloped right before graduation with Wayne Edwards, a man five years older and one none of her friends knew. The newlyweds had moved to Escanaba, but the marriage had been rocky from the start with many separations. Since then, Maggie had seen Carrie only half a dozen times on her visits home, and always alone.

Carrie lighted a cigarette and blew smoke toward the high ceiling. "Funny how money can help you make up your mind—about a lot of things."

Maggie rarely pried, but their friendship went back a long way, which was the reason she dared ask such a personal question. "He was abusing you, wasn't he?" Physical, mental, emotional—there were many forms of abuse and Maggie had long suspected that Wayne Edwards was guilty of at least one.

Inhaling deeply, Carrie nodded, wondering if proof of her defective judgment was stamped on her forehead. "Yeah, the son of a bitch. But I got him, Maggie. He's in jail now and I hope he rots there." Forcing a smile, as she'd had to do all too often, she visibly brightened. "But that's all in the past.

Did you hear that I opened a boutique off the highway? Carrie's Closet. How's that grab you?"

For the first time today, Maggie smiled. "That's wonderful. You always loved clothes."

"It's nothing like the stores you're used to in Manhattan, I'm sure, but for this area, it's fashion city." Her practiced eye examined Maggie's classic look. "You'll have to stop in, not that you need help with picking out a wardrobe."

"Thanks, I'd like to see your shop." Maggie saw Fiona motioning to her that someone was leaving and she needed to say good-bye to them. "But more importantly, let's get together for a long visit. Like old times."

"You bet we will." Carrie ground her cigarette out in a nearby ashtray. "We'll compare notes. Are you still with Rhett or Brett or whatever his name is?"

Maggie's chin moved up a notch. "Chet, and no, like you, I finally ended things."

Carrie grinned. "Feels good, doesn't it?"

"Yes, it does." She gave Carrie a warm hug. "Call me. Soon."

"I will."

As Maggie turned, she noticed J.C. Chevalier, Grady's deputy, waiting patiently nearby, his eyes on Carrie. She leaned in close to whisper in Carrie's ear. "Don't look now, but old crushes are coming out of the closet."

Carrie glanced up and spotted him, then sighed heavily. "Why is it we can never seem to fall really hard for the good guys?"

"I've often wondered that myself." Maggie squeezed her hand, then watched her amble over to J.C. in that slow, undulating walk she had. Probably most everyone in the room thought Carrie was still wild and fast, but Maggie had a feeling her oldest friend had been to hell and back.

Dutifully, she bid two couples good-bye, then gazed around, wondering if she dare escape for a few precious min-

utes. She'd done what was expected of her, hugged one and
all, accepted their sympathetic comments and tried to field
their questions about what she was going to do now. How
the hell did she know? She'd just had the biggest shock of
her life. Who could make plans?

Her shoulders hurt from trying to hold herself together and
her eyes burned from hot tears that wanted desperately to
fall. Would they ever leave? Why couldn't they understand?
Whoever started this barbaric custom of entertaining mourners, anyhow?

Immediately, she felt a rush of shame. Scanning the room,
studying face after face, an indisputable fact hit her hard. The
townspeople had come today not only to pay their last respects to a beloved friend, but because they cared about her.
Many of these same neighbors had invited her into their
homes after the untimely death of her mother, trying to ease
her pain by including her. They'd seen her through her awkward teen years, praised her success in college, and bid her a
fond farewell when she'd struck out on her own.

Maggie could see love in their eyes, in the sympathetic
smiles. It was impossible not to feel an affection for these
folks, her extended family who knew her, warts and all, and
cared anyway.

Turning, her eyes found the man from the cemetery, the
one who'd stood silently staring at her. The one she'd momentarily mistaken for Chet. On closer examination, away
from the shady tree, she could see that the resemblance was
slight. He was rawboned and rangy with an angular face that
reminded her of a younger Harrison Ford. She wasn't sure
who he was, though someone had said he worked with
Wilbur Oakley.

Just then, he shifted and looked over, his eyes colliding
with hers. Maggie held his gaze and saw he didn't waver,
didn't even blink. There was a challenging air about him that
set her already raw nerves on edge. She badly wanted to turn

away from that probing look. Emotions clogging her throat, she moved down the hall to her father's study, entering the cooler sanctuary with an audible sigh of relief.

She left the door slightly ajar in case Fiona needed her, then stepped out of her black pumps. Slipping a hand beneath her hair, she rubbed at the tension at the back of her neck.

This was her father's favorite room. *Had been,* she corrected herself, and brushed a stray tear from her eyelashes. Two walls of bookcases, solid oak, floor-to-ceiling, filled with well-read and beloved books from the classics to the comics, from westerns to biographies, from history to popular fiction. Both of them avid readers, they'd spent many a wonderful hour in this inviting room, curled up in matching easy chairs and ottomans in front of a fire, conversation often unnecessary.

Padding in her stockinged feet across the thick gold carpet, Maggie moved behind Jack's chair, touching the brown leather as soft as butter, the indentation of his head still visible. Heart in her throat, she caressed the headrest, trailing fingertips down to the armrests.

Damn it, Dad, why'd you have to die? Foolish thought, for she'd never known a man who loved life more. Yet Fiona had hinted that lately, she'd seen signs of unrest, of an indefinable sadness. Had he learned he was sick and didn't tell her? She'd check that out with Dr. Alexander tomorrow. Had he grown tired of working, become careless? But he'd always loved construction. Creating visions, he'd called it. Was the business perhaps in trouble? She'd have to go through his papers and find out.

Guilt had her facing another possibility. Was it because she'd moved away? But why a reaction now, six years later? She'd known he hadn't been pleased about her relationship with Chet, but that had ended. So, why had he been asking her to come for a visit so vehemently? Had some worry he hoped to discuss with her caused him to abandon a lifetime of almost fanatically careful ways and get distracted enough to lose his footing on a scaffolding two stories up? Maggie shook her head. She'd probably never know.

Slowly she walked to the far wall made entirely of Michigan fieldstone with a huge fireplace in the center bisected by a wide mahogany mantel. Above it hung the portrait she'd had painted by a New York artist she'd met her first year away. Using her favorite snapshot, Terry Sheridan had captured the essence of the man, Maggie had always thought.

Jack stood on his hill in a casual pose, eyes as deep blue as hers, skin tan and leathery from years spent outdoors. He wore jeans and a plaid shirt, a leather belt with a large silver buckle, and hand-tooled boots. Not your usual portrait, not your usual man.

He looked tall, strong, invincible. *Only you weren't, were you, Dad?* "What were you going to tell me that couldn't wait, Dad?" she asked the silent room. When she'd phoned to say she was coming, he'd been elated, reeling off all they'd do during her stay. Then he'd sobered and quietly said they had to talk, that he had some long overdue things he needed to say. "Oh, God, I wish I hadn't waited. I'm so sorry, Dad. So sorry."

Finding a tissue in her pocket, Maggie dabbed at her eyes. She'd already cried so much, yet there were more tears. "I miss you already. This house, without you, is . . . is awful. Why? Why did this have to happen? We were going to have such a good time. Hunting for antiques, stuffing ourselves on pasties, fishing for walleye. It's been the two of us for years now. You had no business leaving me with no warning. No business!"

Head bowed, she waited for the pain to pass, then blew her nose. Drawing in a shuddering breath, she knew she had to get back to her guests, the people Dad thought so much of.

Turning, she took two steps and stopped.

He was standing by the door, his hand on the frame, silently studying her with those intense gray eyes the color of the sea on a rainy day. Annoyed at being caught weeping and talking to a portrait, wondering how long he'd stood there, her voice turned sharp. "Who are you? Why are you here, following me around, watching me?"

"I apologize for stumbling in on a private moment." Ben had learned very little from the priest and Carrie had been engrossed in a conversation with the deputy. So he'd gone looking for Maggie. Passing the den, he'd heard her voice and pushed open the door, then stood there listening for only a few moments. Long enough to witness her anguish. "I'm Ben Whalen from National Fidelity."

Maggie tried to think through a headache that seemed to get worse every hour since early morning. "Insurance? Wilbur Oakley handles all our insurance. Do you work for him?"

"Not exactly. I'm an investigator for the Home Office." He let that sink in, his eyes never leaving her face. Just now, she'd seemed so genuine in her sorrow, in her heartfelt words to her father. He couldn't help being touched, yet he reminded himself that he needed to remain objective.

She wrinkled her brow. "What are you investigating?"

Ben stepped inside. "Whenever two men in one small town who happen to be lifelong friends die accidentally within three months of each other, the suits on the top floor get nervous." He prowled the perimeter of the room, seemingly casual yet noticing everything—an impressive collection of well-read books, several tennis trophies proudly displayed on lighted glass shelves, an old safe in the corner, and framed photos of Jack Spencer with a variety of friends. Like a patriarch, he definitely dominated the room.

And then there was the picture on his desk of a blond teenager hugging her father, her face radiant with love. That photo spoke volumes.

Maggie rubbed at her headache again. "Two men?"

"Yeah, two. Do you remember Reed Lang, a good friend of your father's?"

"Oh, yes, of course. Dad called me about Mr. Lang. He was pretty broken up about his death. Fell down some stairs, didn't he?" She walked over to slip her shoes back on. The man was so tall that she needed the extra height. She felt vulnerable enough. At least in heels, she'd been nose to nose with Chet, but not with this man. "Did your company insure both of them?"

"Yes." He picked up a paperweight in the form of a big red apple from the desk, tested its weight, and set it back down. Looking up, he noticed dark smudges beneath her eyes and decided to back off. This was not the time or place. "Listen, I need to ask you a couple of questions when you're feeling up to it, but I can wait. I realize this is a very bad day. I'll call you in a day or two." He started for the door.

Tired, but anxious to get this over with, Maggie frowned. "Questions? What kind of questions?"

All right, if that's how she wanted it. He turned back. "Questions like have you looked through your father's papers yet and found his insurance policy?"

Maggie tucked a lock of her hair behind one ear. "I've hardly had time. We never discussed insurance, Dad and I, but I'm sure everything's in order. He was meticulous about keeping his books and records."

"But you never discussed insurance?" The only child of a widower, wouldn't she at least have been curious?

Maggie stiffened. "There seemed no reason. But then, I don't imagine Dad thought he was going to die at fifty-four. At any rate, I can't imagine that he carried much coverage. I mean, he has . . . *had* the business and this house, and there's only me."

Ben shrugged. "Depends on what you consider much coverage."

She was truly not in the mood for games today of all days. "All right, Mr. Whalen. Since you obviously are dying to tell me, how much?"

He moved so he was facing her. "A million dollars, with double indemnity for accidental death."

"Holy shi . . . a million! You must be kidding!"

"I never kid when the stakes are that high."

"Unbelievable." Stunned, she sat down on the ottoman. "Why would he do that? He was a frugal man. This house was his most extravagant expenditure and he built it himself, slowly over five years, he often told me. It was paid off years ago. My God, he drove a four-year-old car! The premiums must have been staggering. Why would he need to have that much insurance?"

Ben angled one hip onto the arm of the chair. "You tell me."

She didn't like his tone. "Just what are you getting at?"

Her eyes became fiery as her anger rose, coloring her cheeks. Better, he thought, than the sad, lost look she'd had when he'd found her. As a man, Ben couldn't help noticing that, even in a state of shock, she was one hell of a beautiful woman. As the investigator, he couldn't let that fact affect him. "I have to look at all the angles. Is it possible Jack Spencer might have taken a deliberate dive?"

"A dive?" Suddenly, his meaning became crystal clear. "Suicide? You think my father committed suicide? And I suppose you think Mr. Lang leaped down a flight of stairs just so your company would be liable." Furious, Maggie got up, her hands clenched. "You have a lot of nerve coming into his home and insulting my father."

Ben stood, aware that most people hated the mere thought of suicide. It made everyone feel both vulnerable and guilty, for things done and not done. "You said you wanted to hear the questions. Are you aware that, according to Spencer Construction records, profits started sliding down recently? Way down. There are people who can't handle financial setbacks and . . ."

"I'm not going to listen to this." There it was, that same go-for-the-jugular ruthlessness she'd learned to despise in Chet. She turned, took several steps, then whirled about. "And I suppose Reed Lang's business was also declining?"

"Maybe. I'm looking into it." Shoving his hands in his pockets, he walked closer. "Look, I don't want to upset you, certainly not on this day, but . . ."

"Well, you've done a remarkable job of doing it anyway." The nerve of the man. "You didn't know my father, or you'd never suggest suicide. He loved life, loved people. He laughed a lot and he was fun to be with. Ask anyone out there." The nagging conversation she'd had with Fiona about her father's recent uncharacteristic mood shifts wasn't something she wanted to think about just now. "No, it's simply not possible that he would 'take a dive,' as you so quaintly phrased it." Her eyes narrowing, she glared at him. "Is charm school a requisite for your line of work?"

Ben ignored the sarcasm. Grieving still, she was entitled to her contempt. "All right then, if he didn't fall from a careless move and he didn't jump, there's only one other possibility."

"I can't wait to hear still another hair-brained theory."

"Someone pushed him."

"Pushed him?" The color drained from Maggie's already pale face as her hand flew to her mouth. "Dear God!"

The door opened wider and Fiona came striding in. "There you are, Maggie. Some of our guests are leaving and . . ." The housekeeper took note of Maggie's shocked face and the stranger's sober expression. "Is everything all right? Would you be needing some help in here?"

What she needed was to get away from this man, from the terrible things he was suggesting. Sucking in a deep breath, she turned her back to him. "No, Fiona. I'm going." Without even a glance in his direction, Maggie hurried out of the den.

For a long moment, the older woman took Ben's measure as he stood unmoving. He didn't look like a troublemaker, nor like a man who'd turn from trouble, either. Still, she didn't want Maggie distressed any more than she was. "If you're finished, let me show you the way out," she said, her voice crisp with Irish brogue.

Oddly pleased at the housekeeper's protectiveness, Ben nodded his thanks and left the room. With no siblings to help her through this, Maggie would need the woman's strength. At the double doors opening onto the front porch, he spotted her saying good-bye to a small group of friends. Crossing over the wide threshold, he couldn't resist glancing back over his shoulder.

Her eyes were on him, icy blue and angry. He followed the circular drive around toward his Jeep 4 x 4, deciding that it was time to leave. He'd upset enough people for one day.

Chapter Two

Sheriff Grady Denton wore his tan uniform like a badge of honor, rarely choosing civilian clothes even on his days off. His father had been sheriff as well and had taught Grady that the law was a demanding mistress, one you could never shed. Grady believed it.

Seated behind his gunmetal-gray desk, leaning back in his swivel chair with his hands folded over his slight paunch, he regarded the young insurance investigator who'd stopped in to see him. There was something about the man that reminded Grady of a hunting dog he'd had years ago. He could see determination, patience, and a tenacity that he admired even as it annoyed him. If there was one thing Grady hated it was an outsider coming in to question the way he enforced the law in Riverview.

"Just what is it you want from me, Mr. Whalen?" he asked in his lazy drawl. The Dentons had moved from Alabama when Grady was ten and he'd never quite lost the Southern inflection. Early on, he'd discovered that people in the North thought slow-speaking Southerners also were slow thinkers. He often exaggerated his accent with strangers, knowing it gave him an edge to have them consider him slow-witted while his quick mind got the jump on them.

Ben tried to get comfortable in the straight-back wooden chair across from the sheriff's desk and wondered if inflicting discomfort on his visitors had anything to do with Grady's choice of furniture. "I stopped by to compare notes with you, to check how your investigation into Reed Lang's death is going. As I mentioned yesterday at Jack Spencer's funeral, my company's anxious to find out exactly what happened in both these cases."

A greenhorn, Grady decided, trying to impress the brass. "Don't know as though I've got a lot to tell you. I checked out the site of both occurrences, determined the cause of death, and made out my report. What exactly beyond that would you want done?" Removing a pocket knife from his top drawer, he proceeded to clean his fingernails.

This country bumpkin routine was a put-on, Ben was certain. "Could I see those reports?"

Taking his time, Grady appeared to consider the request, then finally straightened. He thumbed through several folders on his desk, found the right one, and handed across two sheets of paper before returning to his manicure.

It took Ben half a minute to read each skimpy report listing name of the deceased, location of the body, approximate time of death, and probable cause. Grady's signature was at the bottom, signed with a flourish of capital letters. Ben glanced up. "Is this all you have?"

"Yup." Grady pocketed his knife with a sigh. "What more were you expecting?"

Ben held on to his temper, just barely. He'd worked with small-town lawmen before, but this guy seemed to be deliberately baiting him. "All right, let's start with Reed Lang. Did you interview any of the neighbors around the house where he died? How about his secretary at the real estate office, his business partner, anyone else who might have seen him that night? Did you get the log book of appointments from his office, maybe his mileage records, his phone register?"

Grady hadn't moved. "Go on."

Ben tried to keep the annoyance from his voice. "Okay, moving on to Jack Spencer. Your report here says he was found about nine by a passing jogger and the medical examiner put the death around *dusk,* an ambiguous time at best. Would that be six, seven, eight? On a summer evening, it was probably still light enough that someone might have seen something, a guy out walking his dog, a motorist driving by. There's no listing of anyone questioned, not even the jogger, nor is the M.E.'s report attached." Frustrated, Ben tossed the pages back onto Grady's desk. "Not much to go on."

The sheriff sat up abruptly, his chair protesting the shift of weight. "Are you suggesting I'm not doing my job, Mr. Whalen?" he asked in a deceptively calm voice.

Go easy, Ben warned himself. Pissing off the law wasn't going to get answers. "I'm not suggesting anything. I am telling you that I need more information. And I'm asking your cooperation."

Grady folded his big hands on his desk blotter. "Why would you think I'd go to all that trouble for two deaths, both ruled accidental?"

"I'm not sure they were accidental."

The sheriff's thick dark brows rose. "I can't imagine whatever gave you such an idea." Shaking his head, he removed a plug of tobacco from his center drawer. "Son, I've been sheriff of this community for 'bout twenty years now, and my father served the good citizens before that. We get a little petty thievery, some vandalism, a couple of speeding tickets during the summer season. Mostly visitors, always in a damn hurry. But this is a real nice little town. We haven't had a murder here since, oh, going back about forty years, I'd say. Dad handled that one. A tourist caught his wife cheating on him and shot her in one of the rental cabins along the river."

The recitation was as simplistic as it was unrealistic. "No community is immune to violence in this day and age, Sheriff."

Grady peered at Ben from narrowed eyes, wondering if he'd underestimated the man. "Now, don't you go stirring people up and making trouble in my town, you hear me, son? There's anyone doing wrong here, *I* know it and *I'll* take care of it. You just fill out your little reports and go on back to your big city. We take care of our own."

My town, was it? Certain he'd get nowhere further today, Ben stood. "Thank you so much for your help. Here's my card with my beeper number, in case you think of anything else." Before he said things he might later regret, he left.

Thoughtfully Grady leaned back in his chair. Damn nosy insurance people. That boy would bear watching. He'd have to lean on that pansy Wilbur a little, tell him to straighten the kid out and send him on his way before he got anyone else all riled up. There was far too much at stake here to let a loose cannon go off half-cocked.

Swiveling around, he gazed up at the portrait of his father as sheriff in full uniform. Henry Denton had worn size thirteen shoes. Grady wondered if he'd ever be able to fill them.

Dr. Steven Alexander strode into his office, his lab coat hanging open over his crisp white shirt as he rushed to greet one of his favorite patients. "It's so good to see you, Maggie." He shook hands warmly, then stepped back to look her over. "I'm sorry I couldn't attend Jack's funeral. I had a patient in ICU and I couldn't leave."

"I understand, Doctor." She took the chair he indicated as he leaned against the edge of his desk.

"I hope you're not here because you're ill. You look a little pale, but otherwise as lovely as ever."

Maggie smiled at the doctor who'd delivered her twenty-nine years ago. "Thank you and no, I feel fine. I've come to ask you if my father was ill. Had he been to see you recently?"

Dr. Alexander's thin face moved into a thoughtful frown. "Not in over a year. Why would you ask?"

Crossing her legs, Maggie tried to put her concerns into words. "It may be nothing, but Fiona tells me that Dad had seemed very down lately, as if he were worried about something. And he'd been urging me to visit for several weeks. When I finally found the time to make the trip and told him on the phone, he said he was glad because he needed to talk with me about something. Naturally, I immediately thought it could be his health."

The doctor shook his head. "I really don't think so, Maggie. As you know, he and I played tennis every Sunday morning at the club. Singles isn't an easy game after a certain age." He chuckled. "I ought to know since I'm fifty-eight. Jack was in top form in our last game, scarcely breaking a sweat. He wasn't overweight, got plenty of exercise, didn't smoke, didn't drink much."

She hated to spoil Dr. Alexander's rosy memory of her father, but she had to know more. "Fiona dropped a few hints that lately he'd been drinking more."

He looked surprised. "Really? Well, I never saw signs of it. If he'd been experiencing worrisome symptoms, I don't believe he'd drive to Escanaba or elsewhere to see another doctor. I believe we had a good rapport as well as a deep friendship."

"I know you did. It's just that I'm at a loss to explain his recent behavior. Uncharacteristic at best."

"Actually, I did notice that he wasn't as lighthearted as usual during our Friday poker games. But then, with the interest rates fairly high, construction's down. He might have been worried about the business." Alexander straightened, fingering the stethoscope dangling from one pocket. "I should tell you that Reed's death hit him hard. Their friendship dated back to their grade school days."

Maggie nodded. "He mentioned that during our last phone call." But it was Ben Whalen's upsetting words that had had her tossing all night. "Doesn't it strike you as strange that both Dad and Mr. Reed had fatal accidents three months apart, two apparently healthy men only in their early fifties?"

Alexander made a noncommital gesture. "Sometimes it happens that way. We never know when it's our time." A cliché, but a true one. He wished he had more to offer Jack's daughter. "Death in any form is hard to accept, Maggie. Give yourself some time."

Maggie rose. "One last thing. Do you feel Dad was the sort of man who . . . who would commit suicide?" It was the thought, the fear she'd wrestled with until dawn, because a yes answer would mean she was even guiltier than she felt, guilty of not noticing the signs.

The doctor's frown was back and deeper. "Whatever gave you such a notion? Certainly not. Jack was a man full of life. Besides, he'd never have climbed up onto one of his own buildings and jumped, leaving you with the horror of that." He slipped an arm around her waist as he led her to the door. "Don't overthink this, Maggie. It was an accident, pure and simple."

She wished she felt as certain. "Thank you for your time, Doctor."

"There is a way to put your mind more at ease." He paused, moved by the sudden flair of hope in her eyes. "I'm sure the sheriff ordered an autopsy. Dr. Fielding is the Medical Examiner at County General Hospital. I can check with him, if you like, to see if he discovered any signs of a disease that might have set Jack to worrying."

"If you wouldn't mind, I'd appreciate knowing."

"Certainly. I'll check with him and call you." He took her hands in both of his. "Take care of yourself, Maggie. And give yourself time to grieve. Otherwise, I'll be seeing you back in here for more than just a talk."

Maggie found a smile for him. "I will and thanks again." Walking to the parking lot where she'd left her dad's tan Ford Explorer, she wasn't sure if she felt better after this visit, or worse. Maybe Dr. Fielding's findings would relieve her worries.

At that moment, Dr. Fielding was in his office at County General on the outskirts of Riverview, checking his watch. He had two autopsies scheduled yet today and this insurance investigator wanted an interview. He pushed his horn-rimmed glasses higher up on his nose. "I can only spare you a few minutes. I'm running behind today as it is."

"I appreciate that, Doctor," Ben said. He'd already handed the medical examiner his card and explained his position with National Fidelity. "I'm investigating two recent deaths, that of Reed Lang and Jack Spencer from Riverview. I was wondering if you'd allow me to see their autopsy reports."

Fielding scratched a spot in his thick auburn hair. "The names don't sound familiar."

"Lang died in March, Spencer five days ago. Sheriff Denton would have been the one who called you in on the cases." Ben watched the man trying to remember. "Both men fell, one down a set of basement stairs, the other from a two-story unfinished building."

"No, I'm sure I didn't handle those cases." Briskly, he marched to his filing cabinet, pulled out the top drawer, and began scanning the files. "These are all year-to-date. I have a pretty good memory for names and . . . no, no files on either name in here." He slid the drawer shut. "Sorry."

Puzzled, Ben frowned. "Who else would have done them if not you?"

The doctor shook his head. "I'm it for several hundred miles, the only pathologist on staff at County General. Apparently, no autopsy was ordered."

Ben's frown deepened. He was running into more damn brick walls and the fault lay with that lazy-eyed sheriff. "That doesn't make sense."

"I'm sure you're aware that autopsies aren't usually called for in accidental deaths unless foul play is suspected." Fielding glanced at his watch again. "I've got to go. Better check with the sheriff."

"Right. Thanks." Ben left the office, slowly strolling out to the hospital parking lot bathed in hot afternoon sunshine. Damn Grady Denton, he thought. No suspicion of foul play as far as he was concerned, no autopsies ordered and now, both men were buried. It would take probable cause to get a court order to exhume the bodies. At the moment, he doubted that he had enough case to convince a judge to sign an authorization.

"Son of a bitch," Ben muttered as he climbed into his Jeep. Despite the pleasant summer day, he felt gloomy.

In her father's den, Maggie propped her feet on the leather ottoman and placed the metal box on her lap. Leaning back in her chair, she sighed. During one of her visits home, Dad had told her he had all his important papers in this steel box, which he kept in a locked safe he'd had bolted to the floor in the far corner of his den. He said he needed immediate access too frequently to use a bank safe-deposit box that held only his will and a few old documents. She remembered listening with half an ear when he'd given her a slip of paper with the safe's combination. She'd dutifully placed it in her wallet, and forgotten about it. It never occurred to her she'd need to use it this soon.

Slowly, she pushed back the lid. With trembling fingers, she began perusing the papers that made up the legalities of Jack Spencer's life. His navy discharge, honorable, with commendations. His marriage certificate. A copy of her birth certificate, which she hadn't known he'd kept, for she had the original. Her mother's death certificate.

Maggie swallowed hard and took a sip of her iced tea. She'd never particularly felt the lack of doing without a brother or sister, for she'd had a lot of friends. But right now, she'd give a great deal if only she had a sibling to help her through this. She'd thought fleetingly of asking Carrie, then dismissed the idea. She had no right to burden her friend with something she should take care of alone.

Several minutes later, she'd glanced at the papers of incorporation for Spencer Construction, some sort of investment in a limited partnership she'd study more closely later, the deed to the house, and the discharge of lien when the mortgage on the house had been paid off. The title to the Ford Explorer. And finally, the National Fidelity life insurance policy.

Carefully, she unfolded the thick document. And there it was: Jack Spencer insured for a million dollars, original beneficiary, Noreen Spencer, wife. Updated beneficiary, Margaret Spencer, daughter. And on page two, the double-indemnity clause in case of accidental death. Maggie let out a whoosh of air, sending her feathery bangs flying.

It was one thing to hear it and quite another to see it, all legal and authentic, in writing. Yet it still seemed unreal to her. A tear slipped down her cheek. She'd trade it all, every last cent, if only her father would walk through that door with his lengthy stride, give her one of his dazzling smiles, and pull her to his solid chest for a big hug.

She couldn't look at any more right now, Maggie decided. But as she refolded the policy, something jumped out at her. The date of issue was thirty-two years ago. That was the year

Dad had graduated from college, the year he and her mother had married. The policy wasn't a new one.

Why in the world would Ben Whalen be all upset about his company paying off on a policy that had been in force for so long? It wasn't as if her father had had some sudden nefarious agenda, taken out a huge insurance policy on himself and then committed suicide.

She checked the yearly premium and saw that it was hefty, even by thirty-year-old standards. Still, Dad had managed to keep up the payments or National Fidelity wouldn't have sent their obnoxious investigator to see if he could find something that would get them off the hook.

However, a question still remained unanswered and that was why Dad, as a young man of twenty-two, fresh out of college and getting married, about to start a business, had felt the need for such a big policy. Maggie's next thoughts centered around Reed Lang. How much had he been insured for, and who was the beneficiary? She knew that Mr. Lang had never married and had no children. A while back, he'd been dating someone quite seriously, but she remembered her father telling her that they'd broken it off.

The whole thing was very odd. Maggie put everything back into the box and returned it to the safe, closing the door. It was time she did something she'd been putting off ever since returning. A glance at the mantel clock told her it was only four in the afternoon. She didn't want to go, but she knew she wouldn't rest until she'd seen for herself.

The late afternoon was warm, but had turned cloudy, the sun nowhere to be seen when she pulled up at the building site. The large tract of land had been leveled to form a new subdivision and Spencer Construction had won the bid to build the homes. The unfinished model home her father had been inspecting was exactly as on the evening of his death, according to Theresa, Dad's secretary, when Maggie had called to get directions. The yellow tape put up by the sheriff's department was still stretched around the perimeter to warn curiosity seekers to not cross over. Grady Denton probably planned to leave it in place until the estate was settled and a decision was made about the disposition of the company. Something else she'd have to think about.

Maggie grabbed the keys and stepped out of the Explorer, leaving her shoulder bag inside. She stood looking up at the wood framework, the scaffolding, the angle of roof outlined against a gray sky. The billboard out half a mile by the highway advertised the price of the homes to be built as "from $200,000 up." A big house.

She stepped over the tape and walked around to the side, then stopped abruptly when she spotted the chalk outline on the ground. The delineation of a man's body. Maggie felt a shiver take her.

The cruel reality of death hit home again and had her trembling as she stared at the ground. This is where Jack Spencer had lain after the fall for some time before he was found. Had he been alive for a while? Would he have had a chance if someone had happened along sooner? Had he been badly frightened, guessing he was probably going to die unless help arrived in time? If it had to be this way, she prayed he'd died instantly.

Something caught her eye and she stepped around a small pile of lumber. Her father's tape measure in its silver case, his initials on one side. Mom had given that to him the first year they'd been in business. Her vision blurring, Maggie reached for the tape measure, then gazed upward to the scaffolding swaying in a light breeze. Had he been standing there checking measurements? Had he fumbled with the tape and misjudged his next step? Had he . . .

"A long way up, isn't it?" a deep voice coming from behind her asked.

Her heart slammed into her chest wall as she swiveled

about, clutching the heavy tape defensively. When she recognized Ben Whalen, she nearly threw it at him. "Do you get a kick out of creeping up on people, me in particular?"

"I'm sorry I spooked you." How was it that he found himself apologizing to this woman much more often than anyone else? "I wasn't trying to be quiet. I thought you heard me approach."

She looked past him and saw no car. "How'd you get here?" The area wasn't built up yet, this subdivision the first housing development going up with access through only a narrow side road, until permanent paved streets would be added. Thick woods were bisected by a stream where a few cabins had been built years ago. On the other side of the wooded section toward the back were some small older homes, but they were at least a mile away.

"I parked down a ways and walked over. I wanted to get the feel of the place." And to question anyone he ran across about that night. He shot another look upward. "Did Jack do that a lot, check out his buildings after his men were through for the day?"

Maggie stepped back from the chalk drawing, hating the sight of it. "This project was really important to Dad. He'd outbid two contractors from neighboring cities and won the contract by a hair. So I imagine he checked on the progress frequently since his reputation with these new developers was riding on how well things went." As she spoke, she couldn't help wondering if perhaps one of those other contractors who'd lost the bid had arranged her father's accident.

Stop! She warned herself, frowning at her own paranoia. Now she was beginning to think like this suspicious man.

He caught the flicker of annoyance on her face and wondered what had put it there. "Did you think of something?"

Irritated that he'd intruded on yet another private moment, she stepped around a pile of scraps and bent nails. "I don't know what you mean."

Ben stepped in front of her, forcing her to stop, to look at him. "Maggie, I'm on your side."

Lord, but she felt weary. "Are you? Why don't I feel that?"

"You're not one to trust easily, are you?" When she didn't answer, just stared back at him, he nodded. "That's good. There're too many people out there who'd take advantage. Only I'm not one of them. I just want to get some answers so we can get to the truth."

"The truth is my father had an accident. And so did Mr. Lang. Unusual timing, but there it is. Coincidences really do happen. Why can't you just let it go at that and go back to your Home Office?" Why he made her uncomfortable, she couldn't have said. She only knew that he did.

"Because ignoring inconsistences, coincidences, evasions, and half-truths are not what I'm paid to do. And when answers I get only arouse more questions, I begin to worry and wonder."

He had her attention now. "Care to explain that?"

"I paid a visit to the medical examiner awhile ago. It seems that Riverview's beloved sheriff, a close friend of both Jack and Reed, didn't classify either death as suspicious, as a possible homicide, so no autopsy was ordered by the Medical Examiner. We could have learned a lot from that report."

Now she'd never know if her father had learned of a medical condition that might have worried him. Ben Whalen seemed as upset by this piece of news as she. "Why wouldn't Grady have wanted to know all he could?"

Ben shook his head. "I don't pretend to know the workings of Grady Denton's mind. I have the feeling he wouldn't share information with me if I stumbled across him holding a smoking gun."

Maggie was puzzled. "Is that usual, law enforcement personnel not cooperating with insurance companies on these investigations?" However, she knew that Grady was fiercely protective of what he viewed as his territory.

"Nothing about this case is usual." He glanced around the area he'd been inspecting for half an hour before she'd arrived. "I guess that means I'll have to figure things out without their help."

Grady had talked with her like a Dutch uncle yesterday, Maggie recalled, but he'd avoided answering direct questions. Maybe she could learn more from Ben. If she could overlook his baiting remarks. "Have you learned anything yet, aside from the fact that no autopsies were done?"

"I discovered that J.C.'s the jogger who found Jack's body. I thought it was odd that that information wasn't in Grady's report, but once I had a name, I went to talk with J.C. myself. Hell of a nice guy, much more straightforward than Grady."

"Was he able to tell you anything new?"

"Only that he'd seen a dust cloud swirling on the dirt path as he jogged on the side of the main road, as if a car had just left the area in a big hurry."

"What time was that?"

"About eight-thirty and fairly dark, so he ran over to investigate. He spotted Jack's Explorer parked about where you have it now. He called his name several times, then began looking around. Finally, he found the body. No pulse, still warm, not yet rigid."

He saw Maggie swallow hard and belatedly realized his harsh description had given her an insensitive mind picture. He watched her pull herself together and found himself admiring her gutsiness.

Turning, Ben pointed toward the chalked outline of Jack's body. "Now that I've seen this, I feel fairly certain that your father didn't commit suicide. If he had, the body would have landed more in a crumpled heap, consistent with a jump. See the way his arms were stretched out and upward, away from his body? People don't jump in that position, as if they were doing a belly flop into a lake. It appears as if he'd been surprised, either by a misstep of his own or by a push from behind. You get the impression he probably screamed, his arms jerking out as if trying to grab onto something or trying to break his fall. That's an involuntary reflex action."

Maggie was staring at the outline in that pale, frightened way again. Yet she appeared to be considering his theory. "Everyone I've talked with mentioned how careful Jack had been all his life, which means that, although it's not impossible, it probably wasn't an accident. I know you don't like to think about it, but personally, I lean toward a push."

Maggie's stomach turned over. No, she didn't like to think about that.

He went on, almost as if he were thinking aloud. "A misstep usually sends a man off to one side or even has him falling on his back. But hitting frontal body first, that's more often than not the result of a strong shove from behind." He sought her eyes. "Was your father in the habit of taking people up with him, say a home buyer or an interested friend, when he climbed up to inspect the work in progress? I realize this is an unsold model, but I'm trying to establish his work habits."

"Not that I know of, not when I lived at home. When I was in my early teens on summer vacation, I used to ride my bike to where Dad was working to take him his lunch. It all looked fascinating to me and I'd beg him to take me up. He never did. Civilians don't belong on a construction site, he used to say."

Ben stared at the framework in the fading light. Of course he'd protect his daughter, but did Jack take others up? "I wonder if later he changed that policy."

Maggie studied Ben's profile as he spoke. A five-o'clock shadow darkened his stubborn jaw and his nose looked as if it had been broken once, maybe twice. He had on a gray T-shirt the same silver color as his eyes, black jeans, and Nikes so white he must have bought them this morning. His skin was nearly as tan as Dad's had been, which seemed odd for a man who didn't really work outdoors.

She supposed there were women who would find him an attractive man, if they could put up with his take-charge manner, his brash confidence. However, she'd been down that road before with Chet and had found it full of potholes. "You sound more like a cop than an insurance investigator."

"Used to be one, in another life."

An ex-cop. She should have guessed. "Are you aware that the insurance policy on my father is thirty years old?"

He fell in step with her as she walked toward the yellow tape. "Certainly. I have a copy of it."

Maggie stopped. "Then why did you suspect suicide earlier? Surely you didn't think Dad's been contemplating killing himself for all those years."

"No. He bought the policy back then for reasons of his own. But knowing he had it and the payoff would take care of his debts and his daughter, he could have killed two birds with one stone. It was one theory I pursued. But after visiting the site, I don't think so."

"You think someone followed him, tiptoeing on little cat feet behind him on the rafters, waiting for the right moment, then shoved him off. Is that your scenario?"

There was pain beneath her sarcasm so he let it go. "Much worse than that. Despite his no-civilians' policy, I think it was someone he allowed to talk him into letting them go up with him, someone he knew."

"What?" Maggie couldn't believe her ears. "You're crazy. I thought so yesterday and I still do. Didn't you see nearly the entire town turn out for his funeral? Everyone loved my father. No one he knew would *ever* do such a terrible thing." She stepped over the tape and headed for the Explorer. If she didn't stop having these heart-to-heart discussions with this man, she'd wind up smashing her fist into his face.

Unhurriedly, he went after her. "I know you don't want to believe that. Are you aware that upward of eighty percent of all killings are done by someone the victim knows?"

Hand on the door handle, she turned to him. "What possible motive would anyone have to kill my father? *I'm* the only one who stands to gain something." She cocked her head. "This is where you ask where I was on the night of the murder, isn't it?"

Again, he admired her spirit even in the worst of times, but he didn't think she wanted to hear that just now. "No, I don't think you were involved."

"But you checked me out?"

He placed his hand on the door, preventing her from opening it. "Maggie, I'd check out my own mother if I found reason to."

"What *reason* could I have? I loved him."

Two million reasons, he could have said. That kind of money gets the vote over love in many a relationship. But he didn't want to make her even angrier by voicing his opinion. "I told you I didn't think you had anything to do with your father's death."

"Should I thank you for that? If you knew how badly I want to hit you right now." Her free hand flexed and unflexed, her chest heaving with each angry breath. Why hadn't she left the moment she saw him?

"Go ahead. It might make you feel better."

His expression was unreadable with no hint of amusement. She still wanted to punch him. "You're not worth the bother. Get away from the truck. I have to get home."

Ben did, then threw out his hook. "All right, but I thought you'd want to go with me."

Yanking open the door, she glared at him. "I can't imagine wanting to go anywhere with you."

"Not even to examine the house where Reed Lang died?"

Her shoulders sagged as the fight drained from her. "You don't quit, do you?"

He stepped closer. "Look, Maggie, you're an intelligent woman. I think you realize in your gut that neither of these men died accidentally. Two careful, middle-aged men both fall to their deaths within weeks of each other? Frankly, I don't believe in coincidence and I doubt that you do, either. Don't you want to know how it really happened and what's the connection, if any? Don't you want to know *who* caused your father to die?"

She closed her eyes briefly, torn between wanting to leave and needing to know. When she opened them, she saw that the sky was darkening quickly with a hint of rain. "I really don't think so."

Her hesitant tone told him she was weakening, despite her words to the contrary. "Listen, my Jeep's just up there. Why don't I follow you home, then we'll go to the house together?"

This was crazy and Maggie knew it. But she badly wanted to show this overconfident investigator that his theories were all wet. She'd go and prove him wrong, if only to see that smug, knowing look slip from his face. "Okay." She climbed behind the wheel. "But Mr. Whalen?"

He met her eyes. "The name's Ben."

"All right, Ben. Don't make me regret trusting you."

Chapter Three

A light rain had begun to fall as they approached the city limits of Gwinn. It was only seven but the streetlights had popped on due to the gloomy skies. Through her cracked window, Maggie inhaled the scent of summer rain, the damp earth, growing things. She missed that in the concrete jungle she'd chosen to live in. Rain rinsed off the dust and decay that masked the ugliness beneath. The ugliness she hadn't suspected was here, in the place where she'd grown up.

Seated alongside Ben, she watched the road ahead. "It's funny. I grew up in Riverview, yet I've never been to Gwinn, only driven past it."

"According to Reed's partner, there's not much here." He swung the Jeep off Highway 35 and took a left, following the makeshift map Loren Thomas had drawn him earlier this afternoon. He'd stopped in at Riverview Realty after his chat with the M.E. and been pleasantly surprised to find the surviving partner cooperative and willing to talk about Reed's last night on earth.

"I'm shocked he gave you the key without checking with Grady. Our sheriff runs a tight ship."

It wasn't the impression Ben had, though Grady did have a strong network of residents most likely reporting his every move to the Sheriff. "Actually, he said he'd suggested to Grady that someone look into Reed's death as other than accidental and been ignored."

"Think Grady'll be upset if he finds out?"

"I'm sure of it. He as much as told me to stop stirring up trouble and get the hell out of *his little town*. The sheriff doesn't cotton to strangers poking around where everyone else in Riverview fears to tread."

Maggie felt a need to defend Grady. "I don't see how you can blame Grady for wanting to protect the residents. That's what a sheriff's supposed to do." She spotted the street sign for Hendrix Avenue as Ben turned right. "I can only imagine how the owners of this house feel about having someone die in their former home."

"Older couple named Miller own it and they're not happy, according to Loren Thomas. They were personal friends of Reed's, so that only makes it worse. They've taken the house off the market for a while." The windshield wipers swished lazily on low and in the headlights, he could see a thick woods straight ahead where Hendrix came to a dead end. The small ranch-style brick house was the last one on the right. He pulled into the drive.

Maggie felt an involuntary shudder. "How would you like to buy a house where someone's died violently? I wonder if the Realtor will tell the buyers when it's finally sold."

Ben dug in his pocket for the keys Reed's real estate partner had given him. "Legally, I don't think he's required to, but ethically, I think he should." He saw that she looked apprehensive as she gazed at the dark house and wondered if bringing her along had been such a good idea. "You want to stay in the car?"

"No." The woods looked shadowy and forbidding with the rain falling from a darkening sky. Not a light shone in the windows of the house next door. The last thing she wanted to do was stay alone out here.

"Then let's go." Ben grabbed a large flashlight from the backseat and led the way. It took only a few moments to get the front door open, step inside, and turn on a table lamp.

Following him in, Maggie stuffed her hands into the pockets of her linen slacks, unwilling to touch anything. A musty smell permeated the rooms as they carefully strolled through them. And another odor, something indefinable—the smell of death. Shadows danced along the cream-colored walls and doors creaked when opened. She watched Ben peer into closets and flash his light on the floors, searching for clues, she supposed. She wished they'd have put this visit off until tomorrow, in the daylight, in full sunshine. It felt eerie poking around someone else's home, even if the Millers were no longer living here.

Ben examined the kitchen even more thoroughly, noticing that the sheriff hadn't bothered to call in a forensic team to dust for prints. Why would he when in his infinite wisdom, he'd decided with one quick look that the death was accidental? The killer, if there was one, had probably worn gloves, but you could never tell, and once in a while, you got lucky.

He wondered if he could get some help from the Home Office, some power that be who'd listen to his suspicions and get outside detectives involved. After all, National Fidelity would have a lot to gain if it could be proved that these deaths weren't accidental after all. However, he'd be risking royally pissing off Grady and his Keystone deputies. He'd have to give that some thought.

Maggie stared at the door off the kitchen. "He must have fallen down the basement stairs since there's no second floor."

"That's what the report stated." As a precaution, Ben removed his handkerchief when he opened the door and even used it to switch on the light, although the sheriff's men probably hadn't bothered being careful. Steep wooden open steps leading down. "Are you coming?" he asked.

She wasn't nuts about the idea, but she also didn't want to appear fragile and fearful. "Right behind you."

"Hold on." Going ahead, he tested the railing and found it sturdy enough. He started down. Three steps from the bottom, he stopped. "I can't believe they didn't even clean up."

Maggie peeked around him and saw the dark splotch, then drew in a shocked breath.

"Wait here. There's no point in you going farther." He didn't want her passing out on him, although she didn't strike him as the fainting type. Careful not to disturb anything, he went the rest of the way, then bent to study the stain.

Ignoring his directive, Maggie moved to the last step, struggling with a horrible fascination. "There had to have been a lot of bleeding to form such a large patch."

Ben spoke almost to himself, trying to reconstruct the scene. "Reed must have hit headfirst for this much blood. Grady's report indicated death from a head injury only, no gunshot wounds anywhere. Loren told me that Reed's body hadn't been found until the Monday after the Friday evening he died."

"All that time and no one missed him?" What a terrible thought. Perhaps that was why her father hadn't been generous with details when he'd called to tell her about Reed's death back in March.

"Apparently not. No family in town and he lived alone."

"Why did he come here on a Friday evening, to check on the house in winter? For that matter, how'd anyone know where to find him?"

"Loren found a scribbled notation in the office log book in Reed's handwriting. It seems that he'd taken a late call from someone named J. Marsh and made an appointment to show the Miller house at seven. Nothing else, no address or phone number of the prospect. Loren doesn't recall ever dealing with anyone by that name, but it's not something I've ruled out. I want to check the records at Riverview Realty going back a ways, just to be sure."

Maggie's mind was still on the caller who'd asked to see the house. "Did Grady try to locate this J. Marsh?"

"No mention was made in the sketchy little report he showed me."

"Maybe it was someone Mr. Lang knew personally." Which was exactly what Ben had suggested about the person who might have been with her father the evening he'd died. Maggie felt a shiver race up her spine. "Or maybe the person changed his mind and didn't show up. And just maybe, Reed actually did trip and fall." Would they ever really know?

Ben stooped on his haunches, his flashlight beamed on the bloody spot.

"What is it?" Maggie asked. "Did you find something?"

"Right on the corner here by the bottom stair, there's a set of small crisscross lines, as if a boot with a textured rubber sole might have stepped on the edge. You know the kind I mean, like tire treads for traction in snow."

"Yes, I see them. But there must have been several people here afterward. Grady and J.C. Chevalier, his deputy, the EMS guys, maybe even Loren and the owners. They had no reason to be careful since they figured it was accidental. Anyone could have made that mark."

Straightening, Ben looked doubtful. "Someone stepped there when the blood was wet. The rest of the people came three days later. The blood would have dried by then."

"It was winter and cold. Blood probably couldn't dry that fast in March." She was playing devil's advocate only because to accept that Ben was right would be to acknowledge that Reed had been killed. Which increased the possibility that her father hadn't died accidentally, either.

He shook his head. "Loren said the heat is always left on in vacant houses they list in the winter so the pipes won't freeze and break." He glanced around the basement with its bare walls and cement floor. Nothing much here except the furnace on the far side and the capped connections for washer and dryer. He shone the flashlight on the stairs, looking closely for bloody smudges. Nothing. "Let's head on up."

Maggie didn't have to be coaxed. Outside after Ben closed up the house, she didn't even mind the rain. Standing under the overhang on the porch, she drew in a lungful of humid air and exhaled slowly. "I'm glad that's over. I'd have made a lousy detective."

Ben peered through the darkness at the house directly across the street. "Looks as if someone's home over there. What do you say we go talk to those people? Maybe they saw something that night."

"All right." Anything to get away from this house with the lingering death smell.

The grass alongside the drive was damp and slippery as they hurried across. "Guess we should have brought jackets," he said, ducking his head against the drizzle.

"It's just a summer rain," Maggie answered.

The front door was ajar with the screen hooked up high. Ben stepped closer into the half-moon of light that spilled out. He could smell fried onions and hear a television in the background, the canned laughter of a sitcom. A man who looked to be in his seventies was reclining in a Barca-Lounger angled so he could easily look out the open door and still watch his shows. "Hello," Ben called out.

"I saw you coming." The man was thin with stooped shoulders and rimless glasses riding low on his sharp nose.

"Don't get many visitors out this way. What can I do for you?"

"I'm Ben Whalen from National Fidelity Insurance and this is Maggie Spencer. We're investigating the death of the Realtor across the street last March."

"March the tenth. I remember 'cause that's my son's birthday. He lives in Tennessee."

"Can we bother you with a few questions, Mr. . . . ?"

"Dodson. Gerald Dodson. I don't mind talking, but I don't walk so good. Can you ask 'em through the screen? I just took my medicine. My legs hurt like hell."

"That's fine." Ben glanced across the street and back to the man. "You can probably see most everything that goes on around here from that chair, especially that house over there." Of course, he wouldn't have had his door open in March, but the house had a large picture window in front. "Did you happen to see anything the night Mr. Lang died?"

Dodson ran a bony hand over his bald pate. "Saw a Buick pull into the drive 'long about seven. I recollect 'cause *Jeopardy* was just coming on. The guy went in and right away turned lights on all over the house. I figured it was that Realtor fellow. I sit over there by the window in the winter, next to the heater so I can see out. I like to know what's going on."

The man was sharp despite his age, Maggie thought.

Ben had been told Reed drove a Buick. "He was alone?"

"That's right. Few minutes later, another car drove up and parked in front. The driver got out and the first fella was waitin' for him with the door open. They went in together."

Ben felt a rising ray of hope. There *had* been someone with Reed Lang. "Did you see when they left?"

"Nope. Got interested in my show. Watching *Jeopardy* keeps the mind sharp, you know. Next time I looked out, the house was all dark and the car in front was gone. The Buick stayed right there in the drive till couple of days later when the cops came. Must've belonged to the Realtor that fell down the stairs. I read about it in the paper." Gerald pulled a red handkerchief from his pocket and blew his nose long and loud. "Damn allergies."

"About how much time after the second person arrived did you notice he was gone?"

"No more'n fifteen minutes. I looked out at the commercial break."

"And you're sure the lights were all out after the second car left?"

"You betcha."

Ben pressed on. "The second person who parked in front, could you describe him a little? I know it was dark and snowing when he arrived."

"Can't say. Wore a hooded coat of some sort, was all I could see."

"How about his car? Recall the make or color?"

Dodson puckered his mouth thoughtfully. "Wasn't new, some dark color. Black or navy blue. Couldn't figure out the make. Damn cars all look alike these days. 'Cept I know Buicks. Used to drive one, before I had to quit. Legs no good anymore."

Ben spotted a second similar chair to the right of Dodson's and took a guess. "How about your wife? Could she have noticed anything?"

"Doubt it. She's been dead three years." He cackled at his own joke.

"One last question, Mr. Dodson. Did the sheriff or one of his men come over and ask if you'd seen or heard anything?"

"No, sir. Guess they think I'm too senile, don't you know." He chuckled. "But my mind still works pretty good."

"Yes, it does." Ben gave the old man a two-finger salute. "You've been a big help. I'm leaving my card in your door with my beeper number on it. If you think of anything, please call me."

"Will do. Come on back and we'll talk again."

Maggie smiled and waved to the surprisingly observant old man and followed Ben to the Jeep, dodging raindrops before climbing in alongside him.

She felt tired and depressed. Hugging herself, she pictured in her mind's eye all too vividly what might have happened down that basement. The thought was positively chilling. "I can't believe all this. Is it possible that the man in the second car shoved Reed down the stairs, turned off all the lights, and calmly drove away?"

Ben was trying to sort things out. "It's certainly possible. Then again, Reed could have shown the house to a prospect, say this J. Marsh, who then left, and he could have fallen while groping to turn off the basement light switch."

"Then how do you explain that all the other lights had been turned off? Surely, Reed wouldn't leave the basement light to the last, then have to make his way to the front door in the dark."

"You're right. That's not logical." He'd wanted her to see it for herself, to begin to suspect something was terribly amiss.

"Oh, God." Maggie sank into her seat. "I didn't want to believe you when you first brought all this up. I mean, Reed Lang was a little on the boring side, rambling on with stories we'd all heard before, and he was terribly vain about his looks. But he was kind and sweet. Who would want a nice guy like that dead?" And could that same person have climbed up on that building with her father?

Turning on the windshield wipers, Ben drove down the quiet street, his mind racing.

Maggie was lost in her own thoughts until the Jeep turned onto the highway. "I don't imagine Grady's going to be happy that you found a witness who's been right under his nose all this time."

Ben held the steering wheel in a loose grip, his long fingers relaxed. "I don't think I'm going to tell him about Dodson just yet."

Slowly, she turned to look at him. "Why not? I know you don't think much of him, but he *is* the law around here." She was exasperated with his distrust of their sheriff. "Look, Grady's not J. Edgar Hoover, but he's not Andy of Mayberry, either."

"No, Andy was at least funny—intentionally." Catching her cool look, he switched tactics. "All right, let's look at this. We have an old man, probably every day of seventy-five, wearing glasses, sitting by a window, occasionally glancing out after dark across a fairly wide street through a snowstorm. How believable does that make what he claims he saw?"

"You don't believe Dodson?"

"Actually, I think I do. But will Grady? Or will he hold me up for ridicule and I'll lose the little credibility I have?" He shook his head. "I'd rather keep this information to myself"—he glanced at her—"to *ourselves,* and use it to figure out how this might tie in with your father's death. Like I said, I've already asked Loren Thomas if I could examine the company's appointment book, their client list, and phone records, just in case something was missed, and he agreed to get them together for me. I want to work on this on my own, for now. Then, if and when there's more, I'll go to Grady."

Maggie crossed her arms over her chest. "I don't agree."

Ben frowned as he adjusted the windshield wipers. The rain was coming down harder now. "Why not?"

Shifting the seat belt, she angled her body to face him. "Because this isn't some game, the ex-cop-turned-insurance investigator against the small-town sheriff. I need to know what happened to my father. The more people working on this, the sooner that'll happen."

"Really?" He kept the sarcasm out of his voice, but just barely. "The gun-toting lawmen of Riverview have had three months to 'work on this.' Have they come up with anything? And while we're asking questions, why is it that Grady, a good friend of both of these victims, didn't wander across the street and question the old man? Or ask to look at Reed's office records and try to find this J. Marsh? Or mosey around the neighborhood where your father fell to his death and ask area residents if they saw anything unusual that night, like I did this afternoon before I bumped into you at the house?"

He hadn't found anyone who'd seen or heard anything at the few homes bordering the building site, but he'd try again later. "If that's how Grady interprets the law around here, we're in trouble."

Maybe he had a point, but to Maggie, it seemed as if these two hardheaded men were locked in a game of one-upmanship. "Are you sure you turned your badge in? Sounds like you still think of yourself as a cop."

"No, I don't. I think of myself as an insurance investigator with five years' experience and one hell of a record. You want to check that out, you can." Signaling, he eased into the passing lane to get ahead of a lumbering eighteen-wheeler.

"Why'd you quit the force, Ben?" Suddenly, it seemed important to know, to figure out his motives. Had he overstepped his boundaries as an officer, gone against regulations, as he seemed willing to do now? Maybe if she knew more, she could see where he was heading with this investigation. And then decide if she should trust his instincts.

A muscle in Ben's jaw clenched. Her question was too damn close for comfort. "I don't want to talk about that. It's irrelevant."

Irrelevant. Maggie doubted that. "I don't think it is. You've been critical of Grady Denton from the start. It appears to me that you have trouble with authority." She looked over at his rock-hard profile. "Is that why you're no longer a cop?"

"No, it isn't." His words were terse, clipped.

She went on as if she hadn't heard his denial. "Because if it is, if you can't handle working with the law around here, maybe you'd better get National Fidelity to send someone else."

His hands tightening on the wheel, Ben kept his eyes straight ahead. "I told you, I'm damn good at what I do. I work hard, I get to the truth, I solve cases."

There was that word again. "Cases. You want to solve cases. Well, Mr. Lang and my father aren't 'cases,' they're real people or, at least, they were to those of us who cared about them. You're sent by this obscenely wealthy insurance company that has more money than God to see if you can find a loophole so they won't have to honor the double-indemnity clause. You dig around and question everyone in Riverview, wanting us to open a vein and bleed out our stories for you to dissect so you can find that fatal flaw that makes you a hero to your superiors." She didn't bother to hide her distaste. "What a lousy way to make a living."

He could've retaliated, asking if she was worried she might miss out on her second million. But, although he didn't know Maggie Spencer very well, his gut told him that wasn't the case. She was hurting, wanting answers, needing to lash out.

Wearily, Ben scrubbed a hand over his face, trying to push back the sudden rush of anger, the memories. Internal Affairs had warned him to watch out, that from time to time some incident or comment might push his buttons, that certain things would bring back the rage. The sleeping tiger he must never let loose again. He might confuse and frustrate Maggie by not rising to the bait, but it was the best choice for both of them. He took a deep breath, knowing the fault was more his than Maggie's. She couldn't possibly know all he was dealing with, nor did he want her to.

"Maybe you're right." Noticing that his hands were trembling with tension, he swore under his breath. He needed a little time to regroup. "I saw a sign advertising a place up ahead that offers home cooking. I haven't eaten since noon and it's almost nine. You game to try it?"

His out-of-the-blue suggestion after her heated accusations threw her off balance. She was certain as she looked over at him that her face reflected her feelings.

"I don't want to fight with you, Maggie," Ben admitted, well aware of her confused expression. "I'm not your enemy. We have the same goals, even if you don't think so. Let's go have something to eat and then I'll take you home."

He sounded like a man who had neither the energy nor the inclination to shore up further argument tonight. Truth be known, neither did she. "All right."

Marmaduke's was off the highway, a white brick building with a bright green roof and a matching painted door. The atmosphere inside was cozy with checkered tablecloths, red oil lamps on each table, and yummy fragrances drifting from the kitchen to chase away the gloom of a rainy night. Ben ordered fish and chips while Maggie sat staring at the menu. She really wasn't hungry, her stomach clenching with nerves. But, because she knew she should eat something, she ordered a bowl of soup.

While waiting for the food, she sipped her coffee, trying to think of something to say to get them past their last disturbing conversation. She hated strained silences, even with someone she scarcely knew. She noticed that Ben seemed to be doing the same and wondered what he was thinking as he held his cup in both hands as if trying to warm them. She searched for an opening.

"Is your home base in Detroit?"

He didn't answer right away, his eyes downcast, his face inscrutable. Finally he looked up. "Do you know a man by the name of Warren Harper?"

The non sequitur had her blinking and slow to respond.

"Uh, Warren Harper. No, I don't recall anyone by that name."

As a matter of self-protection, Ben had learned that if he didn't want to answer a question, he'd simply change the subject. Better to be thought odd than to spill your guts to someone who might wheedle something out of you that you didn't want to reveal.

He set down his cup. "When I was talking with Loren, I asked him if he knew anyone Reed might have had a falling out with lately, someone who might not be too happy with him. He told me that last year, Reed and a guy named Warren Harper from Marquette had formed some kind of a limited partnership for the purpose of investing. Apparently six months or so into the deal, Warren, who was running the show, screwed up somehow and Reed lost a lot of money. He even threatened to call the police on Harper."

A possibility and, slim though it was, she was ready to grasp at straws. "Does Loren know Harper and where we can find him?"

"No, but he was going to look through some papers and see if he could come up with an address." The food arrived and Ben sat back, relieved she'd accepted the subject change.

Maggie remembered something, but waited until the waiter left before mentioning it. "You know, when I was skimming through Dad's papers, I ran across some investment document, but I didn't read it."

"I'm not surprised. Loren told me the third investor was your father."

Excitement had Maggie's eyes widening. "Maybe we're on to something here. If this Harper felt cornered, perhaps he lured Reed out to the vacant house using a false name, then pushed him down the basement steps. Next, he went on to stalk Dad, learned his habits, crept up on him one evening, and shoved him off the second floor. What do you think?" She tore off a piece of cheese bread, hating the thought that someone might have murdered her father in cold blood, but relieved to lay the blame on a stranger rather than someone from Riverview.

He felt more at ease and could afford a grin. She certainly had a fertile imagination. "I think you think like a detective, despite what you said earlier. However, all that's a bit premature. We have to find the guy and see if he's got an alibi for those nights. A lot of people have grudges against others without killing them."

"But it is a lead." She got down a few spoonfuls of soup and decided it wasn't bad. "I'll get that document from Dad's strongbox and check it out. I don't suppose Grady knows about Harper."

"I doubt it." Ben dug into his fish as his mind worked through possibilities. "Another person Loren mentioned who wasn't terribly happy with Reed is a woman named Nancy Evans. Ever hear of her?"

"Hmm, the name sounds somewhat familiar, but I can't place her."

"Nancy moved to Riverview about two years ago, a short, middle-aged, bleached blonde with a spreading derriere. Loren's words, not mine."

Maggie glanced up. "A charming description."

"Loren tells it like it is. He said she looked over the field and settled on Reed, who was just about the only single male in her age bracket for miles around. They began to date and Reed fell like a ton of bricks, even talked of marrying her. But someone talked sense into him by checking into Nancy's background. It seems she'd already buried two husbands who'd both died shortly after the wedding, with Nancy as the only heir. So Reed broke it off and she moved away. That someone was your father."

"I remember Dad mentioning that Reed had been serious about someone, but he changed his mind." Maggie set aside her soup bowl as the waiter returned to refill their coffee cups. "Did Reed have a big insurance policy, too? I wonder. And I also wonder if this woman found out about it."

"A million, the same as your father's. Left it all to a sister in Escanaba who's sixty and never married, either. As for Nancy, she certainly had access to the information. While she lived here, she worked for Wilbur Oakley." He'd only learned of the woman this afternoon and intended to question Oakley tomorrow.

Maggie leaned back in her chair. "Another suspect with a motive for harming both men. First there were none, now suddenly there's two. Hard to believe."

"Hard to believe that these men, both owners of successful businesses, both with big insurance policies, could piss off several people over a period of years? Not hardly. There are probably more. On the way to the top, you often make enemies." He finished his dinner and reached for his coffee.

"What is hard to believe is that over the course of several months, Grady hasn't discovered any of this, and in three days, you have. Must be the cop in you." Or it could be that, unlike the older, gentler Grady, Ben enjoyed ramrodding his way through people and didn't give up until he got his answers.

"Maybe he knows about Warren Harper and Nancy Evans and chooses not to tell me."

Maggie didn't buy that. "What would be his reasoning? What could he be hiding, what could be his secrets? I never thought of Grady as a man with a lot of secrets."

"Everyone over the age of three has secrets. Some are just better at hiding them."

Maggie studied him over the rim of her cup. "That's rather cynical."

Ben shrugged. "But true. Our past, happy or troubled, follows us around, and often, we'd prefer others didn't know it all. Baggage. We all have some." He leaned forward resting his elbows on the table, wanting to lighten the conversation and maybe learn something about her. He didn't stop to ask himself why he wanted to know more than was required for his case. "What's yours, Maggie?"

"Me?" She shook her head. "I've led a charmed life, everything perfect. No skeletons in my closet." She tossed him a smile to show she didn't mean it.

Ben found a stray french fry, popped it in his mouth. "Come on, 'fess up. What's the real Maggie Spencer like and what made her that way?"

She wasn't sure she liked the direction of their conversation. "Nothing exciting, I assure you." She finished her coffee and set down the cup.

"Your mother died when you were ten?" he prompted, unwilling to drop the subject.

"Twelve, actually. Then it was Dad and I against the world." She drew in an unexpectedly shaky breath. "I adored that man. He was everything anyone would wish a father to be." She cleared her throat and blinked rapidly.

Ben hurried on, hoping to prevent tears, asking a question he'd been wondering about. "Why'd you leave Michigan?"

"Economics. After college, I couldn't find a job I liked here. I answered a newspaper ad, went for an interview in New York, and was hired by a small advertising firm. A couple of years later, I was asked to join Innovations, one of the largest PR companies around." She'd left out more than she'd told, but she saw no reason to tell him more.

"You like living in Manhattan?"

Maggie shrugged. "I've got a decent apartment, small but it's rent stabilized, and I walk to my office, which means I don't have the expense of a car. I very much enjoyed what I did, until I quit my job recently. End of story."

This he hadn't learned in his background check on her. "You quit, just like that?"

"It was time for a change." In more ways than one. Surprising herself, for she valued her privacy, Maggie realized that she'd recited her life story in a matter of minutes to a near stranger. Chalk it up to vulnerability after shock, she told herself.

"I still think you left something out. A woman who looks like you—what about men?"

Maggie raised a brow. "Men? I like men. Did I say I didn't?"

He drained the last of his coffee. "Are you saying there's been no one special man in your life?"

This line of questioning seemed to go above and beyond the reason they were together, namely the two *accidental* deaths. She decided to answer vaguely. "There has been a man, there isn't one anymore. End of subject." She had no intention of discussing the only man she'd ever seriously cared for with Ben Whalen. Especially since she wasn't quite sure what to make of him.

The truth was that most of the time, he set her teeth on edge. But spending a few hours with him today, she had to admit to a fair amount of curiosity about his background, about why he'd left the police force for a more sedate job. He didn't strike her as a man who'd prefer calm and safe over dangerous and challenging.

"All right, your turn. Tell me about your life—the good, the bad, and the ugly."

The trouble with requesting someone's life story is that they inevitably wanted something back, Ben thought as he took a sip of ice water. He hated talking about himself, always had, but he knew he had to give her an answer or she'd clam up on him. And he needed her cooperation. "As with you, not much to tell. I quit college after my dad died, enrolled in the Police Academy, worked my way up to vice, then made detective and went undercover. Six years ago, I quit that and went to work for National Fidelity. So much for my very boring life story."

And more left out than told, Maggie thought. She hadn't

wanted a litany of his work experience, yet that's what he'd given her. Potatoes without the meat. And he'd made himself sound like a quitter, a man who couldn't decide what he wanted to do. She was certain there was far more to his decisions than that. She decided to get as personal as he had. "How about women, a wife?"

"I don't have a wife," he said. "At least not anymore."

"Divorced?"

"No."

"She died."

"Yeah, she died." His throat was closing in. Time to go. "Ready to leave?" he asked, reaching for his wallet.

"Yes." The look on his face had her deciding to respect his privacy on what had to be a painful subject. She opened her shoulder bag. "Let me pay my share."

"You can pick up the next one." Ben went to find the waiter.

Who said there'd be a next one? Maggie asked herself.

The ride back with only the headlights of an occasional passing car to split the darkness was a silent journey. Ben seemed lost in his memories, his profile hard and unyielding. Maggie let the quiet linger, not wanting to intrude on his musings. They were, after all, two relative strangers hurtling along in the night. She couldn't help wondering what ghosts were riding in the backseat.

The rain stopped about the time Ben pulled into the driveway of Jack Spencer's home and noticed that the housekeeper had left lamps burning for Maggie. How long had it been since someone had left a light on for him? Annoyed with the direction of his thoughts, he shoved the car into park and got out to help Maggie step down.

But she was already jumping down and walking toward the front porch, keys in hand. A nineties' woman, Ben thought, independent, one that knew her own mind and had everything going for her. A great house, a career she loved, neighbors and friends who cared about her, and no excess baggage to haul around, or so she said. And let's not forget the two million dollars.

At the door, Maggie swung around, surprised he'd trailed after her. Ben Whalen didn't seem like the chivalrous type. "Thanks, for asking me along, and for dinner."

"You're welcome."

"Will you, that is, can I tag along when you check out those other leads? I just hate sitting around and wondering." She hated to ask him, but the truth was that her visit to the house where Reed had died and the fact that the old man across the street had been so certain there'd been someone with the Realtor, had raised even more questions in her mind. She wasn't absolutely convinced there'd been foul play, but she felt she owed it to her father to know more.

"Sure." Funny how she wanted to go with him even though she didn't approve of his delay in reporting to the sheriff, or his job with National Fidelity and, most probably, his methods.

"I'd appreciate that." She unlocked the door, then swung back once more. "Ben, why won't you tell me the reason you quit being a cop?" His eyes in the porch light were a fathomless gray as he held her gaze, but he didn't answer. "Were you in trouble or experiencing burnout? Were you running away or running toward something new?" She wanted to understand, to know which, though she couldn't have said why.

Ben scrubbed a hand over his face, feeling older than Gerald Dodson. "You seem to have all the answers, Maggie. Pick one." He turned, walked to his Jeep, and got behind the wheel. He didn't race off, but rather drove carefully around the circular driveway before exiting onto the road.

The night was still with shifting shadows and Maggie felt an uneasiness she'd never noticed before in this, the yard of her childhood home. It almost felt as if someone or some thing was out there, hidden and watchful, waiting.

With a shudder, Maggie went inside and double-locked the door.

Staying well behind the Jeep, a dark sedan followed the insurance investigator, unnoticed, unseen.

Ben Whalen was too nosy for his own good, hanging around, asking questions, poking his nose into other people's business. A check of his job credentials had been simple enough to obtain. Top man in his field at National Fidelity. Bulldog tenacious with street smarts and a keen mind. A former cop.

The smile came easily. All that would do him no good.

The plan had been carefully thought out, every detail, every possibility. No one must rush things before the allotted time, nor get in the way when the time was at hand. No one must hinder the mission or it would cost them. Only those on the list would pay for their past sins, pay with their lives for the lives they stole, the happiness they ruined.

The Jeep turned off the main road and into the graveled parking lot of the Riverview Motel. The sedan slowed, then stopped alongside the hedges that weren't too thick, allowing a clear view of the individual cottages. Squinting, it was just possible to make out Number 10, the last in the row, the one Whalen entered. In moments, the light went on and one could imagine that Ben was preparing for bed, feeling secure. He had yet to learn that no place was safe enough for the wicked.

The light inside the cabin went out and slowly, the sedan left the area as quietly as it had appeared.

Chapter Four

A hazy sun was trying to break through the clouds atop the hill as Maggie stood at the kitchen window sipping a cup of strong English Breakfast tea. She'd spent a restless night and by six, she'd given up wrestling with the sheets and gone in to shower.

She'd even beaten Fiona downstairs this morning, which was remarkable since the woman seemed never to sleep. Last night when Maggie had come in close to midnight, she'd walked past the housekeeper's room and seen the door ajar, heard the television on. But she'd been in no mood to stop in for a chat.

Her last conversation with Ben had swirled through her mind all night like the wispy fingers of fog just outside the window. Perhaps she'd had no right to press, but he'd asked her some mighty personal questions, so she'd followed suit. *Why won't you tell me the reason you're no longer a cop? Were you in trouble or experiencing burnout? Were you running away or running toward something?* she'd asked him. Perhaps she shouldn't have pried, but he'd opened the door to personal questions. His reply had been less than satisfactory. *You seem to have all the answers, Maggie. Pick one.*

The answers. Hell, she scarcely knew the questions. She could have asked herself the same thing she'd asked Ben. Had she run away from her life in New York, a life that had become deeply disappointing? Had she run to her childhood home where she'd always felt safe and well loved? The answer to both was probably yes.

Joke's on you, Maggie, she told herself. The misery she'd left behind was still in her mind and heart, and the safety she'd sought had been an illusion.

She drained her cup and went to pour a second helping from the cream-colored pot decorated with shamrocks that Fiona had brought over with her from Ireland. The housekeeper thought that the devil himself had invented coffee and wouldn't have it in the house. Oddly enough, her father, who'd never let anyone bully him, had gone along with Fiona and there was never anything but tea in the Spencer kitchen. But Maggie's mind wasn't really on tea.

Insulated, Maggie thought as she seated herself at the sturdy oak table in the breakfast alcove. All her growing-up years here in Riverview and even while attending college in Marquette, she'd felt insulated from danger, safe and secure. Perhaps moving to Manhattan should have frightened her, but in her early twenties, she'd been eager to taste life, excited about her new job and, with the arrogance of youth, she'd thought herself invincible. It hadn't taken her long to learn to be careful in the largest city in the country until taking extra precautions had become a way of life. Somehow, she'd managed to avoid ever feeling truly in jeopardy.

Yet now, visiting a vacant house and seeing that terrible bloodstain where a man had died brutally, and staring at the chalked outline of where her father's body had landed after a fall that might not have been accidental—all that had made her see that she'd been living in a fool's paradise.

Murder, for God's sake! Murder in this sleepy little town where no homicide had taken place during her entire lifetime. The thought was too much to comprehend, too staggering to understand. The question *why*, was a disturbing chant at the back of her mind. Followed by *who*. Who was doing this? What madman was stalking her small hometown, tainting the innocent atmosphere with his horrifying agenda? If only she knew. If only . . .

"You're up early, lass." Fiona came bustling into the kitchen with her long-legged stride, tying an apron over her middle as she made her way to the sink. "It's worried I was, with you coming in so late last night and it raining and all. Are you all right, child?"

Only a housekeeper who'd raised you could get away with calling a woman of twenty-nine "child." Putting on a smile, Maggie turned from the window. "Yes, I'm fine. I'm sorry if I worried you." Six years on her own, it hadn't occurred to her to check in with anyone. "I should have called but I . . . I got involved." To say the least.

Fiona poured herself a cup of tea, then bent to retrieve a frying pan. "I don't want you to think I'm watching your every move, for it's a grown woman you are. I'm a worrier, is all. Old habits are hard to break." The good Lord knew she'd worried many a night about Jack Spencer, especially the last few months of his life. "I'll make us a nice breakfast."

Maggie opened her mouth to protest, to say her second cup of tea would do nicely since she seldom ate breakfast in New York, but stopped herself. Fiona seemed lost without someone to fuss over and, although she didn't want the housekeeper's hovering to become a habit, she didn't have the heart to refuse this morning, despite a long list of things she needed to do today.

"I've fresh eggs," Fiona went on, gathering things from the fridge. "And bacon I'll cook crisp the way you like it.

And cinnamon toast. Will that do?" Placing bacon strips in the pan, she rushed on without waiting for a reply. "I remember growing up how you always loved cinnamon toast." The older woman swiped at a nostalgic tear, annoyed because she couldn't seem to get them to dry up these days.

Maggie walked over to her, her own eyes misting, and leaned in to hug the slender frame. "That will more than do, and yes, I remember that you make the best cinnamon toast in the universe."

Fiona closed her eyes a moment, absorbing the comfort, the affection, then stepped back to examine the lovely face of the young woman who was the daughter she'd not given birth to. "Are you holding up all right, Maggie?"

"I'm working on it. What about you?"

Turning back to the stove, Fiona nodded. "Me, too. It's just that I keep expecting him to walk through the door and call out in that booming voice, 'Fiona, I'm home. Where's my tea?'"

"Only lately, he'd asked for whiskey more than tea, isn't that right?" Fiona had hinted, but they'd not really talked it out.

"Oh, no. He never asked me for whiskey, knowing I'd not be pleased he didn't stop with one or two, like he used to be content with. He'd do his drinking alone, evenings mostly, shut away in his den." Expertly, she flipped the bacon, then slipped two slices of bread into the toaster as she talked. "Brooding was what he was doing. You'd have thought the man was Irish like the men from my village who'd go to the pubs and fret with a pint of Guinness in front of 'em."

Maggie opened the silverware drawer to set the table. "When did you notice this starting?"

"Long about last fall, though, he seemed to cheer up at Christmas when you came to visit. It was after his friend died in March that Jack's dark moods got worse and more frequent." The bacon drained on paper towels as she cracked eggs into the pan, not breaking a single yolk, then pushed down the toaster.

Pausing, Maggie tucked a loose strand of hair behind her ear. "Something evidently was bothering him. Do you have any idea what it might have been?"

"I wish. He said not a word to me. I hadn't seen him like that since your mother—God rest her soul—took sick and died. You know how cheerful and smiling your father usually was." She slipped the eggs onto two plates, added bacon, and quickly buttered the toast.

Maggie carried the plates to the table while the older woman topped off their tea. She was moving into cholesterol overload, Maggie thought as she savored the smoky taste of bacon. But what the hell, she rarely indulged herself with Fiona's home cooking. "Mmm, this is heavenly," she said, surprised she could eat.

"You need to stay awhile and let me spoil you a bit." Fiona nibbled on toast, not really hungry herself. But she knew that if she hadn't fixed breakfast for two, Maggie wouldn't have eaten. And she had a few questions needing answers. "Have you thought about what you're going to do now?"

She should have realized Fiona would be concerned about her own future, Maggie thought with a pang of guilt. She knew the housekeeper to be in her early fifties and, although she'd been well paid all these years, for Jack Spencer had been a generous man, Maggie had no idea if Fiona had saved her money and wanted to leave. Or hadn't and needed to stay. Or perhaps just *wanted* to remain.

Which reminded her that she needed to get to the bank, to meet with Kurt Becker and get Dad's will from his safe-deposit box. She remembered the day Dad had had her sign a signature card so she'd have access. His will and a few old papers were all he'd kept in it, to her knowledge. She was certain her father had left something to Fiona after all these years of faithful service. Just one more chore to add to her growing list.

"I don't know how to answer your question, Fiona." She thought about her life back in New York and knew she'd reached a crossroads, even before Dad had died. Things had ended badly with Chet, so much so that he'd made it impossible for her to continue working at the company he'd started ten years ago and still owned. Which was a shame because she loved her job and knew she was good at it.

She'd left suddenly after their last terrible quarrel, but the very next day, she'd called all her accounts to explain. She had no idea what Chet had told them, only that they'd been less than receptive. So be it. There were other jobs, though the prospect of looking for one was daunting.

When she'd originally decided to visit her father, before she'd learned he'd died, she'd thought she'd be gone about a week. But now, she really faced no serious timetable, which was good because, since becoming suspicious about the way Dad had died, she wanted to see things through here. How could she return to New York and go job hunting not knowing?

"I can't go back just yet. There're too many loose ends to tie up here."

That pleased Fiona, but she wouldn't rest until her future was more settled. Thirty years of service was a good many. She'd come to the States from County Cork as a young woman scarcely twenty. She'd left nine siblings and farming parents who barely could keep food on the table, and moved in with an aunt and uncle who'd migrated to Detroit years ago and sponsored her. For two years, she'd stayed, working and helping out without wages to repay them, then looked for work elsewhere, for they had seven other mouths to feed and she'd had a yearning to get on with her life.

Tall and raw-boned with a face even those who loved her had labeled homely, untrained in anything but domestics,

Fiona had answered an ad for a housekeeper and interviewed with the Spencers. Noreen had just learned she was pregnant and was already somewhat sickly, and Jack had wanted her to have help. Fiona had moved in that very day and lived nowhere else since. She'd made the family her own and never looked back, scarcely feeling the lack of children of her own, so attached had she become to Maggie. She'd mourned Noreen's death and now Jack's. If Maggie planned to sell everything and stay permanently in New York, Fiona wasn't sure she'd be able to bear it.

"You don't know what you'll be doing with the house, then?" the housekeeper finally found the courage to ask.

Maggie's face registered surprise. "The house? Keep it, of course, and you with it, if you'll stay." She reached across the table to clasp the older woman's hands, the ones that had bathed her, changed her and, occasionally, swatted her behind for misbehaving. "You're all the family I have left now, Fiona."

The housekeeper couldn't hide the quick rush of emotion, though she tried. "And you I," she answered in a ragged whisper. "But still, I wouldn't be wanting you to keep the place just for me. I've a little money put by and . . ."

"No, it wouldn't be just for you. It would be for me *and* you. New York's where I live, for now, but this house, this is my *home.*"

"All right then." No nonsense as always, Fiona gave Maggie's hand a squeeze and wiped her eyes with a white handkerchief bordered in lace. "We won't need to speak of it again."

Used to the woman's abrupt ways, Maggie rose to clear the table. "Fiona, I need to ask you something." She looked into clear blue eyes and chose her words carefully. "I know you said Dad had been acting worried and despondent for several months and drinking more than usual. Do you think he might have climbed up onto that building after drinking that night and been despondent enough to . . . to . . ."

"No! Never, no." The mere suggestion had Fiona vehemently shaking her head. "I told you, he shut himself in his study and never left the house after drinking. If you're suggesting he might have been depressed enough to take his own life, that's not possible. Not Jack Spencer. He was too devout a Catholic, for one. And not the sort who'd run from his problems like that and leave you to face them alone. Whatever was bothering him—and we may never know what that was—I'll never believe he killed himself over it."

Maggie nodded, grateful to hear her own beliefs put into words. "Thanks. I needed to hear that."

"It's my fault, you know," Fiona stated, her voice suddenly quivery. "Jack's accident. It's all my fault."

Maggie raised a questioning brow. "Your fault? How could that be?"

Fiona blinked rapidly, then brushed aside an uncharacteristic tear. "It's my cowardice that killed him. I knew something was bothering your father, knew it and, as usual, didn't speak up. I should have asked him, should have insisted he tell me. But no, I hid my concern and kept my mouth shut. I never once in all these years let him know how much I . . . how very much I . . ."

Suddenly, it was all so very clear, Maggie thought. "That you loved him," she finished for the poor woman.

Her expression anguished, Fiona looked into eyes filled with understanding. "You knew all along, did you?"

"Not until now, but I should have guessed. You did everything for him, more than anyone should have, and never complained."

Fiona swallowed a sob. "Everything but let him look into my heart, so afraid was I that he'd laugh or send me packing."

"Oh, Fiona, Dad would never have sent you away."

"Perhaps not. But my own pride would have made me leave, knowing he didn't return my feelings." She found her handkerchief, sniffled into it. "A coward doesn't ask so the dream never dies. I never thought the time was right. I . . . I thought we still had years left and one day . . ." Her voice faded into a whisper. "Who'd have dreamed he'd go so quickly?"

Maggie moved to hug the slender woman to her, wondering just what her father would have done had Fiona confessed her feelings. Now, they'd never know.

In control once more, Fiona stepped back. "Let that be a lesson to you, child. Live your live to the fullest and never be afraid to speak your feelings. That way, when you're older like me, you'll not have to live with regrets."

Maggie squeezed her hand. "I know in his quiet way that Dad loved you."

Fiona closed her eyes briefly, then smiled at Maggie. "Thank you for saying that, Maggie."

"And I love you, too. You know that."

Fiona gave her a quick, hard hug, then turned aside, picking up the dishcloth. "I shouldn't be holding you up. I know you have things to do."

Maggie glanced at the wall clock. "I do have a few errands to run, but I'll see you later, okay?" At the older woman's nod, she walked to the doorway, then turned back. "And, Fiona, don't worry about me if I don't check in. I'm a big girl now."

Fiona smiled. "Not to me, you aren't."

"Nancy Evans is not the sort of person I would hire under normal circumstances," Wilbur Oakley said, tugging down the ends of his vest for emphasis. He circled his antique desk and sat down in his very expensive leather chair, needing the feeling of authority it gave him. Here, in his office, he was in charge, and no ragamuffin investigator who'd tried to unnerve him by beating him to his own door this morning would get the best of him.

"How so, Wilbur?" Ben asked, dropping his lanky frame into one of the fussy little chairs facing the irritating little man's sad excuse for a working desk. The thing belonged in a museum displaying French period pieces or in some whorehouse, but not in an insurance office in this remote little country town in the Upper Peninsula.

"It just so happened that my secretary, Roberta Lodenbauer, who'd been with me for twenty years, retired rather abruptly the week my wife had one of her spells. I had to stay home with Mildred, but I couldn't leave the office unattended. An agent I know in Marquette recommended Nancy and I hired her sight unseen. A foolish move I was to regret. But I was desperate." Wilbur hated having to provide explanations to this unkempt individual, but it wouldn't do to let him know.

On the credenza behind Wilbur was a silver-framed photo of a small woman with hair the color of dung tightly pulled back from a thin, unsmiling face, undoubtedly the long-suffering Mrs. Oakley. Hell, he couldn't smile if he had to face Wilbur every day, either, Ben thought. "What kind of spells does your wife have?"

"She has a delicate nature and . . . actually, it's not your concern." Wilbur folded his hands on his desktop and tried to assume a patient attitude. "What does Nancy Evans have to do with your investigation into two accidental deaths?"

"I get to ask the questions, Wil." He leaned back, balancing his weight on the fragile carved legs of the chair, watching Oakley's face. "What about Nancy displeased you?"

Wilbur struggled to keep his thoughts from showing. *The same things that displease me about you. You're both coarse, common, and vulgar.* His hands gripped one another as he watched the big ox teeter on his Louis XIV chair's legs. "Let's see. Where to begin? She couldn't spell, her typing was atrocious, and her phone manners nonexistent. She probably hadn't read a book since her high school days and every time I walked in here, she was listening to country music with all those guitars twanging. She stuffed a size eighteen body into a size twelve dress, wore enough eye makeup to keep Maybelline in the black for the balance of the century, and the color of her hair changed monthly."

Amused, Ben straightened. "Don't hold back, Wil. Tell me how you really feel." He got up and roamed the room, checking an array of artifacts on display, a watercolor on one wall and a stack of *Playboy* magazines on the bottom shelf of the bookcase next to a leather-bound copy of the Bible. Two trophies for placing in marathons with Wilbur's name inscribed on each sat at opposite ends. He'd have never pegged the prissy little man as a runner. "Did you let her go when you returned after your wife was over her spell?"

"Not right away." Wilbur caressed the silk of his conservatively striped tie. "Good help is hard to find in small towns."

"I'll just bet. While you were home with the missus, Nancy had access to all your files in here, right?"

Wilbur's mouth twitched with nerves. "Well, to the extent she'd need to in order to answer clients' questions, perhaps file claims, or talk with the Home Office. Why do you ask?"

Ben set down a copy of *Ulysses* that had been checked out of the local library. "Ah, ah, there you go again, Wil, asking questions. To clarify things, Nancy Evans could have looked up the insurance records of most any resident of Riverview insured by National Fidelity on that computer over there or your filing cabinets, right?"

Flustered, Wilbur toyed with his gold cameo ring. "I suppose so. What has this to do with . . . ?"

With a look, Ben stopped the question, then decided to answer. "Maybe nothing. Maybe something very important. How long did she work here?"

"About six months."

"I understand she was dating Reed Lang pretty seriously for a while, then they broke up. Did Nancy leave right after that breakup?"

"I believe she did. Reed should never have taken up with that woman. He was no prize, but even he could have done better."

"Do you know of any other romantic involvements Reed might have had?"

Wilbur's lips pursed. "I don't keep track of that sort of thing. I have a business to run here."

"Sorry, I forgot." Ben realized his sarcasm was lost on Wilbur as he stepped away from the man's desk, rubbing his nose as the heavy scent of aftershave drifted to him. Oakley had to apply it with a sprinkling can. "Do you have a forwarding address for Nancy?"

"I believe she returned to Marquette. Just a moment." Wilbur riffled through his Rolodex, found the card, and quickly copied down the address. Rising, he held out the note, hoping Whalen would consider himself dismissed. The man really got under his skin, yet he had to ask one more question. "Why is it you're investigating these two deaths as if they weren't accidental? Do you have reason to suspect otherwise?"

Ben pocketed the address. "I'm just a naturally suspicious fellow, Wil. Things aren't always what they seem."

A discreet knock at the door had both of them turning to see the office secretary stick her head in. "Sorry to bother you, Mr. Oakley, but Line One's for you and . . ."

Wilbur glared at her. "I thought I asked that you not interrupt us?"

The woman glanced at Ben hesitantly, then back to her employer. "I know, but you said to always put Ms. Doran through, no matter what."

Sitting up taller, Wilbur waved a dismissive hand at her.

"Yes, fine." His manicured fingers curled impatiently around the phone as he swung his attention back to his unwelcome visitor. "You'll have to excuse me. I must take this call."

"No problem, Wil. I'll be in touch." Ben left the office, closing the door behind him. The secretary was back at her desk. He watched as the red light on her phone stopped blinking, indicating that Wilbur had picked up Line One.

He smiled charmingly at the mousy little secretary he'd met while waiting for Wilbur. Andrea Taylor looked to be in her late twenties with short brown hair and a slender build that could be labeled boyish, quite a contrast to the flamboyant Nancy Evans that Oakley had described. He decided to go on a fishing expedition. "The lady who called, is she Mary Jane Doran, by any chance?"

Andrea's plain face looked puzzled. "Why, no. It's Phoebe Doran, the head librarian at Riverview Library. I don't believe I know a Mary Jane Doran."

Neither do I, honey, Ben thought. "My mistake. Is Phoebe Doran insured through this agency?"

"I don't believe so. I can check." Andrea stood and pulled open the file drawer behind her, wishing she'd worn her new yellow dress instead of her old blue shirtwaist. She knew that Ben Whalen had been sent by the Home Office, but she hadn't known he was so attractive until he'd walked in this morning. Efficiently, she scanned the folders. "No, there's no file on her." She turned back to see a frown on his handsome face.

"Does she phone often, maybe even drop in?"

"I guess you could say that." Suddenly nervous, Andrea wondered if she should have answered his questions without checking with Mr. Oakley. Her boss had quite a temper. "Is anything wrong?"

"You've been a big help. Thanks."

Curiouser and curiouser, Ben thought, strolling outside. If the librarian wasn't a client, was she perhaps calling about the copy of *Ulysses* Wilbur had in his office? Did they belong to a book discussion group? Or was the reason Oakley seemed anxious to be rid of Ben just now because he and Phoebe Doran had other more personal things to discuss?

Hard to believe the proper little man would be involved with another woman, Ben thought as he strolled along Main Street. But you could never tell. That old adage about still water running deep. Maybe he'd just wander on over to the library and stop in. Not that he considered Wilbur a suspect in either death, but as a detective, he'd investigated enough crimes to know that one minor thing often led to something major. Especially if something seemed out of sync, like a middle-aged man with a sickly wife getting nervous and jumpy over a call from a woman who was to be put through to him "no matter what."

It was a beautiful day for a walk, Ben decided, and he had a little time before he was to meet Loren Thomas at Riverview Real Estate to pick up Reed Lang's papers. Imagine, a small town in this day and age that still had a Main Street, he thought. Riverview's broad avenue consisted of several long blocks with small businesses and public buildings lining both sides and cars angle-parked in front with not a meter in sight. The flag in front of the post office flapped in a light breeze and the high school was visible just beyond. Main Street gave the impression of a bygone era with its old-fashioned globe lampposts, decorative trees in redwood planters and reclaimed brick roadway. He wouldn't have been terribly surprised to see a horse-drawn carriage clip-clopping along, like on Mackinac Island.

Across from Oakley's Insurance was the Green Thumb, a florist and nursery with a colorful window display featuring an antique bridal gown surrounded by flowers. How many June weddings could there be in a town of less than nine hundred permanent residents? he wondered.

There was a dry goods store alongside Bailey's Barber

Shop with the obligatory rotating red-and-white pole. Next door was Opal's Beauty Parlor, the shop run by Grady's second wife, displaying an assortment of colorful wigs in its window.

Walking past Kowalski's Meat Market, he peered in the glass door and saw an overweight man wearing a white apron whacking away with a cleaver behind the meat counter. A small woman with a matching apron was sliding trays of lunchmeat into the lighted display case at the far end. Ed Kowalski, Ben knew, had also been a close friend of both Jack and Reed, the three having attended college together. He wanted to talk with Ed and would, but not today.

Overall there was a sense of pride here in the downtown section of Riverview, in the street kept clean of debris with the remnants of the Memorial Day Parade of last weekend swept up. Pride and neighborliness and charm. Stuff you couldn't get in big cities for all their sophistication and cosmopolitan offerings and fancy architecture. Ben had grown up in a large city, but had often yearned for the tranquillity of a small town.

Yet he couldn't help thinking that hidden behind the facade of friendliness, there was someone who was methodically destroying the very fabric of Riverview.

Down a ways was Riverview Bank, managed by yet another of Jack's chums, Kurt Becker. A close-knit bunch, the poker pals. Did any one of them suspect that either Jack or Reed had died other than accidentally? Would they admit as much to him, an outsider? Or could one of them be involved in the current mayhem?

He glanced across the street at Riverview Drugs where George Cannata, another classmate of the two dead men, was the pharmacist. Someone else he needed to interview to get some insight into Jack and Reed. Next to the drugstore was the sheriff's office and alongside that, the small jail. Grady's black Ford Bronco with the sheriff's insignia on the door was parked in front. Why, Ben wondered, were both Grady and Wilbur as uncooperative and unpleasant as could be? Because they resented his presence in their tight little community most likely.

Next to the jail was Spencer Construction, a narrow, unimaginative structure that housed Jack Spencer's office. Surprising that a builder with a fine reputation wouldn't have put up something more eye appealing. Peeking inside, Ben wondered who was running the show now that Jack was gone. To his knowledge, Spencer had had no partners, only a secretary with probably little authority. Had Maggie taken over or put the business up for sale?

Maggie. He stopped short, gazing up at a picture-perfect sky but seeing her face last night when he'd left her unsatisfied on her own doorstep. Her curiosity once aroused was unrelenting. He liked that in a woman, but wished she hadn't focused those gorgeous eyes on his past. He wasn't someone who easily confided in anyone. After all, it wasn't as if he envisioned a future with her, or anyone else, for that matter.

He was a rolling stone, here today, gone tomorrow. Involvements and emotional entanglements are what cut the heart out of a man. He didn't need any of that shit to muddy up his mind. He'd been there, done that, and never again, thank you very much. He was drawn to Maggie, no denying that. But it was strictly hormonal. He wouldn't mind a romp in the sheets, but beyond that, he wasn't interested. Not now, not ever again.

Maggie was different. She was intelligent, quick-witted, and she had him shaving with more care these days. He'd had a relationship or two since his wife's death, for sexual satisfaction and because he genuinely liked women. Liked their softness, the way they smelled, their gentleness, the unique way their minds worked.

But each one had known the score and been as footloose as he. Ben had a feeling that Maggie stood apart from the herd, a woman who could bring a man to his knees if she set her mind to it. That was yet another reason to stay away from her, he reminded himself.

Turning around, Ben found himself in front of an impressive stucco structure with twin concrete lions flanking its tall double doors and a discreet overhead sign that read: RIVERVIEW LIBRARY. Awhile back, someone had decided to paint everything white, but time and weather had chipped off much of the paint, giving the building an old, tired look. The slanted green roof looked as if it, too, could use a little renovation. Ben walked up the six wide steps and went inside.

The atmosphere was hushed and cool despite the sunshine pouring in through several high arched windows. The main room was divided into sections by floor-to-ceiling double-sided book shelves, six to be exact. Off to one side was a small grouping of chairs arranged as if in a reading circle. On the opposite wall were two long tables, presumably for note-taking, and more chairs. He saw a young mother with two toddlers in the children's section and an old man browsing through magazines.

Immediately in front of him was a waist-high circular oak counter behind which was seated a woman with soft brown hair and oversize glasses. Though he could only see her from the waist up, she appeared small in stature with delicate features and slender hands. Her eyes were a deep blue the same shade as the cotton blouse she wore. As he stepped closer, he guessed that she was probably in her fifties, yet there wasn't a line or wrinkle on her face.

"Hello. Can I help you find something?" Her voice was warm and welcoming, as was her generous smile. Her brass nameplate indicated she was Phoebe Doran.

Ben returned her smile. "I'm new in town and I was wondering if you have any books on Riverview, the Upper Peninsula and this whole area, so I could acquaint myself with your town." As an improvised excuse, it wasn't half bad.

"I don't believe there've been any books written specifically on Riverview, but I do have some brochures on our general location and all it offers for tourists. Would that do?"

It was a start. "That'd be fine."

"I'll get them for you." Rising, she unlatched the half door and walked to a filing cabinet, returning in moments. "Here you are. Several of these list specific titles you might want to look into for particular interests, such as fishing or agate hunting, the copper mines of the past, the Indian influence."

She'd apparently taken him for a tourist. "Thanks." He'd been right, she was small, coming scarcely to his shoulder. No wedding ring, no jewelry at all except for a small gold pin in the form of an angel attached to one shoulder of her blouse. "That's an unusual pin."

Phoebe's hand moved to caress the pin lovingly and a soft smile formed. "Yes, isn't it? A gift from a dear friend."

He wished he had the guts to ask if her dear friend was the very married Mr. Oakley with the conveniently sick wife, but Phoebe Doran's manner was so ladylike, so kindly, that Ben didn't want to even suggest something improper. No, he decided, this woman wouldn't have anything to do with that creep. They must have some business to discuss and his overactive imagination had leap-frogged that call into something up close and personal.

"I'll return these," he said, indicating the half-dozen folders she'd given him.

"No need. They're free. If you need more information, please drop by again, Mr. . . . ."

"Whalen. Ben Whalen." He watched the smile slide from her face and disappear, saw the kindness in her eyes shift to suspicion. It was a little like witnessing a smiley-face balloon deflate into a wrinkled frown. Phoebe just stood there, unmoving, looking as if she regretted not having asked his name sooner.

Ben said good-bye politely and walked out into the sunshine. He'd have to think about Phoebe and Wilbur later. A glance at his watch told him he'd better hurry across the street to Riverview Realty or he'd be late for his appointment with Loren.

Maggie leaned back on the tan leather couch in Kurt Becker's private office and sighed heavily. "Then you have no idea why suddenly Dad's interest in the business all but disintegrated starting sometime last fall?" she asked, her voice strained.

Seated beside her, Kurt Becker smoothed back his salt-and-pepper hair, his heart aching for the young woman he'd watched grow up along with his own two daughters. "If something happened to Jack to trigger his disinterest, I haven't a clue what it was. I did notice that he didn't spend as much time working on-site as before, or even in his office. He gave his foreman, Rosco Cadell, more and more responsibility."

As a banker and confidant of most of the men and women in Riverview, Kurt felt oddly responsible if things went wrong in their lives, most especially if it happened to someone close to him. Yet he also felt honor bound not to discuss a friend's problems with anyone without specific permission to do so. "You know how far back your father and I go, Maggie. But he wasn't one to talk about his problems. Sure I noticed he was more moody and that he'd begun drinking at our Friday night poker games. I even mentioned it to him once, but he laughed it off saying a man was entitled to enjoy himself."

"Did he drive home after drinking?" Dad had lectured her so much about drinking and driving that she couldn't imagine he would.

Kurt's face was serious, almost melancholy. "No, Jack never drove a single mile when he'd had a drink in him, not since the . . . well, since his college days."

Maggie glanced down at the last P & L statement from Spencer Construction that she'd found in her father's strongbox. "Profits were down the last two quarters, but not enough to do real harm to the company, unless the trend continued. Dad knew as well as anyone that building booms and slow periods are cyclical. He'd always ridden them out and even diversified his investments so all of his eggs wouldn't be in the same basket. I found stock certificates, bonds, CDs. What I can't figure is why he suddenly lost interest in a business he'd loved all his life."

Kurt rose to his full six-two height, a slim man in an expensive suit, one who cared a great deal about his image in the town of his birth. "One of the last conversations we had, Jack confided that he was tired, bone tired. I advised him to get a medical exam, that maybe he was rundown or perhaps low blood sugar was draining his energy. I don't know that he followed my advice."

"Dr. Alexander said he didn't but that he still played a vigorous game of tennis and never complained to him." She shoved the papers into a thin leather briefcase. "I'm at a loss to even make a serious guess at what was troubling him." Earlier, she'd stopped in to see Bruce Gorman, her father's attorney, but he hadn't been able to shed any light on what, if anything, had been bothering Jack Spencer.

Slowly, Kurt Becker walked to the window and stood staring out, his back to Jack's daughter. "He was a deep thinker, your father, more sensitive than the rest of us. Outwardly, he was always joking and laughing, but inside, things gnawed away at him. Where his friends might dismiss a problem and go on, Jack would worry it to death. He'd always been like that, even when he was much younger."

Frowning, Maggie rose. "Are you trying to tell me something, Mr. Becker?"

Drawing in a deep breath, Kurt turned, putting on a fatherly smile. "Only that Jack Spencer was a fine man who worried overly much. Oh, he'd had his wild moments in college, as we all did, but then he grew up, as we all must. He was a man who wouldn't harm a fly if he could avoid it. I miss him terribly."

Which hadn't really answered her question. Still, what was she hoping for, a miracle reply that would illuminate the situation and everything would suddenly be crystal clear? "Did you ever hear Dad discuss suicide? Do you think he could have taken his own life?"

Kurt appeared to consider the question. "I don't believe so. Jack may have been worried, maybe had a problem he was working through. But kill himself? Doubtful."

Doubtful wasn't as emphatic as Fiona's absolutely not, but it expressed the same view. "Thank you." It was time to leave. "And thanks for going over these papers with me, and for emptying Dad's safe-deposit box." It had contained one item only, Jack's will.

"Anytime, my dear. I know that Jack's death is hard to accept, Maggie. Give yourself time. Relax and rest up. Perhaps you'd like to go fishing with me this afternoon? I know you enjoyed going with Jack. Out on the river, it's so quiet and peaceful. Problems seem less pressing."

She smiled up at him to take the sting from her refusal. "Maybe another time." At the door, she turned. "One more thing. Do you know a Warren Harper from Marquette? I found some business agreement in Dad's strongbox that indicates he and Mr. Lang were somehow involved with this man."

"Never heard his name mentioned. But, as I said, Jack was pretty closemouthed about most things." He smiled down at her. "Take care of yourself, Maggie. And call if you need me."

She kissed his smooth cheek. "Thanks, I will." Moving out into the warmth of late morning, she was glad to leave the musty old bank. She'd parked the Explorer in the back parking lot. Checking her watch as she hurried around the corner of the building, she wasn't watching where she was headed.

And slammed into the hard, broad chest of Ben Whalen.

Chapter Five

"Whoa, lady." Ben grabbed Maggie's arms to steady her. "You're in one big hurry." He'd seen the surprise in her green eyes turn to annoyance.

"Were you lurking around the corner, just waiting for me to plow into you?" She knew the question was silly, yet it gave her a moment to compose herself as she stepped back from him.

"Yeah, that's me. The Riverview Lurker. Actually, I'm glad you bumped into me. You said you wanted to tag along if I had any leads to run down. I'm going to Marquette to look up Nancy Evans. Want to take a drive?" He hadn't planned to call her, even though she'd asked to go along last night. He worked best alone, without interference from interested parties. But seeing the look of concern on her face, as if she were carrying the weight of the world on her slender shoulders, he found himself inviting her. What would it hurt if he included her? Besides, she still didn't really believe the deaths weren't accidental. He wanted to prove he was right.

Maggie mentally assessed the few remaining errands left

on her list and decided they could wait. She was just curious enough to want to follow this new lead, even if it meant having to thrust and parry with Ben. "Yes, I would. Only I should stop by the house and pick up that limited partnership agreement Dad and Reed had with Warren Harper. His last known address is in Marquette, too."

"I was going to ask you about that. We can kill two birds with one stone." He pointed to the far end of the lot. "My Jeep's over there."

"I'm parked right here. Why don't I run home and you can pick me up in, say, an hour?" She'd have time to go through her father's will that way and let Fiona know what was in it.

"That's fine." He checked his watch. "One hour." He watched her saunter off, admiring her walk. She was wearing one of those big floppy sweaters in yellow over white pants that hugged her long legs. He raised both brows, studying her departure. Nice view.

Ben walked back to Main, wondering what he'd do to kill an hour when he spotted a small bungalow on the far corner with a large flower garden enclosed by a white picket fence. It was the only residential building on the street and probably predated the commercial establishments. Trimming the hedges with a hand clipper was Lucy Hanover, the widow he'd met at Jack's house. He headed on over.

"You've got a real green thumb, Lucy," he commented, stopping alongside her. "Your yard's a showcase."

Lucy beamed. "If you give flowers loving care, they'll give you a lot of pleasure in return. Just like a woman." She peered up at him through her bifocals. "And what would you be doing today, out strolling?"

"Just having a look around. Nice little town."

"It is, isn't it?" She turned back to her clipping, evening out the bush. "Have you got all your insurance claims settled?"

"Insurance companies hate to part with a dime until the last possible minute."

Lucy stopped, frowning up into his tan face. "Do you know you've got this bad habit of answering a question *without* really answering? Drives a body crazy."

Of course, Ben knew. He'd perfected the technique years ago and knew it worked, except on people sharp enough to persist, like Lucy. "You caught me. To answer your question more directly, no, the claims haven't been settled quite yet."

Her eyes twinkled with curiosity. "Have you run into something suspicious?"

He smiled at her. "I'll bet you're a big fan of mysteries, right?"

"Well, yes. I read a fair amount." She glanced past Ben as a scruffy, disreputable old man shuffled into view around the hedge. "Hello, Freddy. I got two bags full for you alongside the garage."

As the man came closer, Ben saw that he was much younger than he'd originally thought, somewhere in his thirties perhaps. He wore thick glasses, sliding halfway down his nose. His brown hair stuck up in unruly clumps all over his head and badly needed cutting and a good washing. He wore droopy jeans and a plaid shirt buttoned to the throat topped by a ratty sweater. On his feet were threadbare canvas shoes in a faded turquoise. Curiosity aroused, he watched as Freddy stepped off the sidewalk into the street to avoid walking too close to Ben.

"Thanks, Ms. Lucy." He swiped a soiled sleeve under his nose, not even looking up as he ambled toward the garage, talking to himself.

"Who is that?" Ben asked as Freddy disappeared from sight.

"A sad creature," Lucy said, resuming her clipping. "Thelma Becker's son, from before she married Kurt. She's never said who his father was, but the man raised the boy somewhere in Ohio until his midteens, and he must have been harsh with him because Freddy has trouble relating to men. Seems afraid of most of them, even Kurt, who's as kind as they come. Freddy's what they call learning disabled. Never had much schooling. I save my cans and bottles for him and he turns them in and gets a bit of money."

"Does he live with the Beckers?" He'd seen the immaculately dressed banker and his wife at Jack's funeral and couldn't imagine this sad, unkempt individual living in Kurt's home.

Lucy shook her head. "About fifteen years ago when his father dumped him here, his mother bought a cottage for him over by that new subdivision of houses going up. The small cabin had been there in the woods for years. He does odd jobs for people, lawn work, sells bait, and he raises birds. Just loves all feathery creatures."

Ben swung back to look at her. "You mean the housing development where Jack Spencer fell?"

"Yes, not far from there." Lucy shifted to the other side of her hedge.

"You say he doesn't get along with Kurt Becker?"

"Not really. Kurt being a man and all, Freddy's afraid of him. But he sees his mother often and he visits his grandma up in Gwinn. He's not supposed to be driving, you know. Can't read enough to pass the test, but he grew up on a farm with that father of his and learned to drive tractors, I suppose. He takes Thelma's car occasionally and drives up evenings, going along the back roads, not the highway." Lucy sighed. "I feel sorry for the boy. People are afraid of him because of the way he looks, the way he talks to himself, but he's harmless."

Harmless. Ben wasn't so sure as he watched Freddy emerge carrying two bags, not even glancing their way before shuffling off down the street. He lived near where Jack died and often drove to Gwinn at night undetected, in the town where Reed died. Coincidence? Or had Freddy's fear of men turned into revenge for imagined wrongs? "How'd Freddy get along with Jack and Reed?"

Lucy shrugged. "About like with the rest of the men in town. Everyone more or less lets him be and . . ." She looked up, suddenly frowning. "You aren't thinking Freddy had something to do with those two dying? No, no, he's a gentle boy inside a man's body. Besides, I thought they both died accidentally."

Ben shoved his hands into the pockets of his tan khakis. "I'm not so sure about that, Lucy."

"Is that why you're still here in Riverview?"

He grinned at her. "No, I'm here because I enjoy talking with you."

The older woman's cheeks turned pink. "Go on with you. I know an evasive answer when I hear one, and you're mighty good at giving them."

"Can't tell you all my secrets, now can I?" Ben glanced at his watch. "Got to get going. Good seeing you again, Lucy."

"You, too, young man. Come by again."

The road to Marquette was a divided highway, relatively new and made for easy driving. Ben kept it to a reasonable fifty as he cruised along, thinking this might be the perfect time to get a few answers. But in order to get a little information from Maggie, he knew he'd have to give a little. "I talked with the Home Office this morning. They're not going to settle the claims until I finish the investigation."

Maggie had been staring out the windshield, thinking about the phone call she'd received before Ben had picked her up. Chet Garrett. Of all the people she hadn't been expecting to hear from, he'd been at the top of the list. Especially after their last quarrel, the bitter way they'd parted, the emotional afternoon when she'd cleaned out her desk.

He wanted her back, Chet had said. He was sorry. He'd

been wrong. Please come home. Where had she heard that song before? Different words, for Chet rarely admitted he was wrong, but the same tired tune. She'd been stunned to hear his voice, but she'd been cool and in control talking with him. Calmly, she'd said they had nothing left between them to salvage. Then she'd hung up and noticed that her hands were trembling so hard she could scarcely get the phone back in the cradle. Damn the man!

Realizing that Ben had spoken, she turned to look at him. "What did you say? Sorry, lost in my own gloomy thoughts."

He repeated for her, wondering what else besides her father's death had caused her to have gloomy thoughts.

"Well, I can't say I blame them for not settling until all doubts have been erased. Two million dollars is a big pile of money. Did you tell Reed's sister?"

"No, I let Wilbur do that. By the way, do you know Phoebe Doran?"

"Sure. She's been at Riverview Library forever, it seems. At least back as far as when I was in high school, though she was only an assistant then. She's very nice. What makes you ask?"

"Oh, just a hunch. I think she's playing footsie with old Wilbur." Ben guided the Jeep around a wide curve.

"Mr. Oakley? You've got to be kidding! He's devoted to his wife even though she's a whiner. Besides, I can't picture Phoebe having such bad taste." She sent him a quick, apologetic glance at her uncharitable remark. "I mean, the man's a fussbudget, as bad as an old woman and . . . and . . ."

"Obnoxious, irritating, and arrogant. I agree." He told her about the call at Wilbur's office, that the secretary had been told Phoebe was always to be put through immediately, and then his visit to the library and Phoebe's cool reception once she learned his name.

"Well, well. Will wonders never cease? Those two." Maggie shook her head, on the verge of a smile. "Hard to believe. And he's so self-righteous."

"Yeah, the prig." He'd gotten her to smile. That was something. "Maggie, I feel as if I'm working in the dark on this case. I need to know more about everyone, starting with your father. Can you tell me about him?"

"You're still acting like a cop, aren't you?"

"I don't see the cops acting like cops. Someone should, if we're to learn the truth."

She supposed he was right. "What do you want to know?"

"I don't care, anything. Anecdotes, habits, dislikes. Something I can get my teeth into, something that might possibly give me a clue as to who might have had it in for him."

She'd already told him that everyone loved Jack Spencer. However, she had to face a bitter truth, and that was that if Ben was right and someone had pushed her father to his death, someone hadn't shared the town's opinion. "He was born in Riverview, an only child, like me. His father was a carpenter and taught him to build things. You probably didn't notice our kitchen, but he built all those cabinets, hand carved the trim and made a lot of the furniture, too. He and my mother fell in love as freshmen in high school. Can you believe that?"

"No." Fourteen. They'd been kids.

"Me, either. They got married after Dad graduated from college and started the company with five thousand he borrowed from his father. Mom worked in the office and he was out there with the guys, building, overseeing, working with the architects, and hustling for building loans and subdivision rights. But he never took life too seriously and used to say that we should all live each day as if it were our last, because it very well could be."

He glanced over and saw the sadness there. "And do you?"

"Not really, although I know we should. Dad took good

care of himself, went on long walks, played tennis weekly, never smoked. He'd have an occasional glass of beer, but he was death on serious drinking. Back in his college days, he'd been pretty wild, then he was in a car crash that involved a drunk driver. After that, he told me he absolutely never got behind the wheel if he'd had so much as a sip of beer."

"Amen to that." Ben's hands tightened on the wheel briefly, before he forced his fingers to relax.

She studied his hard profile. "Did you have a brush with a drunk driver, too?"

"Yeah, you could say that. My father was a grocer in a suburb of Detroit. One of those independent little stores that have pretty much disappeared by now. He locked up one evening and crossed the street to where my mother was waiting in the car to drive him home. A drunk driver hit him, tossing his body onto the hood of our car. My mother watched him die."

Maggie reached over to touch his arm. "Oh, Ben. How horrible."

"I was in my second year of college, a real hotshot. I used to party with the best of them, drink until I could hardly walk, then climb behind the wheel like the idiot I was. My father's death woke me up. He was a really good guy. Too bad it took his death to make me see that."

"I know what you mean. From the time I started driver's ed, Dad lectured me constantly. That's one lesson that really got pounded into me. Actually, I rarely drink and in New York I don't own a car so I don't have to wrestle with those decisions."

"Did your father get hurt in the accident?"

"Apparently so, but not badly. Still, it affected him greatly. I heard the story so long ago that I forget the details." She wrinkled her forehead thoughtfully. "And now, our housekeeper tells me that Dad started drinking again sometime last fall. Pretty heavily, though he did it at home, locked away in his study. That surprised me, feeling as he did about alcohol."

Ben flipped on his right blinker, heading for the Pioneer Road exit off Highway 553. "Sounds like he was worried about something or upset. Or something happened that triggered a response that was out of character."

"That's what I've been thinking, but Fiona and I can't figure out what. I've talked with his doctor, his lawyer, his banker. They all noticed that he'd gotten moodier, but no one can come up with a reason."

"How about blackmail? Could someone have been blackmailing him?" He caught her incredulous glance. "I know it sounds off the wall, but I'm grabbing at straws here."

"I don't know what they'd have on him. He was such a straight arrow. Clean business dealings. Honest and honorable. My mother's been dead seventeen years and, to my knowledge, Dad never dated anyone after she died." Maggie rubbed at a spot above her left eye. "Maybe we're on a wild-goose chase here. Maybe it was an accident."

"If it was, we'll find that out, too. Either way, I think it's important to know." He reached for the map he'd marked earlier. "How about navigating? I'm looking for Sherman Street north of the Soo Line Railroad. That's the last-known address that Oakley has for Nancy Evans."

The apartment building wasn't hard to find, but when they rang the buzzer, no one answered. "We should have called ahead," Maggie commented as they walked outside.

"I didn't want to tip her off." As he stood on the stoop, hands on his hips, looking in both directions, an older model Mercedes convertible pulled up to the curb. Behind the wheel was a heavyset woman with lots of hair dyed a unique shade of yellow. "I think we just hit pay dirt," he said under his breath.

They waited until the woman stepped out of the car, reached for a hanger draped with a dry cleaner's plastic bag, hefted it into her arms, and started up the steps. As she fumbled for her key, Ben stepped in front of her. "Excuse me, are you Nancy Evans?"

Shrewd blue eyes narrowed. "Who wants to know?"

Ben turned on the charm, giving her his persuasive smile as he held out his card. "Ben Whalen from National Fidelity. We're looking for Ms. Evans in connection with an insurance policy."

"I don't have insurance through National Fidelity." She tried to sidestep him, but found she couldn't because his female companion was standing behind him. "You're in my way."

"The policy was on Reed Lang and we're checking possible beneficiaries." It was a harmless lie and might win the woman's cooperation, Ben decided.

Nancy's attitude did a one-eighty as she studied Ben with renewed interest. "Reed had a policy with me as beneficiary? I didn't see . . . that is . . ."

Didn't see it when she worked at Wilbur's office and went through all his files? Was that what she'd been about to say? "Are you Nancy Evans?" he asked. When she nodded, he went on. "Are you aware that Reed died on March tenth?"

"I heard something along those lines." Impatiently, she shifted the clothes bag. "Exactly what is this about?"

"I understand you were living in Riverview earlier this year, and that you and Reed were quite close."

Nancy let out an exasperated sigh. "Yeah, honey, we were close enough to become engaged. Until Reed's buddies talked him out of marrying me." She shrugged. "Who wants a guy who listens to his poker pals instead of the woman he said he loved?" Again, she shifted her heavy load. "Now, look, if I'm named on a policy and I've got money coming, then let's get to it. If not, stand aside. I'm getting married tomorrow and I've got to hang up this dress before it gets all wrinkled."

"Ah, married." Ben smiled in congratulations. "You've been married before, haven't you, Nancy? And widowed? Twice, right?"

Her chubby face took on a cold cast. "What's it to you, chum? Like I told Reed's little buddies, both of my husbands died a natural death, and I'd like to see them prove otherwise."

Ben stepped aside. "Then you won't mind if I look into those deaths, right?"

Her color rising, Nancy glared at him. "Go right ahead. You won't find a thing out of line."

Ben moved down the stairs, followed by Maggie. "Okay, thanks." He turned toward the Jeep at the curb, then swung back. "By the way, who's the lucky groom this time?"

Nancy used her ring of keys as a pointer. "You go to hell, you hear?" With that, she yanked open the outer door and disappeared into the building.

In the Jeep, Maggie doubted they'd learned anything. "She's obviously used to lying. How can we believe anything she said?"

"We can't." Ben started the engine. "Just to satisfy my own curiosity, I think I'll check out her two departed exes. But my gut feeling is that she didn't have anything to do with Reed's death. She couldn't score with him, so she left town, came back here, and found another sucker. She's after money, not revenge."

"You're probably right. I wonder if Grady ever bothered to look her up and ask a few questions."

Ben pulled back onto Lincoln Avenue. "I still haven't convinced you that he hasn't checked *anything*?"

"It's just so hard to believe. Grady also plays poker Fridays with the guys. He would have known that Reed had considered marrying Nancy Evans. Of all Dad's friends, Reed was the least experienced and most trusting, kind of sweetly shy. If not in his capacity as sheriff then as a friend, you'd think Grady might have been concerned enough to at least look into the woman's past to protect him."

"I don't view Grady as being a particularly concerned fellow." He pointed to the map on the floor. "I circled Warren Harper's address on Rock Street in the lower harbor area. Want to check it for me?"

"I know the neighborhood from when I went to NMU. It's not the greatest." In minutes, they found themselves in a somewhat shabby section of wood-frame duplexes and older homes. The third from the end was the one they were seeking. Two stories high, it had been painted a dull gold some years ago. Black shutters hung at drunken angles on two windows and were entirely missing from the third.

Jumping down, Maggie shielded her eyes against a slowly sinking sun as she noticed a skinny mongrel dog on the sagging porch. "This place has seen better days. Warren Harper, from what I gathered in Dad's papers, is a builder here in Marquette. You'd think he'd live a little better than this."

Ben took note of the dog who opened one lazy eye, then went back to sleep. He stepped onto the porch and knocked on the screen door. Someone was mangling a song on an out-of-tune piano inside. The smell of fresh paint drifted to him. In a moment, a middle-aged woman with a checkered kerchief tying back her dark hair came to the door. Her clothes were paint spattered and she was holding a brush in one hand.

She squinted through the screen. "You the one called about renting the upper? Ain't finished painting it yet, but I can show it to you, I guess."

"No, ma'am." Ben produced his card and held it out. "We're looking for Warren Harper."

The woman grunted as she opened the screen just wide enough to take the card. "Get in line. Lot of people looking for that crook. Stiffed me for two months' rent *and* left the place a real mess." She waved the brush tinted with white paint. "Got to redo the whole apartment. He was a pig."

"When did you last see him?"

"June first. I remember 'cause I usually go over to my married daughter's on the first of each month, spend the day with my grandkids. I came back and Harper'd moved out, lock, stock, and barrel. I was a fool to trust him, but he kept saying he was gonna hit it big." She made a sound deep in her throat. "In his dreams."

Ben glanced at Maggie and noticed her tight expression. He knew that June first was the day her father had died. "I don't suppose you know of anyone we could contact here in town who might know where we could find Harper?"

"If I did, I'd beat you to him. Nah, that shitty little company he had went bust. His car was some old heap and . . ."

Ben turned back to her. "The car. Can you describe it?"

The woman rubbed at a paint spot on her chin with the back of her hand. "A Chevy, I think, or maybe a Ford. Black, two-door. He was forever fixin' the durn thing." She scrunched up her forehead. "Why you lookin' for him? What's he done?"

"Just investigating an insurance claim."

"Don't tell me that thief come into some money? If so, I want my six hundred bucks."

"No, nothing like that." He stepped back. "Thanks for your time."

"Yeah, sure. You find him, you let me know, okay?"

"Okay." Ben left the porch and helped Maggie into the Jeep. Seated beside her, he could see she was still upset. "I know what you're thinking, but it very well could be a coincidence."

"You said you didn't believe in coincidences, and neither do I." Maggie reached in her purse and pulled out the partnership agreement Warren, Reed, and her father had signed. "Harper's business address is on here. Could we check it out? Maybe someone there knows something his landlady doesn't."

"Sure." Ben glanced at the address, checked the map, and started out. "Did your dad ever mention this Harper fellow?"

"No. I'm really surprised he invested with someone outside his circle of friends. It wasn't like him. He didn't have a gambling nature."

"Limited partnerships can work out very well."

"Yes and they can also be a disaster." Why was everything turning into a dead end? Maggie wondered. Were they even on the right track? Was there something shady about Dad's death or, like some insisted, was it merely an accident and she was running in circles. If only she knew.

By six, they were exhausted and no closer to learning anything about Warren Harper. The builder at the address they located said that Warren had worked there, but had no financial interest in the business. That man sent them to a second location and they'd referred them to a third, contractors who'd employed Warren at various times. But none had seen him in weeks.

"A con man is what Harper is," Tommy Lee Robbins, the job boss at the final construction firm, told them. "A dreamer who's always going to hit it big, next week, next month. Hell, he couldn't even afford a decent car. His tools were old and rusty. No carpenter lets his tools get that way. He's bad news, but funny thing. He skipped town before picking up his check couple of weeks ago. It's still here."

"How much is it for?" Ben asked.

"Around a hundred and a half. Not much, but still, a guy like him, he could use it. Left in one hell of a hurry."

"You have any idea why?"

"Nah. He moves around. I remember once I saw this stack of business cards he had and asked to see one. He'd had them made up at a print shop, his name in big letters, a fancy logo and his title. President. Can you beat that one?"

Maggie reached in her handbag, pulled out the agreement, and removed the card stapled to the first page. "Like this one?"

Tommy Lee took the card, then laughed. "Yeah, that's the one. Thought if he made himself a fancy card, he'd be taken seriously. What a clown."

Except someone did take him seriously, Maggie thought. Two someones. How had Harper conned two experienced businessmen like her father and Reed Lang?

"They might have been experienced in business," Ben told her later at Pasquale's Pizza Parlor, a restaurant just inside the city limits of Riverview where they'd stopped for a bite to eat, "but they'd both spent all their lives in one small town working with and for neighbors and friends. Con men can work guys like that, convince them black is white. It's not a mark against Jack and Reed. These guys are good."

"You're just trying to make me feel better," Maggie said, wondering why the fact that he bothered pleased her. She tucked a section of hair behind her ear, her movements slow and weary. "Oh, I know they weren't worldly wise. But they weren't stupid either."

Ben drained half his root beer from the frosty mug and swiped his hand across his mouth. "No one said they were stupid. Even brilliant people get taken in all the time—in business deals and in affairs of the heart. Happens to the best of us."

She stopped tracing the rim of her mug with one finger and looked across the table at him in the dim light. Pasquale's was a joint on the outskirts of town with fake leather booths, dark wood tables with initials scratched in every which place, and a jukebox that dated back to the fifties. But the smells coming from the noisy kitchen had her mouth watering.

And the man opposite her not only had her interest but wasn't half bad to look at. "That sounds like the forerunner of a confession. Did someone con you, in business or in love?"

Ben shook his head. "No, neither. But I know plenty who've had the experience. The first time, you say, okay, that was dumb but I learned. If it happens a second time, maybe you deserve what you get. I'd be willing to bet your dad and Reed fell for this smooth-talking Harper, invested with him even though the papers were probably printed up at the same shop where his phony business cards were, and lost a bundle. But they wouldn't have fallen for it again. Harper took the money and ran while Reed and Jack chalked it off to experience."

"It seems odd that Harper left right on the day Dad died."

"Odd, but it happens. You remember, Reed died on March tenth, quite a while before." Ben saw the pizza arriving and sat back. He was starving and ready to change the subject.

Maggie hadn't thought she was hungry, but the pizza was wonderful. After the first gooey piece, she sipped her root beer, letting her system settle. These hunt-and-search missions took a lot out of her. Ben seemed to thrive on them, but then, he wasn't personally involved.

Ben's busy mind was off in another direction. "I've heard around town about these Friday night poker games your dad was in on. Who were the others?"

"Mostly just the Sexy Six," Maggie said, picking up her second piece. At the look on his face, she smiled. "That's what they used to call themselves back in college. There was Reed, Grady, Kurt Becker, Ed Kowalski, George Cannata, and Dad. The six of them grew up together and have been lifelong friends." Except now, two were gone. "Occasionally, Dad's doctor, Steven Alexander, joined the game, and once in a while, Judge Fulton. Oh, and Grady's father, Sheriff Henry Dutton, before he died last fall."

Ben wiped sauce from his lip. "How'd he die?"

Maggie finished another delicious bite before answering.

"He went hiking around Lake Gogebic and must have fallen and hit his head. They didn't find him for several days, I guess. Of course, he could have gotten disoriented. He was seventy-five. He used to conduct hiking tours, but that was when he was younger."

"You mean he went hiking alone at his age?"

"Guess so. He used to do it all the time. Some people won't admit they should slow down. Carrie told me that Grady was really upset. He'd been close to his father."

Something rang a bell in Ben's mind. "What month did this happen, exactly?"

Maggie finished and picked up her mug. "September, I believe. Why?"

September. Early fall, which was when she'd told him that Jack had begun drinking again and neglecting his business. Could the two be related? Ben kept his features even, not wanting to worry Maggie further. "Just curious. So, did your dad ever tell you why they called themselves the Sexy Six?"

She smiled fondly. "I can only imagine that, as young men of twenty or so, they saw themselves as studs. It's the age for strutting your stuff, right?"

Ben feigned innocence, glad she hadn't picked up on his sudden interest in Henry Denton's death. "I wouldn't know."

She laughed. "Uh-huh. It was pretty much bluster, I think, because, except for Reed, they all got married within a year or two after college graduation."

As Ben signaled for their check, he noticed a couple of young guys at the booth across from them, downing their pizza voraciously and guzzling Cokes, their eyes on the young female waitress. Every once in a while, they'd lean over and whisper something to each other, jabbing an elbow for emphasis, then laughing uproariously. They, too, thought they were studs, along with feeling invincible.

Maggie followed his gaze, her take on the situation a little different. "Do you ever wish you could go back?" she asked wistfully.

"What, and experience all those terrible uncertainties, chemistry exams, and acne and a voice that cracks? No thanks."

"No, not that. I mean to recapture the feeling that you can do absolutely anything in the world, that it's your oyster."

He was quiet a long moment, looking at the teenagers, then at her. "Yeah," he finally answered, his voice soft, "I wouldn't mind that." Draining his glass, he reached for his wallet.

But before the waitress made it back, Maggie noticed Hank Snow come strolling in with his two young sons in tow. Hank was one of the carpenters who'd worked for Spencer Construction for years.

Catching her eye, the tall, sandy-haired man stopped at their booth to say hello, introducing his boys. "We just came from Jeff's Little League game. He hit a homer." Hank squeezed the older boy's shoulder proudly. "Tommy's game's tomorrow."

Maggie congratulated the suddenly shy boy, then introduced Ben. The two men shook hands.

"Yeah," Hank said to Ben, "I heard you were investigating for the insurance company. Guess you got another one to look into now, eh?"

Maggie gasped involuntarily as Ben looked up in surprise. "Another one?"

"Yeah." Hank looked from one to the other. "Guess you two haven't been around today. We came by way of the river. They just pulled a body out. Sheriff's over there now." He frowned worriedly. "I don't know what the hell's going on in Riverview lately. I'm wondering if my family's safe, if some nut's not running around loose."

Ben tossed money on the table and slid out of the booth. "Did they say who it was?"

"The guy I talked to said the man looked like the bank president, Kurt Becker."

Chapter Six

Someone had set up portable halogen lights on the river-bank. The eerie white glow made the faces of the onlookers appear ghostly frightening. A dozen or more people were standing around talking in hushed whispers as folks do when there's been a tragedy. The low keening sound of someone crying out in pain could be heard in the near distance. A lilac bush in full bloom, heavy with purple blossoms, perfumed the air, mingling with the faint odor of fish and the lingering heat of the day. The calm river slowly drifted past under a pale moon hanging in a summer night sky.

Infusing the area was the beginning of fear, along with an almost palpable sense of confusion. It clung to the bystanders like perspiration on their skin, like a stench that couldn't be washed away. Fear that another of their own had been taken from their midst. Fear that too many coincidences, too many accidents occurring in rapid succession no longer seemed accidental. The fear that someone out there just out of sight was stalking them, and they didn't know who might be next, and confusion as to how all this had come about.

Sheriff Grady Denton's blunt features were grim as he stood watching the EMS crew unzip a black body bag and lay it alongside the bloated remains of Kurt Becker.

"Don't look," Ben warned Maggie as they reached the scene. He'd wanted her to stay in the Jeep, but of course, she wouldn't.

"I'm not a hothouse flower," she whispered, then stepped around him. Immediately, she wished she hadn't as her stomach clenched. She swallowed down a wave of nausea as a gasp escaped from between her parted lips.

He didn't look like the man she'd chatted so pleasantly with at his bank this morning. His face and hands were slightly swollen and weeds were tangled in his salt-and-pepper hair. The buttons of his cotton shirt had popped off, leaving the flaps open to reveal a hairy torso. Oddly, he was shoeless.

But the worst thing was that his eyes were wide open, staring unseeingly up at the living who'd come to take care of the dead.

They'd driven at top speed to get here, Ben anxious to view the accident scene before the body was removed. He'd been more than a little surprised that Grady hadn't stopped him from stepping over the yellow tape into the crime scene. Maybe now, with a third death, the sheriff would be willing to consider that these men hadn't died accidentally. And perhaps he'd even cooperate and assist in Ben's investigation. Maggie had been solemn and silent on the short ride over, though she'd clasped and unclasped her hands repeatedly. He knew how desperately she'd wanted these deaths to turn out to be accidental. But now, this was three. Or was it four, with Henry Denton?

He recognized Kurt's wife, Thelma, standing on the edge of the crowd being comforted by her sister, Helen Kowalski, at the same time Maggie did. As she made her way over to the sobbing woman, Ben approached Grady. "Any marks on the body not consistent with drowning, like a bump on the head?"

"None I could see. Go ahead and have a look." He wasn't going to be accused of not cooperating again, Grady decided.

Ben did, bending down. Gingerly, he fingered Kurt's head, looking for a raised lump, knowing he could have fallen inside the boat or even hit a rock under water. Next he checked Kurt's hands and found no rope burns or cuts, nothing unusual. "Do you have any idea how long he's been in the river?"

Grady shifted the toothpick he was sucking on to the other corner of his mouth. "Not exactly. Couple of teenagers saw him put his boat in the water around two this afternoon."

That had been six hours ago. As he straightened, Ben's glance took in the grassy area that flowed down right to the water's edge. "You mean, he launched right here?"

"Nope. Upaways. Kurt usually went upstream and found some small cove. Said the fish wouldn't bite when there were a lot of folks around with portable radios, talking and disturbing the water." Grady turned aside, his face composed, but his insides churning. How could this be happening? First, his father, then three of his closest friends. Gone, just like that. He shifted his nervous gaze to the faces of the crowd, searching for some unknown profile, someone who didn't belong. But only familiar friends and neighbors stared back at him with frightened eyes.

"Were those teens the last to see him alive?"

"Guess so." Grady spat out the toothpick as his men zipped up the bag and began carrying the remains to the ambulance backed up to the edge of the parking lot. "I talked with most everyone here before you came. No one else saw Kurt after two." He reached up to smooth back his thinning hair, his hand a little shaky. "I don't understand it. Kurt's been fishing since we were kids. He was always so careful.

Damn, why didn't he put on his life vest? We found it in the bottom of the boat alongside his tackle box."

This one was getting to him, Ben realized. It was about damn time the sheriff took his head out of the sand. He noticed Kurt's fiberglass boat had been pulled up on the other side of the willow tree. "The body washed up over here. Where'd you find the boat?"

Grady pointed upstream. "Maybe a quarter mile up. Right smack in the middle of the river, just bobbing along." He shook his head. "He must've stood up for some reason and fallen out."

All right, enough. "Has the possibility occurred to you that maybe he *didn't* fall, that someone pushed him overboard?"

The sheriff's small eyes narrowed angrily. "Weren't no one else in the boat."

"Of course not, not when you found it. Do you think the killer's going to stay in the boat and wait for you to find him?" Ben wanted to throttle the man. "That's three, Grady. When are you going to face the very real possibility that someone's killing your friends?"

Four, but who's counting? Grady needed to vent his anger and frustration on someone and here was a handy outsider. "Listen here, hotshot. What we have here are *accidents,* three of them. Until you can prove different, that's what they are. Period."

"Okay, ignore the evidence in front of you. But will you at least call the M.E.? Let's let Doc decide if there's reason enough to order an autopsy. Maybe someone hit Kurt in the head or drugged him. Don't you think we should at least find out?" He watched the hardheaded sheriff struggle with what he wanted to do and what he knew he should do. As an experienced lawman, Grady damn well knew accepted police procedure. Evidence from the scene should have been collected and the victim's hands bagged, for starters. Why wasn't he bothering?

Bunched fists on his hips, Grady stared at the ambulance as the doors closed. "I'll call Doc Fielding." Fishing another toothpick from his pocket, he jammed it into his mouth.

Ben wanted to shake him up just a little, to draw him out of his dreamworld. "I heard about the six of you, all friends from way back and college classmates." He saw that he had Grady's attention. "The Sexy Six, I believe you called yourselves."

"That was a long time ago."

"Yes, it was. Six of you. And now there are three. Who's got it in for you guys, Grady? Who's setting up these *accidents,* one after the other? Aren't you just a little bit afraid you might be next?"

Grady's mouth was a thin, hard line. "Look, just because you're an ex-cop doesn't give you special privileges. I warned you once before, but I'll say it again. Keep your damn nose out of where it doesn't belong." Turning, he marched off, each heavy step filled with frustration.

Ben didn't care if he'd added to the lawman's problems. Someone had to shake the complacency out of Grady. And he'd best not delay in talking to the other two, Ed Kowalski and George Cannata. If they had the sense God gave a rabbit, they'd be scared, too. Scared enough to bring up their guards, to keep looking over their shoulders, to be on the alert.

Carefully, he picked his way over to the beached boat and stood gazing inside. An ordinary tackle box, bait in a bucket, and a sweater tossed to one side. Bait. Just this afternoon, Lucy had told him that Freddy Richmond sold bait. Kurt had been Freddy's stepfather and they didn't get along. Something else to look into.

The orange life vest was there and looked to be completely dry, its black belts still tied around itself. Kurt hadn't had it on at all from the looks of it. Was he a strong swimmer? How deep was this river? Just a few of the questions he wanted to ask, but tomorrow would do.

More than ever, Ben was convinced he was dealing with three murders here. Oh, the killer was clever, setting each scene up carefully so as to *look* like accidental deaths. And, if they hadn't begun escalating, most folks wouldn't get all that suspicious. After all, friends or not, people die all the time.

But their history and friendship linked them and the town all six had lived in all their lives. What else was it that had made these six citizens targets for some madman? Who had they royally pissed off? The suspects he had so far were poor at best. Nancy Evans was a long shot, but he wouldn't totally rule her out until he'd done some more checking. Warren Harper was still missing and therefore suspect. Harper had had a failed business agreement with two of the three, but how did Kurt Becker fit into that scenario? He'd have to check to see if Kurt had had any financial dealings with Harper through his bank.

Systematic revenge killings weren't all that common. More frequent were crimes of passion and killings in order to gain something. But what one person would gain from these three dying? The beneficiaries of their huge insurance policies, for one, but they were all different. That brought a question to mind. He'd have to visit Oakley and see if Kurt had a similar high payoff policy. And the other three as well, something he should have checked before. But until he'd heard Maggie talk about the Sexy Six, and until tonight's so-called accident, he hadn't considered a serial killer. Yet now, the possibility seemed very likely.

Ben turned away from the gently flowing river and saw that Maggie was saying good-bye to Kurt's relatives. He wouldn't mention his theory to her, or anyone else. All they needed right now was the media to pick up on this happening in this sleepy little town. The killer would be much harder to capture if reporters and strangers were milling about, messing up crime scenes and bringing in their TV cameras.

He'd been involved in one of those in a Detroit suburb years ago with the kidnapping of a little girl who'd subsequently been found dead. Her parents had purchased a very large insurance policy on her, supposedly for her education because they considered her very bright. In the end, it had been learned that they'd snatched their own daughter and killed her. For money.

Ben's mouth had a foul taste. The things he'd seen, the things people did to one another, could sour you on life, if you let it get to you. Far better to adopt his survival technique: keep your distance and stay emotionally uninvolved. As he watched Maggie walking toward him, her face tearstained from consoling the new widow, he reminded himself about his resolve.

"Come on. I'll take you home." He slipped his arm around her waist as naturally as if he'd been doing it for years, and herded her through the small group remaining. Worried about what was happening, neighbors and friends had been talking with her, bringing up Jack's death and then Reed's, trying to make sense of senseless deaths. Maggie didn't need a memory shake tonight.

Maggie let herself be led, like a small, distressed child, which is exactly how she felt. Something was going on here in this place that had been the haven of her childhood. Something sinister, evil. Her father and two men she'd called uncle as a youngster had died within three months. Accidentally.

She no longer believed that, if she ever really had. Someone had helped these good men to an early grave. But why? And who? She needed to think, to work with Ben and maybe Grady, to find out the truth.

But not tonight, Maggie thought as Ben maneuvered the Jeep onto the road leading to her house. She was too damn worn out tonight to think anymore. Closing her eyes, she leaned her head back.

It was incredibly easy to mingle with the crowd of shocked friends and neighbors and not be noticed. Everyone was busy whispering about still another accidental death. Little did they know there'd be more to come.

Suddenly the sheriff didn't look so brave, either. But that insurance investigator wasn't letting up, goading Grady on, demanding action. Why can't he let the scenes play out? It was surprising that this stranger had gotten close to Maggie Spencer so easily. She'd arrived with him, held onto his arm, and left with him. Maggie wasn't a target, for she'd done nothing wrong. She'd loved the sinner, but surely would turn from the sin, if she knew of it.

Perhaps there was nothing to worry about. Maggie was smart. Maybe she'd wake up and turn away from him. Whalen would soon learn that he was outmatched on this one. He would get nowhere with his investigation and the company would recall him. The two of them would bear watching. Nonetheless, the mission would be completed with or without interference.

Eyes downcast, the figure melded into the crowd.

Ben drove automatically, glancing over at Maggie often on the short drive. Exhaustion and worry had left its marks on her delicate, almost translucent skin. He wanted to lean over and kiss them away, to watch her eyes slowly open and awareness leap into them. Comfort often was the forerunner of passion. He wanted her to reach out to him so he could lose himself in her, so they could both forget the horrors of the real world, if only for a short time. There'd be no seduction, no morning-after recriminations, just an age-old mutual escape.

You're nuts, Whalen, he told himself. All Maggie wanted

was a soft bed and eight hours of dreamless sleep. She didn't want him or probably any other man just now. She wanted her world returned to normal, or what had passed for normal. She wanted the lunatics rounded up and locked up so she could get on with her life, to grieve in peace and get past the pain.

But none of that was to be until they caught the sick maniac who was undoubtedly somewhere nearby, laughing at them, secure in his arrogance. Not for long, Ben vowed into the still night. If Grady didn't find him, he would. Somehow, he would.

Ben pulled the Jeep into the circular driveway and turned off the engine. He unhooked his seat belt and turned to look at Maggie.

"I'm not asleep," she said, her voice throaty, as if still clogged with tears. Wearily, she sat up and ran a hand over her face, knowing she must look a sight. Blondes with fair complexions shouldn't weep in public. They haven't the skin for it. She opened her eyes and found him studying her. "Thanks for getting me out of there."

He reached out to trail fingers along the silky ends of her hair, something he'd been wanting to do. He wouldn't question why just now. "I'd ask myself in, but you need to rest."

"Maybe, but I'm too wired to sleep." She sat up, flipped off the seat belt, and opened the door. "I'll make us some hot chocolate. Not as much caffeine as coffee." She glanced back over her shoulder. "Unless you want to leave."

He wanted to stay. He took the key from her and opened the door, then wandered the kitchen while she made their drinks. Admiring the work, he ran his fingers along the edge of a cabinet door. "Your father was a real craftsman."

"Yes, he was." The past tense. Lord, how she hated the past tense. With mugs in hand, they strolled to Jack's den. "This is my favorite room. I feel close to Dad here and, tonight, I need that."

Ben waited until she curled up in her leather chair before sitting down on the ottoman facing her. He sipped his drink, letting her set the mood, to talk if she felt like it or just sit quietly if that was what she wanted. She'd had a bad shock and needed time to absorb it.

She'd invited him in because she hadn't wanted to be alone, Maggie realized. Fiona was in her room, most probably awake, but she didn't feel like going into all that had happened tonight with the housekeeper and get her all upset. She wanted tranquillity, serenity, both in short supply these days.

Ben never seemed to get ruffled. Maybe because of his police training or because he was on the outside looking in, things happening to those around him, but not directly to those he knew and cared about. His father had been killed by a drunk driver and that had changed him, but it had happened a long time ago. He could come here or to some other town, deal with victims, dig for answers, and then leave. And always remain untouched. She envied his ability to stay calm and composed, in control.

Yet she wondered if such constant detachment might not dehumanize a person after a while. Perhaps she was far too emotional for her own good, as Chet had often accused her of being. Yet it was the price you paid for caring, for being connected to others. Caring too much was something Chet would never be accused of.

She wondered how Ben saw himself, as she did, or did he put another spin on his indifference? "Tell me, how do you manage to do what you do, living temporarily in this city and that, delving into people's lives, yet not allowing any of the tragedies you witness to affect you?"

Knees spread, he propped his forearms on them and stared into the mug he held in both hands. "It's the only way you can do this job. It's the same for cops and doctors and, in most cases, lawyers and judges. If you don't guard yourself against all the pain and suffering, you'll burn up and be worthless." Who should know better than he?

Maggie could see he believed every word he said. She wasn't certain she did. "But how do you keep yourself from getting involved? I realize you didn't know Kurt Becker, but how can you *not* be moved by seeing a man like him suffer such a horrible death?"

Where was she going with this? What was it she really wanted to know? "Practice," he said, knowing it sounded glib, but at a loss for a better answer. "What would you think of a surgeon who broke down in the middle of an operation if his patient died? Or a fireman who wept when a burning building took the lives of some occupants? Or a cop who stopped to mourn the victim of a hit-and-run?"

"I'll bet plenty of them do."

"Sure, after the fact. While it's happening, they have to stay in control enough to do their jobs."

She finished her drink, set down the mug, and leaned forward. "But my question is *how* do you manage to do it? Don't you ever want to sympathize with the victim, to let them know sincerely how terrible you feel about their loss? Or is it only solving the case that's important to you?"

They'd had a similar discussion before, and he wondered why she wanted to rehash it all. A muscle bunched in his jaw as he considered what to say to her. "Yeah, I empathize and feel sympathy for the victims. But let's remember, these are strangers to me, and I to them. Kurt Becker's widow, for instance, she was glad to have you, an old friend, comfort her. But how would she feel if an insurance representative she didn't know went to her dripping with sympathy? Wouldn't it sound phony or patronizing? I mean, I'm here on behalf of my company and there's no getting around that."

Disappointed, she sank back against the soft leather. "So then it is the job that has top priority for you, not people."

Annoyed, Ben got up and put down his mug next to hers.

"Look, I don't know what you want me to say. That I'm a cold-hearted son of a bitch out to screw the beneficiaries in the name of National Fidelity? Okay, if that's how you see it. Yes, I have an obligation to my company, but that doesn't stop me from feeling bad for the victims. I'm human. Cut me and I bleed. But I can't *show* emotions or I won't be effective. Do you see the difference?"

"I'm not sure. I think it's the case with you, Ben. You need to score points with the Home Office and to do that, to be the best, you've got to riffle through people's lives, find that flaw, and point it out so the company wins. I'll bet never in your career, either as a cop or as an investigator, have you lost your cool. And you're damn proud of that record."

"You don't know what the hell you're talking about." He swung away, shoved both hands in his pockets, and paced the length of the room. "Not a damn thing."

Bracing her elbows on the arm rests, Maggie leaned forward. "All right, give me an example. Just one."

His innate need for privacy warred with the need to jar her with the truth. He didn't owe her an answer, but he was sick and tired of her thinking he was some damn automaton. He marched over to her, stepping close enough to see a flash of fear leap into her eyes. "You want to know? All right, I'll tell you, but you may be sorry you asked." Needing a moment to collect his thoughts, he sat back down on the ottoman.

"I told you I was married once. Her name was Kathy Smith. Are there really people named Smith? I used to ask her. She'd laugh." His voice changed, softened. "We laughed a lot in those days. She was a public defender in Detroit, someone who believed in the system, that everyone was entitled to fair representation, even those who couldn't afford much. Pretty special because Kathy came from money. She could have done anything, lived anywhere, but she knew what she wanted. Her family tried everything to talk her out of it, but she was stubborn."

He kept his eyes downcast on the thick carpet beneath his feet, because it was easier talking when he didn't look at her. "As much as her family hated her being a p.d., they hated me more. I was a cop with a mission, determined to lock up all the bad guys like the drunk who killed my dad. I wanted to take all the punks who do drugs, those who rob and hurt people for a few miserable bucks, off the streets, and put them away. I wanted to change the world." He shook his head, still not looking up. "God, I was so young, so damn idealistic. It should be a crime."

Maggie didn't move, scarcely breathed. She wanted to hear all of it, to let him tell it his way.

"We dated three or four months, and her folks kept trying to break us up. They pointed out what a crazy life she'd live married to a cop, the hours, the danger—and they were right. Kathy didn't listen. One night, we eloped. The Smiths had a fit. My father was gone and my sister already married and living in Colorado. My mother was upset she didn't get to see her little boy get married, but she got over it and even threw us a party. Her family didn't show. We managed to be happy anyhow. For about a year."

A year. Only a year, Maggie thought.

Ben made himself go on, his eyes like silver shadows as he came to the hard part. "They have regulations on the Detroit P.D. that cops have to live within the city limits. We wanted to start a family so we bought this little house. Not exactly a terrific neighborhood, going downhill some, but I told myself it was temporary. I was working undercover and making good money, socking some away each week. We moved in and within three months, she was pregnant."

Maggie closed her eyes briefly. It was going to be far worse than she'd imagined.

"My partner and I were on stakeout this one night. I was putting in a lot of hours because Kathy was six months along and we needed stuff for the baby. I got the call about three a.m. Dispatch didn't know how to tell me, but they had to. Someone had broken into our house, raped Kathy, and left her to die alone."

"Oh, God," Maggie moaned, reaching out, curling her fingers around his arm. Chet had accused her of being a bleeding heart often enough, but who wouldn't be after hearing this, imagining the scene? Her touch was instinctive, as necessary for herself as for him. She held on as he continued, his voice thick with emotion.

"I don't know how she managed, but somehow, she'd dragged herself to the phone and dialed 911. I drove like a madman, sirens blazing, but she was dead by the time we got there."

She squeezed his arm, unable to think of a thing to say.

At last, he raised his head. "I don't remember going after the guy that did it. We had a few snitches we worked with and one told me where the coward was hiding. I remember Bobby, my partner, pulling me off him. I looked down and my hands were all bloody. But I don't have a clear recollection of just what happened or if he said anything after the confession I beat out of him. He didn't die, more's the pity." His eyes were dark, tortured. "I wake up sometimes and I see him. I wish I'd have killed him. I came so close, but Bobby pulled me away. There was a trial and he's in prison, but that's not enough for what he did. Not nearly enough."

But then, no punishment would be enough for snuffing out the lives of his wife and baby. Kathy's parents had come to the funeral, dry-eyed and filled with accusations they hurled at him. He'd stood there taking it, because they were right. Kathy's death was his fault. He'd loved her, yet he hadn't been able to protect her.

"Bobby did the right thing. You'd have been up on a murder charge yourself."

"Do you think I cared about that? I didn't want to live, either. Kathy was everything good, everything fine. And our son . . ." He swallowed around a huge lump, then drew in a deep breath. "She'd just had the ultrasound a few days before." It all came rushing back, the horror, the anger. Afterward, he'd had a call. Kathy had taken out a big insurance policy he hadn't known about. He'd banked the check and never touched a cent of it.

Maggie felt she understood so much now. "Is that why you quit the police force?"

Ben ran an unsteady hand through his hair. "Not exactly. Internal Affairs took away my badge and gun, had me tested, sent me to a shrink, put me on stress leave. After all that, they decided I couldn't work the streets again. They gave me a desk job, but I couldn't stand that. The bottom line was that I couldn't seem to say what they wanted to hear, that I was sorry and I'd never do anything like that again." He held her gaze a long moment. "How could I when the only thing I'm sorry about is that they didn't let me finish the son of a bitch?"

She saw the pain in his eyes. Still so much pain. "On a gut level, I understand what you're saying. But I also can see why they wouldn't let you remain an officer." Because he'd been a loose cannon. Was he still, at times, when someone pushed him just a little too hard, or refused to cooperate? Was that why he had so much trouble relating to Grady?

"I suppose you're right." Ben rolled his shoulders, trying to ease the tension. "Anyhow, all that happened about six years ago. Later, a friend suggested I apply at National Fidelity. It got me away from behind a desk and out into the field again, where I could at least use some of my training. But the real reason I brought all this up is to explain why I can't afford to let myself feel too much or get involved with the victims' problems. I have this dark side that I'm never sure will stay safely tucked away. If I let myself care and something happens, I don't know if I'll handle it, or blow apart again."

There was more—the nightmares, the cold sweats, the lost weekends where he'd walk for hours, then hole up somewhere and work through the pain until he could face living again. But he couldn't tell her all that. There was no reason to, really.

"I shouldn't have accused you of indifference. It was wrong of me to . . ."

"No, that's all right. I wanted you to know that I'm not a cold son of a bitch. But there are reasons why I can't let myself get too close or care too much. Damn good reasons." He stood. It was time he got going. Past time. Baring his soul was not what he'd intended doing tonight, but she'd slipped past his defenses. He'd have to watch that.

Things had shifted a bit for Maggie. She saw Ben Whalen in a different light, a more human view. On the one hand, she wasn't so certain she was comfortable working in tandem with a man who just might go off the deep end again. On the other, she admired him for the control he was able to exert over his emotions in the aftermath of all he'd been through. The experience might have leveled lesser men. Perhaps the admiration was rooted in envy, for she wished she could keep better rein on her own emotions.

Or perhaps her feelings were all tangled up with an attraction for him that had begun without her permission, one she could no longer deny.

She rose, walking him to the front door, then standing aside as he turned to her. "Thanks for letting me tag along today. I know I cramp your style and I ask too many questions."

"I don't mind." The wariness he'd seen in her eyes was no longer there, yet she still appeared hesitant. "I hope I don't scare you, Maggie, now that you know that I nearly killed a man with my bare hands."

His uncertainty won her over like nothing else could have.

"You don't." To prove it to him and to herself, she stepped closer, encircling him with her arms, hugging him.

For a moment, the shock had him standing stiffly, not responding. Then his arms enclosed her and he gently drew her up against his body as he released a sigh of relief. It was so surprising, this need for her approval, the need to know he didn't frighten her. Where had it come from?

Maggie felt his breath fanning her hair and inhaled the outdoorsy male scent of him. Her hands at his back stroked lightly, as a friend might, not as a lover. It was a gentle embrace, an affirmation. And maybe a beginning.

Ben drew back, looking into her eyes, trying to read her thoughts. He saw only acceptance and a hint of female interest that left him with an uneasy sense of hope. Yet as much as he wanted to pull her back, to lower his head and taste her, he knew this wasn't the right time. He smiled down at her. "Thanks."

Maggie nodded. "And thank you. I really didn't want to be alone tonight after . . . after all that happened at the river."

He stepped back, placed his hand on the doorknob. "Call you tomorrow? Maybe we can dig up some more answers."

"I'd like that." Maggie watched him leave until the taillights of his Jeep were no longer visible, until an eerie feeling had her shivering. Suddenly the familiar yard with its dense shrubbery and mature trees seemed to hide watchful eyes and clandestine secrets. Nothing seemed truly friendly anymore.

With no small effort, she shook off the strange mood and closed the door. It had been a long, disturbing day. She hoped she'd be able to sleep.

From alongside the third tall pine tree, a figure moved from the dark shadows, eyes slanted toward the street where the insurance investigator's Jeep had gone, then back up to Maggie's room. Why was a smart woman like Maggie hang-

ing around that man? She didn't need him, not in her personal life nor for anything to do with the Riverview deaths. They were none of her concern. She'd buried her father, like the loving daughter she was, and now she needed to resume her life.

Didn't she know that the guilty must pay no matter how long it takes? Maggie needed to cash her father's insurance policy, and leave, to go back to her life in New York. There'd been no way to know about the policies, of course. Who would have dreamed? Guilt had brought them about. So much money. Blood money was what it was.

Some of them already knew that. The others would soon find out. At the last instant, they'd know. No sinners get into heaven, for their eternal home is in hell.

The light flickered out in Maggie's room where she'd opened a window to let in the warm summer air. She'd been spooked at the river tonight, but then, so had the others. They hadn't gotten used to it yet, but they would. Until everyone's bill was marked paid, the rivers and roads would run red.

A final glance up at Maggie's window. She would have to be warned somehow, so she would leave. No harm need come to her, for she was an innocent with a good and kind heart. Still, no interference would be tolerated, not even from sweet, kind Maggie. She needed a sign to point her in the right direction, away from evil. Justice has many faces. They would all soon learn.

All in good time.

Feet shuffling, the lone figure climbed the hill to the dark car hidden off the road.

Chapter Seven

Rosie's Diner was smack dab in the center of Main Street, two storefronts wide and deep enough to handle ten tables of four, eight booths, and a lunch counter that could seat twelve. Rosie's name was Polish and quite long, one scarcely anyone remembered or could pronounce, but it didn't matter because she was just plain "Rosie" to young and old alike. Her husband, Wally, who was as thin as she was fat, was the cook, and a middle-aged woman named Dolly waited tables. Rosie did a little of everything, taking orders, bussing, and serving the counter. She also arrived at five each morning to start her soup of the day and a big pot of chili. Good home cooking, generous portions, and fair prices kept the place packed from breakfast through lunch and on into suppertime.

Rosie always seemed to know when her customers could use a little privacy, which was why she tucked Maggie and Carrie into the last booth on the far side. Pouring fresh coffee for each, she gave them a wide smile along with menus. "You girls take your time deciding," she said. "I'll be back."

And she hefted her two-hundred-plus pounds three tables over to take an order.

Savoring her coffee as a nice change from Fiona's tea, Maggie smiled at her friend. "I'm glad you called. How are you doing?" Carrie certainly looked good in a yellow jump-suit, her long dark hair pulled back into a youthful ponytail and tied with a ribbon.

"Never better." Carrie sipped her coffee.

"Are you going to tell me what happened with Wayne or would you rather not talk about it?" For years, they'd been close enough to confide the most intimate details of their lives to each other. Being able to share your deepest secrets without censure, that used to describe their friendship. But did it still? Carrie's elopement and Maggie's move to Manhattan had shifted their relationship. Maggie's visits home hadn't always coincided with Carrie's infrequent returns to see her family. Wayne hadn't wanted her to come back at all, knowing they disapproved of him.

Her hands busily searched her large handbag for her ciga-rettes as Carrie shrugged. "Not much to tell. I don't know why in hell I ever married Wayne, except maybe to get even with Dad for imagined wrongs. I hadn't wanted him to re-marry and decided to dislike Opal before I met her. I think I eloped in order to hurt both of them." She let out a mirthless laugh. "Boy, did that backfire!"

"You must have seen something in him. Lord knows you had your pick of the crop in college." Carrie had dated half the senior males, all but the nerdiest ones.

Carrie blew smoke off to the side toward the window. "Es-cape. I saw him as an escape, I realize now. He was hand-some, older, great in bed." She smiled. "Trouble is, he never let me see the nasty side of him until it was too late."

"They never do."

Carrie raised a questioning brow. "You, too? Did Rhett fall off that pedestal you had him on?" The last time they'd talked, which had to be over a year ago, Maggie had given the impression that this guy all but walked on water.

"His name's Chet and yes, me, too. Did you think I was somehow immune? We all make bad decisions, Carrie. And always, we wind up paying for them." She took another swallow of coffee and tasted bitterness. "What surprises me is that you don't fit my idea of the abused woman. You know, downtrodden, undereducated, nowhere to turn."

"You're stereotyping, girlfriend. You'd be surprised how many women from all walks of life put up with that shit. I did. For years. Don't ask me why, because I don't know. I've been to two shrinks and I'm still not sure. Poor self-image, they say. Dates back to your childhood. Not enough love. What a bunch of crap." Carrie leaned forward. "You know what I think it boils down to?"

"What?"

"Some women just fall for the wrong guys and love makes you stupid. I'm finished with it. Never again. No man, *nobody,* is ever going to lay a hand on me again or make me do something I don't want to do. Period." She ground out her cigarette as if she were smashing it into Wayne's face.

"Well, girls, what'll it be?" Rosie asked, pencil poised. She remembered serving these two back when they were teenagers giggling in her back booth, and her smile was genuine. "I highly recommend my omelets—cheese, ham, veggie, or my specialty. Which one will it be today?"

"Just coffee for me, thanks, Rosie." Maggie's appetite was sporadic what with all that was going on.

Rosie pretended shock. "Not eating? You want people strolling by that big window to see you sitting in here not eating? Can't have that." With a flourish, she stuck her notepad back into the pocket of her generous pink uniform. "Listen, girls, you're in luck today. Two-for-one Tuesday is what it is. Two omelets for the price of one." She winked at Carrie, still not sure if the young woman could afford much, despite her fancy outfits and her new shop. She'd heard all the rumors and guessed the rest. And Maggie wore her sadness like a proud blanket. Two of her favorite people, both troubled. A good meal wouldn't hurt either of them. "Now, you wouldn't want to hurt my feelings, would you?"

Carrie groaned, but she gave in. "You win, Rosie. I haven't had an omelet in years."

Rosie's chubby cheeks shifted to include her big smile. "We're about to fix that." She topped off their coffee before rushing off.

Between Fiona's mammoth meals and Rosie's gargantuan omelet, Maggie thought she'd soon be letting out her clothes. "Don't you wish she was right, that a good meal would cure all our problems?"

"Amen to that." But Carrie wanted to shift the focus. "So tell me about Mr. Wonderful's fall from grace. I never met him, but I hate him already."

Despite the seriousness of their discussion, that had Maggie smiling. "I love loyalty. Well, Chet never hit me, but there're all kinds of abuse. His specialty's emotional battering, and he's very good at it."

Silently, Carrie sipped her coffee. She was a reluctant expert on many kinds of battering, including emotional, but she was having trouble believing that Maggie with her fashion-model looks and her valedictorian brains, her savvy and her sense of humor, her style and wit, had been taken in as she'd been. "You're not just saying this to make me feel not quite so stupid for having put up with Wayne all these years, are you? I mean, because you're my friend?"

"I *am* your friend, but no, it's the unfortunate truth."

Their breakfast arrived then, two overflowing plates with hot, fragrant food. "My specialty omelet with sausage, cheese, and mushrooms," Rosie declared proudly. "Homemade biscuits with honey and hash browns. Eat, girls, eat!" Off she trudged.

Maggie took a steaming bite, realizing she was hungry despite the disturbing subject matter. Did that mean she was truly over Chet?

Carrie's curiosity matched her appetite as she broke apart a hot biscuit and decided to nudge the story out of Maggie. "This Chet is still in New York, right? What'd he do and how'd you find the courage to break it off? I mean, I know you're a lot braver than I've ever been."

Maggie shook her head. "Maybe not. It took me two years to wake up. What finally did it? I'd been occasionally suspicious of his explanations regarding his whereabouts, but I wasn't positive. I worked for him, you may remember, and one day, he sent me to Chicago to a business conference. Only it ended early so I took a late flight back that night and hurried to his place to surprise him."

"You weren't living with him?"

"No. We'd both decided to maintain our independence and keep our own apartments. We were a couple, though, dating exclusively, a monogamous relationship. Or so I thought."

"Uh-oh," Carrie said as she scooped hash browns on her fork.

"You got it. The one most surprised at my early return was me. I used my key to get in and found Chet and another account rep having champagne in front of a roaring fire in matching robes."

"What did you do?"

"Not much, not then. He sent her packing and told me she didn't mean a thing to him. Same old tired line we've read in books and heard in movies. What makes us believe them, do you suppose?"

Carrie set down her fork, her face serious. "Because we *want* so badly to believe them. Because we want to be loved."

"I don't buy that. It's too simplistic an answer."

"So what else happened?" Carrie went back to eating.

"I got more suspicious and started nosing around. I

learned several others in the agency had shared his bed, one very much married. He'd talked marriage to two of us, never setting a date, of course. Finally, I confronted him, told him just what I thought of him, and threatened to tell everyone and anyone. That's when he got mean."

"You mean he threatened to hurt you?" The memory was still so raw for Carrie. *Do as I say, bitch, or I'll break every bone in your skinny body.*

"No. He threatened to blacken my name with all the PR firms around Manhattan. Believe me, that could last longer and hurt more than a black eye."

"Obviously, you've never had a black eye," Carrie said dryly.

"What gave you the courage to finally leave Wayne?"

Carrie shoved aside her half-finished plate and swallowed around a sudden lump in her throat. "He beat me so badly that I lost our baby." Her voice sounded as dead as the child who'd never had a chance.

"Oh, Carrie." Maggie's sympathy was swift and genuine. "The bastard. I hope they throw away the key and never let him out."

"God, so do I, but I don't count on it. He's serving two years for battery and violation of a restraining order, but that's not nearly long enough. I'm not looking forward to the day he gets out."

Maggie set aside her plate. "Surely you don't think he'll come after you? You filed for divorce, right?"

"It's already final. But you can't tell with violent men. Wayne's unpredictable."

"Don't dwell on that. Let your dad take care of you now. He's the sheriff here. He won't let anyone get close to you."

"That's why I came back here and I have to admit, he's been great." As angry and disapproving as Grady had been all the years she'd been gone, he'd done a complete about-face and had welcomed her back with tears in his eyes. Opal, the stepmother she'd disliked so as a teenager, had also been wonderful. "It's good being back, taking control of my life again. I feel better than I have in years." The nightmares were easing and she was beginning to relax, to sleep unafraid.

"When did all this happen with Chet?" Carrie asked.

"A few weeks before I heard about Dad's accident." Maggie finished her coffee and sat back. "Not the homecoming I'd envisioned."

"I feel terrible about your dad. He was the greatest."

"He was, wasn't he?" Maggie blinked hard, the tears always so close to the surface.

"Are you staying awhile or haven't you made any plans?"

"I'm not sure what I'm going to do now, because I quit working for Chet after it all hit the fan."

"You can always come work at Carrie's Closet. We could use a fashion consultant with New York savvy."

Maggie smiled. "Hey, you never know."

Carrie studied her friend. They'd shared so much as girls, and now, here they were, back where they'd started, having shared a similar nightmare. "What happened to us, Maggie? Where did it all go wrong? Where'd we veer off the right path?" She'd thought endlessly about that.

"*Life* happened to us. We're not the only ones. It's not a day at the beach out there."

"No, it isn't. I'm so glad we got together this morning. I haven't had a friend to talk with in so long."

"I missed you, too," Maggie said, and found she meant it.

"Good morning, ladies." Deputy J.C. Chevalier stood alongside their booth, his tan uniform neatly pressed, his smile friendly yet a bit hesitant. He'd tried talking to Carrie several times since her return—at Jack's funeral, dropping in to her shop—and each time she'd been hesitant and wary. J.C. knew her history from comments Grady had made through the years, so he couldn't blame her for not being receptive to another man just now. But he also knew he didn't intend to give up. He'd cared about her for so long, yet he'd never let on, not to anyone. He'd been away at college himself when she'd eloped. But now she was back and he wasn't about to let her get away from him again. "I hope I'm not interrupting."

Maggie didn't know J.C. well, but she'd heard only good things about him. "No, we're just finishing. How are things going with the investigation?"

J.C.'s tanned face shifted into a frown. "Investigation? Do you know something I don't, Maggie?"

"I mean the three recent deaths—Mr. Lang, my father, and now Mr. Becker."

"I believe they're classified as accidents. Grady told me not to waste my time on them." His dark eyes narrowed thoughtfully. "Is there something I should be looking into? Do you have some evidence that suggests otherwise?"

There was no point in bucking the system, not until she did have some proof. Perhaps soon, working with Ben, she'd find that proof. "Not yet I don't." She slid out of the booth and picked up the check Rosie had left. "Why don't you two stay and have another cup of coffee? I have an appointment."

"Actually, I've got to get moving, too. I have to open the shop." Grabbing her purse, Carrie scooted out of the booth.

J.C. touched her arm. "I hope you won't mind if I walk on over with you, then." He turned to Maggie. "Nice seeing you again."

She gave him a distracted nod. "Carrie, I'll be in touch."

"You do that or I'll come park on your doorstep." She took a moment to look up at the tall deputy. "So, here we are again. You are nothing if not persistent, J.C." And tall. Lord, but he was tall. At five-eight, Carrie preferred tall men. If she were in the market, that is, which she definitely was not.

He smiled down at her. "Yes, ma'am." He led the way out.

At the cash register, Maggie stared out the wide window

as she waited for Rosie. She watched Carrie lace her arm through J.C.'s, friendly like. Maggie hadn't known of the tall deputy's interest in Carrie until the afternoon of her father's funeral when she'd noticed them together, but she heartily approved. He came from a big friendly family originally from Quebec, and was as solid as they made them. Maybe J.C. was bright enough to see through Carrie's brash ways and notice the sensitive woman beneath. Carrie needed someone steady right now.

Who didn't? she thought, glancing around the diner that was beginning to fill up with the early lunch crowd. She waved to George Cannata from the drugstore and said hello to Ruth from the Green Thumb Florist Shop, as well as the two gals who worked at the dry goods store down the block. Several others she knew slightly smiled in her direction, making her feel warm and accepted. So different from Manhattan where very few even in her own neighborhood ever spoke a word of greeting.

"Are you getting reacquainted with the town, Maggie?" Rosie asked, ringing up the breakfast ticket.

Yes, Maggie thought, it was like that, as if she were renewing old friendships and committing each face to memory to bring out and examine when she was gone from here. "I guess I never realized I had so many friends here."

"We all love you, honey." Rosie handed her the change. "Are you considering staying on?"

"I don't know, Rosie. A part of me wants to stay because of all this support. The other part wants to run back to New York and that other life I've made for myself." Which had fallen apart recently, but could be rebuilt, she supposed.

"Don't rush things, honey. In time, you'll know what's best." She gave her a big smile. "So, did you enjoy your breakfast?"

"It was wonderful. I'll carry every sinful calorie on my hips for weeks."

The older woman shook her head. "Not so. You need fattening up." Rosie waved at her. "See you later."

Maggie walked outside and turned right, strolling toward Oakley Insurance, wondering if Ben had learned anything.

"I'm sorry, Mr. Whalen, but I'm too busy to see you right now." Wilbur Oakley checked the gold cufflinks at each wrist, adjusting them just so. "You really should call and make an appointment if you need to see me."

Ben had about had it with this pompous ass. "I don't care if you're meeting with the King of Siam, Wilbur. I want to see your files on these men and I want them *now.*" He held out a sheet of paper.

Oakley glanced at the list ever so briefly before shaking his head. "I told you, I can't squeeze you in this morning. Perhaps tomorrow." Turning on his heel, he pushed open the door to his office.

With one firm hand clamped on his shoulder, Ben spun Oakley around, finding the stunned look on his pale face almost laughable. He heard the mousy little secretary seated behind him gasp out loud, but chose to ignore her. Ben had been cooling his heels in the outer office for nearly an hour, waiting for Oakley to show up, and his mood wasn't the greatest.

"Now you listen up, Wil, 'cause I'm only going to say this once. I've got a job to do here and I'm going to do it, with or without your cooperation. Now you march on in to your pretty little office and get me these files this minute, you hear? 'Cause if you don't, I'm getting the Home Office on the phone and we're going to have a three-way chat that might just be your last conversation with National Fidelity. Ever. You get my drift?"

As if it were some large, distasteful bug, Wilbur shook off Ben's hand and took a cautious step backward. His face blushed pink with embarrassment that his secretary had witnessed his humiliation at the hands of such a hoodlum. "Perhaps I *can* accommodate you." Swallowing his temper, he walked over to his locked file cabinet and removed his keys from his pocket. "You'll have to look at them in the outer office as I'm expecting a client shortly."

"No problem, Wil." Sauntering in after him, Ben watched the man's manicured fingers search for the files. "You know, if you showed up for work at eight-thirty, like it says on the front door, you might not be so rushed."

Wilbur slapped the first folder onto his desk. "I run each morning for an hour, then shower and change before coming in. It was a lovely morning, though a bit cloudy, and there were half a dozen of us out enjoying the air." He owed this boor no explanation of his comings and goings, but if he kept his mind on something pleasant, he could get through this without raising his blood pressure. Phoebe had taught him mind exercises to calm himself, realizing what a stressful job he had and how high-strung he was. People thought insurance was such a calm occupation. If only they knew. Phoebe understood him as no one else ever had.

Ben crossed his arms over his chest, wondering who Wil's pals were, other than the librarian. "Who was out running with you?"

"Oh, there was Dr. Fielding, our pathologist, and the deputy sheriff, J.C. And Ruth Bishop from the Green Thumb just across the street. She's competed in several marathons. And Sean McCauley from the mortuary." Retrieving the last file, he pitched it onto the stack. "We're all interested in health and fitness. You ought to try it sometime. Good exercise gets rid of hostilities and makes you feel on top of the world." The oaf was probably too obtuse to get the point.

"So does good sex." Ben gathered up the files. "Thanks a bunch, Wil."

Leave it to Whalen to make a crass comparison. "You're

not to take those out of this office," Oakley warned, needing to get in the last word.

Ben tossed a withering glance over his shoulder and didn't bother to answer. Settling himself at a small drop-leaf table off to the side of the anteroom, Ben opened the first file just as the front door opened. He looked up and recognized Phoebe Doran.

Phoebe looked a bit nonplussed, but her good manners came through. "Good morning, Mr. Whalen." She turned to Andrea Taylor, who was enjoying this unusual morning. "I believe I have an appointment with Mr. Oakley."

"Yes," Andrea said. "Go right in, please."

Ben couldn't resist. "Library closed today, Ms. Doran?"

"No, it's my day off." Head held high, Phoebe went into Wilbur's private office and closed the door.

"What do you suppose those two are up to?" Ben asked, grinning at Andrea. He winked as she let out a muffled giggle.

He was finishing the last file when Maggie walked in wearing jeans and an oversize blue shirt, her flyaway hair looking blowsy. How did she manage to look good even windswept?

"Windy out there," she said, aiming a smile first at the receptionist, then at Ben who looked more than a little uncomfortable with his six-foot-plus frame perched on a distressed cherry wood chair with a needlepoint back. "I hope I'm not late." Finger-combing her hair, she tried to rearrange what the wind had mussed.

She had a knockout smile, Ben thought as he straightened the folders. "Just in time." He rose and handed the stack of files to Andrea. He had a few questions, but he'd talk with Wilbur later. "Be sure Mr. Oakley gets these," he told her. "I wouldn't want him to think I'd run off with his important papers." He gave her another friendly wink.

Totally smitten, Andrea smiled up at Ben dreamily. The

ringing phone kept her from having to come up with an answer.

"So, what'd you find out?" Maggie asked.

"I'll tell you on the way over to the Medical Examiner's office." He took her arm and was about to lead her out the door when Andrea called him back. The sheriff was on the line for him. Ben took the phone from her. "Yeah, Grady."

"Thought I'd best stop you before you go all the way over to Doc Fielding's," he drawled, his accent more pronounced today. "There won't be an autopsy on Kurt Becker."

"What? Why not?"

"Simmer down. Doc says death was accidental and he sees no reason to do an autopsy, especially since Kurt's widow is opposed to having her husband all cut up. Thelma wants him to rest in peace." Grady waited for the explosion sure to come. Ben had called him last night and told him he'd be heading over to County General this morning after checking something with Wilbur. He wished he knew what. He'd had that talk with Oakley, told him to not make things too convenient for Whalen in the hope that he'd get frustrated and quit digging. Apparently, he'd underestimated the tenacious ex-cop.

Ben's temper didn't disappoint. "Damn it, Grady. Why'd you let this happen?" Furious, Ben's voice rose in direct proportion to his temper. He'd been counting on this autopsy since his request for exhumation of Jack Spencer and Reed Lang had been refused. He knew without checking that Grady had written accidental drowning as cause of death in his report, which was what the Medical Examiner based his opinion on. Unless something suspicious shows up, the M.E. goes along with the law.

"There's no proof of a homicide," Grady defended.

"That's precisely what an autopsy might have revealed, proof one way or the other. Are you afraid to risk it?"

The toothpick in Grady's mouth snapped in half. "I don't

know about how they do things in the big city, but in my town, we honor the wishes of the family. Live with it, boy." He slammed the phone down. That's what he got for trying, for calling Whalen and saving him a trip. Ungrateful pup.

Still, his words hung in the air. *Afraid to risk it?* Maybe he was, Grady admitted to himself.

Wilbur's door opened as Ben handed the phone back to Andrea. "What's going on out here? Oh, hello, Miss Spencer." Oakley turned his frown on Ben. "I would remind you, this is a business office, not a back alley. Lower your voice or leave."

Ben just stared at him, knowing if he spoke he'd say something he'd regret.

Phoebe moved past Wilbur. "I see you're quite busy. We'll continue another day, Mr. Oakley." Her eyes lingered on his an overly long moment. With a nod to the others, she went out the front door, the gold angel pin on her shoulder glinting in a weak sun.

Ben looked at Wilbur, who'd removed his jacket to reveal paisley suspenders. Pointedly, he stared after Phoebe's departing figure, his silent suspicion hanging in the tense air.

"She, uh . . . Ms. Doran gives therapeutic massages in her spare time. She's also well known in the area for teaching meditation and biorhythm methods of relaxation." Under Ben's piercing gaze, Wilbur nervously reached up to straighten his tie.

It was all too much for Ben. "Is that what we're calling it these days, Wil—massages?"

A red stain crept up from beneath Oakley's starched collar all the way to his forehead. "A man like you wouldn't understand a perfectly platonic friendship, one on a high moralistic plane."

"No, probably not." Ben pointed to the files he'd given Andrea. "Your folders are there, all intact. I have just one question. Why is it you neglected to mention that there are three more policies for a million each on Riverview residents, beyond the three on the men who've recently died accidentally?"

"Why would I? That's confidential information." His lips pursed in irritation as he noted Andrea gleefully eavesdropping. "If you must discuss clients, at least let's go into my office."

Ushering Maggie in, Ben followed, closing the door. He felt sorry for poor Andrea who'd never get to hear the rest of this fascinating tale.

"Please be seated, Ms. Spencer." Wilbur shrugged into his suit coat, striving to recapture his good manners. "How are you faring?" And what on earth are you doing hanging around with this overbearing neanderthal?

"One day at a time, Mr. Oakley," Maggie answered, wondering why there seemed to be so much hostility in the air.

"Let's start with Grady's father, Henry Denton, who died last fall," Ben said, referring to the notes he'd taken. "He had a policy for half a million, with double indemnity for accidental death, isn't that right?"

Wilbur glanced at Maggie, then at Ben. "Forgive me, but I'm not comfortable discussing privileged information with . . ."

"Don't pull that crap on me, Oakley." Ben's voice was impatient. "Maggie's assisting me in the investigation. Now, am I right about the policies on George Cannata, Ed Kowalski, and Grady Denton for a million each, plus Henry for half a mil?"

Feeling as if he'd just run the Boston Marathon despite the all too few pleasant moments he'd spent with Phoebe massaging his tense shoulders, Wilbur sat down heavily in his swivel chair. "Yes. Henry came to the office with Grady and the others. My father-in-law owned the agency at the time. Henry, too, asked for a million. But he was already almost fifty and the underwriters wouldn't authorize more than five hundred thousand, as I recall."

Ben stood, aware that his height was an intimidating advantage. He would use whatever he could to get some facts from this reluctant man. "According to your files, Grady received a million dollars last fall because Henry died accidentally. You knew I was investigating this, yet you didn't see fit to mention Henry or these other policies." Nor had the Home Office put two and two together, apparently. "Why, Wil?"

"I told you why. Confidentiality."

"Bullshit! I work for the same company as you. I'm not here out of idle curiosity." He moved quickly, bracing his hands on the edge of Wilbur's desk, leaning forward so he was literally in the man's face. "You want to try again? The truth this time, Wil. I think you should know, I'm not in the mood for games."

God, how he hated this, dealing with a man of this caliber. But, no matter. Soon, he no longer would have to.

Oakley ran his hand over his carefully combed hair. "I told him it wouldn't work, that you'd find out."

Maggie sat forward, suddenly curious.

"Who? Who'd you tell what wouldn't work?" Ben asked, his voice deceptively low.

"Grady, that's who." Without a second thought, he turned into Judas. "Just so you know, none of this was my idea. Grady called me awhile back and told me to not make things too easy for you, that what went on here in Riverview was no one's business but ours."

Straightening, Ben's face moved into a frown. "Grady told you that? What reason would he have?"

Wilbur shrugged, trying for nonchalance. "I'm not sure, but as you know, the men who died, including his father, were all close to Grady. Maybe he's worried about what kind of dirt you'll dig up on them, that you'll dishonor their memories." Let that stupid lawman sweat a little. It still rankled that Grady had tried to intimidate with that heavy-handed phone call.

"I don't believe that." Ben sat down in the chair alongside Maggie, his expression thoughtful. "Do you? Does that sound like Grady to you?" he asked her.

"I don't honestly know, Ben. I've been gone a long time."

He swung back to Wilbur. "All right, so let's go back about thirty years. One day, six men walk in here, all in their midtwenties. The seventh was Henry Denton, who was sheriff back then. They all want to take out policies on their lives for a million bucks each, with double indemnity, on the same week. I checked the dates." And since last fall, four of them had mysteriously died. "I want to know why?"

Wilbur shook his head. "I don't know what to tell you. My father-in-law was in charge and I was merely observing, learning the business." How he'd hated those years under the thumb of Mildred's overbearing father. The day he'd died, Wilbur had applied for a name change for the agency. "They came in, told us what they wanted, filled out the forms, and went for their medical exams. Subsequently, they were approved and the policies went into force. We don't ask clients *why* they want insurance. Quite the opposite. We point out why they should buy more. As to motivation, you'll have to ask Grady. Or one of the others."

Which was exactly what Ben planned to do. He'd checked the files of the Sexy Six, but maybe there was more. "One last thing, and I want the truth, is anyone else in this town insured with you for high stakes?"

"Not that high. Not even close."

Rising, Ben hoped to hell the man was being straight with him. He'd call the Home Office, have them run a check, just to be sure. "I hope I don't have to tell you that this conversation goes no further, Wil." He waited until Wilbur gave him a conciliatory nod. "Okay. Ready, Maggie?"

As soon as his office door closed behind them, Wilbur sagged into his chair and let out a sigh of relief. Let them sniff around all they wanted. They'd only learn what he wanted them to know. Soon his well-thought-out strategy would bear fruit and he'd be free. Free of this absurd town and the city fathers who ran it. Maybe they'd figure it all out one day, after he was gone, but by then, it'd be too late to do anything.

They never should have treated him so shabbily. He'd been honest and fair, and what had they done in return? Treated him with disrespect and made fun of him and his refined ways. The one time he'd tried to join their little Friday night card game, they'd told him the table was full. Not even an apology. He wasn't good enough to play poker with them, the scum.

It was a waste of energy to dwell on men who were his inferiors. A Realtor of used homes, a carpenter, and a pompous banker. A fat-ass butcher, for heaven's sake, and a druggist who spent his weekends shooting at pigeons. And that Southerner in his silly uniform and badge playing at being a lawman. Laughable that *they* should reject *him*.

Along with having to bear the scorn of lesser men, his wife had gradually become impossible, exhausting his nearly limitless patience. How long should a man have to endure such a mockery of a marriage? The price he'd had to pay for this two-bit insurance agency had become too high. He'd given Mildred the best years of his life and now, he needed to take what precious time he had left and enjoy.

Relaxing at last, Wilbur picked up the phone and dialed. He knew someone who always lifted his spirits, someone who truly appreciated him. Their precious time together today had been cut all too short. He heard a soft voice answer on the other end and smiled. "Hello, Phoebe."

Outside in the clean air, Ben drew in a deep breath. "I wish to hell I knew what was going on."

Gazing up at him, Maggie studied his hard, set features. "You're like a runaway train when you get going, aren't you? Ask no quarter, give no quarter. That what they taught you at the academy?"

He really needed this right now. "What? What'd I do that you don't approve of?"

"Well, for starters, you were a little rough on Mr. Oakley. He's a little prissy and a bit full of himself, but he's harmless. Was it necessary to embarrass him with that business of the massage?" She blinked as a strong gust of wind whipped at her shirt.

"He embarrassed himself. He actually wanted us to believe he was closed in with Phoebe Doran communing with the spirits or having an out-of-body experience. Come on, Maggie. Surely you didn't fall for that. As for the rest, if I hadn't leaned on him a little, do you think he'd have told us what Grady asked him to do?"

"So then the ends justify the means, is that it?" She shook her head. "Are you having a testosterone surge, Ben?"

"No, I'm having a frustrating morning. I thought you wanted to get to the bottom of things here, to find out what happened to your father. Do you think that's going to happen if we sit around politely sharing a cup of tea until the person responsible drops in and confesses one sunny day? Get real."

"And you said you didn't consider yourself a cop anymore." She began walking down Main Street, wondering why every man she found attractive wanted to run the show and run it *his* way.

Ben fell in step with her. "I suppose you'd have handled things differently."

"Just a tad. I've never been real big on humiliation, intimidation, bullying."

They passed in front of the library and he remembered Phoebe Doran's rabbit-caught-in-the-headlights look. "Maybe I was a little overzealous. But damn it, I get . . ."

"The job done. I know. You're the best with a terrific record. You already told me." The persistent wind tossed her hair about, but she ignored it and kept walking.

She had a way of saying things that made him feel lousy. They rounded the bend into the parking lot alongside the bank. As they reached his Jeep, he touched her arm, stopping her. "Look, I told you once before. I don't want to fight with you."

She let out an exasperated sigh. "Then what is it you could possibly want from me? Let's see. Could it be that you want me along to smooth the way for you with the people of Riverview, knowing that if one of their own introduces you, they'll open up, maybe even trust you because they know me?"

He opened his mouth to protest, then closed it, because she was right.

"Didn't think I had that one figured, did you? You want me to fill you in on everyone's background, reveal their secrets if I know any, so you can home in on anyone who remotely appears to be suspect. And intimidate them into revealing more." She saw him start to say something again, but she held up a hand to stop him. "No, don't deny that, either. You want to pry into everyone's personal life, to get at what you call *the truth*, then when that happens and you file your little report, you'll repack your bags and leave us. If some of us are a bit shattered by your probing and meddling, by your airing our dirty linen publicly, well, it's all in a day's work. Am I on track, Ben?"

"You're saying I'm using you to make my job easier and that I don't give a damn about anyone?"

"That's exactly what I'm saying."

His eyes were a stormy gray. "That's a damn lie. I don't deliberately hurt people. And I can do my job just fine alone. I have for years. I don't need you or anyone else to run interference. Sure, it's great if someone involved in a case lends a hand. After all, *you're* the one who asked *me* if you could go along. But if not, I manage on my own. Actually I work *best* alone."

The parking lot was nearly deserted, probably because it was Saturday and the darkening sky hinted at a summer storm brewing. Maggie ignored the weather and drew in a deep breath. For some unfathomable reason, she badly wanted to believe him, if only because all too recently someone else had used her without so much as a qualm. But she doubted that Ben Whalen was any different. "If that's so, if you work best alone, then why did you invite me to tag along? I know I asked to go, but you could have easily refused."

"I could have, yeah." He stepped closer, backing her up against his Jeep. "Maybe I have another reason, a personal one." With that, he lowered his head and kissed her, hard.

Stunned, Maggie's hands flew up only to be caught between their bodies as he drew her close against his rock-hard chest. His hands roamed her back, his strong fingers stroking, coaxing a response. His mouth was the only soft thing about him as he seduced and tempted, his full lips brushing against hers, kissing the corners, then devouring with an ease that was as frightening as it was enticing.

Beneath her palms, she felt his heart pounding as her fingers curled into the soft cotton of his shirt. She heard a sigh escape as he changed angles and took her deeper, but she wasn't sure which one of them had made the sound. The world became a little blurry as she clung to him, letting his fascinating flavors tease her tongue as it crept into his mouth.

It was the sign he'd been waiting for, the assurance that she wanted this as much as he. Arms winding about her, he pulled her closer, his response instantaneous and obvious. It had been a hell of a long time since someone had put him on the edge of explosion with just one kiss. The truth was, he hadn't wanted a woman in years, but he wanted one now. This one.

The kiss went on and on, yet was much too short. Finally, Ben released her, then stepped back and shoved fingers that were none too steady through his hair. "I'm sorry. I probably shouldn't have done that."

Unnerved at how quickly they'd come so far, Maggie took a step back, then another. Breathing hard, she shook her head to clear it, although it didn't work. "You didn't do it alone." She made a stab at clearing her throat. "Ben, I . . . I don't think this is wise. I don't want to get involved."

He braced one hand against the Jeep's door. "Me, either."

She raised her eyes to his face. "Then why are you coming on to me?"

"Because I can't seem to stop wanting you."

The simple statement stopped her in her tracks.

Ben stepped back, digging for his car keys in his pocket. "Don't worry. I'm sure we'll get over it." He forced his mind to focus on where he'd been planning to go next. "Are you coming with me to have a chat with Grady, since we no longer have a reason to see the Medical Examiner?"

She needed some time and a lot of space. "No, I have some things to do." Finally trusting her legs, she set out for the Explorer parked in the next lane, berating herself all the way. Why had she let him kiss her? Why hadn't she turned her head or shoved him away? Why?

Because, God help her, she'd wanted to know what his kiss would be like. And now that she had, how could she keep from wanting more?

McCauley's Mortuary was a sedate red-brick building with a pitched roof and wide double doors at the back entrance. Ben wasn't sure how many permanent residents lived in Riverview, but he was fairly certain most of them had squeezed themselves into the cool, dim building to pay their last respects to Kurt Becker, bank president, neighbor, and friend.

By the looks of the number of flower bouquets, green plants, and arrangements, Kurt had had a lot of friends. Ben spotted a tall, athletic woman with short curly brown hair rushing about, checking the floral displays, bringing in more. He guessed she was Ruth Bishop from the Green Thumb whose business must have tripled over the last few weeks with three separate large funerals.

Standing at the back, Ben let his glance slide over the mourners row by row, starting up front with the widow, Thelma Becker, who appeared heavily sedated and scarcely aware of her sister patting her hand. Helen Kowalski seemed more angry than sad while her chubby husband, Ed, sat staring straight ahead to where the open casket lay, his expression one of dazed disbelief. The two married Becker daughters were also up front, visibly weeping while their husbands looked as if they'd like to cut out for a cold beer. It was a miserably hot Monday morning.

Noticeably missing from the little family gathering was Freddy, Thelma's son, the one Ben had seen in front of Lucy Hanover's.

Strolling to the left, Ben saw Maggie walk in, looking mouthwatering in a black linen outfit with a sedate white collar. It wasn't easy for her to look funereal with all that shining blond hair. The dress was fitted, not loose like everything else she wore, a real bonus since he could finally see that she had full breasts and a great back view along with those long, long legs. Why would she want to hide such a nice package?

Maggie stopped to talk to Thelma and the Kowalskis, then moved on to a tall, solidly built blond man in full Marine uniform. Squinting at the square face and deepset eyes, Ben finally placed him as the Kowalskis' son, Tom, a career soldier he'd seen briefly at Jack's funeral. He couldn't tell if

Tom was mad as hell or if angry was his natural facial expression.

A sound at the side door had Ben turning to watch Grady stroll in, his hand on the elbow of the redhead he'd been with at the Spencer house. His second wife, Opal, resplendent in a multicolor gauzy number and dangle earrings that brushed her shoulders, sat down near the end of a crowded pew. Carrie, Grady's daughter, followed her stepmother in and removed large sunglasses, her eyes scanning the mourners as if searching for someone. Spotting Maggie, she hurried over to sit with her friend. He saw Deputy Chevalier break from a group and wander over to Carrie, leaning down to say something to her. She gave him a welcoming smile and made room for him on the bench. Ben made a mental note to ask J.C. about Carrie.

Grady, wearing his ever-present uniform and mirror sunglasses, spotted Ben and ambled on back. "You wanted to see me?" he asked Ben, his soft Southern drawl low key in deference to the dead.

"I stopped at your office yesterday before noon, but they told me you were gone for the day. Nice hours."

Grady kept his gaze aimed toward the front. "If I'm not there, it doesn't mean I'm not working. What'd you want?"

"Not much. Just wanted to know why you told Wilbur Oakley to give me as little information as possible."

Grady's profile didn't change. "That what he told you?"

"Sure did. Is he lying, or are you?"

Slowly, Grady swung toward Ben. "You don't want to be accusing folks of lying without sound evidence, son. It's not healthy."

Ben raised a brow. "Is that a threat, Sheriff?"

"I wouldn't call it that. Let's just say that I'm real tired of your questions, of you popping into my office every little while with some new dumb notion and of you just being here. What exactly is it you expect to gain by hanging around?"

"A murderer. What do you expect to gain by blocking my investigation?"

Off came the glasses and Ben found himself looking into angry brown eyes. "I've been patient with you, son, but you should know something. I don't answer to the Home Office of National Fidelity like Wilbur does and I don't intimidate real easy. You'd best watch your step. You're a guest in my town, but that could change." Slowly, he put his glasses back on and wandered over to stand alongside his wife.

I'm quaking in my boots, Ben thought. It wasn't the implied threat that bothered him. But the fact that Grady had felt it necessary to give him a not-so-veiled warning. Why? Why wouldn't a man who'd lost his father and three close friends, who might himself be in jeopardy, not want to cooperate with the person sent to get to the bottom of things? The sheriff's attitude was a real mystery.

The side door opened and Wilbur Oakley walked in. When he saw that Grady was right there, his expression grim, Wilbur paled and seemed frozen in place. With a jerk of his head, Grady motioned him outside and trailed after him. Ben wished he was close enough to eavesdrop on that conversation.

Up front, Sean McCauley stepped to the podium and announced that the service was about to begin, then introduced the Methodist minister. Ben figured he wouldn't learn much more here, so he made his way to the back door. Hand on the knob, he glanced back over his shoulder and caught Maggie watching him. He didn't smile and neither did she, but he could see she was remembering that kiss in the parking lot yesterday. Just as he was.

Ben walked outside. Maybe it'd be more interesting to hunt down the man who didn't show up at today's funeral. Getting into his Jeep, he headed for Freddy's shack.

Lucy Hanover had told him approximately where Freddy lived, in a wooded area near a stream that ran along the new section being developed for upscale homes, very near the site of Jack Spencer's death. After driving around the subdivision on rutted dirt roads, each worse than the last, Ben realized he'd have to look for the little house on foot.

He parked his 4 x 4 near a makeshift path and looked around. A thicket of white pine and cedars surrounded the narrow walkway. In the distance, he heard the stream rushing downhill on its way toward the Escanaba River. A bluejay somewhere above squawked a protest as Ben set out, hiking into the woods.

He calculated he'd been walking about fifteen minutes when he caught sight of a log cabin just ahead through the thinning trees. Minutes later, he stopped when he heard some unidentifiable noises. Standing very still, he cocked his head to listen.

They were human sounds, a series of grunts punctuated with sniffling and low jabbering. Trying to walk quietly, he slowly moved closer. Several moments passed before he could see around a thick maple into a small clearing alongside the cabin and near the stream. Someone was digging a hole with a short-handled shovel, troweling up the earth made soft by yesterday's rain. The effort made him groan with each pitch of dirt off to the side.

Two steps nearer and Ben could see that it was Freddy Richmond wearing the same baggy pants and misshapen sweater, his nose running, his lightly bearded cheeks ruddy from his physical effort. Something was lying on the grass beside the mound of fresh soil, but Ben couldn't make out what it was.

"Got to get rid of 'em," Freddy singsonged. "All of 'em. They're sneaky and they kill. Hurt my Pretty Baby." He heaved another shovelful of earth to the side and dipped in for more. "No one understands. I'm Baby's only hope."

The man looked every day of thirty-five, yet according to Lucy, he had the mentality of a nine- or ten-year-old. He was short and squarely built, but flabby, probably from lack of exercise and not eating right out here all alone. A glance at the cabin told Ben it was no more than two small rooms with an overhang that shaded a rickety porch. A barrel containing what looked like stagnant water stood by the door and several bamboo cages containing chattering birds were hung from pegs under the overhang. Lucy had mentioned that Freddy liked birds.

A loud grunt as the boy-man set down the shovel brought Ben's attention back to the freshly dug hole. Freddy bent down and picked up something black and hairy and bloody.

A cat! He was holding a dead cat. Ben stepped forward. "Hey, what are you doing there?"

Startled, Freddy dropped the cat and grabbed a thick walking stick, holding it defensively. "Nothin'. I'm not doing nothin'."

Ben reminded himself that he was dealing with a child in a man's body. "Don't be afraid. I was with Lucy Hanover the other day when you came by for her cans. Remember?"

Freddy sniffed and nodded, but he didn't drop the stick.

Ben stepped closer and looked down at the cat with its head all bloodied. "What happened to your cat?"

"He . . . he's not my cat. I hate cats. They hurt my birds." Freddy stammered out the words, sniffling in between sentences as he pushed his thick glasses further up on his nose.

"Did this cat hurt one of your birds?"

"Yeah. Pretty Baby." Freddy lowered one hand and pointed to a small mound of fresh dirt. "I had to bury her. She . . . she was my favorite and this . . . this awful cat hurt her. He had to pay for sinning."

Ben felt a rush of pity. Freddy should have had help years ago. "So you killed the cat because he hurt Pretty Baby?"

"Sure. 'An eye for an eye.' That's what the Bible says. Mama taught me. Bad people gotta be punished."

Shifting his stance, Ben studied the boy-man, but Freddy

avoided his eyes. "I thought we were talking about cats. What bad people have to be punished, Freddy?"

"All bad men who hurt people. The Good Book says so." He pointed a filthy hand toward his cabin. "Mama gave it to me. I read it every day. I don't read so good, but I know some by heart. 'A tooth for a tooth,' " he quoted.

Ben thought he'd take this just a bit further, though he was probably wrong. "Do you know any bad men who need to be punished, Freddy?"

He swiped at his drippy nose with his soiled sleeve. "Yeah, lots of 'em. They call me names. They laugh at me."

Not liking the direction of his thoughts, Ben nevertheless had to go on. "Your stepfather, Kurt Becker. Is he a bad man?"

Freddy smiled, revealing chipped teeth. "Not no more. He's dead. I told Mama I'm glad." His smile faded, replaced by a worried frown. "She got mad at me. I don't like her to be mad at me."

"Were you over by the river the day Kurt Becker drowned?"

He dropped his gaze. "Only for a little while. He came here first and bought some bait. We had a fight. He's a bad man. He wants to put me away." Suddenly, he brightened. "But he can't no more, can he?" He giggled to himself, then walked over to the hanging cages. "Don't worry none, sweet ladies. I killed the bad cat. No one's gonna hurt you now." Shuffling, he reached into a bag on the porch and scooped up birdseed, placing some in each cage. "Lunchtime, sweet ladies."

Ben watched a few minutes longer, then turned and slowly walked back to his Jeep. If he reported this conversation to Grady, he'd only say that Ben was way out of line, suspecting a retarded boy of a murder, much less several. If he talked with Thelma Becker, asked her just why she wouldn't permit an autopsy on Kurt, perhaps because her son might be implicated somehow, she'd run to the sheriff. He was basically stuck.

But, Ben thought as he climbed behind the wheel, he would definitely keep an eye on Freddy Richmond, and hope he was wrong.

Freddy heard the car drive off and immediately felt better. Why do they come around? Why did they have to build those houses so close to his cabin? Why couldn't everyone just leave him alone with his birds? That man, sneaking around, like a cat, surprising him. He might hurt Freddy like the cat hurt Pretty Baby. Men were like that. You could never trust 'em.

Like the man who used to live with Mama. He came that day, wanting bait he said. But no, he really wanted to nose around. In the house, telling him he lived like a pig, that he made his Mama sad. Freddy knew that wasn't so. Mama loved him. Mama and Granny were the only ones. And his pretty ladies.

He reached in and smoothed the little wren's head. She used to nip at his fingers when he first caught her and put her in the cage he'd made. But no more. She knew he was kind, that he took care of her. He had to make sure no more cats came around to worry his ladies.

It wasn't good to kill, the Bible said. But you had to protect little, helpless ones. Like his birds. Like Mama. Freddy was glad that the man who lived with Mama would never be back. He wanted Freddy to go away to a special school. Freddy'd already tried that and run away. Mama wouldn't let him be sent away again.

Now, the bad man was gone. Mama wouldn't miss him. Mama had Freddy. She didn't need that hateful man. He had wished him gone, had thought long and hard about it, and now, he was gone.

Smiling, Freddy went back to bury the bad cat.

Chapter Eight

Maggie pulled the Explorer into the circular driveway in front of the house and turned off the engine. On the passenger seat beside her was a large box containing contracts, tax forms, P & L statements, and files she'd been given by her father's secretary at Spencer Construction. She needed to go through them, Theresa had said, then meet with the company CPA and attorney in order to come to a decision as to what was to become of the firm.

The building project just begun when Jack died had to be completed, the construction crew needing to get back to work. She'd met with the job boss and told him she'd have a decision for him in a day or two. What in hell did she know about running Spencer Construction? If not that, then how would she go about selling it?

Damn, but she didn't want to have to wrestle with these problems, Maggie thought, climbing down and hoisting the box off the seat. It was heavy so she couldn't dig for her key easily. Instead, she punched the doorbell with her elbow and heard the chimes echoing inside.

Fiona swung open the door, holding it for her. "What have we here?"

"Some papers from Dad's office," Maggie explained, walking past her directly into her father's den. She set it down on the desk where she'd been going through other documents. No, she couldn't face doing more just now. She walked back into the foyer and found Fiona fussing with a vase of long-stemmed red roses and green ferns that she'd placed on the small marble hall table. "My, aren't those lovely?"

Fiona stood back to admire the flowers. "That woman from the Green Thumb delivered them a short time ago. I should have opened the box while she was still here. Downright peculiar is what I call it. These six red ones are as perfect as can be. But there's a white one that has its head snapped right off the stem. It's still in the green tissue paper in the box on the kitchen counter. What do you make of it?"

Maggie inhaled the lovely scent of roses. "How odd. Who sent them?" Surely not Chet. Surely he'd given up by now.

"I left the card in the box." Fiona marched into the kitchen and handed Maggie the small white envelope.

Maggie pulled out the card, read the message, and gasped.

"What is it?" Fiona asked, moving to her side.

"Go back home where you belong before an innocent one dies, too," she read out loud. "There's no signature."

"I don't imagine there would be with such a senseless message." Fiona noticed Maggie's pale cheeks, the hand that shook slightly. "You're not taking this seriously, I hope. It has to be some idiot's idea of a prank."

Maggie lifted the broken green stem and saw the limp white rose lying in the corner of the box. "No one I know would send this to me as a prank, especially with a reference to dying." She pulled her hand back only to prick it on a thorn. "Damn." She sucked on the tiny wound.

"With the cost of roses, I can't imagine anyone going to

all this trouble to get across some vague message only he understands." Half annoyed, half frightened, and unwilling to admit to the latter, Fiona began clearing away the tissue paper and box. "A lot of screwballs out there."

The phone rang as she shut the lid. "Spencer residence," Fiona answered. She listened, then glanced at Maggie. "Hold a moment and I'll check." She covered the mouthpiece. "It's that insurance fellow. Do you feel like talking with him?"

As she reread the card, Maggie thought that Ben's timing was perfect. "Yes and don't throw the box out just yet, Fiona." She walked to the wall phone. "Hi, Ben."

"Glad I caught you." He'd debated about calling, his desire to see her winning out over his common sense. They hadn't spoken at Kurt's funeral or since, but the kiss they'd shared kept drifting through his mind with unnerving regularity. He wanted to see her again, to determine if that kiss had been a fluke or something far more. "I'm planning to have a chat with Ed Kowalski. He looked pretty shaken at the funeral yesterday. I wondered if you wanted to come along." He refrained from adding that he didn't actually *need* her along, but rather wanted her with him.

Going with Ben sounded infinitely better than sitting in the den poring through dusty old papers, not even certain what she was looking for. "Thanks, I would. Matter of fact, I just received an odd gift that I'd like to show you." There was probably nothing to the strange note, yet reading it had given her an eerie feeling.

"A gift? What sort of gift?"

Briefly, she told Ben about the flowers and read him the note.

Listening, his cop antenna went soaring upward, but he kept his voice neutral. "I'll be over shortly." No sense in alarming her, Ben thought as he grabbed his keys from the dresser and left his room. Maybe it was nothing. Then again, could their killer be so bold as to contact the daughter of one of his victims? And why Maggie? Jumping into his Jeep, Ben took off.

Maggie met him at the door and saw he was wearing his stern face today. "I feel silly. This is probably some bored kid or a crackpot."

Ben looked over the flowers in the vase, slowly circling the table. "You put them in water?"

"Fiona did." Maggie glanced at the housekeeper who was standing off to the side, looking irritated.

"What time was the delivery, Fiona?" Ben asked.

"Between three and half past. Ruth herself delivered them." She didn't want this to be anything, didn't want to face the possibility that Maggie could be in some sort of danger.

"Did she say anything?"

"Not much. Handed me the box, said the delivery was for Maggie, asked how I was managing with Jack gone, and that was that. She ran back to her truck and left." What else could it be but a joke? A sick joke, but nothing more, Fiona told herself.

"Where's the box they came in and the card?" Ben followed Maggie to the kitchen where he examined the broken white rose and studied the message. "Plain white card stock, block printed letters, ordinary blue ballpoint pen." He turned to Maggie who was watching him intently. "And you don't know anyone who's a practical joker or someone who might like you out of here?"

Helplessly, she shook her head. "I don't. I've never had a serious run-in with anyone in Riverview. Not since I stepped on Lucy Hanover's geraniums one summer while taking a shortcut through her yard. I was eight."

Ben ignored her attempt at levity. Three men were dead, maybe four. He saw no humor in this. "How about some guy, in New York maybe, who might want you back and this is his cute way of scaring you home?"

In her mind's eye, she pictured Chet, then immediately dismissed him. It wasn't his style, not at all. "I can't imagine anyone I know doing this." Certainly Chet was capable of plenty, but this simply wasn't something she could picture him doing. He'd never been subtle.

"I think I'll have a chat with the lady who runs the Green Thumb. She'll be able to tell me if the person who sent them was local or if it was an FTD order." He pocketed the card. "You coming with me?"

"I sure am." Maggie turned to the housekeeper as she picked up her shoulder bag. "I'm not sure when I'll be back, Fiona."

"All right, but be careful, please." She stood at the open front door looking after them, trying to shake off the unnerving feeling of being watched that had disturbed her lately. You've too much imagination, Fiona, my girl, she told herself. Nevertheless, she quickly closed and locked the door.

The Green Thumb was featuring roses this week, its wide front window decorated with American Beauties plus a cluster of miniature roses in a delicate shade of peach and a rose tree. The bell over the door tinkled as they walked inside. Arranging a large bouquet of daisies at a side table, Ruth looked up. "Hello, Maggie. How are you?"

"Doing well, thanks." She moved to the counter. "This is Ben Whalen, an insurance investigator who's looking into Dad's accident. Ben, Ruth Bishop."

Ben recognized the woman he'd noticed at Kurt's funeral fussing with the floral arrangements.

Ruth wiped her palms on the apron tied around her waist and walked over, offering her hand to Ben. She was tall, at least five-eight, with broad shoulders and most likely had the muscular legs of a runner, he thought, remembering Wilbur mentioning that she ran in marathons. Her hair was brown and cut short to curl around her face. She had on a cotton jogging suit in green and on the table was a pair of yellow gardening gloves with the thumb dyed green. Undoubtedly her trademark.

"Nice to meet you," Ruth said. "You're investigating an accident?"

Like everyone else in town, the woman thought that odd, Ben knew. "The company sends us to accident sites at times to check things out. But today, I'm here about something else. Did you deliver some roses to Maggie earlier today?"

"Sure did." She looked at Maggie. "Was something wrong with them?"

"Well, yes," Maggie answered. "The white one was broken."

"Yes, I know. That's the way the man wanted them sent. I thought it was odd, but then, peculiar requests aren't unheard of in this business. Just last month, I had an order from a man for carnations tinted black for his wife's fortieth birthday."

Ben wasn't terribly interested in her customer's eccentricities. "Do you know the man who ordered the roses?"

"Never saw him before."

"Can you describe him?"

"He wasn't tall, maybe five-five, and he was wearing a bulky jacket and jeans."

"A bulky jacket and it's at least seventy-five out there today," Maggie commented. "That's odd right there."

"I thought so, too," Ruth added.

Ben wanted to know more. "His face, his features, his hair. What can you tell me?"

Ruth smiled. "I thought it was pretty funny. He had on this misshapen hairpiece, sort of reddish brown, obviously a fake, and a droopy-brimmed hat on over it. Plus he had a thick towel draped around his neck that more or less hid the bottom half of his face. I remember his eyes were dark with long lashes."

"Thin, fat, in-between? About how much did he weigh?"

"Oh, I'm not good at this." Ruth screwed up her face thoughtfully. "Kind of chubby. Maybe one-seventy or eighty. Hard to say. His hands were pudgy and had several little cuts on them, like scratches."

Ben's gaze skimmed the single room with a narrow center hall leading to the back. A typical florist shop with refrigerated section, wood counter, several freestanding displays, stuffed animals for sale, and a greeting card rack. There was also a shelf displaying jars of homemade honey for sale. The place was nicely kept and the only flower shop in town. "So this guy came in about what time?"

"Just after I got back from lunch."

"I don't suppose we get lucky and he paid by credit card?"

Ruth shook her head. "Sorry. Cash."

"I might have known. Did you see what kind of car he drove?"

"I didn't see a car at all. He appeared to be on foot. Came in from the left there and walked out heading in the same direction."

"The municipal parking lot's in that direction," Maggie reminded him. "But I imagine the chances of finding someone who might remember having seen him are pretty slim."

"Can I ask a question?" Ruth looked puzzled. "Why are you so anxious to find this guy? I mean, so he sent you half a dozen red roses and one broken white one. Odd, yes, but what's the big deal?"

Ben handed the card to her and watched while she read the message.

"Oh, my." Her brown eyes wide, she looked at Maggie. "Who would want you to leave?"

"I haven't any idea."

"Well, he had that envelope in his hand when he came in

and asked me to tuck it into the paper. He knew exactly what he wanted. Stood right where you are while I broke the white rose and fixed the box just so."

"Did you ask him why he was sending Maggie a broken flower?" Ben asked.

"Yes. He said that she'd know the reason why."

Maggie pushed back her hair. "Wonderful. My father dies, I'm out of a job, and now I've got some creep sending me mutilated roses who thinks I'll get his warped message. Maybe I should go back to New York. It's beginning to look pretty good about now."

"Let's not make any hasty decisions." Ben withdrew his business card from his shirt pocket. "Ruth, I've written the number of where I'm staying on the back of my card and also my beeper number. If you think of anything that might help us track down this guy, would you please call me?"

"Sure." Ruth glanced at the card, then slipped it in the cash register drawer. "Sorry I couldn't be of more help."

"See you later." Maggie walked out the door with Ben following. On the street, she strolled toward his Jeep parked up a ways. "That didn't net us much."

"How long has she owned that shop?" he asked.

"Oh, three maybe four years. Fellow named Herman owned it for years, but he had a heart attack so he and his wife decided to move to Florida. I believe Ruth said she'd read about the shop being for sale in some real estate magazine, bought it, and moved here."

"Where's she from?"

He was doing it again, suspicious of everyone. "Chicago, I believe. I've always enjoyed working with growing things myself, so we've had several conversations about seasonal plantings, what's a good mulch, which plants do well in sunlight, that sort of thing. She really knows her flowers."

"She's not married, I take it."

"No. She lives upstairs above the shop in a little apartment." Maggie squinted up at him. "Inquisition over?"

"Yeah, I guess so." Ben propped an arm on the Jeep's door. "Not much of a life for a woman who's what, forty or so?"

"I suppose not, but Ruth seems happy enough. She's very physical, forever going on these long bicycle rides and hiking and entering marathons. And she sews beautifully, I hear."

"A multifaceted, many-talented woman. I wish she was a camera buff who'd taken this guy's picture." Actually, he had a hunch, yet suspected his idea was totally off the wall. "You know, her description sounds a little like Freddy Richmond."

Maggie raised a brow. "Freddy? Oh, please. Let's not pick on poor old Freddy. I doubt that he could copy that message, much less think it up and write it out. And why would he want me out of town? I've always been nice to him." She shook her head. "Too ridiculous to consider."

"If you say so." He glanced across the street and saw that Kowalski's Meat Market was still open. "Want to go buy some sausage? I hear Ed makes the best."

It wasn't sausage he was after, she was certain. "Might as well get it over with." Although it seemed as if all their visits combined bore very little fruit. If this legwork was typical of the life of a cop, she knew she'd hate it.

A study in white enamel, chrome shelves, and glass-enclosed display cases, Kowalski's was clean and neat, with pungent smells filling the shop and a Wagner opera playing in a back room. Ben studied the variety of sausages hanging from the ceiling as a young woman with a toddler in tow left the store and Maggie stepped up to greet the butcher.

"It's good to see you, Maggie," Ed said, smiling from behind his high counter. "I hope you're going to stick around for a while. We miss you."

"Thanks. Ed, I'd like you to meet Ben Whalen from National Fidelity. He's in town investigating the accidents."

Ed didn't offer his hand, only slid his horn-rimmed glasses higher on his nose. "That so. What's to investigate? Accidents happen. Your company don't want to pay off, is that it?"

"No, sir, that isn't it," Ben said. "There are some inconsistencies that need looking into, that's all. Since you have a similar policy as the three men who've recently died, you can imagine that National Fidelity wants to check everything out so there're no problems later."

His eyes on Ben, Ed closed the sliding glass door to his meat display case. "Oh, you know about that, do you?"

While he wasn't exactly belligerent, Kowalski wasn't friendly, either, Ben thought, and wondered why. "Yes, sir. I understand that you and five others were friends since boyhood. Can you tell me how the six of you happened to take out such big policies right out of college? Most young men wait to get established in business before thinking that far ahead."

"Maybe so, but that's the sort of guys we were, even back then. We wanted to protect our families, to secure their future. We're honest, good citizens, strong family men. We were then and we are now."

Quite a declaration, Ben thought, and far more than he'd asked for. Why was Ed so defensive?

The butcher wiped his hands on the large white apron he wore tied around his rotund body and slid his eyes to Maggie in a deliberate move to change the subject. "Fiona hasn't been in in a while. Would you like some spring lamb? Just came in today." He turned toward his big walk-in freezer and touched the handle. "Special price for you, Maggie."

"Thanks, but I'd better leave the meal planning to Fiona," Maggie told him. "The kitchen's her domain and she gets pouty if anyone interferes." She glanced toward the small back room. "Helen not in today?" His wife usually worked alongside Ed.

"She was earlier, but she left to go with Tom to the doctor. He's been having these headaches, really severe. He's been on leave but I think they're going to give him a medical discharge. The doctors can't seem to find the cause." Ed looked concerned.

Tom had to be that angry young Marine he'd seen at Kurt Becker's funeral, Ben thought. The Kowalskis' only child. "Has he seen battle duty?" Ben asked, less from curiosity than wanting to rejoin the conversation.

"Yeah, the Gulf War. He didn't get hurt, but he seems different somehow. And now these headaches. Tom wanted to be a career Marine." Ed shook his head sadly at the loss of his son's dream. "You never know what road life will take you down."

It wasn't much of a lag in the conversation, but Ben jumped in. "Mr. Kowalski, getting back to the six of you, now suddenly, three are dead, all recently, all by accident. This may seem like an odd question, but would you have any idea why someone might want to harm any of you?"

A scowl appeared on Ed's normally placid face. "No, I certainly do not. We're law-abiding, God-fearing, church-going family men. The wildest thing we ever do is play poker on Friday nights and occasionally get a little drunk. Ask anyone. I . . . I don't know anything else." He turned aside, embarrassed at a sudden rush of emotion.

Ben glanced at Maggie who merely shrugged. He decided that he ought to take another stab at Ed. "Mr. Kowalski, I don't mean to upset you, but . . ."

"You don't understand." Hitching up his trousers, Ed turned around, his face stormy. "Those men who died were my friends, my *close* friends, since I was a boy. I resent you coming around here and asking your damn nosy questions, acting as if we have something to hide. Go back where you came from and tell those guys at National Fidelity that they owe that money to the beneficiaries and they damn well better pay up."

Ben's voice was calm, a direct contrast to Ed's. "I came here to warn you, Mr. Kowalski. Three out of six are gone. You're one of three others left. Something's going on. If you know anything that could stop this, why not speak up? Aren't you worried?"

Maggie placed a hand on Ben's arm. "Ben, perhaps we ought to leave. This isn't helping."

"I'm not here to blame or accuse, Maggie. I'm trying to keep Ed and George and Grady from some *accident* that could cost them their lives." He'd thought that at least she understood.

"I don't want to hear any more of this," Ed stated, removing his apron. "It's past closing time. You'll have to leave."

Feeling defeated as well as annoyed, Ben placed his card on Ed's counter. "You can reach me at one of those numbers in case you change your mind, Mr. Kowalski."

Maggie felt she should say something, but couldn't for the life of her think what. So she simply preceded Ben out the door and walked briskly to the Jeep. At the passenger door, she paused and drew in a deep breath, feeling unaccountably shaky.

Coming alongside, Ben searched her face. "Are you angry with me for what I tried to do?" He knew how far back her friendship with these men went, how terrible she felt, not only about the loss of her father, but of Reed Lang and Kurt Becker. It was all too easy to blame the outsider and he wondered if she did.

Maggie stared up at the setting sun as if she might find answers there. "Not really. I know you're trying to help. On the other hand, I can almost feel how afraid Ed is that he might be next, yet he won't admit to that."

"Do you think he knows something or someone who might have it in for all six of these guys?"

"It's hard to say, but my guess is that he does. Look at how Grady dismisses the whole idea, and now Ed. I'd be willing to wager George would, too. They suspect something, I feel, but they're not certain, and maybe there's no way they can check."

"There's always a way to check, if they'd just trust me."

She shook her head. "You're asking a lot on that one. You've been here, what a week, ten days? This is a small, close-knit community. They don't trust easily. They won't discuss their fears with me, either, and they've known me all my life."

Ben paced back and forth beside the Jeep. "What the hell happened that caused this chain of events to break loose? And does it date back to when these guys were young, or is it more recent, like a business deal gone sour? Who are they protecting?"

"Then again, maybe we're just overreacting. We seem to be the only two who think the deaths weren't accidental."

"I think we're right." He only hoped no one else would die before they learned the truth. "Let's go for a ride, clear the cobwebs." Only he reached into his pocket and his keys weren't there. It took a moment for him to remember. "I left my keys on Ed's counter." Gazing across the street, he saw that the lights were still on in the butcher shop. "I'll be right back."

Thankfully, the door was still unlocked. He went in and found the store empty. Deciding not to call out and upset Ed who was probably somewhere in the back, he walked to the counter. He'd just picked up his keys when he heard a voice trailing down the short hallway.

"I don't give a damn how busy you are, I need to talk to you. And I'm calling George, too. I'm telling you, Grady, I'm worried." Ed's voice sounded anxious, then he paused to listen to the person on the other end. "Yeah, I know, you keep telling me, no one knows a damn thing. But this insurance guy's not stupid and even Maggie thought I was lying. I could tell." The silence stretched for several long seconds. "Right you are, eight o'clock. We'll talk then." With a loud clatter, he hung up the phone.

In the front of the store, Ben tiptoed out, hoping the faint sounds of the opera were enough to drown out his footsteps. Walking to the Jeep, he found himself frowning. So at least one of the three remaining Sexy Six was getting worried, maybe more. He'd been right—they were hiding something. But what? Maybe if one got nervous enough, he'd spill the beans. Ben hoped so.

"When you think about it, there's no such thing as a really safe place," Maggie said. "Your father got killed right in front of his store, my dad less than three miles from home, and Mr. Becker on a quiet river. How can you guard against something happening?"

Strolling slowly with her along the bank of the stream that backed up to the Spencer property, Ben shook his head. "You can't. There have always been and probably always will be people out there who can't be defined as normal who either accidentally or deliberately fixate on someone, and there's no stopping them."

Maggie ducked her head to avoid the low-hanging branches of a weeping willow that trailed its leaves into the clear water. "You mean a sociopath, someone who fools people into believing they're normal, and yet their actions prove they're not."

"That's one explanation, although most criminals, even murderers, aren't sociopaths, which is one reason they're usually easier to catch."

Stopping, Maggie looked up at him, admiring the way the moonlight made his gray eyes seem silver. "Why is that?"

Ben flopped down on the thick grass and waited until she'd joined him. They'd left Main Street and driven all the way to Negaunee to a tiny restaurant that served fish so fresh it was still flopping on the plate, or so the owner told them. Then they'd come back to Maggie's and decided to take a walk along the stream. The night was warm and peaceful, a contrast to their serious subject matter. "Because when an average person kills, he quite often does it in a rage, a spontaneous jealous fit or to avoid being detected for a more minor crime. The killing isn't well thought out." Ben leaned back against the thick bark of the tree.

"Small mistakes are made by even the smartest criminals—like wearing a cologne that's easily recognized or dropping a cigarette butt that's clearly their brand at the crime scene or maybe wiping every surface clean of prints at a murder scene, erasing even the victim's fingerprints. But sociopaths are different. They have no conscience and so they can and do use means that even hardened criminals would reject."

"Like what?"

"Like using family members or children, animals, sacred objects, anything to achieve their goals. They're unemotional about inflicting pain on others."

Maggie had on a knit top and full summer skirt that skimmed nearly to her ankles, yet she felt a chill. Unconsciously she moved closer to Ben, her thoughts uneasy. "Is that the kind of person you think we're dealing with here?"

She looked tense, a little afraid and heart-stoppingly beautiful in the moonlight. More for himself than her, Ben drew her closer so that her back was up against his chest, his hands resting on her crossed arms. With no small effort, he groped to remember her question. "No, I don't think so, although all three deaths seem very well planned out beforehand, certainly not spontaneous or impulsive. This is a very clever, very patient person, one who has a hidden agenda. I wish to hell I knew what it is, what motivates him."

Maggie could see Fiona moving around in her bedroom at the back of the house, her window open. She hadn't gone in when they'd returned and Ben had parked in front, but the woman had cat's ears and probably knew exactly where they were. She'd left a light on downstairs for Maggie each evening and hadn't scolded her for not checking in since their last discussion on that subject. Still, it was odd how Maggie felt she ought to report in periodically, something that hadn't concerned her in Manhattan.

Manhattan. Home for six years now. Or was it?

"I wish this whole thing was cleared up, that it was over and we knew what was happening and who was behind it. I dislike chaos. I need order in my life and I haven't had it for some time." She became aware of strong fingers moving along her bare arms, gently stroking, lightly massaging. It felt good, and just a little disturbing.

Ben wasn't sure he agreed. "Every time I try to get my life in order, something happens to mess things up." College hadn't seemed the same after his father had died, so he'd quit. Then just when things were going well on the police force, his marriage had ended so tragically and, afterward, he'd been unable to handle the desk job. He liked working for National Fidelity, the freedom, the variety. No ties. That's how he liked his life. Yet, even so, he felt dissatisfied at times. "Sometimes it's better to just drift along."

"Your work doesn't exactly lend itself to order with new cases all the time and so much traveling involved." Now his hands were on her shoulders, gently rubbing. He'd found the tense muscle there and was working on the knot, slowly, gently.

"That's part of it. But I've learned it's a waste of time making plans, trying to carry them out in an orderly way.

What good does it do? Some madman comes along and bingo! Everything changes."

She knew why he felt the way he did, yet it seemed so cynical. "Should we just give up then, give in?"

"I get tempted. Personally I think the gods sit around and laugh at us as we scramble about making our little plans, working toward our little goals. Then, when we're feeling smugly secure, they send us a zinger we hadn't even considered, and it's all over."

There was just enough moonlight to see his eyes as she tilted her head. She saw sadness there and very little hope. She could only imagine he was thinking of his wife and child. "Perhaps it is all over, for that dream. But you can always begin a new one."

He reached up to stroke her cheek, the feel of her skin smooth as satin to the touch. He wasn't all that much older than Maggie, but light-years ahead of her in experiences, the kind he hoped she would never know. "Is that what you plan to do, Maggie? You've said there's no longer a special man in your life and you also said you're out of a job. I assume the two may even be connected. So are you going to pick yourself up, dust yourself off, and start all over again with a new dream?"

She hadn't thought of it quite that way. "Maybe. One day. I can't think about that just yet. It's only been a matter of weeks, and I think I'm still hurting too much to begin something new. Besides, I need to have some sort of closure on Dad's death. But for you, well, it's been six years, as you've said."

He gave her a touching smile. "I used to think time healed all wounds, that given enough time you'd forget anything. It isn't necessarily so."

She covered his hand with her own, then took it into both of hers. "You need to *want* to heal, to want to get past it, I think. Don't you?"

"Perhaps. Are you saying I'm wallowing in my sadness?"

She smiled then. "No, I'm saying I think I am. I'm hugging the pain to my chest like some sort of shield, thinking it'll keep me from making another foolish mistake, from trusting the wrong man again. But I don't know that it will."

"Do you want to tell me what happened?" He wanted to know, but he wouldn't push.

She sighed, sitting cross-legged now, her full skirt spread out around her. "It's a short, not very pretty story. My first job in New York was with Butler and Sons, a very good PR firm. And I was doing quite well, climbing the old corporate ladder, slowly getting a few new clients, but good ones. Then one day, I met Chet Garrett. He's ten years older than I and the owner of Innovations, the firm I told you awhile back that I worked for."

"I remember."

"Innovations is big with some real power clients. It didn't take Chet long to coax me over for lots more money and that stupid corner office. I'm disappointed in myself that I caved in so easily, but I did. Young, impressionable, ambitious. Anyhow, I worked mostly with writers, doing book tours, arranging signings, setting up ad spots, television bookings, that sort of thing. Chet had been married and divorced and said he never wanted to walk that path again. That was fine with me. I was intent on my career, not marriage. Only I made a mistake. I fell for him."

"It happens to the best of us."

"I suppose. He wanted me to move in with him, but I held out. Maybe because I couldn't face giving up that last little bit of independence." She paused a moment, searching for the right words. "You see, Chet's overwhelming. He's very confident, bulldog determined, and pretty arrogant. A person could get lost in his shadow. But, of course, I didn't think I would. Naive of me."

He was rubbing her shoulders again, lightly, casually, almost playfully. "You wouldn't be the first to misjudge."

"Oh, but when I do it, I do it up right."

"Let me guess. He told you you were the only one even without the gold band, and then you caught him with another woman."

Slowly, Maggie nodded. "Pretty predictable to everyone but me." She had no idea how defeated she sounded. "We'd had this so-called *understanding*. No wedding bells, but no playing the field, either. To me, it was like a promise. To Chet, it was a line, one I belatedly discovered he'd used before. Oh, he tried to talk his way out of it after I caught him, but I'd heard other rumors and checked them out. They were true and he was not." Maggie dropped her head forward, letting his clever hands work on her neck.

"End of story?"

"More or less. He called, apologized in a manner of speaking, as if he'd breached some rule of etiquette, nothing serious. He said he'd never betray me again. After all, everyone made mistakes and why was I being so provincial." Not just once, he'd phoned repeatedly. Finally Maggie stopped taking his calls. She'd even hung up on him when he'd called her here.

"But you didn't go for it."

"No. He lied to me and he hurt me. I couldn't ever trust him again. I despise deception." She made a purring sound low in her throat. "If you ever want to stop playing cops and robbers, you can take up massaging. You have great hands."

"I haven't wanted to put my hands on a woman in a long, *long* time." His one hand trailed to the front, caressing the silk of her throat. "You have the most incredible face, the softest skin. I never see you that I don't want to touch you."

Languid from the summer night and the shoulder rub, she was too relaxed to go on alert, finding more humor than lust in his comment. "I thought you leaned toward wanting to clobber me most of the time."

"In the beginning." There was a subtle change in his voice, a thickening, as his fingers moved up to lazily thread through her hair. "What would you say if I told you I've lain awake nights thinking about doing just this, being with you, imagining what your bedroom must be like?"

The same bedroom where she'd lain imagining him. She'd come to admire Ben Whalen, the way he was able to ferret out important facts from the most innocuous conversations, the way he doggedly pursued the smallest thing and looked at it every which way before discarding it as irrelevant. They'd crossed swords several times and might again. She had him pegged as a single-minded company man, a bit ruthless in his dealings.

Yet underlying all that was a male-female awareness humming just beneath the surface that neither of them could rightfully deny. Maggie felt an electrical tension radiating between them, a seductive energy she was certain Ben felt, too. It was there in the way he looked at her with those quick-silver eyes that seemed to see far more than she intended, in the way his hand lingered overly long each time he touched her. He had a habit of standing a hairbreadth closer than good social manners dictated. She was certain he invaded her space intentionally, hoping for a reaction, and was rarely disappointed.

Sensing a change in the way he was touching her, she tensed as his hands tangled in her hair, bringing her closer. "Ben," she whispered, startled by the sharp stab of desire the contact aroused in her.

"You make me think of things I'd pushed out of my mind—like a soft summer night and the way your hair smells and moonlight on satin sheets." He dipped his head lower and touched his lips to her cheek, the tip of his tongue trailing down to kiss the corner of her mouth. "Mmm, I love the way you taste."

"Ben," she tried again, knowing the effort was halfhearted, hearing the catch in her voice. "I thought we weren't going to . . ."

His mouth swallowed the rest of her words as he drew her up tight against himself.

Passion exploded, immediate, frantic, racing like a speeding bullet through his veins. The kiss in the parking lot had been but a practice session for this mindless mating call that had him dizzy with need in mere seconds. Seeing her daily, trying to ignore the attraction, had heightened the craving. Arms wound around her, her heart beating against his, Ben let the separate sensations wash over him.

Emotions swirled then collided inside Maggie, leaving her trembling. His mouth was warm and wet and wonderful, chasing away all rational thought. His dark, masculine flavors burst on her tongue until she was seeped in him, in pleasure. She'd known passion before, but never had she suspected she could feel more, so much more. On a throaty moan, she angled her head and invited him to deepen the kiss, to show her more.

The moon slipped behind a silken cloud and the soft breeze had the willow branches swaying just above them. The stream flowed lazily over polished rocks, splashing and gurgling on its constant journey. A night bird called encouragement from somewhere nearby. Ben saw none of it, heard none of it, with his lips fastened to the pulse pounding at her throat. Pounding for him. His hands shifted, moving around front, impatient to touch bare skin. Inching beneath her knit top, his fingers found her breasts, and he heard the moan she couldn't suppress.

Her heart pounded beneath his hand as he caressed trembling flesh, then dipped his head to taste. Maggie's hands moved into his hair and pressed him closer. He felt her buck as he drew on her, then shifted to swallow her cries. Their mouths locked together in fiery demand, in frantic need. They rolled on the fragrant grass until each was breathless and panting.

Ben was stunned to his core, unable to function beyond holding her, caressing her. Needs whipped at him, making his mind hazy. He wanted her desperately in his bed, his to love all night long. But not out here where the moon dappled down on them and anyone could walk by. Breathing hard, he eased back a fraction.

Through a brain still cloudy, Maggie struggled to think clearly, to make sense of what had just happened. A hurricane, an avalanche, a tidal wave or something no less forceful. She needed time to assess the situation and her feelings. She needed some space. She scooted over, sitting up and taking in a deep gulp of air as she adjusted her clothes.

Ben sat up and ran a hand through his hair, then touched her shoulder. He placed a fingertip on her chin and made her look at him. "I want you and I think you want me, too."

"No. Yes." Maggie shoved both hands in her hair and drew her knees up, spreading out her skirt. If she could just get her heart to slow down, she could sort this out. "What I mean is that we can't do this, not here where I used to play as a child in plain sight of Fiona's bedroom." Praying her legs would hold her, she got to her feet.

"I agree." Ben stood. "Let's go to my room at the motel."

She knew everyone in town, and they all recognized her. How could she go to his room with Hector, the desk clerk at the Riverview Motel, making note of everyone's comings and goings? There were other reasons as well, but she wasn't sure she could make him see. "If we were in Manhattan, it might be different. But I don't feel right about going to the motel here or to my room, nor out here, either." She saw the disappointment on his face and his struggle to accept the rejection. To soften her decision, she touched his arm. "Please understand. This is a small town."

"Yeah, in more ways than one." He stepped aside, jammed both hands in his back pockets, and gazed up at clouds slowly drifting along.

"I know we're both free, both old enough to do as we wish. But I simply can't do anything here to invite gossip, especially right now."

He took a moment to calm down before acknowledging that he was acting childish. He turned back and saw her watching him carefully, gauging his mood. Sliding his hands along her arms, he gazed down at her. "I know you're right, about the town. Is there another reason?"

She was glad he'd brought it up. "I'd be stupid to deny that there's something powerful between us. But I've been hurt badly and quite recently. I need time. Can you handle that?"

Finally, he found a small smile. "I've been known to be patient a time or two." He wanted her to come to him willingly, having made up her own mind, not in the heat of the moment. He knew she was worth waiting for. He just hoped she didn't take too long.

"There's so much going on, you know. The problems I walked away from in New York, the possibility that a madman is killing people, the mess my father's estate is in, the decisions I have to make about his company." Maggie shook her head. "And then . . ."

"And then I come along and suddenly, your mind gets even more muddled. I know all that." He drew her closer. "I hope you realize, though, that what just happened between us on the grass over there doesn't happen with everyone." It certainly hadn't happened quite like that for him before.

Remembering had her cheeks warming. "I do know that."

He kissed her lightly, no pressure. Then, his arm around

her waist, he walked back to the Jeep. Before climbing in, he kissed her again. "I'll call you tomorrow."

Maggie nodded. "Yes. Good night." She watched him drive away, then turned toward the door just as a nearby sound startled her into stopping in her tracks. Frowning, she glanced toward the trees bordering the side yard, then beyond to the stream that led to the pond. No movement, no further sound. She was alone, yet she had the odd sensation that someone was nearby, watching, waiting.

She drew in a deep breath. Probably her overactive imagination, Maggie decided as she went inside and locked the door.

Driving south on Manor Drive with the Jeep's windows down, Ben turned on the radio and hummed along with a western tune. He was nearly at the turnoff to the Riverview Motel when the program was interrupted by a news bulletin. Slowing, he turned up the volume.

Freddy Richmond had been arrested and was in jail, according to a spokesman for the sheriff's department.

Chapter Nine

"It isn't just the Peeping Tom complaint, Thelma," Grady said, gazing across his desk at Kurt Becker's irate widow, "it's also the bloody knife we found on Freddy."

Thelma waved a dismissive hand. "That's a bunch of bull, Grady. You know Freddy wouldn't harm a fly. Why, he refuses to dig worms for bait because he can't stand the thought of killing. He picks up scraps at Kowalski's instead."

"Then how do you explain the blood on his knife?"

"It's probably ketchup. Freddy dumps ketchup on everything he eats. He only carries that knife for protection, because so many bullies pick on him. Twisting her hands together, Thelma sat on the edge of the uncomfortable wood chair. "Grady, please. You *know* Freddy. He's . . . simple, not dangerous."

Grady reached for a toothpick and wished for a cigar. He'd given them up years ago because Opal hated the smell, but he sorely missed smoking, especially in difficult moments. "Thelma, let's be patient here. I'm sending the knife to the lab in Marquette. We'll get the results in a couple of days."

"You're not going to keep him in jail until then, are you?" She sniffed into a wadded-up tissue. "Lord, Grady, I just buried my husband and now this. Please, don't do this to me."

Though there were some who wouldn't think so, Grady was a compassionate man. He especially couldn't stand to see a woman cry. "I'll release him to your custody, Thelma, but you've got to promise to keep him with you until we can get to the bottom of this. I mean, what the hell was he doing peeking into the windows of that rental cabin, anyway? Those tourists swore out a complaint. I can't just ignore that."

Frazzled, Thelma shook her head. "I don't know what came over him, but I mean to find out." Rising, she swiped at her eyes. "You know, I've been thinking. Once I get Kurt's insurance settlement, I'd like to sell the house and move closer to my girls in California. I'll get Freddy and me a nice place and then you won't have to worry about us anymore."

"Don't be hasty, Thelma. It's not good to make big decisions after losing a spouse. You need time to adjust." Camilla hadn't died, but run off on him, yet it had taken him a long time to get used to being without her. "Besides, I don't want you making any plans to leave until we settle this thing about Freddy peeping in windows."

"Oh, really, Grady, if that silly woman thought that that poor boy was interested in watching her undress, she's far sicker than he is. Freddy isn't sexual at all."

Frowning, Grady stood. "You know that for a fact?"

"He's got the mind of a ten-year-old, for heaven's sake. Boys that age don't think about girls."

"I wouldn't go that far," Ben said from the doorway.

Grady's frown deepened. "How long have you been there?"

"Awhile. J.C. told me you were back here. Hello, Mrs. Becker." He watched her face change as it dawned on her who he was.

"You're just the man I want to see. Wilbur Oakley says he can't get National Fidelity to release my husband's insurance money until you give the okay. I'd like to know what's going on."

"So would I." Ben stepped into the room, unapologetic for not having approved payment yet or for having eavesdropped. Sometimes listening unobserved was the only way to learn things, especially in a small town run by a reticent sheriff. "I wouldn't be too quick about releasing Freddy, either, Sheriff. I was out at his place a couple of days ago and found him burying a cat he'd just killed. Doesn't sound like someone who wouldn't harm a fly to me."

"How dare you!" Breathing fire, Thelma Becker puffed herself up to her full height of five-three. "My Freddy's a good boy. Who are you to come here hurling accusations?"

Ben held up a hand as he shook his head. "I'm not accusing. I'm stating a fact. Psychological profiles indicate that men who kill cats often kill humans."

"He's *not* a man. He's a boy," Thelma insisted.

"With the strength of a man."

"All right," Grady said, "that's enough. Whalen, I make the decisions around here. Thelma, I'm releasing Freddy to you, but I hold you responsible until this matter is resolved. Are we clear on that?"

Thelma sniffed into her soggy tissue, calming since she got most of what she'd come for. "Yes, and thank you, Grady." With a hostile glare aimed at Ben, she flounced out as Grady buzzed J.C. and gave him instructions. Replacing the phone, he stifled a yawn, which wasn't surprising since he'd been up all night. He needed about eight hours of oblivion, but the determined look on Ben's face told him he wasn't apt to have it soon. "What can I do for you now?"

Ben settled himself in the chair Thelma had vacated. "I'm telling you, Freddy Richmond's not to be trusted. Have you ever been out to that shack of his?"

Grady leaned back in his chair and propped a booted foot on an open drawer. "Lots of times. I buy bait from him when I fish. And I'm telling you, he's harmless. He could no more plot a killing than he could fly to the moon."

"Maybe not, but if someone frightened him or threatened him, he could go into a rage and kill."

"Given the right set of circumstances, I suppose we all could," Grady stated. The face of Wayne Edwards, his son-in-law, the man who'd knocked his daughter around for years, came to mind.

Grady had him there, Ben thought, for he'd nearly done that very thing. "You're probably right. But harmless people, especially retarded ones, don't kill cats or anything else."

"You still on this killer-on-the-loose kick, Whalen? When you going to give it up, go on home, and leave us alone?"

"When are you going to admit there's something going on in *your* town? I . . ."

"Sheriff," J.C. said from the office doorway, "can I see you a minute?"

He was too damn tired to move. "What is it, J.C.?"

The deputy glanced at Ben, then back at Grady. "We just got a call from the head of the construction crew that Maggie Spencer put back to work at the site where Jack fell. Guy was using a backhoe to clear a section and ran into something. Looks like they dug up a body buried on the far side."

Grady wasn't happy that Ben had overheard his deputy's message or that he'd decided to follow him out to the site, Ben knew. But short of ordering him to stay away, there wasn't much the sheriff could do about it since he was well aware by now that Ben didn't take instructions well.

Apparently Maggie had called this morning and put the

men back to work. She'd said something yesterday about pressure from everyone to get the project finished. There was no longer a reason to keep the area roped off.

Or so they'd thought.

Ben parked the Jeep off the makeshift road and walked over to where Grady and J.C. were staring down at a rectangular hole alongside two men in work clothes and hard hats. Stepping up, he saw a pair of men's shoes, some clothes already rotting away, a dark briefcase, and a body already well into decomposition. The skull looked smashed in, as if hit very hard by a blunt object. On a sunny morning, the air was thick with the stench of death and decay.

"You got a pair of long-handled pliers handy, Roscoe?" Grady asked the construction boss.

"Right here." He handed them over, handle first.

A handkerchief over his nose, Grady leaned down, aiming the point of the pliers at a flat object lying alongside what looked to be a large hip bone. Retrieving it, he held the object toward J.C. who gingerly plucked it from between the teeth. "Looks like the man's wallet. See if there's ID in there."

The deputy opened the wallet, his face grim. "Driver's license says his name was Warren Harper. Lived in Marquette."

Grady stepped back away from the smell, his gaze shifting to Ben as he handed back the pliers. "You know this guy?"

"Never met him, but I know *of* him. He was involved in some sort of three-way investment deal with Jack Spencer and Reed Lang. As I understand it, Harper mismanaged some funds and his partners weren't happy with him."

"Uh-huh." Grady nodded, looking pleased. "That's what I heard, too. So, Whalen, looks like we got our killer."

Flabbergasted, Ben stared at him. "How's that again?"

"Well, obviously this Harper fellow was a crook and when Reed and Jack found out, he knew he was in trouble. So he set Reed up, drove to the vacant house, and shoved him down the basement stairs. Then he came after Jack. Only Jack beat him to it and killed him. Accidentally most likely."

If the whole thing wasn't so serious, it would have been amusing, Ben thought. *Accidentally* smashed in his skull? "I see. Then was Jack so filled with remorse that he climbed up onto the second floor and jumped to his own death?"

The sheriff's eyes narrowed with temper. "No. Jack turned his back on his conscience and buried the body. As to his own death, I know he started drinking again, maybe over what he'd done, and he came out here to check on the shallow grave he'd buried this guy in. It was getting dark and he was in his cups. He climbed up and fell. No mystery, no murderer stalking anyone."

Ben scratched his head. "Nice and neat. How do you explain Kurt's drowning?"

"No connection. Kurt fell out of the damn boat. People do, you know." Angry now, Grady turned to his deputy. "Call for help, bag the remains, and have this guy taken to the morgue." Starting back to his truck, he nodded to the construction boss. "Thanks for calling us so quickly, Roscoe."

Ben followed, trying to gauge the man's temper. "I wonder if the M.E. will think a bashed-in skull is reason enough to do an autopsy?"

Grady swung about, his dark eyes blazing. "What's it to you? I doubt Harper's insured with your company. Or did National Fidelity insure the whole damn Upper Peninsula?"

"You know more about who around here is insured by us than I do, especially since you got to Oakley and told him to keep his mouth shut when it comes to my investigation." He stepped to within two feet of the sheriff, his look challenging. "But it's not working, Grady. I'm going to get to the bottom of this if I have to call on all the law enforcement agencies between Escanaba and Marquette along with the FBI. Don't think I won't."

Every bit as angry as the sheriff, Ben marched to his Jeep and took off.

Grady stood watching him leave, a worried frown on his face.

"I'll be fine, Fiona, honestly," Maggie said, tossing the pen she'd been using onto her father's desk. "You go and have a good time."

"It wouldn't hurt me to skip tonight," Fiona said. "I know you're having one of your bad days." She'd heard Maggie weeping through Jack's bedroom walls earlier, the sound nearly breaking her heart. Maggie had been sorting through her father's clothes, packing them up to give to the church, when memories had likely made the task too much for her. Fiona had gone in, then backed out when she'd seen the young woman bent over double, clutching Jack's favorite shirt to her face, tears flowing from behind her closed eyes. Grief, she knew, could hit you unexpectedly at odd moments and needed privacy. She'd had many bad days herself.

Maggie stretched her arms up over her head and yawned. "Yes, well, I'm sure everyone who loses someone they love has a bad day now and then. I'm all right, now. I taped shut the boxes of clothes and stacked them in the kitchen by the back door."

"Yes, I saw them." Fiona stepped closer, concern wrinkling her brow. "I've put a bowl of chicken salad in the fridge for your dinner and hard rolls in the bread box."

Maggie couldn't help smiling. "I won't starve, Fiona. I do know how to feed myself."

"That you do, but you don't do a very good job of it. You've lost more weight."

"I haven't. This shirt's always been loose on me." She rose and walked around the desk, finished for the day. She'd had no idea her father was such a pack rat, stuffing new documents in among old, outdated papers. The chore was very nearly completed, thank goodness, so she'd be able to take the necessary forms over to the attorney's office and to the accountant tomorrow.

Walking with Fiona to the front door, she tried to sound cheerful. "You know you love playing canasta with your lady friends and it's only once a month. Why deprive yourself when you know I'll be just fine right here?"

"All right then." But the worried look wouldn't disappear. "Katherine's phone number's on the pad in the kitchen if you need to reach me. I'll be back around lunchtime tomorrow, unless you want me to start out earlier."

"Of course not. You take your time and enjoy yourself." Maggie picked up the small overnight suitcase and carried it out to the trunk of the gray Plymouth Fiona had had for probably ten years. But then, she only drove it to the grocery store, church, and to Gladstone just south of Riverview for her monthly card club meeting.

Six ladies, all Irish and by now either widowed or never having married, had been meeting at Katherine's large rustic home for about twenty years. Because northern Michigan winters often made the roads impassable, they'd gotten into the habit of spending the night, even in good weather. It was Fiona's only social outlet and Maggie had no intention of letting her miss it.

Slipping on her sunglasses, Fiona got behind the wheel. "You know, I've been thinking. We should get a dog. A big one that would serve as protection when one of us is home alone."

Had the recent deaths in Riverview spooked Fiona, too? "Are you afraid being here alone when I'm not home?"

"Not really. We have solid locks on doors and windows. It's just that a dog is like a warning system should anyone be thinking of prowling about the property." She pulled the door closed and rolled down the window. "What do you think?"

Maggie frowned. "Let's think about it and talk it over after you get back." Maybe a visit with her old friends would calm Fiona's nerves.

"All right, then." She started the engine and adjusted the seat and mirror, a ritualistic habit, since she was the only person who ever drove the car. "What are you going to do with yourself all evening?"

"Oh, I don't know. Relax. Go for a walk along the creek. Eat some chicken salad. Read a book. The usual exciting stuff." She reached in and squeezed Fiona's arm. "Go on before you miss tea with Miss Katherine."

Finally, Fiona smiled. "All right then. Remember to lock up, won't you?" Shifting into gear, she drove along the circular driveway, then turned down the road.

Watching her disappear around the bend, Maggie felt a mixture of relief and loneliness. Relief that she could cry without the risk of being overheard if she felt like it, yet a bit lonely since she'd rarely spent a night alone in her father's house. Still, she'd lived alone in New York and usually enjoyed solitude, especially when she felt blue. Which she decidedly did today.

Back inside, Maggie wandered from room to room, gazing at objects and furniture as familiar to her as the back of her hand. She picked up a small vase made of blue glass from a shelf and recalled that it was the first piece of her mother's collection. Running her fingers over the piano keyboard, she could almost hear the many times the three of them had sat listening to her mother play, singing along for birthday celebrations and Christmas carols. Eyes moist, she walked to the kitchen.

Memories everywhere, of a happier time when they'd been a family, then years of sadness as they'd tried to adjust to Mom dying so young. Somehow, she and Dad had gotten past that in time, but not easily. Fiona had helped, always there for her, and for Dad. She hadn't guessed that the housekeeper had loved her father, but Jack Spencer's heart had been buried with his wife, and was no longer his to give away.

A one-woman man, that was her father. Admirable. And unusual in this day and age. The divorce rates were staggering. Chet, Carrie, Grady, George Cannata, so many New York friends. Would she ever love one man till the end of her life? Certainly she'd been very infatuated with Chet, especially in the beginning, but love? That word had never been spoken aloud between the two of them.

Struggling with a lingering melancholy, Maggie opened the fridge and poured herself a glass of milk, then stood at the sink to drink it. What was she going to do with the rest of her life? Go back to her Manhattan apartment, send out résumés, hope someone would want her and trust that Chet hadn't badmouthed her too badly? Which he was fully capable of doing, especially after his last call when she'd hung up on him.

At first, she'd found Manhattan appealing, fascinating, exciting. But as time went on, the very things that had drawn her began to repel her. The anonymity, the indifference, the noise, the constant surge of humanity. Daily she saw shadowy people, homeless souls, beggars with wasted lives and dull eyes—such a proliferation that in order to get around, New Yorkers pretended not to see and many became desensitized to the endless human misery.

Her apartment at 37th Street and Second Avenue was small, three stories above a Chinese restaurant with its accompanying odors permeating the walls, the furniture. Fumes from traffic clogged the air outside. Tall buildings dominated so that no sun ever shone through her two tiny windows. So very different from the fresh air here, the quiet, the caring neighbors.

Did she no longer belong there? Maggie asked herself.

Perhaps she should stay in Riverview then, live in her

childhood home with Fiona and . . . and do what? Of course, when all this business was settled, she'd have a minimum of a million dollars and a lovely house, free and clear, so a job wasn't a crushing necessity. But at twenty-nine, she wasn't ready to hang it up and live off her investments, become reclusive, and putter around in a garden, viewed by everyone as odd and eccentric.

So what other options did she have? Move to an altogether different city? Start a new career? Go back to college and specialize in . . . what? Her head was beginning to ache, from her earlier bout of tears and from searching for answers that seemed elusive. That was another thing, she was getting too damn many headaches lately. Quickly, she drained the glass, set it in the sink, and went outside.

A walk was in order, some exercise to clear the cobwebs. Locking the door, Maggie stuffed the keys into the pocket of her white shorts and stopped to check the flower beds she'd worked in most of the morning, thinning out the portulaca and petunias, staking the rosebushes, weeding around the geraniums. It had felt good, getting her hands in the rich, fragrant earth. She missed gardening in New York where her total efforts consisted of trying desperately to keep a couple of African violets alive.

She set off along the bank of the stream, hoping a stroll would lift her spirits. The twilight sky was already streaked with orange and gold and purple, the clouds changing color as the sun lowered. A beautiful evening.

Maggie wished she had someone to share it with.

Ben told himself he was stopping by to let Maggie know about Warren Harper's body being found. He reminded himself that she'd asked to be kept up to date. Then he stopped lying to himself and admitted that he wanted to see her. Badly.

He could hear the door chimes echo through the house, but

could hear no footsteps coming to answer. After a moment, he stepped to the side window and peered in. No lights on, no movement. Yet the Explorer was parked in the drive. He walked around back and peeked into the garage. Fiona's car was gone. Had they gone together somewhere? Probably not, since Maggie would probably have driven.

The back door was locked, too. Hands on his hips, he looked around. She probably hadn't gone far, maybe just a walk. But in which direction? Her father's grave was just up over the hill to the north. Chances are she might have walked that way. He remembered going to visit his father after his death, sitting on the grass and talking to him as if he could hear. Maybe he could.

It was a really lovely evening. The sunset must have been spectacular; there were still a few streaks in the moonlit sky. A soft summer breeze ruffled his hair as he strolled along, his eyes getting used to the shadowy light. The grass was damp underfoot where the stream splashed onto warm earth. Wild flowers grew haphazardly around a huge maple at the top of the hill. He could see Jack Spencer's gravestone from where he walked.

But Maggie wasn't in sight.

Still, he kept on going, listening to water sloshing over stones, spotting a squirrel scurrying up onto leafy branches, then cocking his head to look down at him from his safe perch. It was truly peaceful here. Ben recalled Maggie telling him how much her father loved this area, and he could see why. A born-and-bred city boy, he'd never had much use for the country. But lately, he could see its appeal.

Now he could hear the waterfall just ahead. Up over the next rise and he saw its misty spray swirling into the pond at the far end of the stream. And then he saw her.

Despite the light from a full moon, he would have missed her if not for spotting movement. She appeared to be doing laps in the width of the pond, swimming fast, kick-turning and heading back, her hair wet and sleek, her slim arms knifing through the fresh water. Ben walked down, certain she couldn't hear his approach over the sound of the falls.

Twenty feet from him, she executed another swift turn, rushing to the opposite side as if in a race, her face tight with concentration. Was she after exercise or was she exorcising the demons everyone had inside their head? By the time she'd completed another lap, he had his shoes off and was loosening his belt.

As he tossed his shirt under the large maple up the incline, he noticed her clothes in an untidy pile, as if she'd shed them in a hurry, before she could change her mind. He turned back and saw she'd changed directions and was heading for the falls. Stripping off his briefs, he stepped out of them, threw them aside and did a parallel dive into the whirling water.

He surfaced quickly, shivering momentarily as the cold registered on his warm skin. He tossed his head to free his eyes of dripping water and blinked, looking for her. Another minute and he found her standing on the edge of the waterfall, her back to him.

She wore nothing but moonlight and beads of crystal-clear water. Her head was raised to the spray, her hair slicked back, her shoulders and back gleaming with moisture. Her arms were outstretched, hands fanned out, fingers trailing through the bubbles. Then she slowly turned. It took her but a moment to sense she wasn't alone, another to locate him as he tread water some ten yards from her. He thought she looked sad, but not frightened, almost as if she'd been expecting him.

Slowly, with lazy strokes, Ben moved closer. Her breasts glistened as water sluiced down her long, slender body. His own body was heating, despite the cool temperature of the pond. He saw her eyes turn silvery in the moonlight as she watched him approach. Neither of them spoke a word as his feet touched the smooth rocks on the bottom, and he straightened to stand waist high in the water. He couldn't stop looking at her there with the backdrop of the falls like rain showering down on her.

He was beautiful, Maggie thought, with those broad shoulders and the water pearling in the hair of his chest. She'd decided to dive in, to swim until she was exhausted so she could sleep. Yet somehow, in the back of her mind, unreasonable as it seemed, she'd known he'd come. She'd felt his presence, had turned and found him there, as if she'd conjured him up with her need.

Turning again, she walked through the falls to a small grottolike area with a wide rock ledge inside an air pocket. Her back to the ledge, she waited for Ben.

Stepping through, he plunged both hands in his hair and brushed water from his face. Mists from the falls clouded the air as he blinked to clear his vision. He saw that she was waiting, unafraid, all her reserve seemingly washed away by the hurtling water.

He couldn't think of a thing to say, couldn't find the words, so he took two steps closer and held out his arms in invitation. Her choice. It had to be her choice.

Suddenly, here they were in a scene she'd imagined more than once. She'd thrown up barriers to loving again, but Ben had torn them all down. She'd built walls and now heard them crumbling more clearly than the sound of the thundering falls. At least, here in his strong arms, she could find a safe haven that eluded her elsewhere.

Without hesitation, Maggie stepped into his arms and into the kiss that began as a gentle searching. Unhurried, they rained kisses on each other, lips trailing along moist skin as the falls thundered behind them and slivers of moonlight intruded to chase away the shadows.

Maggie wrapped her arms around his neck and pressed her body against his, then heard him suck in a stunned breath. She felt a shiver at the contact as his mouth returned to crush hers. Then his hand slipped around back and inched down, urging her closer as desire shuddered through her. Passion and need mingled and mixed as Ben moved his mouth to taste the long column of her throat.

She was losing ground rapidly, Maggie thought as her fingers moved up to clench his thick, wet hair. Then his hands cupped her buttocks and he lifted her easily, bringing her breasts to his waiting mouth. He drew on her slowly, thoroughly, and she was lost, drowning in sensation as she wrapped her legs around his waist and held on.

With teeth and tongue, he tormented her and himself as needs clawed at him. Driven by a kind of frenzied passion, he feasted on her, the longing to possess her completely shocking him as never before. He let her legs slide down him, then backed her up against the slick wall of the grotto. Drunk with desire, he trailed his mouth over her shoulders and her vulnerable neck, returning to her breasts.

His hands raced over her, followed by his seeking mouth as her head fell backward and a deep moan came from between her parted lips. Then his fingers found her and slipped inside as her knees nearly buckled.

Tossed about on a sea of sensation, Maggie knew a surrender so complete it stunned her. She let him lead her, let him take her, then cried out her release before going limp in his arms. Her breathing ragged, she met his silvery gaze. "More," she whispered, her voice thick.

Lifting her again from the thigh-deep water, he leaned her against the wall and stretched to brush his lips against hers, back and forth, over and around, until she lost all patience. As he watched, she took hold of him and guided him inside her.

His hands cradled her, shifting her weight until they were deeply joined. With her arms draped over his shoulders, he began to move. The time for slow loving was past. The rhythm was wild, both of them impatient and needy.

The thunderous waterfall echoed like a drumbeat in his ears as Ben plunged and withdrew, then plunged again, deeper, harder.

Jolted by the depth of his craving for this woman, he watched her beautiful face as she strained with him. Finally he felt rather than heard her astonished cry join his own as they trembled on the precipice, then slid down into the water.

Struggling to breathe and to keep them both upright, Ben shifted their positions and leaned into the rock wall, holding Maggie close in his arms. Burying his face in her wet hair, he let the sweet waves of pleasure roll over him.

It was long minutes before she felt able to move. At last, Maggie found her footing and took a step back, shoving her hair off her face with both hands. She felt just a shade awkward and embarrassed at how anxious she'd been, how willing and eager. She couldn't help wondering what he was thinking as she raised her eyes to his face and met that unsettling gray gaze. *Play it cool*, she told herself. "I . . . I hope I didn't hurt you," she finally said, her lips twitching.

He smiled then and his eyes warmed. "Just a little, but I heal fast." He glanced sideways through the thinning waterfall to where the lone maple tree stood dappled in moonlight. "I should really give you hell, you know. Walking alone along here in the dark. I thought we agreed there's a murderer lurking around this area."

"I've walked alone along this stream and gone swimming in this pond since I was ten. Besides, I'm the wrong gender for our killer."

He couldn't resist pulling her back to him and nuzzling her. "Personally, I think you're the right gender for me." He kissed her forehead. "But right or wrong, until we get him, I wish you'd stick closer to home after dark unless I'm with you."

Maggie cocked her head at him. "Is that an order, Detective?"

"No, a request." He doubted she'd pay attention either way. "What were you doing, just needing a swim?"

Maggie dropped her eyes to his chest and raised a hand to tangle in the dark curls. "Just out for a walk and wound up here. I always loved this pond. Dad taught me the dog paddle here and the breast stroke and . . ." Her breath caught on a sob. She had to stop doing this, stop reminiscing.

Ben watched her try to regain control over her emotions and it touched him. "I know you don't believe this just now, but time does help."

Maggie still looked skeptical. "When I lost my mother, it was years before I could think of her without crying. But at least then, we knew because she'd been sick for so long. But Dad's death was just so damn sudden."

"It was the same with my father. And Kathy. No time to prepare yourself, that's the hardest, not that any death isn't difficult to handle."

Maggie looked up, contrite. Here she was again, wallowing in her grief when he'd been through so much. "Thanks, for understanding." She stepped away, needing some action to chase away the blues. "Race you to the maple tree?"

Ben was proud of her, that she'd set aside her sadness in a deliberate attempt at lightening the mood. She was trying, he'd give her that, and no one knew better than he how damn hard it was to replace tears with smiles. "I don't know. You look a little like a water nymph, like this was once your playground. That gives you an edge."

"You're right. This was my own private pond." Her hands moved languidly in the water in deceptively lazy circles. "What's the matter, are you chicken?" With that, she jackknifed into the water, skimmed around to his other side, and gave a shove to the backs of his knees, neatly taking him under. With a swift kick, she took off on a strong side stroke, swimming under the falls, and didn't come up until she was some distance away. Tossing her hair out of her eyes, she looked around for him.

He was nowhere to be seen.

Treading water, she narrowed her eyes, searching the surface, trying to spot him, certain he'd ambush her from one side or the other any moment. No movement. It took another few seconds before panic set in. "Ben, Ben!" she called out, and got no answer. Frightened now, she swam frantically toward the spot where she'd pulled him under.

And heard a loud masculine laugh behind her.

Swirling about, she saw him standing a few yards from where she'd been looking for him, his arms crossed over his chest, a grin on his face. Damn him for scaring her. Slowly, she stroked back toward him, vengeance on her mind. "That was mean."

"And dunking me wasn't?"

"No, that was playful."

"I'll show you playful." His long arm reached out and with a quick tug, he took her under, then pulled her back to him.

Maggie came up sputtering and found herself within the circle of his arms. She swiped water from her face. "You don't play fair."

"Never said I did. I grew up on the mean streets of Detroit. If you wanted to make it to your next birthday, you learned that fair didn't always count."

Her hands rested on his biceps as she floated with his arms holding her up. "It's hard for me to imagine that kind of upbringing."

Ben took in the neighborhood watering hole, the full moon, the peaceful night. "It's a whole lot nicer growing up here."

"It was, until someone came along and made us all afraid to leave our homes. Fiona said she wants us to get a dog."

Reality was intruding its ugly head, bringing with it thoughts of the recent deaths. "Did you learn anything new today?"

Yeah, he had, but this wasn't the time or place. Later, he'd go into it all with her. He shook his head. "Tonight, we don't talk." Leaning in to her, he licked droplets of water from her cheeks, her chin. "We only feel."

She met his eyes and knew he was right. *This* was right and the devil take the high road. "Mmm, Mr. Whalen, are you trying to seduce me?"

"Yeah," he said, his lips at her ear. "How'm I doin'?"

She shivered as his warm breath shot through her. "Not bad."

"Did I see right, that Fiona's car isn't in the garage?"

"She goes to play cards at a friend's house once a month. Tonight's the night."

"And she comes home . . ."

"Around noon tomorrow." She smiled up into his grinning face. "Why? What'd you have in mind?"

"Well," Ben said, drawing the word out, "it's not that I don't love waterfalls and all. But my skin's beginning to pucker. I vote for dry land, maybe a soft bed. What do you say?"

"I thought you'd never ask."

With that, he scooped her up in his arms and walked out of the stream bed.

Chapter *Ten*

"What a ridiculous conclusion," Maggie said, setting down her mug. "I think Grady's losing it."

"My thoughts exactly." Seated across from her at the kitchen table, Ben sipped his tea, wishing it were strong coffee instead. He hadn't awakened until eight, late for him. He'd reached for his clothes, but she'd come out of the bathroom and handed him a clean towel, after he'd taken a quick shower. When he'd come downstairs, she'd offered to make him breakfast, which he'd turned down, but he couldn't refuse a cup of tea. He couldn't be out-and-out rude, not after last night.

Maggie had asked again what he'd learned yesterday, having guessed there was something. The fact that she was beginning to read him too easily bothered him almost as much as the delay in leaving. The old restlessness was back, urging him to get going, and he was having a hard time sitting still. Maggie was probably going to misinterpret his desire to be gone, but that couldn't be helped. Later, maybe he could explain, though he wasn't sure about that. He'd told her about the men at the site finding Warren Harper's body and Grady's take on what had happened the evening her father had died.

"Frankly," Maggie went on, "I think he's simply not used to crimes of this magnitude, four people now dead, and he's willing to blame anyone, come up with any cockamamie theory, just to put an end to things."

On this, at least, they were in complete agreement. "I don't get it. He's not a dumb man. He ought to know that sweeping this under the rug isn't going to make it go away."

"You'd think so, especially with you here, breathing down his neck." She drank more tea, sensing his unease, wondering at its source. Wasn't it usually the woman who had regrets the morning after? "Will the medical examiner be able to tell the exact date that Harper died? I mean, wasn't June first the last day he'd been seen in Marquette as well as the day Dad fell?"

"They can determine the general time of death, maybe, but not always the exact hour, depending on conditions. We don't know if an autopsy was done on Harper. But even if both deaths occurred the same date, what would that prove? Only that more than likely the same person did them both in. Surely you don't believe that your father would have taken a blunt instrument, say a shovel, smashed it over this guy's head, and then buried him in a shallow grave right at his own work site, no matter what beef he had with him?"

"No, of course I don't think that for a moment. But you know how often we've said there are no coincidences?" His fingers were now lightly drumming on the table, she couldn't help noticing. Here the two of them were, calmly discussing a murder after spending an amazing night together where neither of them had managed more than two hours' sleep, so hungry for each other had they been. Yet in the light of day they couldn't say what was really on their minds to each other.

"Not *no* coincidences, just damn few." Ben drained his cup and wondered why she was keeping this conversation going when she had to realize he was anxious to leave. Maggie was sophisticated, a career woman who'd lived on her own in a big city for five or six years. Surely she was aware that spending the night together, as great as that had been, didn't imply further obligation. After all, there'd been no seduction. She'd been as willing and ready as he.

Usually quite open, her expression this morning was hard to read. She sat across from him looking calm and collected, only a slight trembling of her hands hinting at nerves. Did she want to end this scene as badly as he and was searching for a way out?

"Did you learn anything else? I spent most of the day in Dad's den with his papers."

He managed not to sigh in frustration, but just barely. "Freddy's been released into his mother's custody." He told her about the encounter with Thelma Becker in Grady's office. "Naturally, I'd expect a mother to stick up for her son. But I don't think she sees him clearly."

"Do you think Freddy's capable of all those deaths? He's awkward and clumsy, for one thing. How could he have gone up onto the scaffolding and shoved Dad off? The basement steps, maybe, but on what fabricated story could he ever have gotten Reed to agree to meet him? He's not clever or devious. As to Kurt's drowning, that makes no sense. Kurt was his stepfather, for heaven's sake."

Ben toyed with his empty mug. "Yes, and Lucy Hanover told me that Freddy is frightened of men because of the way he was raised, *all* grown men, including his stepfather."

Maggie shook her head. "I still don't buy it. You have to have means, motive, and opportunity. What could his motive be?"

Ben shrugged. "He has a childish mind. Just not liking men, especially men his stepfather's age, might be enough.

He could view them as threats. You have to agree, he had the means and the opportunity. He pretty much skulks around this town and is one of those people everyone scarcely notices, this shadowy figure they see but don't really notice because he's so familiar. That gives him free rein to wander about practically invisible."

"Skulks? My, aren't we dramatic today? Well, using that criteria, I'd say half the town had the means and opportunity. The key is the motive, and I disagree with your dislike theory. Freddy may be uncomfortable around men, but he isn't a killer." She got up to refill her cup. "Want some more tea?"

His eyes followed her. She was wearing a long yellow robe and no makeup, fresh from her shower, her hair shiny and clean in the morning sun coming through the window. He felt a stab of desire slam into him, but he studiously ignored it as he got to his feet. "No, thanks. I've got to get going."

Maggie decided to pass on a second cup herself. "All right." She looked up at him, uncertain what to say next.

He just stood there staring at her for long seconds, then shook his head. "Maggie, I . . . never mind." He ran a hand through his shower-damp hair, annoyed with the conversation, with himself. Regardless, he was what he was and there was no use pretending whatever they had between them was going to work into something permanent. If she knew everything about him, she'd be shoving him out the door herself.

He looked like a man facing a firing squad, Maggie thought, with no small amount of dismay. She thought she knew exactly why. "You're thinking this was a mistake." It wasn't stated as a question.

"More like a tactical error." Hell, that didn't sound any better. Why did words always fail him when they mattered the most? "Look, Maggie, last night was great and . . ."

"Yes, for me, too. But it was just that, Ben. A great night." She wouldn't cry, wouldn't let him see the hurt. She would, instead, help him out just a little and deal with her feelings later. "Please don't think anything's changed, because it hasn't. Not for me. I want nothing more from you than before we slept together. Does that ease your mind?"

Damn, if stated that way it didn't make him feel like six kinds of a fool. "I wasn't worried about that." Which was only partly true. "I do want you to know it was very special for me." He stepped closer, slipped his arms around her, and kissed her lightly.

She stood still, wondering why he held nothing back in physical intimacy, but was ready to run from another sort of intimacy.

It was then that Ben heard a key turn in the front door and realized the housekeeper had returned. "Shit!" He'd intended to be gone before she came back. It was early. Why in hell had the woman rushed home?

Puzzled at his reaction, Maggie lay a hand on Ben's arm. "It's all right. I'm a big girl now, and Fiona knows that."

"But the other night, you said . . ."

"I said I didn't think we should make love under her bedroom window or down the hall from her, but this was different. Are you . . . upset at being found here with me?" She was beginning to get irritated.

Ben scowled. "Of course not. I was thinking of you." Or was he?

Fiona's footsteps drew nearer. "Good morning," she said, her eyes moving first to Maggie wearing only a robe, then to Ben's guilty look, surprise evident on her thin face. Recovering nicely, she glanced at the empty stove. "Would you be wanting me to fix some breakfast?"

"No, thank you," Maggie said, trying for a little normalcy here. Dear God, she was nearly thirty. Why did she feel as if she were about thirteen and just caught sneaking a boy into her bedroom? And why was Ben acting as if she'd dragged him to bed, kicking and screaming, and he now regretted the whole night? "How was your trip?"

"Very nice, thank you." Fiona threw another quick glance at Ben, then turned. "I'll just go up and unpack." With that, she trotted to the foyer, picked up her bag, and marched upstairs.

Ben let out a long breath. "Like I said, I've got to get rolling."

Something seemed very wrong here and it appeared to be more than morning-after regrets. "Ben, what's the matter?"

"Nothing." He was acting like a jerk and unable to stop himself. If only he'd awakened first or if she'd have let him go right away. Maggie didn't deserve this from him, yet he saw no way out except to go into lengthy explanations, which he definitely didn't want to do. How could he tell her that his anxiety had little or nothing to do with her?

Ben swung around to face her, one hand rubbing the back of his neck. "Sometimes, I freeze up and I need to go off by myself. Call it strange or temperamental or moody." Black moods was what the shrink had labeled his odd spells. But there was more, so much more. "I don't have a better explanation. I should have warned you, probably."

She stared up into his troubled eyes. She didn't know what to think or believe. Had going to bed with her put him into this odd mood? He seemed sincere enough, yet his timing sure was rotten. She wasn't going to stop him, or interrupt, either. She also wasn't going to make it any easier for him. "All right. Now you've warned me."

"Right." He dug his keys from his pocket. "Thanks for the tea. I'll be in touch." Walking to the door and out to his Jeep, he all but ran and didn't look back. He was halfway down the road when he realized she hadn't said good-bye. Angry with himself that that should matter, he revved the engine and sped around the bend.

In the kitchen, Maggie methodically placed the two mugs

in the dishwasher, then stopped to stare unseeingly out the window. She hadn't expected a lot, certainly not words of love or even promises of a repeat performance. She'd expected very little, really. Mutual respect maybe, affection perhaps, surely something other than a stilted conversation with a man who suddenly wanted to be gone as much as last night he'd wanted to be with her. Was that so much to ask?

As if viewing a scene in her mind, Maggie retraced the night's events, followed by the morning's painful awakening. What had she done to cause such a reaction in Ben? Nothing she could think of. Then it would follow that it was something within him, something that had him reaching for her in mutual need, yet distancing himself from anything resembling a different closeness.

Sucking in a deep breath, Maggie turned from the window. She was not going to take his rejection—if that's what it was—personally. Whatever Ben's problem was, she'd have to let him solve it himself. And she'd steer clear of him until he did. The last thing she needed was someone with a deep-rooted problem to work through. She had enough on her plate at the moment.

Climbing the stairs, she almost convinced herself.

"There, there, pretty ladies. I know I missed your feeding yesterday." Freddy poured more birdseed into the cup, carefully closed the door of the first cage, then moved to the second. "They kept me for hours even though I told them I had to get home to take care of all of you. No one ever listens."

Sniffling, he backed away from the cages and sat down in his rocking chair, gazing at his little feathered friends. They were so grateful to have him back. They were the only ones who really cared about him.

And Mama.

But she'd been mad this time. She didn't listen, didn't understand that he'd only been looking in the window of that cottage searching for the gray cat those renters had brought with them, the one they let loose at night. The cottage was too close to his cabin for comfort. Twice he'd seen that awful cat roaming around his home, stalking his birds. Freddy knew just what that terrible animal wanted. His pretty ladies.

Why had it upset everyone so much that he wanted to make sure the cat was inside? He'd asked the man who'd come running outside after the woman screamed where his cat was. But instead of answering, he'd taken one of those little phones out of his pocket and called the sheriff. Patiently, Freddy had waited for Grady Denton, thinking he'd tell him about the cat who was after his birds. But when the sheriff arrived, he was wearing his mean face and wouldn't listen, just shoved him into his Bronco.

Freddy didn't like the jail. The door clanged shut and they left him alone in there with only a cot and one bright lightbulb on. He'd been afraid until Mama had come to get him out. He'd known she would. Even though she didn't want to hear about the cat, either, she did get him out. But she'd warned him that he must not do any more bad things or they'd put him back in jail.

Didn't they know that the man with the cat was the bad man, not Freddy? Scowling, he swiped his sleeve along his nose. He'd have to teach that man and that cat a lesson. He'd have to get even so his pretty ladies wouldn't be hurt.

"An eye for an eye," he muttered. In his heart, he knew who the sinners were, like the Bible said. They'd have to pay.

Ben swallowed the last bite of his third piece of toast, took a sip of his coffee and sat back in the booth at Rosie's Diner. As always, after one of his spells, he'd been ravenous when he'd awakened. Six years and the pattern hadn't changed much.

They happened less frequently now, not every few months like at first. More like every eight to ten months, unless he was really under a lot of pressure. He couldn't predict when or what triggered them. Posttraumatic stress syndrome the shrink had labeled his condition. Shrinks always had labels for what someone had or did. Otherwise they couldn't justify those outrageously high fees.

The Department had paid the fees, yet the doctor hadn't really helped. Oh, he'd maybe identified the problem, that seeing Kathy—or what was left of her—like that, then nearly killing the perp, the violence, the enormity of his loss, all apparently triggered a reaction in him that was deeply buried. Infrequently now, but occasionally, it reared its ugly head.

It would start without warning. He'd awaken restless, depressed, sweating. He'd go out usually, trying to walk it off, afraid to get behind the wheel. He'd lose all track of time and later not remember what he'd done during those lost hours, or where he'd gone or even who he'd seen, if anyone. Hours later, he'd somehow find his way home as the black mood began to wear off, but he'd have this incredible headache. He'd more often than not be dirty, sweaty, dehydrated. He'd take a long, hot shower, drink lots of water, and fall into bed for twenty hours or so. And he'd awaken hungry enough to eat a bear.

Sometimes he was gone ten or twelve hours, once thirty-six, and each time, it scared the hell out of him.

Most often, he'd return with bruises, scrapes, once a black eye. Had he been in a fight or fallen? Ben didn't know. Try as he would, he couldn't remember. He didn't think he'd done anything illegal—the shrink had said that usually didn't happen, that a man wouldn't act out of character, even during a blackout. Nor did he think he'd ever been with anyone, man or woman. His guess was that he'd just walk and walk, trying to get calm, fighting the memories, while his headache built into a real beaut, until he was too exhausted to take another step.

This morning, he'd awakened slowly and something unusual had happened. He remembered something, that it had begun when he'd been with Maggie, and that he'd probably hurt her by leaving like he had. How, he wondered, could he make it up to her, how to explain the unexplainable? Time, the shrink had said. In time, the black moods would ease and finally stop altogether. Yeah, sure.

So he'd just polished off a gargantuan breakfast, and as he sipped his final cup of coffee, he gazed out the window, getting his bearings. He couldn't imagine how it had gotten to be the Fourth of July weekend almost upon them, but folks outside were putting up flags and bleachers and poster announcements, preparing Main Street for the annual parade.

Across the way, the VFW guys were putting together a booth that would sell flags. He'd overheard some teenagers in the booth behind him talking about the float they'd finally completed. Another group had rushed off to practice with the high school marching band. The citizenry of Riverview were planning a large patriotic bash.

Uncharacteristically, Ben fleetingly wished he were a part of things, that he felt a connection to a hometown where people all knew and looked after one another, where holiday plans were shared. Frowning, he drained his coffee and wondered if he was getting soft in the head. A month in this hokey town had affected his brain. Next thing he'd be attending 4H meetings and making plans to go fishing with the boys.

He was city bred, not a country boy, Ben reminded himself. He valued his privacy and enjoyed solitude. He didn't want anyone to know his business, much less a whole town. There must be something in the drinking water.

It was Maggie's influence, that was what it was. She'd chosen to leave all this behind and move to the busiest city in the world, but Ben believed in her heart, she still lived here. She knew everyone in Riverview, and they all knew her. What must it be like to be on a first-name basis with the butcher, the baker, the candlestick maker? Ben couldn't even imagine, having grown up in a city the size of Detroit. His mother had shopped at huge supermarkets and the banks were cavernous old buildings and schools had graduating classes of five hundred each year. Working parents often didn't even know their next-door neighbor. Nor did most of them want to.

But he'd seen the people who'd come to offer their condolences to Maggie on the day of Jack's funeral. Not only did they know her, they wept with her, hugged her, kissed her.

Kissed her. Memories of kissing Maggie flooded his mind and warmed his blood until he found himself shifting on the fake leather seat. Under the waterfall, she'd stood like some kind of fantasy, waiting. He'd held out his arms in invitation and she hadn't hesitated a moment. She hadn't held back, either, honest and open in her lovemaking. She was one in a million.

At first, he'd thought it was pheromones or endorphins or whatever. Purely physical. If only it was just sex tugging at him. But no, it was the way she smiled, her scent, her voice, the throaty sound she made when he filled her.

He didn't deserve her, and he'd hurt her. She didn't know and he wouldn't tell her, but she was better off without him. He was a man shackled to the past, haunted, tormented by mind pictures that wouldn't erase, dreams that had been cruelly crushed and hope forever gone. He'd seen too much, experienced too much pain to ever be like other men, men who could offer her a solid home, a sane partnership, children.

She must want that, especially now that her whole family was gone, her mother taken from her by an illness and her father by some madman. He'd sensed in their first time together that she'd been as driven by passion as he. But later, in the bedroom of her childhood, he'd watched the dawning of tenderness on her face, and felt the touch of someone who found herself caring more than she'd planned.

Perhaps that more than anything had set off one of his black moods, though he couldn't be certain. She was a forever woman unconsciously seeking a mate despite her denials, and he was not the answer to her needs. He wished with everything he had that he could be, but he knew he'd only hurt her more if he let this continue. She'd delivered a fine speech in her kitchen about nothing changing between them because of that night, but her voice had trembled ever so slightly, and her eyes wouldn't meet his. She was too smart to believe her own lies, and so was he.

If only they could have just had sex and let it go at that. Apparently, they'd both done without a long while and the attraction had been smoldering between them since the day of Jack's funeral. They were both free. What was the harm? Only something had happened that night that neither had foreseen, something beyond merely satisfying a temporary need. Something that under other circumstances might develop into more. If he backed away now, she might be angry, but she'd get over him. It wouldn't be easy, having to remain in town until this whole mess was cleared up, running into Maggie and brushing shoulders with her regularly, and be unable to reach out, to touch her.

But how the hell else could he keep from hurting her more?

"More coffee, young man?" Rosie asked at his elbow, the pot already in her hand. It was late morning with rush hour long over, the diner nearly empty. She'd been watching the insurance investigator for some time, noticing that despite his effort to keep his face expressionless, he was obviously wrestling with some mighty heavy problems. Rosie had done her share of that in years gone by and empathized. "How about a Danish to go with a fresh cup?" He'd eaten like a lumberjack even though he was lean and all muscle, but maybe he had a little room left.

Ben had stopped at Rosie's place several times and liked the solid little woman because she treated everyone as a friend. "I couldn't eat another crumb," he told her. "Best breakfast I've had in I can't remember when." Picking up the check, he left a generous tip and slid from the booth.

"Thanks. Guess we know how to do a few things in small towns as well as they do in the big city." Rosie stepped behind the cash register.

"Better. Much better." He paid his check and left her with a smile, heading back to his motel room. He had a few phone calls to make and he wasn't looking forward to them.

But when he entered his room, he saw that someone had been there and ransacked his things. Damn!

Two days later, the Fourth of July dawned bright and sunny. By midafternoon, it was downright hot. Ben parked his Jeep in the lot next to the bank and strolled toward Main Street, glad to be out of his motel room. He'd made a lot of contacts over the last few days, but he wasn't sure how much forward progress he'd made.

The Home Office call hadn't been fun. They wanted results and they wanted them yesterday. His manager, Pete Williams, a hard-nose, by-the-book type, had asked if Ben wanted him to drive up for a personal look-see. They both knew that he'd never taken this long settling claims before. But then, there'd never been so many at one time in one small town, and for such large amounts of money. He'd gotten a reluctant reprieve, but he knew Pete's patience wouldn't last too much longer. After all, he also had people he had to answer to.

Next he'd phoned the Medical Examiner. Dr. Fielding hadn't been too happy to hear from him, but he'd checked his files. There'd been no autopsy work done on Henry Denton, Grady's father, back in September, which didn't surprise Ben since that first death, happening the way it had, probably had looked more like an accident than any of the others. It was only when you began to add them all up—Henry, Reed, Jack, Kurt, and most recently Harper—that things began to look suspicious.

To his credit, Grady had listed Harper's death as a homicide so there'd been an autopsy. Although the Marquette man hadn't been insured with National Fidelity, Fielding didn't know that and told Ben the results. Death due to a hard slam to the head by a blunt instrument, such as a shovel or a piece of lumber. The skull had been crushed causing the M.E. to rule out a possible self-inflicted accidental head bump. Fielding had added that he felt the killer must be fairly strong to deliver such a blow.

Ben had already figured that out. The probability of someone slight shoving a big man off a scaffolding without himself falling, or out of a boat even, would be small. His thoughts drifted back to Freddy.

Mentally incapable of passing a driving test, he nonetheless drove and could have gotten to all of these places. Who could prove he wasn't sly? Certainly not his mother. He could have used a false name and lured Reed out to the vacant house. An argument, a shove, and that was that. He could have crept up after Jack in the twilight and pushed him off. He could have appeared up the river where his stepfather was fishing and waved him over with some excuse, then climbed in the boat, and managed to nudge poor unsuspecting Kurt over the side.

As to motive, wasn't it Socrates who'd said that fear is an excellent motivator? Freddy was a fearful boy-man. Improbable but not impossible that he was the perp. Especially after what he'd learned yesterday.

Ben rounded the corner and stopped to lean against a lamppost as folks started arriving and picking out spots along the curb to best watch the parade already assembling at the far end of the street. He'd had the Home Office check out Freddy Richmond right after his arrest and they'd faxed him their report earlier this morning. It seems that Thelma Becker had had her son in a special school outside of Detroit in his late teens. After only one semester, he'd been expelled.

A phone call to the school had finally located someone Ben had been able to charm into reading him part of Freddy's records. He'd been fascinated with small animals, furry ones, and seemed to enjoy killing them. Ben had also learned that Freddy had a minor arrest in Detroit for indecent exposure—urinating in a public park and frightening nearby children. Thelma had gotten him released to her custody again, and that's when she'd hustled him up to Riverview and bought the cabin for him.

No question that poor Thelma had had her hands full with Freddy all these years. Perhaps after the first few incidents, he should have been institutionalized. Easy for an outsider to say, Ben thought with a sigh. A parent might feel differently.

He'd come to watch the town turn out today, hoping to spot someone or something unusual, out of sync, suspicious. He hadn't said the words out loud yet, although his manager had, and that was that the possibility of a serial killer loose in this town was no longer conjecture but most likely fact. The overused term struck fear in the hearts of everyone, which was why he hoped no one in Riverview would put all the pieces of the puzzle together until he could at least have a solid suspect. He especially hoped no one in the media would get wind of what was apparently happening in this small town.

Before that happened—and happen it would—he had to find out who and why. The motive would surely reveal the killer. Maybe if he strolled up and down the avenue, looking into faces, studying those who were participating and those who were not—perhaps something would jump out at him.

Something he'd missed before. Ben was the first to admit he was getting desperate.

As to the ransacking of his room, he'd quickly checked and found nothing missing. The intruder had been an amateur, Ben had decided, for most of his possessions had been rearranged and disturbed with no effort made to disguise the uninvited visit. Even his police issue gun had been in the nightstand drawer where he'd left it.

Since he wasn't a random thief, what had the guy been looking for? The door had been locked, yet Ben supposed it wouldn't be all that difficult to get a key or pick the lock. Had Grady sent someone to snoop through his belongings for information? Or had the killer decided that Ben was getting too close?

He'd questioned the desk clerk and the maid, but no one had seen anyone suspicious around the motel. Ben decided he'd keep a sharper eye out from now on. His gut instinct told him that his visitor had been the killer and that he wanted Ben to be aware he could break in easily. It had been done as a warning, he was certain.

Across the street, he noticed Grady in full uniform, toothpick in place, watching the crowd much as Ben was, his eyes hidden behind mirror sunglasses. A little further up was J.C., the young deputy, talking with Grady's daughter, Carrie. Ben still hadn't stopped in at her boutique for a visit. He'd lost a couple of days there and he'd had to prioritize his time. Not that he suspected Carrie Denton of anything, although at five-eight or more, she certainly appeared strong enough to flatten a man with a piece of lumber. Again, it boiled down to motive and Carrie seemed not to have one.

Speaking of tall women, Ruth from the Green Thumb was dashing about checking on the geranium baskets she'd placed along the path of the parade. Hot as it was, she was wearing one of those nylon jogging suits in pale pink. He wondered if she went out for her runs covered from neck to ankle. Weren't runners supposed to let their skin breathe?

As his eyes scanned the gathering crowd, he felt more than saw someone move into his peripheral vision. Turning, he looked into the calm blue eyes of Maggie Spencer. Caught off guard, he forced a smile. "Well, hello. How've you been?"

She'd driven Fiona in with her contributions to the bake sale and had seen Ben almost immediately. To the casual observer, he looked relaxed. But she knew him better and he appeared tense, his eyes even more haunted. Was the job worrying him, not finding a solution? Or had she somehow brought about this change in him? "Fine. And you?"

God, she looked good. Yellow was certainly her color, the dress light and airy like the summer breeze ruffling her hair. It was all he could do not to reach out and run his fingers through the golden strands. Not long ago, he'd done just that as she'd lain with her head on a pillow, that gorgeous hair spread out around her lovely face. Pushing back from the post, he ran a hand along the back of his neck. "The same." Shifting his gaze to the skies, he continued the inane conversation. "Nice day."

He was doing it again, acting like an uncomfortable stranger. "Did you find out anything new regarding the investigation?"

Safe ground at last. "A couple of things." He shouldered them both away from a family with small children who were jockeying for a space curbside and walked with her across the street to the shrubs bordering Lucy Hanover's house while he told her about the few things he'd learned. "I also went through all the office stuff Loren Thomas gave me on Reed Lang and couldn't spot a single discrepancy or a name that rang a bell. Plus I checked out Nancy Evans's ex-husbands and, odd as it sounds, they both died of natural causes within a year of marrying her."

"Not much to go on. Frustrating, isn't it? This must be what police work is like, only more so." Normal chatting. Finally he'd relaxed a bit.

"Pretty much."

"Maybe he's finished or taking some time off. We haven't had anyone harmed in some time, not counting Harper who'd been killed awhile back. Maybe you frightened him off."

Ben shook his head. "Maniacs don't do R and R. The more he gets away with, the worse he gets. At least, that's been my experience." He glanced toward the neat bungalow behind the hedges. "Funny thing, I had a message at the motel from Lucy Hanover. I was out when she called. She said she wanted to talk with me, but she was leaving for Canada to visit her daughter. Said it wasn't urgent and she'd call again when she returned, whenever that will be. I wonder what she has in mind."

"I'm sure she'll let you know. She's a little gossipy, but Lucy's one of Riverview's oldest residents and knows everyone. She may have come up with some theory." Maggie knew she shouldn't pry, but she had to ask. "Are you all right?"

He hadn't planned to, but he decided to tell her about the break-in. Immediately her features registered concern.

"Is anything missing? Did you call Grady?"

"No to both questions. What could or would Grady do besides tell me I was hallucinating?"

She knew he was probably right. "Then what are you going to do about it?"

"Be more alert." Ben huffed in a big breath. "Listen, about the other morning . . ."

"No." She touched his arm, stopping him. "I meant what I said. No rehashing. Nothing's changed. Let's just be friends. Can we do that?" She needed to let him off the hook. He'd hurt her, but mostly, it was her own fault. She'd invited him into her bed and now she'd have to live with the aftermath.

For long moments, he stared into her eyes, those deep blue, honest eyes, and wished he'd never met her. She would be his downfall, he knew, the one he couldn't turn from, despite his best resolve. Hadn't he known that since day one when he'd seen her standing on a windy hill at her father's grave? "Friends," he repeated. "We could give it a try. How long do you think that'll last?"

Maggie shrugged, uncertain what he was thinking, feeling. "Would you rather I walk away and stay away?"

His determination fled as her words sent a chill up his spine. "No. No, that's not what I want."

He had her emotions in a turmoil, but she was determined not to let him see. "What is it that you do want, Ben?"

Taking another deep breath, he took the plunge. "A little time, Maggie. Please, a little time." For what, he wasn't sure. Time for the black moods to pass, time to finally and forever come to grips with all that had happened, time to again be able to accept love, to be able to love again?

She knew it cost him to ask. She had no idea what was troubling him, though she felt it had more to do with his past than anything they had together. What did she have to lose by going along with his request? Only her heart. "All right, Ben."

His hand trembled as he reached up to touch the ends of her hair, to trail the backs of his fingers along her soft cheek. He'd never met a woman who could bring him to his knees so easily, so effortlessly. Not trusting his voice, instead he held out his hand to her.

Her eyes locked with his, she laced her fingers through his and found a smile. "Let's go watch the parade."

It was the end of the week and Ed Kowalski was grateful. Saturdays were always busy days in a meat store with everyone shopping for the weekend, especially since he'd been closed on Wednesday for the Fourth. His feet hurt and he was tired, but he'd have Sunday and Monday to rest up. When he was younger, he'd stayed open six days a week, but he wasn't up to that rigid a schedule anymore.

Wearily, he cleaned the cutting block one last time. Truth be known, he hadn't felt good since all those accidents had begun. Something was going on, Ed was sure of it. But he couldn't get Grady to listen seriously, probably because to admit that the deaths weren't accidental would be to admit he wasn't doing his job as sheriff in keeping Riverview safe.

And George! He was so damn arrogant. Yeah, he'd said the evening Ed had insisted all three of them meet, it's possible someone might be stalking them all. Quite possible because they all knew what had happened that terrible night thirty years ago this fall. But he could take care of himself, George claimed. He was an expert marksman, a man who'd hunted large and small game for years, one who had an impressive gun collection. And he knew how to use them all. No one would get the drop on him, accidentally or otherwise, George had stated firmly.

Rinsing his cleaning rag under running water, Ed frowned. Great for George who was a sharpshooter. Grady, too, obviously knew all about weapons. That left Ed who'd never been in the service, never even held a real gun. Besides, the men who'd died, his lifelong friends, Reed and Jack and Kurt, none of them had been dummies or fools, nor strangers to guns. Yet someone, if Ed's suspicions were right, had managed to catch them unawares and end their lives, clever enough to make the deaths all appear accidental.

Thoughtfully, he dried his hands on a clean towel. The killer was probably living right here among them and had been for years. The trouble is, they had no way of knowing who that person was, while the six of them had always been very visible. Riverview's permanent residents numbered around nine hundred, often doubling and sometimes tripling during summers. Who could possibly know them all, their backgrounds, their agendas?

It wasn't quite five yet, but Ed decided to call it a day. Moving slowly, he hit the switch turning off the overhead lights.

Or was he just paranoid? Ed asked himself as he checked to make sure all of the sliding doors to the display cases were closed. That's what both Grady and George had told him.

He heard the door open and frowned as he looked up. Tired though he was, he smiled. "Oh, hi. I was just getting ready to close. I've put most everything away, but if you need something for dinner, I can get it."

The customer smiled back, checking out the skimpy remains in the display case.

Always the salesman, Ed had a suggestion. "I just got in some lamb chops. Really nice and I remember you love lamb."

"That would be perfect."

"I'll get you a couple." Ed turned around and opened the door to the walk-in freezer, the light going on automatically. He moved to the small shelf at the rear and his hand touched the lamb package he'd placed there a short time ago. Just as he did, he heard the freezer door slam shut and the lock click into place as the light went out, leaving him in darkness.

The truth slammed into him as fear struck his heart. At last, he knew the identity of the killer. Too late.

Chapter Eleven

"Fiona said I'd find you back here," Ben said, walking toward Maggie. She was sitting beneath the large maple tree that shaded her father's grave. She wasn't crying, she just looked infinitely sad. It broke his heart.

She hadn't been expecting him, yet wasn't really surprised to see him. When it came to Ben, the unexpected was usual. They'd spent time together the afternoon of the Fourth, more or less as two friends might. But she hadn't seen him since. Now he popped up on Saturday evening wearing that hesitant half smile that always got to her. Maggie supposed he didn't know what to expect from her any more than she did of him.

"Twilight's my favorite time of day," she told him, her arms hugging her bare knees.

"I like it, too." He sat down next to her, stretching out his long legs, and noticed a book in the grass. He picked it up and read the title. *The Secret Garden*. It was an odd place to read, alongside a grave, but he figured she had her reasons.

Maggie thought she ought to explain. "I used to read that

book aloud to Dad when I was young and my mother was ill. I don't know if you know the story about an unhappy young orphan girl who finds herself living in a Victorian manor with a cold, unfeeling uncle. The only thing that saves her is time spent secretly restoring a neglected garden, pouring her love and care into it. That small act changes the lives of everyone around her. Dad used to say that maybe one person can't change the world, but by bringing love and beauty into one small place, we can affect the lives of people around us."

"Do you believe that?"

"Yes." She gazed at the headstone. "Don't laugh, but I come out here once in a while and talk to Dad. I know he can't hear me, but it makes me feel better."

He set down the book. "I'd be the last one to laugh. I used to do the same thing when my dad died. And I'm not so sure they can't hear us, either."

Maggie shifted to look at him in the waning light. "You never stop surprising me. I'd have bet good money that you were too cynical to believe that."

He smiled. "Oh, I'm a card-carrying cynic. But I think there's a whole lot we don't know, and maybe will never know." He was feeling melancholy, and with good reason. The Home Office had had it with the Riverview case, or cases. If he didn't come up with something solid by the end of next week, they were calling him home.

"You look unhappy. Anything happen?"

He told her about his conversation with Pete Williams.

"Does that mean they're going to consider all three deaths as accidental?"

"Apparently. They may send in what my manager calls *a team* to look into the matter, but if they can't come up with proof of wrongful death, they'll have to close them out."

"They're replacing you?"

"Threatening to. They gave me until the fifteenth. It appears that some of the heirs, namely Thelma Becker, are phoning constantly, demanding settlement, threatening court action since the sheriff's office has classified each death as accidental."

He was leaving, by the fifteenth, was all she'd really heard. At least now she knew why he'd stopped by. The good-bye scene. Hadn't she known all along that he would go, whether he solved the case or not? She tried to shove back her feelings and concentrate on what he'd said. "I thought insurance companies stalled as long as humanly possible, hating to pay off?"

"That's right, but I think, in this case, they're nervous about publicity. If a newspaper reporter gets wind of a possible serial killer here, they wouldn't like that at the Home Office." A soft breeze carried the womanly scent of her to him, the one he remembered so well, the one he'd lain awake nights recalling while he twisted in his lonely bed. He couldn't seem to stop wanting her.

No longer able to maintain eye contact, afraid she'd reveal too much, Maggie stretched out her legs and flopped back in the grass. "I don't see why that makes them nervous. Either way, accidental or murder, how could the insurance company be at fault?"

"Beats me how they come up with these things. That's why I'm not wearing a suit and sitting in an office, I guess." That and a hundred other reasons. No, he didn't want to work in an office. There was a long list of things he didn't want to do, and never seeing Maggie again was at the top.

Impulsively, he leaned down to kiss her, the element of surprise on his side. She didn't stop him and, grateful, he kept the kiss slow, easy, tender. He felt her stir and knew the instant she began to respond. An explosion of heat all but had him gasping. She was the most responsive woman he'd ever known. Or was it just that the chemistry was right?

Before he got in over his head, he eased back and looked into her eyes, too bright even in the hazy light remaining.

"What was that?" Maggie asked softly.

"Well, if you don't know, I must have done it all wrong."

"No, you did it right." Arousal and confusion warred within her. "I'm just not sure this is smart. I'm getting a lot of mixed signals from you and . . ."

The sound of a very loud engine coming closer and a car turning into the Spencer driveway startled them both. Maggie sat up and peered down the small incline. The silver sportscar came to a screeching stop mere inches from Ben's Jeep and the driver stormed out, hurrying to the door. Impatiently he jammed his finger to the bell, pounded on the wood, and yelled something she couldn't make out. "That's Tom Kowalski," she said, rising.

Already on his feet, Ben offered her a hand up. "I wonder what's got him so hot." They started toward the burly young man who was by now shouting both their names.

"Maggie! Let me in. I know he's in there with you. I want Ben Whalen *now*!" Tom's thick fist thudded against the door.

"Tom," Maggie called out as she rounded the corner past the two vehicles, "what is it?"

Swiveling about, Tom spotted Ben and, tucking his chin in, came ramming toward him, fists clenched. "You son of a bitch! You killed my father. Now I'm going to kill you."

Ben sidestepped the first punch, quickly realizing he'd have to outwit the guy who outweighed him by at least fifty pounds, all solid muscle. "Hold on, hold on," he said, turning back toward him.

"The hell I will." Tom shifted and shot out a powerful left jab that grazed Ben's shoulder. But before he could follow through with the right, Ben grabbed the fist, twirled him around, flung him onto the ground face first and twisted his arm painfully behind his back. Eating dirt and crying out in sudden pain, Tom yowled fiercely.

"All right, calm down and tell me what happened."

"You know damn well what happened!" The big guy spit out a mouthful of grit.

Ben saw the backward kick coming and dodged it, then dropped both his knees hard onto Tom's lower back. He heard the grunt and hoped the fighting fool would finally quit. He didn't want to hurt him, but he hadn't grown up in Detroit without knowing how to fight dirty if he had to. And tonight, he'd had to. "You going to tell me what this is all about before I break your arm?"

Maggie had watched the whole thing, wondering why it was that men always thought smacking each other around would solve any problem. She'd heard Tom say something about his father and wished the hothead would stop yelling and explain. "Tom, please. Don't do this. Talk to me." He was obviously filled with anger toward Ben, but maybe not her. "What happened to Ed?"

"He's dead, that's what." Suddenly, the fight drained out of Tom Kowalski. "Some bastard locked him in his own freezer." Losing control, he lowered his head and began to sob.

Cautiously, Ben let go and stepped back, moving to Maggie's side. Even he had begun to relax, begun to think the killing spree might be over. It'd been two weeks since Kurt's drowning. Never drop your guard, he reminded himself, not until the murderer's in custody. A cardinal rule of police work.

Maggie stooped and touched Tom's shoulder. "I'm so sorry."

Shifting his bent arm painfully, Tom sat up and wiped his face on his sleeve, then glared up at Ben. "It's his fault. None of this happened around here until *he* came around." He made as if to stand up, his eyes blazing.

Ben regarded him, feet wide apart, arms loose at his sides. "I wouldn't if I were you. I had nothing to do with your father's death, or any of the others, either. I'm trying to find the person who's responsible."

"That's what you say." Angry and embarrassed, he shook off Maggie's hand and scrambled to his feet, grimacing in pain as he brought his arm forward.

"Tom, listen to me," Maggie implored him. "Reed Lang and my father died before Ben ever stepped foot in Riverview. He's honestly trying to find their killer. I know because I've been working with him." She gave him a moment to absorb that. "Tell me how it happened."

Cradling his arm, Tom swallowed around a huge lump in his throat. "Dad was late coming home and Mom got worried. He usually closes about five, but sometimes, if there're people in the store, he stays later. Around eight, she called the store and no one answered the phone. So I went down."

He blinked rapidly. "I knew something was funny when the front door was unlocked. I called out, searched the back, couldn't find him. I don't know what made me think to look in the freezer. He . . . he was on the floor, already stiff and cold and . . ."

Maggie moved to his side, reaching a hand out in comfort. "I know. I know just how you feel." Eyes moist, she glanced over at Ben who was standing very still. "Ben knows, too. His father was killed by a drunk driver when he was quite a bit younger than you. I know you want to strike out at someone right now, but Ben's an ex-cop and trying to help. He's the wrong man to blame."

Tom sucked in some air, but couldn't quite spit out an apology. "I gotta go home. Someone's gotta tell Mom."

"You came here straight from the store?" Maggie asked.

"Yeah." Calmer now, but still simmering, his pain-filled eyes were on Ben. "I thought I'd find *him* here."

"Is it possible that Ed might have accidentally locked himself in the freezer?" Ben asked. "Maybe he went in and the door closed behind him. What kind of lock is it?"

"No, not possible. My dad's worked that store since before I was born. He'd never be that careless. We have a key on a nail alongside the freezer, outside in the store itself. None inside. He always left the door open wide when he went in to arrange meat because there's not even a handle on the inside. Someone had to close the door on him. *Had to*."

"They ought to put handles on the inside of those doors," Maggie said to no one in particular. A little late for Ed.

"Did you call Grady?" Ben asked.

"Yeah, but he wasn't around so J.C. came. He's over there now. I don't want my mother to see Dad, not like that. I carried him out and tried to revive him, but . . ." He shook his head and walked away. Gingerly, he climbed back into his car, then glanced back at Ben. "If you really are trying to help, why don't you go have a look? I don't think Grady and his sidekick know what the hell they're doing."

"I will." Ben let him clear the driveway before opening the Jeep's door. "Maybe you should skip this one," he suggested to Maggie, remembering how upset she'd been seeing Kurt Becker's body at the river.

"I think you're right." She closed the door as he started the Jeep. "Don't be too hard on Tom. He's had a lot of problems since coming home. Remember when we were in the store and Ed told me he was worried about Tom, that he'd been having bad headaches and they were running some tests on him? He was over in the Gulf War for most of it. Posttraumatic stress syndrome, I think they call it. He'd planned on making the Marines his career and now . . . well, I don't think he's coping well."

Ben understood far more than she knew. "I don't blame him for coming after me. Hell, I might have done the same if I'd have been around when that hit-and-run driver killed my dad." The need to blame, to seek revenge, was a fearsome emotion.

Maggie wasn't sure she should ask, then decided to after all. "Will you let me know how things go?"

Hadn't she noticed that he couldn't seem to stay away? "Count on it." Knowing it was probably a mistake yet unable to resist, he leaned out the window, cupped the back of her neck with one hand, and gently grazed his lips over hers. Slowly, he pulled back and stared into her eyes for two heartbeats. Then he pulled her into a very long, very thorough kiss.

If he had to leave her, he wanted to leave her remembering that kiss.

Unlike Grady, J.C. had called Dr. Fielding immediately and asked the Medical Examiner to come to the scene. Ben admired him for that. Standing back as the tall pathologist did a preliminary exam on Ed Kowalski on the floor of the butcher shop where his son had placed his body, Ben waited alongside the deputy. Everyone else had been cleared out, thanks to J.C. The ambulance and attendants waiting outside had naturally attracted a small, curious crowd.

Fielding checked his watch and wrote eight-forty-two on his pad. "I'd say he's been dead a couple of hours. It wasn't only the cold that killed him, but he used up all the oxygen in that small insulated freezer. He could've been in there around three hours, give or take thirty minutes. I'll know more when I get him on the table."

"That would be just about closing time," J.C. commented. "The hours posted on the door indicate the shop's open from nine to five Tuesday through Saturday."

"I don't suppose anyone outside saw anything or anyone leaving the shop around that time?" Ben asked the deputy.

"I questioned five or six folks standing around, but they'd all arrived after Tom called me. No one remembers seeing anyone leaving the place earlier."

Ben craned his neck in the direction of the cash register. "I wonder if Ed kept a receipt book of his sales. Maybe it'd be helpful to know who his last customer was." He spotted a small spiral notebook on the counter. "That might be it."

J.C. glanced at Ben. "You were a detective once upon a time and it shows."

Ben shrugged. "Guilty as charged."

Quickly, the deputy scanned the small book, then held it out to Ben. "Look at the carbon of the last entry."

Ben read it aloud. "Four-ten. Two pounds of scrap meat. One dollar. Freddy Richmond." His eyes met J.C.'s. "Wasn't Ed Freddy's uncle?"

"Sure thing. Freddy uses scraps for fish bait." He shook his head, thinking that this whole mess got crazier almost daily.

"This might or might not be something, fellas," the doctor said. Using tweezers, he held up a well chewed toothpick. "Found it in the folds of the victim's apron. Do either of you know if Mr. Kowalski was given to chewing on toothpicks?"

The look on J.C.'s face confirmed Ben's thoughts, that someone else they both knew had the habit. "Don't know," J.C. told Fielding.

"If you had a suspect, we could maybe run a DNA check," the M.E. suggested, slipping the toothpick into a small plastic evidence bag.

J.C. sighed. "But we don't have a suspect as yet and somehow I don't think it's feasible to collect saliva samples from everyone in Riverview at the moment. People are fairly jumpy around here. That just might set them off." He turned to the doctor. "Are you finished for now?"

Fielding closed his bag. "Yes. Tell Grady I'll do the autopsy first thing tomorrow morning. My report should be ready by midafternoon." With a nod to Ben, he left the store.

J.C. signaled the men alongside the waiting ambulance outside to come in and get the body.

"You don't want to call a team in and dust for prints?"

Ben asked, trying not to become annoyed at the way this small town handled a homicide.

Letting out a sigh of exasperation, J.C. shook his head. "You know Grady'd have a fit. Despite what the son thinks, there's no proof here that the man didn't let the door slam shut on him accidentally." He ran a frustrated hand over his short hair. "That's the damnable part of all these deaths. Each one in its own way appears to be an accident. But I'm beginning to wonder."

It was about damn time someone representing the law here did some thinking. "I've felt for some time that there's more going on than we know. Are you planning to question Freddy?"

"I suppose, for all the good that'll do. He just talks in circles. Sure, he was here. The carbon of the receipt's undoubtedly right. But could or would he lock a man in the cooler and calmly walk out the door? I doubt it. He's afraid of his own shadow."

Ben thought he might just follow up and talk with Freddy himself later. "How about that toothpick?"

J.C.'s loyalty flared. "I hope you're not suggesting that Grady did this. That's just impossible."

Nothing was impossible. Who had better ease to come and go as he pleased without question than the sheriff? Did Grady have a beef with all of his old school chums? Was he systematically knocking them off? Was that why he was so uncooperative? But what would be his motive?

The only thing Ben could come up with was that they had something on him and he'd had to shut them up. But his own father? And if he was right, what would be so terrible that it would justify killing seven men, including Harper? Ben decided that his newest theory was too far-fetched.

Or was it?

He stood aside as the men moved the rolling gurney toward the ambulance, then stepped over to J.C. "By the way, where is Grady that he was unavailable tonight?"

"Ishpeming on business. Left this morning. Took his wife along and decided to make a day of it, I guess. He should be home soon. I'll leave a message to have him call me." Walking out with Ben, J.C. took the keys Tom Kowalski had given him and locked the store. Then, because he always went by the book, he grabbed his roll of yellow crime scene tape from his car and sealed off the scene.

Ben waited until the deputy had dispersed the few folks still hanging around. "Thanks for including me." He liked J.C., much preferring him over the grumpy, uncooperative sheriff.

"No problem." J.C. glanced at his watch, then frowned.

"Late for an appointment?" Ben asked, curious.

"Not exactly. I was with Carrie when I got Tom's call." J.C. studied Ben Whalen from under lowered lashes. He knew more about the insurance investigator than the man might imagine since Grady had run a check on him. Ben Whalen had not only been a cop but one with a hell of a fine record. His take on a situation would be worth listening to. "You worked in law enforcement for years. I wonder if I could run something by you?"

Ben leaned against the Jeep as the ambulance drove away. "Sure."

"You know Carrie Denton, Grady's daughter?"

"I've seen her, that's all, but I know a little something about her background."

"You know about her abusive husband, the one who's in jail now?" J.C. saw Ben nod. "Well, here's the situation. Despite the fact that he beat the hell out of her, he's not considered high risk. I just heard they've got him on a work-release program, doing construction work down in Gladstone. A truck load of guys from the jail are taken over every morning and back each night. Mostly road cleanup, park maintenance, that sort of thing."

"And you're thinking he'll take off and come after Carrie."

"Hell, yes, that's what I'm thinking. They're not in chains, naturally, or they couldn't work. I looked into it and there's a supervisor on premises, but how can he watch a dozen men every minute all day?"

"You don't think he's learned his lesson, that he'll serve his time and get on with things?" Ben had seen a lot of battery cases in his day, and knew that some went on to abuse other women. Then there were the few who became obsessed.

"The last thing he said to Carrie as they hauled him away in cuffs is that he'll make her pay."

A rowdy group of teenagers drove by, music blaring, but noticeably slowing down when they spotted the deputy's car. "Does Carrie know he's out on work furlough?"

J.C. jammed his hands into his pants pockets and shook his head. "I went over to her place tonight intending to tell her. Then this call came in. I don't know if I should so she'd be more careful, more watchful. Or if it'll spook her. I told Grady and all he said was to keep a closer eye on her, as he's doing."

Ben sent him a questioning look. "Is this dangerous situation the only reason or are you in love with her?" It mattered only because a man's judgment became clouded when he cared too much, as Ben certainly knew firsthand.

Hands in his pockets, J.C. looked up at the evening sky. "Oh, I've only been in love with her since about the eighth grade. I was pretty nerdy back then. I had asthma and couldn't go out for sports. She was a cheerleader and had all the jocks hanging around her. Well, just look at her! She's gorgeous. I didn't feel I had a chance so . . ." He shifted his gaze to the pavement, at a loss to explain.

"So you never let her know."

"Right. I can't tell you how much I regret not telling her years ago. Maybe if I had, she'd never gotten involved with that creep in the first place, much less married him."

"Don't be too hard on yourself. You were young. It's never easy to confess your feelings to one of the best-looking girls around."

"So I've told myself, but you know what? I think in the long run, most of us wind up regretting things we never did far more than things we did."

"You're probably right. So what's your question? Do prison authorities often release low flight risk felons on work programs? Yes, mostly because of overcrowded jails. What are the chances her ex will chuck it all and come after her? I wouldn't even hazard a guess, not knowing him or her. But I will tell you this, if the woman I loved was facing this, I'd sure as hell stick close to her. Fortunately, you're in a pretty good position to do that in your line of work."

"I have been. I use any excuse to drop in on her and watch from a distance every chance I get. But I'm still worried. These guys are devious as hell, you know. It's like they've got this mission to destroy someone so no one else can have them."

"I agree. They become obsessed." Ben pushed off from the Jeep and dug in his pocket for his keys. "If it'll help, I'll try to lend you a hand in keeping Carrie under quiet surveillance. If you have to be away on business, here's my card. Beep me and I'll spell you. Between you and Grady and me, we ought to be able to keep her safe."

"Hey, thanks. I appreciate that."

Ben opened the Jeep's door. "I'm not sure you should tell Grady I'm involved. I'm not his favorite person."

J.C. shook his head. "When it comes to his daughter, I know he'd appreciate any help you can give."

"Good luck with Carrie." Ben decided it was too late to go

back to Maggie's, that he'd go to his room and update her from there.

"I think we've attended far too many funerals lately," Maggie commented as she and Ben stepped out of the gloom of McCauley's Mortuary into bright sunshine. There would be no graveside service as Ed Kowalski was to be cremated.

"I agree. I wonder why Tom Kowalski wasn't up at the front with his mother. I . . ." Turning to glance up Main Street, he saw the big truck with Channel 7 emblazoned on the side, the television cameras, the female newscaster holding a mike up to Tom's furious face. "Well, there's my answer."

Maggie slipped off her sunglasses. "I was afraid he was angry enough to do something. Do you think he called them or they got wind of things here and phoned him?"

"My money's on Tom contacting the media." He noticed a black car pull up and angle park. A slight man in a rumpled suit jumped out, pad and pen in hand, along with a tall fellow who reached back inside for his camera equipment. "Newspapers, too. It's going to be a zoo around here." The Home Office was not going to be happy.

Ed's friends and neighbors were filing out of McCauley's, glancing toward the commotion up the street. Ben noticed bearded George Cannata, the only other remaining member of the Sexy Six along with Grady, but the man seemed in a hurry to be gone. Ruth, the florist, was carrying several arrangements to Helen's car. The sobbing widow seemed hardly to notice.

Maggie saw Grady separate himself from Opal and move toward the camera crew. "He's just going to make it worse if he orders them away. They'll think we have something to hide."

Ben took her arm. "I'd like to get close enough to hear what Tom's saying." But stay far enough away so that the loose cannon wouldn't spot him and point an accusatory finger again. That would be all he'd need, to be on the six o'clock news.

"The sheriff's department in this town stinks," Tom was saying, his angry voice carrying over the crowd inching forward. "Four of our finest citizens have died within a short time and they keep saying these deaths are accidental. Well, I'm here to tell you that no way did my father *accidentally* lock himself in his own meat cooler, not after being a butcher for thirty years."

"What do you think is going on, Mr. Kowalski?" the striking brunette with the microphone asked him, knowing full well it was a loaded question and she had a volatile subject.

"The truth? I think there's a serial killer loose in Riverview." There was an audible gasp from the people gathered around, the ones who'd just paid their last respects to Ed Kowalski, and others passing by who'd stopped to see what was going on. Low murmurs could be heard as Tom's tirade continued. "The insurance company's sent an investigator and *he* can't find who's doing this. Sheriff Denton's got his damn head buried in the sand, picturing us as the perfect little all-American town. Well, guess what, folks? A killer's stalking our citizens and *no one* is doing a damn thing to catch him."

Scanning the crowd, Ben noticed that Grady hadn't gone over to break things up after all. He was just standing aside, quietly chewing on a toothpick, his eyes hidden behind those damn sunglasses. A hard man to figure, Ben decided, moving alongside him. "Quite a show, eh?"

Watching the reporter, listening, Grady didn't respond to Ben's comment or acknowledge his presence.

Annoyed, Ben stepped closer. "When are you going to do something besides watch from the sidelines, Grady? There're only two of you left now. Isn't there anything you want to tell me?"

Slowly, Grady swung toward Ben, his expression stony. "When I want to tell you something, I'll call you." Turning, he walked over to where Opal stood on the sidelines, took her arm, and headed for his Bronco.

"Damn," Ben muttered as he strolled back to where Maggie was now talking quietly with J.C. and Carrie.

"I see you got nowhere with Dad," Carrie commented. She held out a slender, beautifully manicured hand. "I don't believe we've met but I've certainly heard an earful about you, Mr. Whalen."

Ben shook her hand. He had to admit, as J.C. had said, she was gorgeous in a black pantsuit that must have set her back several hundred dollars. "And I about you, Miss Denton." His look took in J.C. and he wondered how much Carrie had been told about the situation with her ex that he and the deputy had discussed two days ago. "How are things, J.C.?"

"Oh, terrific." He waved at the television cameras, Tom's rantings and ravings, the flashbulbs popping across the street as the newspaper reporter interviewed various residents. "As you can see, wonderful."

"Do you have any idea why Grady is turning from all this?" he asked, truly puzzled at the sheriff's nonaction.

"I wish to hell I knew."

"Can I see you a minute?" Ben asked J.C. He waited until the deputy stepped aside with him. "About that matter we discussed the other night, Carrie's ex-husband, did you tell her?" He didn't think so by Carrie's unworried expression.

Watching the woman in question over Ben's shoulder, J.C. shook his head. "Not yet. I just don't want her running off somewhere because of it. She's safer here where we can keep an eye on her."

Yes, except this would be the first place her ex-husband would look, Ben thought, wondering if J.C. was trying to force a showdown. "All right. It's your call, buddy."

Twenty feet away, Maggie wrinkled her forehead. "What do you mean, confess?" she asked Carrie.

A knowing smile creased Carrie's face. "You know perfectly well what I mean, girlfriend. You and the macho insurance man. You've been seeing him, right?"

Maggie tried a bluff, not quite ready to discuss her tenuous relationship with Ben. "Pretty hard not to since he's in my face daily about this investigation."

"Uh-huh. Tell me, have you been to bed with him?" No one had ever accused Carrie of beating around the bush.

"Carrie! Honestly. We're not high school teenagers anymore and . . ."

"Can the bull. Yes or no?"

Maggie turned so her back was to Ben, certain he could guess their conversation by the look on her face. "I don't see what possible reason you'd have for wanting to know."

Carrie's grin widened. "You have. I can always tell. Well, hot damn. We got us a love affair going on right in the middle of this here murder investigation. How was it?"

Her friend was relentless when she went into her Southern mode. The only way to handle her was to turn the tables. "I might ask you the same thing. Seems as if J.C.'s hanging around your shop at all hours. Did he suddenly develop an interest in women's fashions?"

Carrie frowned as she glanced over at J.C. "You know, I've been wondering about that, too. I can't make a move that he doesn't show up. I've known the man since grade school and he scarcely even sent me a glance. Always had his nose buried in a book. Why now?"

Glad to have the focus shifted, Maggie smiled. "Who can predict the ways of love?"

With lights turning off, loud shouts and the slamming of doors, the television crew packed up their truck, having gotten their story. Ben and J.C. rejoined the women, watching the media rush back to wherever it was they were from.

"They don't give a rat's hind end about us," Carrie commented. "They only want to report a *breaking story* at six and eleven."

"I hope Tom's satisfied," Maggie said, noting that the ex-Marine got into his car without a word to his disapproving mother and rushed off with tires squealing.

"I don't know why you can't control your son," a loud female voice from behind them said. "Now the whole country's going to hear about our problems."

Turning, Ben saw that Thelma Becker was addressing her sister, Helen, Ed's widow. Not another altercation, he thought, yet with little surprise. Everyone's nerves were on edge, certainly the relatives of the four men who'd so recently died.

"*Me* control *my* son?" Helen countered. "What about Freddy? *Your* son was in the shop shortly before my Eddie died, they told me. I'm not so sure he's as innocent as you're always telling us he is."

Thelma's cheeks flamed and she shook one small fist at her sister. "Don't you dare talk against my Freddy. He's just a boy. A sweet boy who never hurts anyone. You've never liked him, that's all."

"That's not so. But lately, well, things just aren't adding up. Where is he, anyhow?"

"At his cabin, I'm sure. You know he's uncomfortable around so many people." Thelma sniffled into her handkerchief. "I hate this, all of it. I'm thinking of taking Freddy and moving away."

Helen's emotions, bounding all over the place, overflowed and she began to openly weep. "Oh, Thelma, don't leave. I seem to be losing everyone. First your Kurt, then my Eddie, and Tom's not well. How can this be happening to us?"

Blood being thicker than pride, Thelma slipped an arm around her sister's shoulders. "Come on. I'll take you home."

Maggie watched the two older women walk away, each carrying a heavy burden, and felt like weeping as well. So many people's lives turned upside down lately.

"What did Helen Kowalski mean about Tom not being well?" Carrie asked J.C. She'd always thought the big jerk was a bully and could have predicted he'd join the Marines so he could have a reason to bash in a few heads, then come home and brag about it.

"It's in the record so I guess it's not a secret," J.C. answered. "Tom recently received a medical discharge. It seems he gets these violent headaches, goes into rages, and even attacked his commanding officer."

"He's lucky they didn't lock him up," Ben said, remembering how Tom had come at him.

J.C. agreed. "I guess Ed pulled a few strings, even asked Grady to write a letter."

Carrie shoved both hands through her thick dark hair, straightening what the wind had rearranged. "That's our cozy little town for you." Squinting, she peered down the street. "Do my eyes deceive me or is that Wilbur Oakley and Phoebe Doran from the library strolling together?"

They all turned to look, but Maggie spoke first. "It surely is." In the silence that followed, she felt she had to say something. "There's probably a good explanation."

"Sure there is." Carrie all but rolled her eyes. "When was the last time anyone saw Wilbur's puny little wife? For all we know, he's buried her under the tulip bed or she's up in the attic in her rocking chair, mad as a hatter."

Ben had to smile at that picture. "I vote for the attic. That's why Wilbur can't marry his true love."

"No," J.C. said, catching the craziness, "I think she's in the garden. Have you ever seen such healthy tulips anywhere?"

They all laughed, but Maggie shook her head. "Listen, we

shouldn't be joking out here. We just buried a man, an old friend."

"We can't help Ed Kowalski anymore, Maggie," Carrie said. "With all that's going on around here, I happen to think it's healthy to laugh a little. Otherwise we'll be the crazies in someone's attic."

And she didn't even know all that was going on, Ben thought as he nodded in agreement. "You're absolutely right, Carrie."

She cocked her head at him. "You know, you're all right, Ben Whalen." Without taking her eyes from him, she addressed Maggie. "I approve. Go after him, girlfriend."

No one noticed that Maggie didn't join in the laughter.

Chapter Twelve

Something was wrong, Maggie decided. Had to be. Staring at the phone she'd just hung up, she struggled with her unreasonable fear.

She wasn't normally a person who worried about the safety of others, imagining their car running off the road and winding up dead in a ditch somewhere or run over by a bus. Why, then, was she a wreck over the fact that Ben had said he'd call before coming over around seven and, at a little past nine, she still hadn't heard from him? After all, he was a grown man, an ex-cop, strong and capable and cautious.

But where in hell was he?

They'd spent only small snatches of time together since Ed Kowalski's funeral two days ago because he'd been going over each and every accident, trying desperately to come up with even a small lead that would buy him some time with the Home Office. After this last death, they seemed to believe Ben's theory that someone the victims knew was methodically killing them. However, they demanded results and had increased the pressure on Ben.

Maggie's fear wasn't just that there might be a killer loose in Riverview. What she worried about more was that that murderer might have turned his attention to the one man who made no secret of the fact that he was looking into the deaths as homicides. If five other healthy, aware, and alert men had somehow been blindsided, Ben might have been also. No one was infallible.

She picked up the phone and dialed the Riverview Motel number that rang straight through to Ben's room. Impatiently, she let it ring eight, nine, ten times. Hanging up, furious with him for doing this to her, with herself for allowing him to, she paced the kitchen. Fiona was up in her room and all was quiet in the house. She felt like screaming with frustration as she gazed out at the night shadows.

A new, equally worrisome thought had crept into her consciousness. Maybe shortly after they'd talked this morning, he'd left town, ordered back to the Home Office because he'd failed to close out the cases. And, with that failure sitting uneasily on his broad shoulders, he'd quietly driven off, not knowing what to say to her. Maybe, in a few days, she'd get a curt note of explanation including a terse good-bye.

Maybe she was getting paranoid.

Another half an hour passed painfully, slowly, before she called again. Still no answer. Nearly ten now and she was really worried. All right, she'd jump in the Explorer and drive to the motel to see if he was there, to make sure he wasn't sick or hurt. She wouldn't even mind if he simply didn't feel like being with her tonight. She just had to know he was okay.

Driving along, windows down to let in the night air clogged with humidity and the very real possibility of rain, she called herself twelve kinds of an idiot. For going, for caring for a man who didn't want anyone to care. She would probably arrive to find him perfectly fine and he'd think her a fool for checking up on him. Maybe he'd fallen asleep and

couldn't hear the phone. Or perhaps the phone was out of
order.

Shit!

The moment Maggie turned the corner and drove into the
parking lot, she saw Ben's Jeep parked near Number 10, the
last in a row of cabins. The Riverview Motel was a bit off
the beaten track, not nearly as modern as the newer Holiday
Inn just off Highway 35. But the individual cottages were co-
zier, more inviting, with an old-fashioned charm. She wondered if that's why Ben had chosen to stay here instead of in
a slick high-rise with all the amenities.

Heart thudding, Maggie pulled in beside the Jeep and
turned off the engine. Sitting there a moment, she wondered
if she dare get out and see this through.

Finally, she jumped down and walked over, noticing that
the drapes on the one fairly large window were open, but the
room was dim. A lamppost in the parking lot lent a bit of
light. Taking a deep breath, she leaned in close, cupping her
hands on either side of her face so she could see inside.

The bed was unmade and rumpled looking, as if someone
had been wrestling in the sheets unable to sleep. Some of
Ben's belongings were scattered on the dresser, on the desk,
hanging in the doorless closet and in an open suitcase on a
stand. But no sign of the man himself.

It took Maggie only a few minutes to check out the
motel's coffee shop, which was just about to close for the
night. She even peeked in at the small cubicle of an office
and saw the night man dozing in a chair in front of the television where a sitcom was blaring forth. Hugging herself, she
wandered back toward his room, wondering what to do next.
Stay or go, wait or give up?

Pacing seemed to get rid of some nervous energy. The lot
wasn't paved but rather covered with white gravel, which
didn't make for easy walking. Still, she walked, back and
forth, back and forth. What was she doing? Maggie asked

herself repeatedly. Had she truly lost her mind or just her heart? Did she love this man, even though he'd all but drawn her a picture showing he didn't want her in his life? Was she a masochist or just a woman in love?

Maybe he'd gone for a walk, a simple explanation. But for three hours? Glancing up at a cloudy sky, she felt the first few drops of rain. Wonderful.

Maggie checked her watch. She'd give him another half an hour, then she'd leave. Enough was enough.

Moving at a brisk pace, Ben saw the lights of the motel just ahead as he walked on the shoulder of the highway, his own shoulders hunched against a light summer rain that was quickly escalating into a storm. He didn't mind because this time, the gods had smiled and he'd been able to walk off the headache that had come out of nowhere. It had started hours ago and had scared the hell out of him, coming so soon after the last one. But maybe it'd been nothing more than the type of tension headache others had all the time.

After all, he had plenty of tension in his life. Six deaths including Harper, all unsolved, all clueless. A sheriff that refused to cooperate, to even admit there might be a murderer in their midst, still insisting each death was an accident. The media locally and nationally putting Riverview on the map and causing no end of problems. Millions in insurance benefits due and beneficiaries screaming for payment. The Home Office about to give up on him because he couldn't get a handle on things. His murky, mixed-up feelings for Maggie Spencer. His disturbing past that kept him locked in a nightmare. The combination of all of those would make most strong men weak.

Nevertheless, his headache was gone for now and he felt pretty good. Wet and tired, but good. A lightning bolt split the sky as he rounded the bend into the parking lot, his shoes crunching on the gravel. When he spotted a shadowy figure leaning against the door to his cabin, he stopped in his tracks, his entire body going on alert. He still had his police issue .38 and now he cursed himself for leaving it in his room.

The figure moved, head turning toward him. Straightening, taking a hesitant step forward, then pausing. Through the rain he saw blond hair and a slim frame. "Maggie?"

Feet flying, she closed the short distance between them in moments, hurtling herself into his arms, oblivious of the rain. Stunned yet pleased, his arms went around her as she pressed her face into his neck.

She couldn't look at him, could only absorb his strength, inhale his wonderfully familiar scent mingled with the sweet smell of summer rain. He was here, with her, whole and in one piece, despite her wild imaginings, her ungrounded fears. "You didn't call and I got worried," she murmured.

Gently, Ben eased back from her until she looked at him. "No one worries about me. No one." It shocked him to realize it, to say it out loud. The remaining members of his small family—his mother and sister—had long ago decided that he could handle himself and went about their own lives. Which was the way he'd always liked it. And yet . . .

"Someone does now." She frowned, swallowed, feeling as if she were standing in shifting sand. Then suddenly the words came tumbling out. "I probably shouldn't have come. I know you don't want me to worry or to care about you, but I don't know how to stop. I don't know anything anymore. God help me, I only want to be with you. Only you. Please don't send me away."

Ben was sure the sound he heard was his heart flipping over. "Oh, lady, I have no intention of sending you away." And he crushed his mouth to hers.

Inside, out of the rain, into the warmth. Soft bedside lamp enveloping the room in hazy light. Drapes drawn for privacy, an inviting king-size bed. Damp hair towel-dried slowly, then the gentle brushing of fingers along a silken cheek, stopping to linger, to look, to enjoy.

Ben loosened the buttons of her oversize cotton shirt, then tugged it from her shoulders, his eyes locked with hers. He saw an unexpected shyness and a heartbreaking need. He let her pull his shirt from the waistband of his jeans, then yank it off over his head, too impatient to mess with buttons. Her fingers splayed on his chest and he knew she felt his heart pick up its rhythm. But when one hand slipped lower, he stopped her.

"No, not this time. This time we go slowly. We have all night." He would hold back and savor, for her. He would love her as she deserved to be loved, with reverence, with feeling. The last night they'd spent together, they'd been wildly hungry, hands and mouth seeking, their need huge. His hunger was no less tonight, but he wanted to cherish her, to let her know with his lovemaking what he couldn't put into words.

"It isn't necessary," Maggie whispered, oddly afraid to break the spell. As long as he wanted her, that was all that mattered.

"Yes, it is." His experienced hands unhooked her bra, let it fall to the floor, his eyes filled with wonder, as if it were the very first time he'd seen her. "So beautiful. Do you know that each time I see you, I want you? That even when you're not with me, I see you. At night, I close my eyes, and you're there." His fingers trembled over the lush curve of her breasts, surprising him. He couldn't remember the last time a woman had made him tremble. Had it *ever* happened before?

Now his thumbs brushed over her nipples as he watched her close her eyes and suppress a soft moan. Color moved into her lovely face and he saw that she was finding it difficult to stand still. He'd brought her to this, Ben thought, pleased, and he'd show her much more.

Maggie's hands curled around his upper arms to steady

herself. She leaned into his touch, both tender and rough at the same time, as he caressed the damp skin of her shoulders, her back, and traveled around to cup her breasts as vivid colors exploded behind her closed lids. His fingers glided as if over something fragile, something precious. She opened her eyes and saw him intently watching her.

"I've never wanted like this. Never." She had to tell him, to let him know. "Only with you." She'd made love before, even with him, yet she'd never seen such need in a man's face, nor felt it inside herself quite like this.

He had no answer except to frame her lovely face, to kiss her willing mouth, then trail feather-light kisses over her face, her shoulders, her throat, pausing at the pulse point. There he felt her heart pounding, throbbing, for him. Only for him as he kissed his way back to her waiting mouth.

Slowly, making her ache with the waiting, he eased his hands into her hair, thrusting through the damp strands and massaging her sensitive scalp with long, lingering strokes. Her head fell back, her eyes filled with fierce desire. "You make me lose my mind, Maggie. Because of you, I can't concentrate like I used to. Why is that?" His voice was hoarse and thick to his ears.

She didn't know, knew only that she was glad she could make him feel a little when he made her feel so much. Steeped in him, in the way his hands and lips moved over her, she had no breath left to answer. Then she felt his mouth close over the peak of one aroused breast, and her knees buckled as she moaned low in her throat.

He lowered her to the mattress, his eyes on her face, his mouth drawing on her. Unable to lie still, she shifted and writhed, shoving her hands into his hair, urging him closer. With teeth and tongue he pleasured her until she was bucking and straining.

"Now. Oh, please, now." Maggie felt delirium closing in on her. No one had ever made love to her with such infinite care, with such tenderness, each touch whisper-soft, as if her needs were all that were important, as if she were fragile. Trembling, she sighed his name as she reached for him.

"Not just yet," Ben said, easing back to slowly peel off the rest of her clothes. Kneeling over her, wearing only his jeans, he let his eyes feast on her perfection before he sent his hands on a lazy journey, reacquainting himself with her lovely limbs. His open palms caressed every inch of her sleek arms, her flat, quivering stomach, her incredibly long legs. He saw a shiver take her as he lay down alongside her. "I want you to remember this night for all the rest of your days."

Outside, the wind threw rain against the window and the old wood cabin groaned with each gust. Her scent tangled his senses and her taste lingered on his lips as he bent to her.

Eyes on her face, he skimmed his hands down one leg, then the other, along her rib cage slowly, then picking up speed. Over and over until he had her squirming, thrashing. He knew the moment she stopped feeling vulnerable and gave herself willingly over to him, letting him take her where he would. At last he trailed his fingers up the inside of her thigh and closed over her. He watched her arch as he sent her soaring, felt her heat pour into his hand and wanted to shout at the beauty, at the passionate way she responded with wholehearted abandon.

But he was far from finished. Not giving her time to re-cover, he put his mouth to her, into the fire. In seconds, she crested again, a sound like a sob escaping from her parted lips. Finally, she shuddered and curled into his arms.

He'd begun this for her pleasure, Ben told himself, but he was the real winner. He'd wanted to reach her as no man ever had before, and instead, he'd found a craving, a longing such as he'd never known before. The seducer had become seduced, he thought with no small amount of surprise.

Naked and damp, Maggie lay with muscles quivering, trying to catch her breath as she watched him rise and quickly shed the rest of his clothes. Surrender was a new word to her vocabulary, one she'd thought she'd never apply to herself. But surrender she had, to his way, to his lead, to her own unleashed desire finally set free. She was shaken to the core, to the point of no longer being able to hide it or care if it showed.

He was a gorgeous specimen, she thought as he returned to her. Long and lean and tan, hard and strong, as close to male perfection as she'd ever seen. Incredibly, she wanted more and reached for him. His eyes darkened as he slipped into her as naturally as if they'd been lovers for years. She kept her gaze locked with his as he filled her, as the heat built and built inside her. She knew he'd held off as long as he possibly could, that slow was what he'd intended, but his control was shattering.

She watched him struggle, then saw his need take over as he plunged, driving himself into her mindlessly. She gloried in seeing him like this, his dark desire and his hunger like a living thing, pushing him on. Her hands bunched on his back as she rode with him, as the heat engulfed them both.

At last, she arched upward, straining to hold in the pleasure just a little longer. But she lost the battle and let go of the room, of reality.

Blood rushed like a thundering river in Ben's veins, hot and dark and insistent, as he neared the summit. His vision blurred, his heart all but burst free as he finally emptied himself into her.

"Do you want me to get up?" Ben asked, some moments later, too comfortable to want to move, but aware that his weight was heavy on her.

"No, it's all right. I think you've killed me so it doesn't matter if you get up." She let out a long, contented sigh. With a great deal of effort, she overcame the marvelous lethargy and raised a hand to her hair, which must look a sight after being soaked by the rain followed by the ravishing.

Placing a kiss on her ear, Ben eased back. "You don't look dead. You look wonderful."

"Oh, I'm sure."

He reached to disentangle her hand as she tried to finger-comb her hair. "It's the truth. A woman is at her most beautiful after being thoroughly and completely loved."

There was that word, but she decided to let it slide, for now. The things he'd said, the words he'd used, the tender way he'd made love, had her wondering if he were preparing her for the good-bye scene. She wanted to ask, yet hated to. "You've made a study of this, I imagine. On hundreds of women."

Rising, he shook his head. "I think I'll take the Fifth on that one."

"You'll probably take the Fifth on another question I'd like to ask, but I wish you wouldn't." She didn't want to blow this mellow mood, but there were things eating at her and she needed some answers. There was no point in postponing the inevitable.

Ben sighed, as if he'd been expecting this all along. He took his time bunching the pillow behind his head just so, then lay down and pulled the sheet over both of them. It was easier to think if he didn't have the distraction of her lush body. There was no doubt in his mind. He owed her some kind of explanation. "All right, shoot."

Maggie wasn't quite certain how to begin. "I know how devastated you were by your wife's death and the loss of your son. I understand how difficult it must be to let yourself care about someone else, even so many years later. There's always the fear that you'll lose them, too. My question is: Is that why you run from me, why you don't want to accept my feelings or acknowledge your own?" A long speech but at least she'd gotten it out.

From the beginning, he'd known she was smart and that she'd figure it out. But she didn't know everything. "Mostly that, yes. I know it seems unreasonable . . ."

"No, it seems perfectly natural. But, Ben, things happen in life that we can't stop or control, like someone we love dying. I've experienced that, too. But it's not a reason for shutting out the world. No one can live in a vacuum."

He scrubbed a hand over his face, realizing he should've shaved, that he must have scratched her. "I've been working on the premise that if you don't let yourself care again, you won't get hurt. Works for me." Or rather it had, until now.

Holding the sheet to her breasts with one hand, needing the small protection, Maggie sat up. "How do you stop yourself from caring?"

He stared into those deep blue honest eyes for a long while and knew that if he could blot out his past, overcome his memories, she'd be the one he'd want by his side. "Obviously, I'm not able to. I know you think I don't care about you because . . . because of the way I've behaved lately. Not true. I do. But there's more, and after I tell you, maybe it's you who'll do the running away."

"You're wrong. I'm here and I'm not going anywhere."

She sounded so certain, so positive. He wished he shared her confidence.

Ben shifted his eyes toward the window and heard the rain still coming down, but there'd been no thunder, no more flashes of lightning. The storm was in his mind and heart. "I started having them shortly after Kathy died. Black moods the shrink called them." In detail, leaving out nothing, he told her about losing whole days and nights sometimes, of walking he knew not where, of returning dirty, tired, and with the mother of all headaches, and the healing sleep that finally had him waking, thirsty and starving. And scared.

"You can't know what it's like to lose time like that and not remember. That's why I went walking tonight, because a headache started and I wasn't sure if it was going to be the big one, or if I could walk it off. I was lucky and it went away. Other times, I'm not so lucky."

She'd listened without interrupting as the questions piled up. "Did the police psychologist put a name to this, like post-traumatic stress syndrome? I've read about that, mostly in connection with veterans like Tom who've been in combat."

"Yeah, that's what he said, or a variation of it. Shrinks have names for everything."

Maggie touched his arm. "Lots of people suffer with this, Ben, and manage to live productive lives. And for many, in time, they become less frequent and finally stop altogether. Is that what's keeping you from . . . from allowing yourself to care for me?"

He turned to look at her, his expression troubled. "You deserve better. I have no idea what to expect, when these will come again, what I do when I go walking. Afterward, I can't remember, not even snatches. Nobody should have to live with that. It's awful, not knowing, always wondering."

She'd read something about this in a newspaper article written about a celebrity who'd overcome a similar problem. The one thing she especially remembered was that the psychiatrist explaining the syndrome had stated that even in that state, the victim wouldn't do anything he wouldn't ordinarily do. Something illegal or immoral. She told Ben about the article and that she believed the premise.

"Yeah, that's what they told me, too. But how do I *really* know? And what's causing them to continue for so long?"

"Those are valid questions, but nothing is quite so terrible if you have someone at your side to go through it with. I want to be that someone for you, Ben. Together, we can lick this thing."

His look was more than a little skeptical. To make himself

that vulnerable, to open himself that way to someone. Together they could lick this, she'd said. He still had his doubts
and he hated being pinned down, feeling uncertain as he was.

She was as quiet as he, sorting out all that had been said,
Ben supposed. And all that hadn't. It made him nervous. He
didn't want to lose her, yet how could he commit to her, feeling as he did? Would she feel the same after watching him
go through one of his spells?

Shifting, he nudged her onto her back and leaned over her.
"I didn't come here to get involved, Maggie, and I know you
weren't looking for anyone, either. But here we are. So what
am I going to do about you, lady?"

Maggie felt on safer ground. Small victories, she told herself. The rest will come in time. He cared even though he
wouldn't admit it, not out loud, and not yet. Keep it light, she
warned herself. They'd had enough serious talk for one
night. "I'm taking suggestions." Then she wiggled her hand
between them and closed her fingers around him.

Ben's eyes widened, but he smiled. This he could understand, could handle with no trouble. "Good suggestion," he
said before pressing his mouth to hers.

It was time, Ben thought the next afternoon as he pulled up
in front of a small brick house. Time he had a chat with
George Cannata, who besides Grady was the other survivor
of the Sexy Six. He'd dropped in at George's drugstore several times, but the pharmacist was always too busy to see
him. Finally, he'd agreed to meet Ben at his home after closing.

George was a short, stocky man who'd lost his hair years
ago and had concentrated instead on his neatly trimmed gray
beard and full mustache. His yard alongside a vacant lot was
as tidy as his beard, the trim on the house recently painted
and there was a flower box with red geraniums in full bloom.

"Come in, come in." George held the door wide, then led

the way to a large back porch with louvered windows. There were two cushioned rattan chairs, a couch, assorted tables, and a big-screen television. "Want a beer? The air-conditioning went out in the pharmacy today. Damned hot." He picked up an empty beer bottle from the table and made his way back to the kitchen.

"Sure," Ben called after him as he sat down and crossed his legs. There was a slight musty smell even on the porch, but the interior from what Ben could see was spic-and-span despite the fact that George lived alone, having been divorced for over twenty years, according to his file.

"Here we go." George handed him a frosty bottle before tilting his head back and taking a long pull on his. Wiping around his mustache, he leaned back. "I suppose this visit's about everyone dying, right?"

"Yes, sir. What do you make of it?"

George shrugged his shoulders. "What does anyone make of accidents? Damn shame, but there you are."

An odd reaction, Ben decided as he tasted his beer. The man didn't look as if he had his head in the same sandpile where Grady kept his. "Doesn't it seem unusual that there've been so many *accidents* in Riverview in such a short time, all centering around your old friends? The Sexy Six, I believe you used to call yourselves, wasn't it?"

George let out a chuckle. "Yeah, that was us. Unusual, maybe, but if not accidentally, then what's your theory on what's happening?"

"I think someone's methodically killing in Riverview, and he seems to be targeting the Sexy Six. Surely the thought had to have occurred to you, too. Only you and Grady are left. Doesn't that worry you?"

"Not really." Leaning back, George pointed to a glass-enclosed gun rack on the far wall of his dining room, clearly visible through the open archway. "See those? Twenty-two of them, all kept up to snuff. I've got a fistful of sharpshooter medals. I could blow a man's head off at two hundred yards. There'll be no *accidental* death for me."

Ben wasn't impressed. "Have you noticed that this person has gotten the drop on four other able-bodied men, plus perhaps Grady's father, a former lawman who undoubtedly knew how to handle weapons? I think our killer's enormously clever and probably living right in this town." He watched George chug down more beer, still looking unconcerned. "Can you think of a reason anyone might want to hunt down the six of you, all friends from boyhood?"

Thoughtfully, the older man set down his nearly empty bottle. "Probably because of that incident that happened 'bout thirty years ago, the auto accident. Hard to believe, though, that anyone would hold a grudge that long and come gunning for us."

Trying not to look too interested, Ben sat up taller. "What incident and what accident?"

"Well, I suppose the statute of limitations has run out by now, so there's no harm in telling you." He crossed his hands over his flat stomach. "It was Thanksgiving weekend and snowing like all hell, I remember. The six of us were on our way back to school in Marquette after being home for the holidays. We'd all been drinking, but we weren't really drunk."

Really drunk. What did that mean? "By the six of you, you mean Jack and Kurt, Reed and Ed, you and Grady, right?"

George nodded. "That's right. We'd piled into Jack's old Ford and we were all in a good mood. Laughing, telling stories, joking around. Had a couple of bottles in the car. Back then, they didn't make a fuss about drinking and driving, you know. Didn't have seat belts, either."

"I suppose not."

"So it was snowing and we were zipping along when we saw this car coming toward us some distance away. Someone suggested we try a game of chicken, you know. We were kind of a wild bunch back then. Never know it now, 'course."

"Who was driving?"

George stroked his beard, his eyes downcast. "Can't remember. Anyhow, we challenged this car to a game of chicken and we were winning. But they chickened out and sped off. We were laughing it up, you know, like kids do, when suddenly there was this other car straight ahead of us. I swear it came out of nowhere. I've thought about this a million times, and I don't know where he came from. It was impossible to avoid hitting it."

"Who was at fault?"

"Not sure. All of us, I guess. The impact threw most of us out of the car, but that old Ford was built like a brick shithouse. None of us were badly hurt 'cause the snowbank cushioned our fall. I think Jack had a concussion and Kurt's nose was broken. Scrapes and bruises for the rest of us. That was all. We were damn lucky, I've always said."

"And the occupants of the other car?"

"Not so lucky." George finished off his beer and belched into his closed fist. "There were four of 'em, a man and woman plus two young children. The couple died and so did the four-year-old. The older kid—eight or ten, I can't remember—lived, but was badly hurt. The family had been returning to Detroit after spending Thanksgiving with relatives around the Marquette area. Or maybe Ishpeming. Up that way somewhere. Hell, it was a long time ago. I don't remember all the details." He pushed to his feet holding his empty bottle. "Want another?"

"No, thanks." Ben waited while George got himself another beer. That must have been the accident Jack Spencer had been in that made him swear off drinking, the way Maggie'd told it. He watched George sit back down and take another long swallow, thinking that this was probably a nightly ritual for this guy.

He couldn't help wondering how many George had had before answering his door. Of course, Ben wasn't about to discourage his drinking tonight. Alcohol loosened the tongue and made a man say things he might otherwise keep to himself. And he needed more answers. "What was the family name of the people in that car? Do you remember?"

"Let's see. Thurgood, I think. No, Thurmond. Yeah, that's it. Thurmond."

"Was there a hearing, an investigation of the accident? Had to be if three people died and another was badly hurt."

George shifted uneasily in his chair, his glance evasive. He swallowed more beer and ran a shaky hand over his bald head. Then he must have decided there was no good reason not to tell the rest, so he picked up his story, his words slow and his voice thicker.

It seemed that Grady's father had been sheriff and he'd taken statements from the boys, advising them to swear that the other car had crossed over the line and hit them. It'd been a bad night with snowy roads and there'd been no other witnesses so their version was believable. Then an aunt of the family or a sister or some relative of the Thurmonds filed a wrongful death suit. So the sheriff had taken the boys to a lawyer friend of his who'd taken their depositions.

Later, all six of them had been summoned to appear in Judge Perry Fulton's chambers for a settlement hearing. In a small town, they often took care of these matters in chambers rather than in court, according to George. The police report showed that the accident was due to weather and the only witnesses, the six college kids all from good families, swore they'd been hit by the Thurmond car. The judge dismissed the charges due to lack of evidence to the contrary.

Ben had listened, growing more and more appalled. "Then the surviving child and the guardian wound up with nothing?"

George chugged more beer, wiping his mouth with the

back of his hand. "Nah. The auto insurance company paid all the kid's medical expenses."

Ben wondered if George knew how shabby that sounded. "So basically Sheriff Henry Denton and Judge Perry Fulton saw to it that all of your records remained clean?"

George nodded as he picked up his empty bottle and got up to get another.

Thoughtfully, Ben regarded the man as he returned and sat back down somewhat unsteadily. George Cannata had lived with this terrible secret all these years, as had the others. This had to be the reason Grady avoided him, unwilling to confess that he'd been involved in a fatal accident years ago that his father had helped cover up. And why Jack had begun drinking after Reed's death, why Ed had called a meeting of the remaining three. They must all have suspected their sins had caught up with them. The buried guilt might also be why George was draining beer bottles so freely. "Do you think it's the surviving child, who must be thirty-eight or forty by now, who's involved in these deaths?"

Again George shrugged. "Makes sense, doesn't it? Can't imagine anyone else holding a grudge against every one of us."

"But who is this person and why did he wait so long?"

"I wish to hell I knew. I'd blow the bastard's friggin' brains away."

Apparently, George had divorced his conscience, too. "Thurmond," Ben mused. "Do you know anyone in town by that name?"

"No. I tried looking into things after Ed got so worried. I looked through local county records for deeds, marriage certificates, birth records, deaths. No one by that name around here."

"Is that why all six of you, and Henry Denton, took out such big insurance policies?"

"Right. It was Jack's idea. During that court case, the one

that ended in our favor, the kid was still in the hospital. Jack said that later, some member of the family could conceivably come after us. We wanted to protect our own in case the kid sued us again, to have a big policy we could borrow against if the cash value wasn't large enough."

"Did the survivor ever sue or contact any of you?"

"No, never."

Not until he went on a killing rampage, that is. Ben's eyes narrowed as he studied George. "You know who was driving, don't you, George?"

The druggist drew in a deep breath. "Yeah, we all know. But we made a pact never to tell because we were all egging him on to drive faster, to race that first car. We were shouting and cheering. We never dreamed that this other car would suddenly be there in our path and be unable to avoid us. Shit, we didn't mean to kill anyone. We were just kids, out having a good time."

Did the man realize how lame that sounded, how foolish now coming from someone in his fifties, supposedly a respected businessman and responsible citizen? "Did any of you ever tell your families the truth about the accident?"

George shook his head. "No one other than Grady's father and Judge Fulton knew the whole story."

Ben stood, having lost interest in his beer. "Thanks. You've given me a lot to chew on."

George walked to the door with him, his steps heavy. "Look, maybe I'm barking up the wrong tree. It's just a theory, you know. I wouldn't want you to go making any trouble about this with anyone."

No, Ben was sure he wouldn't. On the porch, he turned back to look at him through the screen. "Are you aware there's no statute of limitations on murder?"

George frowned. "It wasn't murder. The worst they could call it is manslaughter."

"Murder is what it was. Manslaughter's a defense plea."

Holding his empty beer bottle between his hands, George scowled. "It happened a long time ago. Best to let sleeping dogs lie, don't you think?"

Not when there are five dead men and their grieving families to consider, Ben thought. Without answering, he went down the walk to his Jeep.

As he opened the door, he caught a glimpse of Freddy Richmond standing alongside a row of shrubs in the vacant lot alongside George's house. He was carrying a satchel slung over one shoulder, his eyes huge behind thick glasses as he stared at Ben.

Gripping the door handle, Ben stared back. Freddy was in his mid-to-late thirties. He'd checked the insurance records and knew that Thelma Becker was fifty-four, a year older than her husband had been. Instead of his birth mother, could Thelma be Freddy's aunt, who'd taken him in to raise after the accident? Something to look into, Ben mused as he got in and started the Jeep.

At this point, Freddy was their best suspect.

Chapter Thirteen

It was wrong to steal. Ben knew that, but he snapped off one of Lucy Hanover's roses anyway, down low on the stem. The sweet little old lady wouldn't mind, he told himself, not if she knew he planned to present it to a sweet young lady.

Back in his Jeep, he headed for Maggie's place. He'd never given her anything but worry. A single pale yellow rose wouldn't make up for that, but it was a start. Besides, he wanted to soften her up and see if she'd drive to Marquette and Ishpeming with him tomorrow. Maybe he could learn something there about a family named Thurmond.

His talk with George had made him uncomfortable. He wasn't certain how reliable the man was, but if what he'd told Ben was true, that meant that Jack Spencer had been guilty of a cover-up also. Maggie wasn't going to take that news well. He planned on telling her the bare bones of what George had said until he had proof positive. He saw no reason to upset her unnecessarily.

As the big white house with the pillars came into view, he saw the florist van from the Green Thumb parked in Maggie's circular driveway. His lips tightened into a thin line as he wondered if the man who'd sent the first batch of roses including the single dead white one was at it again. He stopped the Jeep behind Ruth's van just as she came outside. He picked up the stolen rose and climbed out, holding it behind him.

"Hi, there," Ben greeted her. She was wearing purple today, a nylon jogging suit with a white stripe down each pant leg and circling her wrists. Again he wondered how she could stand such a hot outfit when the temperature earlier had hovered around eighty. "More unusual deliveries for Maggie?" he asked as he approached her.

Ruth gave him a smile as she shook her head. "Not this time. A special bouquet wired from New York."

"Oh." New York. That Chet person perhaps. Did her former boss and lover want Maggie back after all? With a bitter taste in his mouth, Ben waved to Ruth. "Nice seeing you again." He rang the bell.

Maggie came to the door holding a small white card and wearing a welcoming smile. "What a nice surprise."

He kissed her distractedly, his mind on the delivery. "I ran into Ruth. More flowers? Not from our mysterious dead rose man, I hope." He wanted the explanation to come from her.

Walking slowly to the kitchen, she shook her head. "No." She glanced down at the card. "They're from Chet."

The flowers were still in the box, an enormous tropical bouquet with anthuriums and three orchids along with a bird of paradise nestled among some greens. "That must have set him back a bundle." He studied her face as she reread the card. "He wants you back." It wasn't a question.

Sighing, she looked up slowly. "Yes."

Ben felt his heart twist. So much for that, he thought.

Carefully, Maggie ripped the card into four pieces, tossed them on top of the flowers, tucked the green florist's paper around the bouquet, and put the top back on. "I don't want him or his stupid flowers." Annoyed that Chet would think she'd fall at his feet for the price of a floral bouquet, she hauled the box to the back porch and shoved it into a tall trash can.

Returning to the kitchen, she saw that Ben was watching her with an odd, unreadable look on his face. He didn't say a word, just stood there with both hands behind his back. "What? What is it?" she asked him.

He shrugged, opting for nonchalance, wondering how he could edge backward to the trash can and toss in the poor pitiful stolen rose he held without being noticed. "Nothing."

Maggie cocked her head. "Yes, there's something." She stepped closer, then angled her head and peeked behind him. "Is that for me?"

Frowning, he brought the rose forward, noticing that it was beginning to droop in the heat of summer without water. Much as he felt. "Not much compared to what you just dumped. And stolen, at that. From Lucy's yard." She might as well know.

Carefully, she took the delicate blossom from him and buried her nose in the soft petals, inhaling the lovely scent. "It's beautiful." She stepped closer, went up on tiptoes, and kissed him thoroughly. Leaning back, she looked into his shadowy eyes. "Thank you."

Irritated with the unknown Chet and with himself for letting him matter, Ben shrugged. "It's not much compared to . . ."

"Don't! Don't ever compare yourself to him. He's not half the man you are. Please believe me."

His answer was to pull her close and kiss her until they were both breathless. Only the buzzing of his beeper stopped him from continuing. Stepping back, he checked the number, then frowned as he recognized it as the sheriff's office. "I need to use your phone. It's Grady."

Maggie waved him to the wall unit and busied herself placing the long-stemmed rose into a tall, thin vase while he dialed, all the while praying the call wasn't to inform Ben of still another dead Riverview resident.

"Ben, it's J.C.," came the reply on the first ring. "I need some help."

"Sure. What do you need?"

"Grady's home sick with a summer flu and I need backup. I just got word from the jail. Wayne Edwards, Carrie's ex, didn't return from work release tonight. Sure as hell he's headed for her." J.C.'s voice was loud, urgent.

"What do you want me to do?"

"I've called her home. No answer. Called the shop and the phone rang and rang. I know she keeps the place open till seven on Friday nights with a young clerk, just the two of them. I'm on my way over there. Can you meet me at Carrie's Closet? You know where it is?" The words tumbled out of him as fear took up residence inside him.

"Yes. I'm on my way." Ben hung up and explained the situation to Maggie as he raced to his Jeep. "I'll call you as soon as I know anything."

"Do you have your gun with you?" She'd seen it in his room.

"I'll be all right. Go back inside and lock the doors." He drove away, taking the turn out of the driveway on two wheels.

Maggie read between the lines. His evasive answer meant he didn't have his gun and he could very well be facing a man who had nothing to lose by hurting more people.

Obsessed was what Wayne Edwards was. She'd spoken with Carrie last night and knew she wasn't aware of the work release program, nor had Maggie known until Ben told her just now. Carrie'd thought Wayne was behind bars, unable to get to her, at least for several more years.

No place and no one was truly safe, Maggie decided as she went inside and did as Ben asked.

J.C.'s black Bronco, a couple of years older than Grady's, was angle parked in front of Carrie's Closet as Ben pulled up and jumped out. Cautiously, he entered the store and immediately heard a woman toward the back sobbing and J.C.'s voice, low and controlled. He hurried over, then stopped in the doorway.

Carrie was lying on the floor, her face puffy, swollen, and bloody, and one arm was twisted behind her head, but she wasn't moving. A redheaded teenage girl, bleeding from the nose and sporting a bruise on her chin that was already darkening, was huddled in the corner as J.C. stooped beside her, trying to get information. Ben knelt to check Carrie.

"Can you tell me what direction he went, Angela?" J.C. asked gently, though his nerves must be jangling.

The young girl hiccuped out several breaths as she held a bloody handkerchief to her nose. "I couldn't see, but it sounded like he turned alongside the building, going north." She reached to gingerly touch a bruise on her head and groaned as her fingers came away wet with blood. "Oh, God, J.C., you've got to find him." She glanced over at Carrie. "Has he . . . killed her?"

Ben had found Carrie's pulse to be weak but pumping away. "No," he told the young girl. "She's knocked out, but she's alive." He looked up at J.C. questioningly.

"I checked her vital signs as soon as I got here," J.C. told him. "They're good. Her arm's probably broken, maybe a few ribs. And her face may need some surgery. But she'll make it. She's tougher than she looks."

Ben thought that the deputy seemed too calm, too controlled. Then J.C. turned and Ben saw his eyes. There was rage there and something he instantly recognized. The burning need for revenge.

"I've called Doc Alexander," J.C. went on, "and he's sending two ambulances. You wait here with them. I'm going after that bastard."

Ben straightened. "No." He could hear sirens in the distance wailing closer. "They're almost here. I'm going with you." It was like *déjà vu* only he was on the other side of the equation. J.C. was in no shape to go alone. No one knew that better than Ben.

J.C. narrowed his eyes for the flash of an instant, then nodded. "Hang on, Angela," he told her. "Help's on the way." He spared a brief moment to gaze down at the beaten and battered face of the woman he'd loved since he was a kid. "It's the last time, Carrie, I swear." He touched a shaky hand to her hair, then raced for the Bronco.

On his heels, Ben jumped in as J.C. shifted into Drive. "Any idea what vehicle he's got?"

"Angela said he took Carrie's red RX convertible, after he hit her repeatedly in the face with her ring of keys." J.C.'s face darkened and he drew in a couple of deep breaths, seeming ready to hyperventilate. He wasn't one to lose his temper normally, but inside, where it did more damage, he must be seething.

He was driving very fast and erratically, Ben thought, but he understood the pain the poor guy was feeling. "Do you know what happened?" he asked, hoping to slow him a little by distracting him.

At high speed, J.C. careened over a double set of railroad tracks, rattling the Bronco until he nearly lost control. But he righted it and kept his eyes straight ahead. "Angela said this short, stocky man apparently snuck in and waited until all the customers had left, then pounced on Carrie and got an arm around her throat. He threatened to hurt Angela if she didn't do everything he said, all the while keeping Carrie in a choke hold."

"The bastard," Ben muttered, thinking of another day, another man who'd victimized a woman.

"He ordered Angela to give him all the cash in the drawer and in their wallets. He started to drag Carrie out the back way when she somehow broke free and tripped the silent alarm that goes straight to the sheriff's office. I had her in-stall it recently, just in case."

"Damn lucky thing."

J.C. kept his eyes on the road that stretched ahead, an older north-south route that was scarcely used since Highway 35 had opened. It wound and twisted and turned through hilly farming country with little traffic. He was watching for that flash of red that would mean they'd taken the right path, that they'd spotted their prey. "Only I wasn't in the office and neither was Grady. I was on my way there when the prison reached me on the mobile phone, so I got the message anyhow. I put on my siren and maybe that's what spooked him. Angela said that when he saw Carrie hit the button, he got furious. He started beating her with his fists and the ring of keys, ranting like a madman." J.C.'s jaw clenched. "Carrie told me once that he used to be a boxer." J.C. swore under his breath. "I should have told Carrie he was on work fur-lough. She might have prepared for his possible arrival. But I didn't want her to take off and now, look what happened!"

Ben knew all about blaming yourself for letting harm come to someone he loved. There was nothing he could say to J.C. at the moment, so instead, he kept scanning the horizon until finally, he spotted something. "Look up ahead. Isn't that a red car whipping up all that dust?"

J.C. pressed the pedal all the way down. Rolling out of a cloud of dust, he spotted the red convertible zigzagging all over the road as Wayne tried to floor it over potholes large and small. "That's her car. That's him."

The big Bronco inched nearer, closing the gap between them. Ben could make out a man's dark head in the driver's seat. "You going to try to force him off the road?" The Bronco was certainly sturdy enough to make mincemeat out of the smaller sportscar.

"Yeah. Just let me get close enough." Ben could tell J.C. was remembering Carrie's face for an instant, letting the adrenaline pump through his veins, needing the strength to focus.

Ben guessed J.C.'s plan, knew all the signs. "When you get to him, you can't let yourself lose it, man. Trust me, I know what I'm talking about." He glanced over at the deputy's rock-hard profile and figured he was merely spitting in the wind.

"When we get him out of that car, you remember, he's mine," was all J.C. said.

Closer and closer until he was on the bumper, lightly tapping. Wayne kept on, skimming around a turn. To the left was a rocky hillside, on the right a fallow field bordering a thicket of trees. J.C. bumped harder and felt the RX jolt.

Suddenly, Wayne yanked the wheel hard to the right into the field, racing over unplowed land. But the low-slung little car didn't get far before it sputtered and stalled. Leaping out, looking over his shoulder, Wayne headed for the trees at a dead run.

They'd lost several valuable seconds backtracking after the unexpected swerve of the RX, but made up time nicely with the Bronco easily chugging over the field. They came to the edge of the trees just as Wayne entered the shadowy woods.

J.C. was out and running almost before the Bronco came to a full stop. Ben leaped down and raced after him. "Hey, he may have a gun," he yelled after the deputy.

"I have one, too," J.C. called over his shoulder. "Besides, I doubt it or he'd have used it on the women." His legs pumped as he dashed around trees and headed straight in.

A summer dusk was settling in, the moon already out, but it was darker in the woods. Some light was available from overhead since the trees weren't thick with foliage but young scrub oaks.

Still, J.C. appeared to have lost him, so he stopped to listen. As Ben came charging up the rear, he held out a hand to quiet him. There was no wind and few night sounds. Suddenly they heard a moan sounding close by. Hands balled into fists, he moved toward the faint noise.

In moments, they found him huddled under the sparse protection of a small tree, his face gritty from where he'd apparently fallen.

"I got a broken ankle here. Get me to a doctor." The voice was shrill, angry, frustrated.

J.C. bent down and grabbed the sniveling creep up by his shirtfront. "I'll get you to a doctor, all right. But first, I'm going to make sure you really need one." With his other fist, he smashed into Wayne's simpering face, almost smiling at the satisfying crunch.

"Okay, J.C.," Ben said, taking hold of his arm. "Let's get him to the Bronco and . . ."

"Not . . . quite . . . yet!" With each word, J.C. thrust a fist into Wayne Edwards, his face, his gut, his shoulder.

"That's enough!" Ben called.

J.C. stopped, looking down at the poor excuse of a man who'd caused so much pain. "I ought to finish you. For two cents . . ."

"Go ahead, tough guy," Wayne said, wiping blood from his mouth with the back of his hand. "I'll sue your ass off. Police brutality. You heard of it, you big, dumb cop? That's my wife back there and I got every right to teach her a lesson."

"Your *ex*-wife and you've got *no* rights, you slimy shit." J.C. took another step toward the man on the ground, but again, Ben jerked him back.

"Oh," Wayne said, drawing the word out, as if a sudden new thought just struck him. "I get it. You're sticking it to her, aren't you, Bucko? You're hot to trot with my wife. I got you dead to rights and . . ."

It was his last word as J.C. swung with an uppercut that jerked Wayne up, then sent him flying back down with a heavy thud. Instantly, J.C. was on him, straddling him, fists pummeling. "You scumbag," he got out through gritted teeth. "You aren't fit to wipe her shoes." And the pounding resumed.

Ben's ears rang with a rush as he relived the nightmare. No, it couldn't be happening again. He wouldn't let another man go through what he'd lived with for years. With a gigantic effort, he pulled J.C. off Wayne and shoved him to the ground. Holding a clenched fist near the deputy's face, he glared down into eyes filled with fire. "You have to stop, or I'm going to have to stop you. I was in your shoes once, and I nearly killed the bastard. Six years later, it still haunts me, that I could have killed a man, that I wanted to. Don't do this to yourself, J.C. Or to Carrie."

The last three words did it. The fight drained out of J.C. and he relaxed, rolling over, rubbing his sore knuckles. He took a moment to level his breathing.

Slowly, Ben got up and walked over to Wayne, more surprised than J.C. to find himself the calm voice of reason. He applied two fingers to his throat and felt a pulse, then he breathed a sigh of relief. He wasn't certain who was more shaken at what had happened in the woods today, he or J.C.

When he turned around, J.C. was on his feet. "Come on, help me get him in the Bronco. We'll cuff him to make sure, but he's out cold."

J.C. rolled his shoulders to relieve the tension, then bent to pick up what was left of Carrie's ex-husband.

By the next day, Carrie was awake in her hospital bed, a bandage at her hairline, her arm in a cast, and her face a mass of swollen bruises. Through puffy lips, she tried to smile as J.C. walked in with a huge bouquet of flowers, but she couldn't prevent a few tears from trailing down her battered cheeks. Walking behind him was Ben Whalen carrying a big stuffed animal.

Maggie rose from the chair alongside the bed. "See, I told you you'd be getting more company. Hi, fellas."

Ben greeted Maggie, but J.C. had eyes only for Carrie.

"How are you feeling?" he asked, moving close to the bed, but afraid to touch her.

"I'll be all right." Her voice was croaky from a bruised throat when Wayne tried to choke her sometime during the ordeal. For the life of her, Carrie couldn't think of one witty comment or smart quip. She hurt too much in more ways than from the beating. "I don't know how to thank you."

"No thanks necessary. I just wish I'd gotten there sooner and you wouldn't be here like this."

Maggie took the forgotten flowers from J.C. "I'll put these in water."

Carrie looked over at Ben. "And you, too. Thank you. Maggie told me all about what you two did."

Ben looked as uncomfortable as the next guy in hospitals. "You're welcome." He handed her the stuffed bear, saw her embrace it with her good arm, then stepped back.

"I saw Grady in the hall," J.C. told Carrie. "He's really mad that I didn't call him, but you know, he was sick and all."

She touched his hand. "It's all right." But his fingers felt odd and she looked down. "Oh, Lord. Look at your hands. I'm so sorry."

J.C. shook his head. "Don't be. You should see the other guy."

Carrie blinked, then swallowed. She hoped never to see the other guy as long as she lived. "Is he really put away this time?"

"Oh, yeah. No more work furloughs. He's going to have a lot of years tacked on for aggravated assault, the escape, and a few other charges." Wayne's cellmate had come forth and sung a sweet song for the sheriff. Apparently Wayne had talked about getting even, getting out and killing his ex for putting him in the slammer in the first place. J.C. decided that news could wait. "You don't have to worry about him ever again."

Noticing the dreamy way the two of them were looking at each other, even with their obvious wounds, Maggie set the vase of flowers on Carrie's bedside table and signaled to Ben. "I think we'll take off." She touched Carrie's arm. "Get well, girlfriend. We have some catching up to do."

Carrie tried another smile. "Thanks, Maggie. You, too, Ben." Emotions high, she felt more tears slide down her cheeks. She watched them leave and saw J.C. lean a hip onto the side of her bed as he took her good hand in both of his. "I can't believe what you did for me. That bastard could have killed you."

"Nah. He's a little shit. That's why he picks on women." He took a tissue from the box on the table and dabbed at the moisture on her cheeks ever so gently. "Don't you really know why I went after him like that? I mean, part of it is my job, but there's more. A whole lot more."

"Tell me," she whispered.

He leaned down, so his face was close to hers. "I've loved you forever, it seems, Carrie. I just never had the courage to tell you."

She wrinkled her brow, then wished she hadn't as a pain sliced through her. "You don't even know me, J.C."

He smiled into those wonderful blue eyes. "I know you. Love begins here, you know." He tapped his head. "In your thoughts. And I've thought about you for years. Then it moves here." He touched his heart. "That's when it becomes permanent."

Though swollen, Carrie's mouth twitched. "I thought it was sex that started in the mind."

J.C. grinned. "No, that begins considerably lower."

She smiled back and realized that her tears had stopped. For now, at least. Despite her broken arm, her bumps and bruises, she felt better than she had in years. She squeezed J.C.'s hand and hung on.

Freddy Richmond shuffled along the street in his worn turquoise canvas shoes looking for abandoned cans. It was seven on a Saturday evening, a good time to find them after teenagers partying on Friday night threw them out their car windows. He hated running into any of them. They always teased him, made fun of him. They were bad.

Sniffling once from a cold that never seemed to leave him, Freddy paused to reach into the sling pouch he'd rigged to hold one of his ladies. It hung around his neck, allowing the sweet bird to cuddle into the warmth of his chest while he walked. It wasn't so lonely that way.

Lovingly, he petted the downy head and was rewarded with a low cooing sound. God's creatures knew who was kind and good. They trusted Freddy. Happily, he resumed his search, the large canvas bag slung over his shoulder still only half full as it bounced against his thigh, alongside his fishing knife. It hadn't been a very productive night so far.

He came to the vacant lot next to Mr. Cannata's house. Freddy knew kids often crept behind the protection of the shrubs to drink beer. Lights were on in the house, but not in the back porch so Freddy didn't think the druggist would spot him. Slowly, he trudged into the field, his myopic eyes scanning the grass through his thick glasses. Another few steps and he spotted two cans. Bending, he picked them up and slipped them into his pouch.

It was then that he heard footsteps.

Startled, instantly afraid, he stopped and stood there as if rooted, his hand grabbing his knife. He saw a tall figure step out of the shadows and walk along the side of Mr. Cannata's house, going toward the back. Recognition dawned on him and he relaxed. There was nothing to fear.

At his breast, the bird chirped, probably picking up on his

nervous reaction. At the sound, the figure halted, turning toward him. Freddy walked closer. "Hi," he said. "I'm glad it's you. I thought it was that insurance man. He keeps hounding me."

"What are you doing out here?" The voice was low, a gruff whisper, decidedly annoyed.

"Pickin' up cans. I turn 'em in for money." Wanting to please, he removed the bird from its pouch. "Want to see my baby?"

They were to be his last words.

Moments later, the tall figure dropped Freddy's knife from a gloved hand onto his still form, then quietly hurried off, the plan, for now, aborted.

From the sidewalk, two ragged turquoise tennis shoes could be seen protruding from between the hedges.

"You've the appetite of a longshoreman, and that's the truth," Fiona said as Ben leaned back in his chair at Maggie's table. Clearing the empty plates, she gave him one of her infrequent smiles. "It's a pleasure to cook for you, Ben Whalen."

"The pleasure, Fiona, is decidedly all mine. You can't know what a wonderful change this is from coffee shops and diners." He glanced at Maggie's plate and saw that even she had nearly finished the delicious lamb stew that Fiona had heaped on both their plates.

Maggie got up to get their tea. "You're going to fatten him up, Fiona. How's he going to chase the bad guys with a big belly?" She'd relayed the story of how Ben and J.C. had captured Carrie's ex-husband and, since Fiona had always had a fondness for Grady's motherless daughter, that effort had turned the corner in the older woman's feelings about Ben. She'd been the one who insisted on making him a *fine Irish Saturday night dinner*, as she'd put it.

"I doubt that'll happen," Fiona stated in her no-nonsense

manner. "I cooked for your father for thirty years and over all, he gained no more than five pounds from the young man he was when we met." She set sugar, cream, and sliced lemon on the table. "Moderation's the key, as they say."

Behind her, Maggie winked at Ben. "In everything, I would think." They'd spent a lovely day fishing upstream, hadn't caught a thing but it had been fun. He'd told her about visiting George Cannata and the odd theory he had, which worried her. Ben had asked her to go with him on Monday to Marquette and Ishpeming to see if they could learn something about the Thurmond family. She would put aside real concern until then because it was a beautiful evening and they had tomorrow to spend together as well.

Ben kept a straight face. "I couldn't agree more." He felt good, better than usual. The incident with Wayne Edwards yesterday had energized him, not so much because he'd been able to help, but rather because he'd been able to stop J.C. from killing a man in a rage. Carrie was on the mend and even Grady had been grateful to him. Not grateful enough to agree to a meeting about Ben's conversation with George, but at least he was loosening up. After his visit up north, he intended to pin Grady down and not take no for an answer.

Sitting down, Maggie poured tea all around. "So, Fiona, what do you think about Wilbur and Phoebe running off like that?"

One who thoroughly enjoyed gossip, Fiona looked disapproving even though she was hungry for details. "I still can't believe it. Just how did you hear of it, Ben?" He'd insisted she call him Ben, though she'd hesitated at first, not really knowing him all that well. But she had a feeling, with the way Maggie kept looking at him, that this man was more than a passing fancy. And about time, she thought.

The girl could use a heavy dose of happiness. She'd prayed endlessly that Maggie wouldn't miss out on a love of her own, as she had. Perhaps they'd even settle in Riverview, fill the house with babies, and keep her on. The thought warmed her heart.

Ben recognized the woman's eagerness and was glad to oblige. It hadn't been easy winning Fiona over. "Actually, it was Helen Kowalski, Ed's widow, who first brought the situation to my attention. She'd called Wilbur about Ed's insurance policy and the secretary had told her that he wasn't in, but she'd see to it that Mr. Oakley got the message. Three or four days went by and Helen decided to pay old Wilbur a personal visit. She arrived just as the secretary was cleaning out her desk. Wilbur had, as they say, flown the coop."

"His secretary told Mrs. Kowalski that he just up and left?" Fiona asked, thoroughly intrigued.

"She told Helen that she'd gotten a long-distance phone call from him saying that he'd left a severance check on his desk in his locked office, that she was to pick that up, clear out her things, and lock the door. When she went in, she found that the place had been cleaned out, nothing left except her check."

"Is that possible, to just walk away from an insurance agency and leave everyone hanging?" Fiona was appalled.

"No, ma'am. National Fidelity, like most insurance companies, is a member of National Insurance Crime Bureau, which works with law enforcement and acts as a go-between for insurance agencies and the law. They police their members. If an agent dies or decides to close shop, he has to go through several steps of dissolution with the parent company, making sure all clients are taken care of. Wilbur skipped those steps, cleaned out the company account as well as his personal bank account, and skipped town, taking his new love with him."

"Still water runs deep, wouldn't you say?" Maggie asked before tasting her tea.

"But how would you know Phoebe Doran's involved?" Fiona wanted to know. "I mean, who told you? She's a lady if ever I saw one. I'd have bet the farm she'd not take up with the likes of Wilbur Oakley."

"Apparently they've been seeing each other for months. When Helen came to see me, we both paid a visit to Mildred Oakley."

Fiona made a face. "I used to see her occasionally at the market. A dried-up prune of a woman, she was. A bit of a recluse now, I hear."

Ben took a swallow of tea and wished he had coffee. "And a hypochondriac, according to Helen," Ben added. "She's a very bitter woman about now. She claims she'd begun to suspect Wilbur, even followed him a couple of times and caught him meeting Phoebe at her place."

"This gets better and better," Maggie said, trying to picture a refined, educated woman with prissy old Wilbur.

"Mildred was about to confront him when she found his note saying *sayonara*." He turned to Maggie. "And you were angry with me awhile back for suggesting that her massage therapy might be more like hanky-panky."

Smiling, Maggie nodded. "I admit it. You were right and I was wrong."

"Maggie always looks for the best in people," Fiona said in defense.

"Maggie was never a cop," Ben stated, knowing that hardly explained all of his skepticism, but a goodly portion. "But there's more. I talked with the Home Office. It seems that Wilbur was both owner and beneficiary of a rather large insurance policy on his wife and another on himself. He cashed both in last week. And, as if that's not enough, he also took *all* of the files on all of the policies in effect in Riverview. I swear I think that's a thumb-your-nose gesture at everyone who'd ever criticized him, and I'm at the top of that list."

"Well, I'll be," Maggie said, stunned. "I never thought old Wilbur had it in him to be *that* devious. And I wouldn't beat myself up, if I were you. Half this town thought Wilbur was a real schmuck."

"His grand gesture sure has thrown National Fidelity into chaos. Suddenly, everyone's calling, checking their coverage, wanting refunds, canceling policies. What a mess." Ben felt a pang of guilt, thinking he should have guessed Wilbur was up to something.

"There's a lesson to be learned here," Fiona concluded. "You truly never can know another, now can you?"

"I don't know about never, but it isn't easy," Maggie answered, her eyes on Ben's.

"Maybe we're better off not digging too deep."

"Said like a true cynic," Maggie told him.

"A true cynic answering an optimist," he said, smiling.

The phone rang, halting the discussion effectively. Maggie walked over. "Five will get you ten that it's for you," she told Ben. She was right. "It's Grady." Handing him the instrument, she felt her heart skip a beat. *Not again, please, God.* Hadn't they had enough?

For several long seconds, Ben listened to Grady, his face unreadable. "I see. You think it fits our man's M.O.?" Again, he listened. "Well, that's at least different. This can't be construed as an accident, nor was Warren Harper's death. Maybe now, you'll listen to me." After a moment, he spoke again. "All right, I'll check with you tomorrow. Thanks for letting me know." Slowly, he hung up.

"What is it?" Maggie asked anxiously, afraid to know after what she'd overheard, yet unable to turn away.

Ben ran a weary hand over his face. "They just found Freddy Richmond's body in the field alongside George Cannata's house. He's been stabbed with his own knife."

Chapter Fourteen

Kneeling on a hard wooden pew near the back of St. Matthews alongside Maggie, Ben half listened to the mass, his eyes scanning the pitifully small turnout. The mourners at the funeral for Freddy Richmond didn't take up but a third of the church, unlike the ceremonies for the solid citizens who'd died recently. He felt a wave of pity for the man inside the plain bronze casket at the front of the center aisle, for the way he'd had to live and the way he'd died.

In the first pew, clinging to her sister, Thelma Becker seemed to have shrunk since he'd last seen her. Ben had been shocked when he'd seen her walk by, her skin pale and drawn, her shoulders sagging as if carrying more burdens than anyone should have to bear. Helen Kowalski held on to her as if the poor soul might topple over without the additional support.

As usual, when he saw the devastation that the murderer had generously visited on so many members of this nice little town, Ben gritted his teeth. He struggled with an impotent anger that had his fists clenching and his stomach knotting.

Attending a church service while dwelling on all manner of things he'd like to do to another human being probably wasn't right. But he couldn't help it.

He wanted to put that bastard behind bars so badly he could taste it.

Sensing his tension, Maggie placed her hand over Ben's fist and leaned closer. "You're grinding your teeth."

"That's not all I'd like to grind," he whispered into her ear, thinking he'd like to smash his fist into the killer's face.

The mass ended with the choir singing "Amazing Grace," though they weren't able to drown out Thelma's sobs that escalated as the six pallbearers moved the casket toward the double rear doors. At least, Ben thought, Freddy's death had managed to reinforce the bond between the two sisters, united once more in their shared grief.

Outside in the bright sunlight of a Monday morning, Ben led Maggie away from the small crowd, noticing that several persistent members of the press were hanging around hoping for an interview with some shock value. He was pleased to see the few mourners present brush on past them with disgusted looks. "I think I'll skip the graveside and get going," he said to Maggie. "I'd like to get this trip to Marquette and Ishpeming behind me. If you feel you'd rather stay . . ."

"I'm coming with you. Can we swing by the house so I can change real quick?"

Shrugging off his sportcoat, Ben nodded. If the traffic was light, they could make Marquette before lunch.

The best library for their purposes in Marquette, according to Maggie who'd lived there while attending Northern Michigan University, was Peter White Library downtown on Front Street. An hour and a half after they left Riverview, they were pulling into the parking lot.

"Ah, memories," she said as they walked up the steps of the old white masonry three-story building with the large pillars in front. "Northern University Library is best for research, but this place has a much wider selection of general fiction."

"I'll bet you were straight A's, acing all your exams." He held the door for her.

"Don't I wish," Maggie said, lowering her voice automatically. It was cooler inside and the same hushed atmosphere prevailed that she remembered. She headed straight for the microfiche section upstairs. "The *Mining Journal* is Marquette's only paper. We'll get back issues and see what we can find."

They got lucky, for the microfiche section was deserted. Seated at a reader/printer with film for every issue of the *Mining Journal* from mid-November to the first of December thirty years ago, Ben inserted the first spool Maggie handed him and followed the instructions taped to the front of the machine. He threaded the film under the lens and onto the pickup reel and began scrolling. "I'm not sure we'll find a report of the accident since it took place on the highway. Even so, the Thurmond name probably wouldn't appear in print here unless the family had some relatives in Marquette."

"We don't know if they did, so we have to check. Besides, not that much goes on in small towns, so they may have reported an accident where three people died, even if it happened some distance away." She got the next film ready as he scanned page after page.

It was slow going and tedious, skimming through local events and farm reports, deaths and births, new arrivals, trying to spot the name Thurmond in each small item. After half an hour, Ben straightened, rubbing his neck, tense from leaning forward and trying not to miss anything.

"Here," Maggie said, threading in the next spool, "let me have a shot at it." They changed places, with Ben behind her chair, reading over her shoulder, handing her new spools.

Some ten minutes later, they hit pay dirt. "Look!" Maggie said, her excitement rising as she adjusted the lens to bring the article into sharper focus. "This is dated the Tuesday after the Thanksgiving weekend and there it is."

Ben leaned forward and read the brief four-sentence news report buried on page six. An accident on Highway 35 before the fork at Route 553, two cars colliding head-on around nine in the evening. Six college boys from NMU were in one car traveling north and a family of four in the other, traveling south. Three members of the Thurmond family had died and the fourth was in critical condition. They'd been visiting a sister, Mary, in Ishpeming for the Thanksgiving holiday.

"That's it? That's all they printed? I can't believe there isn't more." Disappointed yet determined, Maggie scrolled on.

When she got to mid-December without finding another reference, Ben straightened and let out a frustrated sigh. "I don't think you're going to find anything else." He returned the films into the correct files while Maggie printed a copy of the small article.

"I can't believe there's no follow-up piece. What hospital did they take that child to? And what about the court case that was resolved in the judge's chambers? Shouldn't an account of that be in here somewhere?"

"A newspaper picks and chooses what to print, what they consider to be of interest to a majority of its readers. Besides, we don't know what date the court handled the case. Could have been weeks, even months later. However, all is not lost." He smiled knowingly. "The courthouse will have the information we want. It's all a matter of public record."

She returned his smile. "You're so smart."

The first order of business, according to the Clerk of the Court, a Delores Remick who wore her hair in such a tight bun that Ben worried about her eyes becoming slanted, was to fill out a request form. After that, they handed the form to the stern-looking woman and were told to have a seat.

Wiggling on the hard wooden bench, Maggie watched the woman walk out of sight, presumably to get their file. "I hope she doesn't go on her break and forget us."

"Not real friendly, is she?" Ben paced the small area, tired of sitting. They were getting close. He could feel it.

It was a full fifteen minutes before Delores returned and motioned them over, holding out a sheet of paper. "The Thurmond case is Docket #6537. The case folders are kept downstairs, filed by number. You can take those stairs and someone will direct you to the correct section."

Thanking old prune face, Ben hustled Maggie down and found the man in charge who checked the number and pointed to a large filing cabinet. Eagerly, they went to it and began thumbing through the folders. Missing it on the first pass through, Ben frowned. He began a second search, more slowly, more thoroughly. But to no avail.

"I don't get it. I find #6536 and #6538, but not the one in between." Frustrated, he took one more slow journey through the old files. "It's definitely not here."

Maggie called over the man who'd sent them to this cabinet. "The one we need doesn't seem to be here." She held out the paper Delores had given them. "Can you help us?"

Repositioning his glasses, the man glanced at the docket number, then bent to the task. After several moments, he shook his head. "Nope, not here."

"How can that be?" Maggie wanted to know.

Shoving in the drawer, the man sighed. "Well, you could have the wrong docket number. Happens all the time. Or the folder could be misfiled, especially if it's a thin one. Easy to slip one of these inside the other, don't you know? The only other possibility is that it's still an open file. Only closed files are down here." He started walking away. "You'd best check back upstairs."

Annoyed but trying not to show it, Ben led the way back up and again stood in front of Delores Remick. In short order, he told the woman the problem.

A look of irritation flitted across Delores's tight features. "Impossible." Without another word, she left them, her high heels clicking on the wood floor as she went into the next room. This time she was back in five minutes waving still another sheet of paper. "Here's the docket schedule for that period. You'll note the number I wrote down for you is for a wrongful death lawsuit filed on behalf of Lee Thurmond, a minor, the plaintiff, and lists six names as defendants. You'll also note the date of filing is filled in as well as the date of disposition. Therefore, the number is correct and this file *was* closed out." Her reputation intact, she looked up at them. "As to whether the folder is misfiled, that I couldn't say. That's a different department altogether."

"Lee Thurmond," Maggie said softly. "At least we've got the kid's name."

"I don't suppose the name Mary Thurmond is listed there somewhere?" Ben asked hopefully, pretty certain he was wasting his breath.

"*All* those particulars would be in the file," Delores said.

"The file that's misfiled or lost or whatever," Ben added.

"That, sir, is not my problem." She paused, looking down her nose at him, waiting for his next attempt.

"How about the attorneys' names? Are they listed?"

Looking aggrieved, Delores all but rolled her eyes. "Wait here." Again, she hustled out and returned several minutes later. "According to docket files, the plaintiff had a court-appointed attorney, Joshua Smith from Marquette, and representing the defendants was Homer Cromwell from Riverview."

Ben nodded. "Terrific. We can probably find them in . . ."

"Not Mr. Smith." Tough as she was, Delores was beginning to feel sorry for them and softened her expression. "He went into private practice later here in Marquette, and hated that, too. He moved to Mexico about ten years ago. The building he had his office in is now a bookstore."

"That's just wonderful," Maggie said, "because Homer Cromwell died before I started college. He was a friend of Dad's."

Sure, the attorney Grady's father had hired for the boys. His frustration rising, Ben felt like giving up. "Well, thanks anyway." Taking Maggie's hand, he left the building.

Sharing his disappointment, Maggie walked with him. "Nobody promised us this would be easy."

Ben unlocked the door for her. "Yeah, I know." He waited until she'd climbed in, then walked around.

"At least we have the kid's name. That's something. Maybe if we go to Ishpeming and ask around, someone will remember Lee Thurmond and his aunt, this Mary Thurmond."

"We don't even know if the woman is the father's sister or the mother's, which would make her last name different." Ben pulled out into traffic.

"I guess you're right." Yet she saw he wasn't quitting, was instead heading toward Ishpeming. "Where do you propose to begin?" She was really growing fond of playing detective.

Ben decided to look ahead, not behind. "First, I guess we should try the obvious and see if there's a Thurmond listed in the phone book. If not, the courthouse has all kinds of records we can check. For instance, tax rolls might be a good place to begin. If the lady owns a house, she'll be listed."

Maggie smiled at him. "I knew you wouldn't give up."

Only there was no Mary Thurmond or M. Thurmond or *anyone* named Thurmond on the tax rolls in the old mining town of Ishpeming, not currently and not in the recorded past. Maggie blew at her bangs in frustration. "Well, damn. Another dead end."

"Let's not give up quite yet. We've got other places to look." But after checking the only name they had for a marriage license, divorce papers, criminal record, business license, probate for the possibility of a will, only to come up empty-handed, even Ben had to admit he was getting discouraged.

Maggie had long since lost her energy and her earlier enthusiasm as they'd gone from one department to another, searching through dusty files, more microfiche and huge books with information often recorded by hand. By three o'clock, she'd had it. "If we don't take a break and get something to eat soon, I'm going to sit down and cry right here on the courthouse floor."

Ben was well aware that when he was hot on the trail of something, he forgot to eat, even to rest, especially if he sensed that he was getting close. And he had that feeling now. There was something here, in this town, some secret he needed to unearth that held the key to the killer. He felt it deep inside.

But one glance at Maggie, looking more wilted by the minute after spending hours in old buildings without air-conditioning, and he threw an arm across her shoulders and led her outside. "All right, let's go eat."

The Depot was an old railroad station, hardly more than one large room, that had been converted into a pleasant restaurant off the main drag. They ordered the specialty of the house, fried chicken with the works, and tall, frosty glasses of iced tea with big chunks of fresh lemon.

Finally off her feet, Maggie drained half her glass and sat back while her stomach gurgled in anticipation. "You really think we're going to find a clue to this Mary Thurmond's existence in Ishpeming?" she asked Ben, noticing that he didn't look tired but rather anxious to eat and get moving.

"Yes, I do. Just a gut feeling, of course. At least we can say we gave it our best shot." He stirred sugar into his tea.

Maggie was resigned to more hunting and searching, reminding herself that she'd asked to come along. But at least she'd get to eat first, she thought as the young, attractive waitress set the baskets of chicken and fries, biscuits, and coleslaw in front of them. "I'm hungry enough to eat the basket," she said, picking up a drumstick.

It did smell good. Ben dug in, watching Maggie chow down. He loved watching her do most anything, for she seemed to do everything with such gusto. "Hey, slow down. This isn't your last meal, you know."

"Feels like it." She chewed on a french fry and sighed. "Sinfully delicious."

They ate in silence for several minutes, until the main thrust of their hunger was satisfied, then Maggie's curiosity got the better of her. Ben was in his cop mode and willing to talk, and she didn't want to miss anything. "All right, so suppose we find this Mary Thurmond. What then?"

Ben tossed the last chicken bone into the basket and wiped his hands on his napkin. "Then we question her about the surviving nephew—where he is now, what his physical condition is. Remember the report said he'd been in critical condition after the accident. He might have died later and if so, this whole theory's out the window."

"It's probable that if this Thurmond kid did survive, this Mary Thurmond had something to do with raising him since she went to court on his behalf. Maybe there was insurance money from the deaths of his parents."

"That's certainly a possibility, one George didn't mention. He did say that the auto insurance paid for the child's medical bills."

"Well, at least, that's something. So as to what we know so far, for whatever reason, maybe physical limitations, Lee Thurmond didn't take action all these years. But then something must have happened to trigger his need to get even, and he insinuated himself into the Riverview community where he'd learned the six college boys, now grown men, lived. It had to have been awhile back and, quite obviously, he had to have changed his name since there's no one in our town named Thurmond."

"Right. Offhand, can you think of some names of guys between thirty-five and forty who are fairly new to Riverview?"

Maggie pushed aside her empty basket and sipped her tea thoughtfully. "Not really, but then, I've been gone six years. And there're a lot of men who work on construction who are in town seasonally. The same with hunting and fishing guides, fish and tackle shop owners, hiking leaders. I can only think he has to be one of those, someone who's in Riverview, but not really a part of the community."

"Maybe."

"What's *your* theory on why he's killed all these men? Is it to get even for his family being taken from him? If that's so, it's a puzzle as to why he's waited so long."

Ben shook his head. "I can't say why he's waited but, yeah, I think his motive is revenge. That's a huge motivator. I ought to know and now, so does J.C."

"I can't condone it as a valid reason to kill."

"Of course not, on an intellectual level. But I was a cop too long not to believe in vengeance killings. Pure and simple and unadulterated vengeance. How can you not understand it if you believe someone deliberately shoved your unsuspecting father to his death?"

Maggie studied his intense face for a long moment. "You have a real taste for blood, don't you?"

"Maggie, you're getting off track and making this personal." The conversation and her assessment of the situation were beginning to annoy Ben. "Let me tell you a story," he said, leaning forward. "About ten years ago, I was working Homicide when we were alerted that a 911 call had come in from a neighbor of this woman who was screaming for help, pleading for the person in there with her to stop hitting her. My partner and I arrived and had to damn near break the door down. We find this big guy leaning over this tiny woman who's got blood all over her face. She looked far worse than Carrie the other night."

Maggie pressed her lips together, wishing she'd never brought up the subject.

"This was no slum project in the inner city, but rather an upscale suburb. Turns out the guy's a doctor with pots of money and an attitude. Told us the law was on *his* side because he caught his wife flirting with another man and as her husband, he had every right to beat the hell out of her if he so chose. So my partner calls for an ambulance and I'm reading the guy his rights and cuffing him when I spot a picture on the table of a boy about six or seven. I ask this clown if that's his son. He says yes and wouldn't answer anything else. So I shoved him into a chair and went upstairs."

Hand to her mouth, Maggie knew what was coming, just knew.

"There he was, small for his age, still in his Bugs Bunny pajamas. The son of a bitch had shot his own son when the kid dared step out of his room to see why his father was beating on his mother. The husband later told me, real proud like, that children must obey their parents, as if that excused what he'd done, as if that explained everything."

In an effort to calm down, Ben drained his iced tea and made himself put the glass down carefully. "So you ask, do I believe this jackass should lose his life for taking that boy's, for beating his wife so badly she required plastic surgery? Damn right I do. But did he? Hell, no. He's in prison while his kid's dead and his wife's probably afraid to leave the house or trust another man ever again. Stories like that are why you don't meet too many cops who don't believe in capital punishment."

"But you didn't hit that man when you went back downstairs after finding the boy, did you? Because his punishment and vengeance aren't up to you." She kept her eyes on his until he finally looked up.

"No, I didn't touch him, but I wanted to. Oh, man, I wanted to."

Maggie reached over and took his hand. "Wanting to and doing it are miles apart. I might have wanted to if I'd been there, too. That's only human. You can forgive yourself for being human, Ben."

"I guess so." At least, he prayed it was so. He'd gone too far just once. He had to believe, after the other night in the woods, that he'd never cross the line again.

"You're too hard on yourself, you know."

"Maybe." He glanced at the clock. "Listen, why don't you sit here and have another glass of tea. I'm going to get a handful of quarters and go over to that pay phone and make some calls before these offices close for the day."

"All right, but will you tell me who you're calling?"

"I want to check if Mary Thurmond had a driver's license or an auto registration or a voting card or a social security number assigned in Michigan. I can find the phone numbers I need in the yellow pages. Be right back." At the counter, Ben paid the bill, got his quarters, and walked over to the pay phone.

Maggie finished a glass and a half of iced tea before Ben returned, but at least he seemed excited. "You got a lead?"

"Not a good one, but a possibility." He sat down for a moment. "Mostly, I struck out. Mary Thurmond doesn't have a driver's license nor a car registered and no voting card. The social security I couldn't check out because the damn line was busy every time I dialed until the last time when a recording told me the offices were closed, to call back. I hate dealing with government agencies."

He took a sip of her tea. "So I got to thinking that the kid had to go to school and there's only one grade school in Ishpeming, Roosevelt Elementary. It took me a while since it's summer vacation, but I got the name of the principal, called her, and she gave me the name of the woman who'd been principal back twenty-five, thirty years ago." He glanced at his scribbled notes. "Doris Hodgkins. Lives on Cedar Street the other side of the railroad tracks. She agreed to see us if we went over right now."

Maggie stood, revived by the food. "Great. I'm ready."

The house on Cedar Street was made of cinder block, painted a perky yellow and had flower beds overflowing with petunias and a big apple tree in the center of the yard. Mrs. Hodgkins, a widow, was a small, birdlike woman somewhere in her seventies, but she had a firm handshake and a ready smile.

"I don't have much time," she explained, leading the way into her living room and directing Ben and Maggie to her overstuffed couch while she settled into a wing-back chair by the small fireplace. "My bridge night, you see. The girls will be over soon." She repositioned a hairpin in her white hair fussily. "What is it I can do for you?"

"As I mentioned on the phone," Ben began, "I'm an insurance investigator for National Fidelity." He handed her his business card. "My company's looking into some accidental deaths in Riverview that are somewhat suspicious. We have reason to believe that a young boy named Lee Thurmond, a nephew of a woman named Mary Thurmond, may somehow be involved. He would have been eight or ten, thirty years ago. He may have moved here and possibly been raised by his aunt Mary after a hospital stay. He'd been seriously injured in an automobile accident that also killed his parents."

"Oh, how terrible. The poor lad." Mrs. Hodgkins crossed her feet clad in blue crocheted slippers. "And you think he might have attended our school?"

"Yes. Is it possible you recall someone named Thurmond since you were principal of Roosevelt Elementary around that time? I realize you must have worked with literally hundreds of children, but I have to ask."

"I was actually principal for twenty-two years, and before that, I taught eighth grade for eight." She stroked her chin thoughtfully. "But I honestly can't remember a boy by that name. You don't have more information on him, a description perhaps?"

"No, I'm afraid not." Ben cursed the newspaper for not providing more information. "Can you suggest how I might go about checking the school records dating back to those years? This is very important. Several lives may depend on what we can learn."

"That may be a problem. You see, we had a fire at Roosevelt twelve years ago. The storage room where we kept all the records was the hardest hit. I'm afraid all those files dating back to the time you mentioned are destroyed."

Maggie felt like groaning out loud. So near, yet so far.

Ben, also, had a hard time not shouting out his frustration. "Mrs. Hodgkins, can you think of *anyone* who taught at Roosevelt back then who might have some information we could use in trying to locate this Mary Thurmond? She would have lived near the school or at least in the district. The boy possibly had some physical injuries from the accident, or perhaps missed a good deal of school while he was recovering, so he could have been a grade or two behind, or even a slow learner needing extra help. Anything, anything at all? We're desperate."

"Oh, dear, I can see you are. Let me think." Her hand worried a cross hanging from a gold chain around her neck while her brown eyes behind wireless spectacles blinked in concentration. "Well, perhaps Martha Enright might be of some help."

Ben hoped this wasn't another lead that would die on the vine. "Who's Martha Enright?"

"Just about the finest teacher I've ever known. Martha took a personal interest in every child, boy or girl. She not only taught sixth and sometimes seventh grade, but she helped with remedial reading, she counseled troubled children, she took them on outings on weekends. A wonderful woman. If this boy attended Roosevelt, especially if he was handicapped in any way, Martha would know him, and probably his guardian as well, for she often dropped in at the home of students to have chats with parents."

Ben's hopes inched up. "Sounds good. Where can we find Ms. Enright?"

"Right now, she's in Hawaii. A niece took her for a month's vacation in Maui, rented a condo for her family and Martha. I don't know where they're staying, but I can look up when she's due back." Doris got up favoring her right knee, then walked to her desk and rummaged until she found her calendar. "Martha is a member of our bridge club so I keep track of her since I set up the weekly games." She thumbed through several pages. "Yes, here it is. She'll be back on the weekend, Saturday or Sunday."

And this was Monday. Five or six days to wait. Ben sighed. They'd waited this long and so far, this was their best lead, slim though it was. Doris could be wrong and Martha's memory might be no better than her own. Still, he had to follow up. "I wonder if you could give me her phone number? Does she have an answering machine? I could leave her a message to contact me when she returns."

"Certainly, and yes, she does." It took Doris a few minutes to find her address book and write down Martha's phone number for Ben. "If you like, I'll also leave her a message stressing the urgency of your call."

Ben rose, taking Maggie's arm. "I'd appreciate that. My beeper number's on the card if you think of anything else."

The doorbell rang, a cheerful melody. "That's one of the girls," Doris said, smiling in anticipation. She hurried to open the door and quickly introduced Ben and Maggie to two older ladies, near carbon copies of Mrs. Hodgkins.

"Thanks again for your help," Ben said as the retired principal waved to them from behind her screen door. He helped Maggie into the Jeep, then sat looking at Martha Enright's number. "I'll call and leave a message as soon as we get back. I sure hope this pans out."

"Me, too." Maggie stifled a yawn. "I don't know why I'm so tired tonight."

Ben did a U-turn and headed back toward the highway. "I think it's not so much physical fatigue as mental. Attending a funeral in the morning for poor Freddy, browsing through musty old records, getting close, then having our hopes dashed constantly. All that's wiped you out."

Maggie fastened her seat belt before glancing at him. He looked as fresh as ever. "You look like you're just getting your second wind. Are you immune to the weaknesses of the flesh that we mortals fall prey to, Mr. Whalen?"

He placed a hand on her thigh suggestively. "Wait until we get back and I'll show you how immune I am to the weaknesses of the flesh." But he put his hand back on the steering wheel because a thick fog had rolled in off Lake Superior.

Maggie yawned again. "Mmm, maybe I'd better rest up." She leaned her head back and closed her eyes.

It took longer than usual to drive back to Riverview due to the fog that whirled about them nearly the whole way. It was exactly nine when Ben parked the Jeep in front of his cabin.

The sudden quiet awakened Maggie. She blinked and looked out the window, then at Ben. "Your place, eh?"

"I hoped you'd stay. I didn't wake you to ask, but if you'd rather, I'll drive you home." Which wasn't what he wanted to say at all. He'd stolen glances at her during the drive, her lovely features relaxed in sleep, and he wanted nothing more now than to take her into his big bed and lose himself in her. But as always, he would let the decision be hers. Their relationship was too tenuous, too tangled, for him to call the shots.

Maggie liked that about him, the way he never pushed when it came to this. After Chet, who'd been such a control freak, it was a refreshing change. "I want to stay, if I can call Fiona so she won't worry." Another yawn had her stretching. "I might have to have a nap before anything important happens. Otherwise, it might border on necrophilia."

Ben smiled as he opened the door. "I'm willing to bet I can take your mind off sleep."

Climbing down, Maggie was certain he could, too.

Neither noticed the person slouched down low by the steering wheel in the front seat of a dark sedan parked at the far end of the lot between two trucks. Eyes narrowed in frustration and annoyance watched Maggie and Ben walk to the cabin, then go inside. Immediately, the drapes were drawn over the wide window.

As if it mattered. Who would sneak over and watch them? One need not behold evil to know it was present. Maggie had been clean, innocent. But she'd been won over by the one who would mess up the plan.

Didn't he know that the business at hand was not over yet? Ah, but he would and, unfortunately, so would Maggie. "Repentance comes too late and revenge is sweet." The Bible pointed the way, but sinners never listened.

The dark sedan had made the trip to her house and back to the motel repeatedly all day. Then a couple of phone calls had revealed the truth. They'd gone to Marquette and Ishpeming.

What were they up to? If only they would back off until the work was done. They were getting perilously close to discov-

ering things that might delay the order of things. The mission was nearly accomplished. Only a few wicked ones remained and soon, they would be joining the others.

Those who got in the way would perish with the guilty, though they be innocent. "Let justice be done, though heaven fall."

Quietly, the sedan came to life and the driver left the lot. It wouldn't be long now.

Chapter Fifteen

"So, Pete, now you know as much as I do," Ben told his manager.

"You sound fairly certain you're on the right track with this Thurmond family lead," the impatient voice on the phone said.

"I am. Today, I plan to talk with the judge who handled the case thirty years ago and the two men left from the six who were in the car that night. Someone's going to break, I can feel it. And by the weekend, I should hear from that teacher who's vacationing in Hawaii. Hopefully she'll confirm what I've learned and be able to tell us more." The call from the Home Office had awakened him from a terrific dream he'd hated to let go of. Then he'd opened his eyes and realized the dream was reality as Maggie had stirred within the circle of his arms, then stretched lazily.

Pete Williams was thoughtfully silent for several seconds. "All right, Ben. There's no point in muddying up the waters with more guys if you're on to something. But I sure hope this breaks wide open soon. We're having one hell of a time sorting out all the requests for information on our policies from Riverview, thanks to Wilbur Oakley. And the media's hounding us like crazy."

"Tell me about it. I've got a reporter staying in the same motel and the TV people are swarming around town like ants. On the positive side, with so much attention and so many people around, it should make it more difficult for our killer to act again without being seen." He heard the shower and pictured Maggie standing there with water rolling down that great body, much like the evening he'd seen her in the waterfall. "Listen, I'd better get going." Shoving aside the sheet, Ben got out of bed.

"Right. But, Ben, you keep me informed, you hear. The suits upstairs are getting nervous."

"I will. 'Bye." He hung up and made it into the bathroom just as she turned off the shower. "Hey," he called through the steam, "don't you know there're restrictions on wasting water in this town?" In one smooth move, he stepped into the tub, took her into his arms and yanked the curtain back into place. "We need to conserve water by sharing showers."

"But I'm already clean," Maggie protested halfheartedly as her arms wound around his neck.

"I can see your education has been sadly neglected. Getting clean isn't the only reason to get into the shower." With a wicked smile, he turned the water back on.

"I thought of something during the night," Ben said as the coffee shop waitress refilled their cups.

Maggie waited until the woman left, then smiled impishly at him. "It didn't seem to me that thinking was on your mind last night at all."

The lazy smile came slowly. "You can say that again. But I mean *after* you fell asleep and *before* I woke you up again. The more I thought about it, the more I feel certain that the reason we could find no trace of Mary Thurmond is that she definitely isn't Mr. Thurmond's sister, but rather Mrs. Thurmond's, because then we'd have found *some* record of her maiden name in the county register. We discussed this yesterday both ways and I've come to believe Thurmond isn't her name. Which stalls us again since we have no idea what her real last name is or was."

"You're probably right. Judge Fulton might know. Maybe he even saw that missing file before it was misfiled."

"Or helped it to disappear, another possibility. It also occurred to me why Grady keeps putting me off and probably why the judge hasn't come forward. They both know about the accident and they know they're guilty of, at the very least, a cover-up. There'd be manslaughter charges for the driver *but* if it came out that a sheriff and a judge had conspired to cover up everything, it would effectively end their careers."

"If that's so, why isn't Grady talking now since his father's dead and the judge is retired?"

Ben finished his coffee and reached into his pocket for his money clip. "Loyalty, maybe. Or it could be that Grady doesn't want to dirty his father's reputation—or his own, for that matter. Would he be reelected if people knew he'd been involved in a cover-up of an accident that killed three people? Meantime, the judge is enjoying his retirement and is highly regarded in the community. How would people treat him if they knew the truth?"

"You have a point there. It would appear there's plenty of guilt to go around." Ben noticed the melancholy look on her face and knew she was thinking of her father's part in all this. "At least now you know what Jack probably wanted to tell you, how badly his conscience was bothering him."

"Yes." Maggie sighed. "I'm having a hard time accepting that he was involved in a thirty-year cover-up. It's not the actions of the father I knew."

"He carried a heavy burden, Maggie, for that night. And he wound up paying a high price for his silence."

Agreeing, she nodded. "I just wish he'd have confided in me." But wishing wouldn't make it so, and she knew she had to put her disturbing thoughts aside. "Where are you going now?"

"To have a talk with Judge Fulton. I was hoping you'd come with me since I've scarcely spoken to the man. As Jack's daughter, you'd be more apt to get him to open up than I." As much as he hated admitting that, it was the truth.

"I'd like to go along, but first, I really need to stop by the house and change into clean clothes." Maggie slid out of the booth as Ben got up to pay the check. The long shower helped, but she'd spent too many hours in the same clothes yesterday.

"All right, but Fiona's going to give me that look again, the one that says I shouldn't be keeping you out late, much less all night." He climbed behind the wheel.

Buckling herself in, Maggie laughed. "Hey, if the shoe fits . . ."

The two-story house on Crandall off Main Street that belonged to Judge Fulton had to be over half a century old. The bottom half was brick and the upper half covered by weathered cedar shake siding beneath a gabled black roof. A screened-in side porch looked out on a rock garden decorated with a variety of green plants, but none that flowered.

"I'm terribly allergic to bee stings," the distinguished-looking man told Maggie and Ben as he settled them on his comfortable couch. At the far end of the cozy room, a chess game was set up on a table flanked by two straight-back chairs. "I make sure there's nothing in my yard that would attract bees."

Wearing pin-striped trousers and a brocade vest over a white shirt open at the throat, the judge sat down in his favorite easy chair and turned his attention to the two young people who'd arrived on his doorstep so unexpectedly. "How are you faring, my dear?" he asked Maggie. "I want you to know I still miss Jack."

Maggie nodded in agreement. "I find myself talking to his portrait."

"Yes, of course. After my Loretta died—it's been seventeen years ago now—I'd visit her grave and have regular chats with her. Occasionally, I still do." His sharp blue eyes shifted to Ben. "And you're with National Fidelity, I understand. Are you going to take over Wilbur Oakley's agency? Terrible thing, him leaving like that."

There was a hint of the South in the judge's voice, Ben noticed. "Yes, it was, but I actually work for the Home Office as an insurance investigator." He was watching the man closely, but there wasn't a flicker of unusual interest about what he'd just heard. However, since Ben had been in Riverview for months now, perhaps the judge already knew more about him than he planned to reveal. "It seems quite a few of our clients who made their home in Riverview have met unexpected deaths recently. You probably knew them all."

"Yes. They were my business associates and my dear friends. So many tragic accidents." The judge suddenly remembered his social manners. "Would either of you care for a cup of coffee or tea? Perhaps a cold drink? It's already hot and it's not yet noon."

They both shook their heads, then Maggie jumped in. "Judge, we need your help. We're convinced that my father and the others didn't die accidentally, but that someone is responsible for their deaths. Someone who may live right here in Riverview."

One of the judge's rather shaggy brows rose in question. "You're suggesting murder, here in Riverview, and by someone we know? Oh, I can't believe that."

Ben was growing impatient and decided to cut to the chase. "Judge Fulton, we've learned that about thirty years ago, there was an auto accident on Highway 35 just before the fork leading to Marquette. It was at the end of the Thanksgiving weekend and six college students from NMU were in one car. All were injured, but not seriously and all recovered. The other car contained four people, three who died and one survivor, a child of eight or ten. Their name was Thurmond."

The judge cleared his throat and crossed his thin legs, carefully arranging the crease just so. "I seem to recall that incident, yes. But what has that to do with Jack and the others all dying lately?"

Sensing the older man's unease and hoping he wouldn't refuse to continue, Maggie took up the story, thinking her tone was softer than Ben's who was used to interrogating rather than questioning. "Ben and I have done some investigating and we think that the child who survived the accident might have changed identities and moved to Riverview with the express purpose of taking vengeance on the six who'd been in the car that killed the others."

Waving a dismissing hand, the judge gave a grunt of disbelief. "I think you're way off track. What occurred that night was an accident and, yes, three people died. Accidents do happen and when you take into consideration the weather and road conditions, it's amazing that more didn't die. Even so, why would this person wait thirty years for revenge, if in fact that's what it is? No, no, the whole thing's preposterous." But his hand shook as he reached into his vest pocket, pulled out an old-fashioned pocket watch, and checked the time.

Ben guessed that they were about to be dismissed, so he hurried on. "Judge, I've spoken with George Cannata and he told me the whole story." He watched as Fulton's head raised and his face seemed to take on a weariness. "George said that the six of them had all been drinking, that they'd challenged another car to play a game called chicken, to see who would give in first. The other car lost interest and drove off. Then suddenly the Thurmonds' car was smack dab in front of the boys and they couldn't avoid hitting it. And he also told me that Grady's father appeared with them in your chambers along with their attorney, Homer Cromwell. George went so far as to suggest that together you and Henry Denton saw to it that all charges against the boys were dismissed. Is that true?"

"No." The word was said quietly, but with unmistakable authority reminiscent of the judge's courtroom presence. He got to his feet and walked to the far end of the room, then turned back to face the two young people. Chickens always come home to roost, his father had often told him many years ago. How true, Fulton thought. Again, he cleared his throat. "Your implication here is that there was a misdeed, and I not only resent that, but I wish to clarify what happened."

Ben decided at this point a little soothing of ruffled feathers was in order if he was to get what he needed from this man. "I meant no disrespect, Judge."

"Mmm. At any rate, Sheriff Denton—Grady's father—came to me and told me what happened. The boys were driving back to college after spending the Thanksgiving weekend with their families. Drinking was never mentioned. He'd taken the boys to Cromwell, who in turn took depositions from all six stating that the Thurmond car hit them, not the other way around. Now understand that we have six fine young men, all from good families, honor students attending the university. I had no reason then, nor do I have now, to not believe them."

Fulton paused a moment to give Ben an icy glare, totally ignoring Maggie by now. "When the aunt of the surviving child filed a wrongful death suit, intending I'm sure to attach the assets of the families of all six of these young men on be-half of the minor child, I had no choice but to dismiss the case without prejudice. I don't know how familiar you are with the law, young man, but when you have *six* sworn state-ments from *six* fine, upstanding young citizens, all stating the same thing, and nothing from any other witness since the surviving child apparently was asleep at the time of the acci-dent and badly injured afterward, there is no case. While my sympathies went out to the aunt burdened with this responsi-bility, I could do nothing for her."

It's a smart man who knows when he's licked, Ben thought as he stared back at the judge. There was a great deal the older man wasn't telling and most probably he was even rearranging the facts. Of course, George could have been wrong about which car was at fault, too, but it seemed un-likely that he'd fabricate a story that would implicate him-self. No, the judge was in on the cover-up, along with his good friend, Sheriff Henry Denton, and all six young men in that car. But proving that was another story.

"It's just so odd, you know," Ben couldn't help adding. "Maggie and I went to the courthouse in Marquette and the entire file on the Thurmond case is nowhere to be found."

The judge's gaze didn't waver. "Files get lost all the time, unfortunately."

Or fortunately for the party who took it, Ben thought. "One more question. Do you recall the name of the aunt who filed the suit on behalf of the child, Lee Thurmond?"

"I'm afraid I don't remember." The voice was cool, tired.

Rising, Ben offered his hand to the judge. "Thank you for seeing us."

Silently, Judge Fulton briefly shook Ben's hand, then found a small smile for Maggie. But as she looked up at him, his smile faltered, became shaky, and he took a step back. "Maggie, you know how fond I was of your father, and the others. Nevertheless, I hope you believe I wouldn't do anything illegal, not even to protect good friends. I took the facts as they were given to me, interpreted them according to the letter of the law, and made my ruling. Thirty years later, I stand behind my actions."

Something there, in his eyes, Maggie thought. A suspicious brightness, but more. Was it guilt? She searched for something noncommittal to say. "My father always spoke very highly of you, Judge Fulton."

Taking another step back, the judge nodded, then slowly turned to gaze out at his yard. "I'm sure you can find your way out."

There was nothing more to be said. Ben took Maggie's hand and they left Judge Perry Fulton alone with his memories and his regrets. They were in the Jeep before either of them spoke.

"What do you think?" Maggie asked as Ben backed out of the drive. "Is he guilty of a cover-up, did he take that file or see to it that it disappeared? And does he honestly think he did the right thing?"

"Oh, he's convinced himself he did the right thing. Almost. But for my money, he's as guilty as the others." He drove down the quiet side street slowly, his mind recapping the judge's words.

"Ben." Maggie's voice had a little hitch in it. "I need to ask you something."

"All right, shoot."

"When George told you the story of what happened that night with the six of them in the car on the way back to NMU, did he tell you which one of them was driving?"

He'd been wondering when she'd ask and realized how afraid of the answer she was. "No, he wouldn't tell me. I asked if he knew and he said yes, that all of them knew, but they made a pact that all were guilty, not just one. Because of the drinking, because the other five had egged the driver on to challenge the first car to the game of chicken. Apparently, they didn't even tell their families the whole story later when they married."

Maggie let out a ragged breath. "Their loyalty to one another doesn't surprise me. Despite what happened, I believe they were men of their word." She felt a headache coming on and absently rubbed her brow. "Maybe there are those who wouldn't feel there was anything to admire about those six when they were young, especially when this story comes out, but later, when I knew them, they were good and honorable men."

Ben reached over and squeezed her hand. "I believe you. It's ironic, isn't it, that one small mistake can affect the rest of your life, and the lives of the people you love, the children you later have, everyone. As we said earlier, I imagine that every one of the six lived every day with a deep sense of regret."

"I wonder if the person who's killing them systematically has any regret? I wonder how he can keep on taking lives, seeing the pain he's causing, and still live among us here in Riverview and pretend nothing's wrong. What kind of person can do that, kill one person after another, then go home and eat dinner, maybe watch television, mingle with his neighbors as if nothing out of the ordinary happened?"

"A psychopath or a sociopath. Take your pick. The world, unfortunately, is full of them. The thing that worries me here is that our man is escalating. The killings are occurring more and more frequently."

"That's right. There were three months between Reed's death and Dad's, and since then, my Lord, it seems like there's one a week."

"I think we can go back farther than that." Ben swung the Jeep into the parking lot behind the sheriff's office and turned off the engine. "I believe his first victim was Grady's father last fall."

"If that's so, why would he wait until March to kill again?"

Ben shook his head. "Only he can answer that one. I'm not sure what Warren Harper's involvement is, but the only one that I feel was an unintentional killing was Freddy. I think Freddy was in the wrong place at the wrong time and the intended victim was George Cannata."

Maggie drew in a deep breath. "My God, Ben, someone needs to warn George to be extra careful. This guy will try again."

"Someone did warn him. Me. Do you know what his reaction was?"

"No, what?"

"He laughed. He told me again how proficient he is with guns, even has two hidden behind his counter at the drugstore, plus one in his glove compartment and often straps a small thirty-eight to his ankle."

"Sounds like he's expecting to need them. Didn't you say he drank quite a bit when you were there that evening? A man who has loaded guns around, then drinks is an accident waiting to happen. Someone could get a jump on him while his reflexes are slowed down from alcohol and get him with his own gun."

"Entirely possible."

Maggie looked out the window for the first time since getting caught up in their conversation and saw that they were in the sheriff's parking lot. "What are we doing here?"

"While you changed clothes, I called J.C. and asked when Grady would be in today. All day, he told me. I intend to go in there and pin the sheriff down about all this, see if he'll open up."

Maggie shoved open her door. "This I've got to see."

Grady's sandy hair looked as if his big hands had thrust through the thinning strands more than once recently as he glanced up and saw Ben and Maggie in his doorway. He nearly moaned out loud. "What are you doing here again, Whalen? I've got nothing to say to you, as I've said more than once." He went back to thumbing through folders in his file drawer, searching for a particular one.

Ignoring his nonwelcome, Ben walked in and folded his long frame in the wooden chair, motioning Maggie to the one next to his. "You can run, Grady, but you can't hide from me forever. I know what happened that Sunday night after Thanksgiving thirty years ago."

Grady went still, even his fingertips going motionless. Slowly, his head swiveled and he looked at Ben. He fancied himself pretty good at reading the truth on a man's face, and Ben's eyes looked confident and unafraid. He wished he could say the same for his.

With a quick, snapping motion, he closed the side drawer and leaned back in his chair. "Just what is it you think you know?"

God, but he was getting tired of the bullshit. "You know damn well what. I know about the auto accident, the head-on collision involving a car you and five other college boys were in and the Thurmond family in the other vehicle that snowy night. Why couldn't you have been honest and up front with me from the get-go, Grady? Maybe together, we could have saved a few lives."

Grady bought himself some time as he dug in his pocket for a toothpick and stuck it into the corner of his mouth. After several moments of consideration, he decided the best defense was an offense. "Look, I don't have time for your dime-store detective theories today. I got the County Board of Supervisors on my back, going over every damn piece of paper in and out of here since God was a child on account of this Freddy Richmond killing. I got the goddamn media camping outside my office *and* my house. I got the phone ringing constantly, reporters, TV people, and just plain nosy folks. And this morning, I got a representative from the state attorney general's office waiting for me when I came in, demanding answers. Get in line, boy. Everyone wants a piece of my ass."

Ben felt Maggie flinch at Grady's tirade but he knew it for the smoke screen it was. He'd had bigger guys than this small-town sheriff try to bluff him when he'd worked vice. "Tell me what you know about that surviving kid, Grady. Let me get to work on this. I need a name, the aunt's, someone. I swear, if anyone else loses his life because you couldn't *find the time* to talk with me, I'll report you myself for obstruction of justice."

Grady straightened in his chair so quickly they all heard the springs pop right before he started yelling. "Get out of my office. I have work to do. Get out now, or I'll personally escort you out!"

Bullheaded and stubborn. "All right, Grady. Let's hope you don't wind up regretting this." Reaching for Maggie's hand, he walked out of the sheriff's office and closed the door.

Grady sank back into his chair, the wind gone from his sails. The whole damn world was crashing in on him and he had nowhere to turn.

Swiveling his chair around, he stared up at the portrait of his father, Sheriff Henry Denton, standing tall, looking invincible, and just a shade cocky. "I don't know how much longer I'm going to be able to keep the wolves at bay, Daddy," Grady whispered.

"Maybe he left on a vacation," Maggie suggested. "Maybe he got to thinking about what you said and decided to absent himself from the area for a while and let things cool off. Or he could have gone hunting, which he does frequently."

"I don't think so," Ben said as they drove toward George Cannata's home. "Hunting season is in the fall."

They'd stopped for lunch at Rosie's and he'd phoned George at the drugstore to ask if he could meet with him after hours. But his assistant had said that Mr. Cannata hadn't been in all day, nor had he phoned in. "When I asked the pharmacist if it was unusual for George to just take off without notice, he said that it was highly unusual."

"So you think George is holed up at home, more frightened than he let on?"

Or worse. "We'll soon see."

At three in the afternoon, the residential tree-lined street was quiet, as if dozing in the sun. A skinny dog ambled past the vacant lot next door to George's where Freddy had died, and didn't even glance their way as Ben brought the Jeep to a stop.

"What do you plan to ask him?" Maggie wanted to know as she followed him up the walk.

"More details about that night and to try to impress him with the need to watch his back. All three of the remaining men should." He stepped on the porch and noted that the front door was closed even though the other evening, it had been open to allow air to drift in through the screen.

"Three? Grady, George, and who else?"

"What about Judge Fulton?"

"Oh, I forgot." The nightmare seemed to Maggie as if it would never end. And George had laughed at Ben's warning, Grady had just blown them off saying he had no time, and the judge had said he was satisfied that he'd done the right thing, as if that would keep him forever out of harm's way.

Ben pressed the bell again and heard the faint echo inside. Moving along the porch, he tried to peer in the front window, but all he could see was his own image. "Come on, let's go around back. His porch is screened in with louvered windows. There's a television in there. Maybe it's on and he can't hear the bell." He hoped that was the case.

"Or maybe he's not home. Did you ever think of that?"

Walking along the driveway, he spotted the detached garage. "Let's check." No windows to peer in, but the handle on the garage door turned easily enough. Ben gave it a yank and up it went. A tan Dodge four-door took up most of the space. Just to satisfy the uneasy feeling he had, he stepped in and checked. The car was empty. Outside again, he pulled the door back into place. "Okay, so his car's here. He should be, too."

"Unless he went hunting with a friend who picked him up."

"Without telling anyone at the store about his trip? Doubtful." Ben moved along the edge of the screened porch, noting that the louvered windows were all closed. He could see no one, but a dim light shone through the archway. "It's only three and the sun's shining. Why would he have a lamp on?" His instincts, honed over years as a cop, told him something definitely didn't look right.

"People often leave lamps burning when they go away, Ben, so the house won't appear empty." Fear, Maggie decided, was making her think up rebuttals for each of his questions. Fear that he was right and she was wrong, that something terrible had happened to George Cannata despite his protests that he could take care of himself.

At the back door alongside the porch, Ben checked out the lock. No dead bolt. It'd be simpler to break in than to break the door. But if George was asleep and they surprised him, he might just be mad enough to report him for breaking and entering. But, listening to that small inner voice that seldom led him astray, he decided to do the deed and explain later.

"Look the other way," he told Maggie.

"Why?"

"Because I'm going to break in and if you don't see me do it, you won't be involved."

"Ben, do you think you should . . . ?" The sound of breaking glass told her she was a shade late with her doubts. She watched Ben reach in through the hole in the glass, fiddle with the lock, and open the door from inside.

"Maybe you should wait here," he suggested, not at all sure what he'd find inside.

"I've come this far. I'm going with you." It was darn spooky out here, too close to the vacant lot where Freddy had been knifed right next door.

Ben pushed the door open. He held it wide and walked in cautiously. "George, are you here?" Ben called out. Only silence.

He bypassed the basement stairs leading down, walked up the two steps into the kitchen and looked into the dining room through the archway straight ahead. He guessed that the bedrooms and bath were down the hall off to the right. Six of one and half a dozen of another as to which way to go, he thought and moved forward.

He could see a lamp burning on an end table in the living room. On the far wall of the dining room was the glass-enclosed gun case that he'd seen the other evening from the porch. Several guns were on the dining-room table, lying on a heavy pad. A can of gun oil sat next to an open bottle of beer, and the armchair at the head of the table was pulled out.

And sprawled on the floor alongside a rifle was George Cannata, his face blown off.

Registering the room's contents in split seconds, Ben turned quickly, hoping to catch Maggie before she stepped in. But he was too late for she'd been right behind him, peering over his shoulder. "Come on, let's get out of here."

But she stood, rooted to the spot, her face drained of color. Then she let out a scream that died in her throat as she began to sway.

Ben caught her just before she hit the floor.

Chapter Sixteen

Ben followed J.C. out the back door of George Cannata's house and watched him carefully place the shotgun wrapped in a large evidence bag in the back of his Ford Bronco. Turning, he checked on Maggie seated in his Jeep. She was exactly as he'd left her, unmoving, head tilted back and eyes closed. Her absolute stillness, her silence, worried him. He'd have preferred that she scream, cry, anything but this utter quiet. Shock, Ben knew, affected people in different ways. But this was eerie.

"Too bad she had to see George like that," J.C. said, joining him alongside the Jeep.

"Yeah, I know. I blame myself for exposing her to that scene."

Peering through the tinted windows, J.C., too, became worried. "Do you want me to call Carrie and have her meet you at Maggie's? Maybe another woman . . ."

"Thanks, but I'll take care of her. How's Carrie doing?"

"She's out of the hospital, recuperating at home. Most everything's healed except her broken arm, of course. She's already talking about going in to the shop."

Ben shook his head. "Looks like you've got a strong-willed woman on your hands."

J.C. tipped his head in Maggie's direction. "Looks like you do, too."

Frowning, Ben followed his gaze. "No, it's not like that with us. I mean, we're close and all, but it's different. I'm sure when this is over, Maggie will go back to New York, and me? Well, hell, I travel six weeks out of eight. No, it wouldn't work." But not for the reasons he'd stated. "You, on the other hand, have been nuts about Carrie forever."

J.C. nodded. "And finally, she's looking at me like a man instead of her father's deputy."

"About what happened in the woods, any nightmares, feelings of regret, anything?" He'd been wondering.

"No, nothing. I did the right thing, thanks to you. I suppose I should be worried, afraid I may lose control again one day, and that wouldn't be good in my line of work. But I don't think I will. It's different when someone you care about is involved." He saw the ambulance pull up behind Ben's Jeep. "One day when you have some time, let's have a beer and you can tell me your story. Because I know you have one or you wouldn't have worked so hard to stop me. I owe you, buddy."

Ben got out his keys. "You don't owe me anything." It might very well be the other way around. Watching J.C. as an outsider, he'd recognized the demon that had once lived inside him. Maybe the deputy was right and it was possible to conquer the monster. "I'm going to take Maggie to my place, if you need me for anything."

"I'll be in touch. I'm having the body taken right to Doc Fielding's for an autopsy. I'd like to know just how much Cannata had to drink, for one thing. You said there'd been no sign of a forced entry, so he obviously had to know his killer and invite him in."

"I would think so. By the way, where's Grady?"

"He had a meeting with the guy from the attorney general's office, told me to take the call. He's got a lot on his plate right now."

Too much to visit a crime scene where a close friend just bought the farm? "I hope he's not going to try to label this an accidental shooting. George may have been cleaning his gun, but the angle, the projectory is all wrong."

J.C. agreed. "That's why I took all those pictures. The killer made a halfhearted stab at trying to make it look like an accident, but no expert on guns cleans his rifle while it's loaded. This is a clear-cut homicide."

Ben opened the Jeep's door. "I sure hope you can convince Grady." He climbed behind the wheel.

"I may need your testimony as to how you two found the body."

"Sure. You know where to find me." Ben shifted into gear and drove off.

J.C. called to the attendants with their gurney and equipment and led the way around back.

She wasn't asleep, Ben knew, as he drove to his cabin. He didn't want to leave her with Fiona, concerned that the hovering housekeeper might upset Maggie more. He'd seen all sorts of cases of shock and knew some people would spin out of control for a short period of time, then end up sobbing. Still others would retreat into a quiet place in their heads to escape the trauma of what they'd witnessed, and it might be hours before they'd emerge to try to cope with their pain. Maggie seemed to fall into the second category, but he had no idea how long this first quiet phase would last.

The gravel crunched beneath the tires of the Jeep as he pulled into the parking lot. He noticed that Maggie stirred, her hand going to her throat, her breathing suddenly erratic. He stopped in front of his door and turned to her. "Maggie, I'm going to take you inside."

She didn't answer, just coughed into her fist, and began to tremble.

Ben hopped out and helped her down, then opened his door. Still coughing, she rushed past him into the bathroom and closed the door after herself. He heard gagging sounds and realized she was sick. He tossed his keys on the dresser, then stepped outside to the Coke machine and got two cold ones.

Back inside, he popped a can open for her, pulled back the bedspread, and drew the drapes, closing out the setting sun and any prying eyes. He turned the bedside lamp on low just as she came out.

"I used your toothbrush," she said softly, walking hesitantly into the room.

"That's fine." He saw that she'd rinsed off her face, noticed her hands were shaking. "Here, drink some Coke. It'll settle your stomach."

Obedient as a child, she took several sips before handing back the can. The oversize blue shirt she wore seemed to hang on her, making her look fragile, and he wondered if she realized she'd lost some weight over the past several weeks. She stood looking uncertain, pushing her hair back from her face.

"What do you want to do, Maggie? Do you want to talk it through or lie down and nap? Something to eat? Tell me." Odd how he couldn't seem to recall feeling quite so helpless in a long while.

Finally, she raised her eyes filled with sadness to his. "I just want you to hold me. Would you, please?"

He scooted onto the bed, his back to the headboard and held her curled into him, her head resting on his chest right over his heart. She was small and vulnerable and he felt a rush of anger that he couldn't have prevented still another trauma from happening to her. She didn't deserve so much pain.

He'd thought she'd go to sleep, giving in to fatigue and a need to escape reality for a short time, but instead, within minutes, he felt the dampness on his shirt and realized she was crying without making a sound. His hand caressed her back, letting her know he was there and he understood. "Let it out, Maggie. Let it all out."

It took several minutes before the storm inside her truly burst free. Her hands bunched in the material of his shirt as hard sobs shook her. The sounds she made were primal, revealing a deep agony and utter helplessness. The tears flowed and she was unable to stop them, crying out for her dead father, for all the other victims, for the injustice of it all.

She let out the fury that had her by the throat, as she railed at the madman who was wreaking such havoc on so many good people. It seemed that once she'd unleashed the dormant outrage, there was no stopping the deluge. She felt powerless, impotent, robbed of all defenses.

Later, Maggie couldn't have said how long she cried, then finally sniffled and at last stopped, moving into hiccuping breaths that shook her whole body. She'd hoped to feel cleansed but instead felt ashamed that she'd given in to self-pity when others had lost more.

Edging back from Ben, she looked around for a tissue and noticed the handkerchief he held out to her. Eyes downcast, she mopped her blotchy face and shoved back her hair, sitting up, unable to meet his concerned gaze. "I'm sorry. I've never . . . I rarely lose it like that. Not even when Dad died. But . . ."

"But you've had a hell of a shock and you're entitled." Ben took hold of her shoulders and turned her to face him. "Don't apologize. There's no need." Placing two fingers on her chin, he tipped her face up. "Do you feel any better?"

"I don't know." She shook her head. "There's so much I don't know." She closed her eyes. "I wonder if I'll ever be able to forget seeing George like that."

"The memory will ease after awhile. Take it from someone who's been there."

Of course. He'd seen his wife beaten and no longer breathing. God, how could she have forgotten? Maggie opened her eyes. He was so understanding, so good to her, setting aside his own bad memories. She reached up and placed a hand on his cheek, loving the feel of him. Suddenly she knew exactly what she needed, what would chase the ugliness away. "Make love with me, Ben, please. Make me forget."

He knew what she was feeling exactly. When a person saw death firsthand, a part of the shock was facing their own mortality. And what better way to reaffirm that we're alive than by making love, the elemental way of celebrating life?

With two hands, he gripped the hem of his shirt damp from her tears and yanked it off over his head, tossing it aside before gathering her to him. He kissed her tear-swollen lips and felt her instant response. As his mouth made love to hers, gently, carefully, his hands busily unbuttoned her shirt and eased off her bra. She rubbed her breasts along his chest, arousing them both.

It was a struggle, removing both their clothes and still not breaking the kiss, but Ben managed it with much wiggling and squirming. Flesh to flesh at last, he realized she wanted to take over, *needed* to, and he let her.

Her hair falling forward like a curtain, Maggie rained kisses on his strong, lean body, working her way down, lingering where she fancied, then slowly moving back up. When he was no longer able to lie still, she smiled, then went back to work, tugging with teeth and tongue on his nipples, nipping at his earlobes and always returning to his mouth. That wonderful mouth that could work such magic on her.

Long moments later, she got up on her knees and straddled him, pausing to look deeply into his silvery eyes, as shiny with need as her own. Finally she took him inside, completely, until they were as close as two shadows. Then she began to move.

Ben watched her toss her beautiful head back, her hair dancing along her shoulders, her lips slightly open as she concentrated. He reached for her, but she stopped his hands. This was her show and she was calling the shots.

Her movements became faster, more frantic. Changing her mind, she took his hands and placed them on her aroused breasts, never dropping the rhythm. Panting now, he met her thrust for thrust, his vision blurring as he felt himself on the verge. Her damp skin shimmered in the glow of the soft light as she moved toward the finish line, her eyes on his.

Seconds later, he felt her shudder and jolt, then collapse forward onto him as he let himself go, holding nothing back. Awareness slipped out of his control just after he felt her lips at his throat and heard her low whisper. "I love you," she said.

Ben lay there in the aftermath, his body still experiencing the waves, his mind clearing more rapidly than usual. The sex had been beautiful, everything he could have ever wanted. Maggie was beautiful and everything a man could want.

But she'd said the words that put fear in his heart.

Perhaps he'd been stupid and naive, thinking they could care for each other, enjoy a great physical relationship, then part as good friends. Was that concept not possible between two consenting adults, a mature man and woman? Why did love and all that went with it—most likely marriage and a forever commitment—have to be a part of the equation?

It wasn't as if he hadn't been honest with Maggie. He'd told her from the start that he wasn't interested in the long term. He'd also told her he had trouble staying away from her, that he wanted her in his bed and in other ways. For now.

It was the forever part that scared the hell out of him.

Because there was no such thing as forever after. People changed their minds, fell out of love, divorced and got hurt, died and left someone grieving and alone and hurting. Which was why he'd decided after Kathy that he needed to stay alone, difficult as the loneliness was at times to handle. Because getting involved, then losing that love for whatever reason, hurt infinitely more. The first time had devastated him. He wasn't sure he'd survive a second time.

But how was he going to tell Maggie all this at a time when she was so vulnerable? Round and round his thoughts raced, like mice in a maze, frantically looking for a way out.

Maggie sensed the change in him and knew exactly what had caused his withdrawal. She hadn't meant to say the words she'd been thinking and feeling, the words she knew might make him turn away. They'd slipped out because her heart had been so full of him, because her defenses were down, because a part of her wanted desperately for him to know.

Well, she'd found out, all right. She'd felt, deep inside, that he'd change his mind, but that hadn't happened. He didn't want love, didn't want to even hear the word. She should have known better, should have heeded his earlier warning. But, as it was often said, love makes you stupid, makes you take desperate measures.

Perhaps it was best she found out now before she made six kinds of a fool of herself. She would get up, get dressed, and go home. She wouldn't let him know how hurt she was, because it wasn't his fault, not really. You couldn't force a man to love you if he truly wasn't interested. Ben enjoyed her in bed, that much was obvious. He even enjoyed her company, or so it seemed. But that was it, the whole package with no extras.

Fiona had advised her to speak up or she might live the rest of her life regretting that she hadn't. That hadn't worked with Ben and it most probably wouldn't have worked on her father, either. Still, she couldn't regret speaking what was in her heart.

She'd heard it said that if you love someone, you let them go. If they come back to you, it was real and meant to be. If they don't return, there was never any love at all. She was about to put that old adage to the test.

Rolling off him, Maggie got up, quickly gathered her clothes, and went into the bathroom.

Damn! Dressing, Ben wanted to slam his fist into something very hard. Maggie was no dummy; he knew she sensed something was wrong. It wasn't in her to press, to make things difficult for him. She'd probably put on a smile, say thanks and so long, letting him off the hook.

Why, then, did he feel like a rotten heel?

The bathroom door opened and Maggie came out, still brushing her hair. "Ben," she began, "I'm pretty beat. Would you mind driving me home?" Eyes on her purse as she put her brush away, she waited, heart pounding.

What could he say? What could he do that would take that wounded look from her face, yet not mess up his life? Nothing. "Sure." He grabbed his keys and held open the door for her.

The drive to the Spencer house was short and quiet. For the life of him, Ben couldn't think of a thing to say. Even parked in her circular driveway, his mind simply stayed locked down. When he saw her hand on the door, he dared look at her face. Just as he'd predicted, she wore a sad smile. "Maggie, I . . ."

"No, Ben. Let's not talk any more right now. Thanks for getting me through a rough time. Good night." And she jumped out quickly, trying desperately to beat the tears that she finally let fall as she stepped inside and closed the door behind her. "Oh, God," she whispered into the dark, lonely night.

Ben stood down a ways from McCauley's Funeral Home as

he watched the mourners trickle out. He'd opted not to go in to pay his respects to George Cannata whose closed-casket service had just ended. He'd attended far too many funerals in this small town. And he hadn't wanted to run into Maggie.

But there was no avoiding her in a small town. He saw her walk out with Carrie, whose one arm was still in a cast, although her bruises had healed nicely. J.C. was on Carrie's other side as the threesome paused to talk. But Ben had eyes only for Maggie.

It'd been a full week since he'd seen her. She was stunning as always, this time in black with that cloud of blond hair and those long, slender legs that just a short time ago had felt so good wrapped around him. He couldn't see her eyes for they were hidden behind sunglasses. She seemed to be listening intently to something J.C. was saying, her face composed, distant, unsmiling. He'd brought that look to her, Ben thought. There'd be a price to pay. There always was. He wondered if she was hurting half as much as he was.

He'd made the right choice, he reminded himself, for her sake as well as his. But right choices weren't necessarily the easy ones.

Ben strolled around the milling crowd, not wanting to risk a face-to-face encounter with Maggie just now. He was almost past the building when he spotted Grady standing alone, chewing on one of his ever-present toothpicks, his face an unreadable mask, eyes hidden behind sunglasses. In his present mood, Ben relished the thought of an encounter with the evasive sheriff.

"Sheriff," he said, none too quietly, "so nice to see you out and about."

Grady turned, saw who was talking, and his teeth clamped down hard on his toothpick. "What do you want, Whalen?"

"Just this. I want to know why you aren't doing one damn thing to find the person killing all your friends. Or do you think George Cannata pointed the business end of his rifle toward his head and then pulled the trigger with his big toe?" His tone was as accusatory as his words, but he didn't give a damn. Something had to get through Grady's thick skull.

Opal broke away from a small group of women she'd been chatting with and came alongside Grady, taking her husband's arm in a possessive, protective gesture. "Mr. Whalen, why don't you let the sheriff do his job and you go about yours?"

Ben allowed himself a small, mean smile. "I'd be happy to, ma'am, if only he would. Seems all Sheriff Denton does is hide his head in the sand." He was aware that several people who'd been standing around outside the mortuary had turned toward them.

Grady noticed that folks were listening, too. Color moving up past his shirt collar, he took a step closer to Ben, jabbing him in the chest with his finger. "You get out of my face, boy, d'you hear?" With that, he shrugged off Opal's hand, marched over to his Bronco, fired it up, and zoomed off in a cloud of dust.

Opal just stared after her husband for several heartbeats, then glared at Ben. "Are you happy now?"

"I'd be a hell of a lot happier if I could get him to talk with me, tell me what he knows. It might just save his life." Knowing he had no business starting in on Grady's innocent wife, Ben turned and headed for his Jeep.

As he passed the open door to McCauley's, he couldn't help but notice that Maggie was staring after him, her stance stiff and disapproving. Had she changed sides, too? Why wouldn't anyone listen to him? Ben wondered. The killer was probably back there in that pack of people, laughing up his sleeve. And no one but Ben thought to be concerned.

At the parking lot, he paused. Lucy Hanover was sitting on her front porch. He crossed over to her, wondering if he was still welcome in at least one place in this town. "Lucy, you're back. Good to see you." He strolled up her walk.

She smiled at him from her porch swing. "Hello, young man. Come sit a spell."

He did just that, choosing the bentwood rocker across from her. "How was your trip?"

"Wonderful the first week. I miss my daughter and grandchildren so much when I'm here at home. But after five or six days, I got to tell you, those energetic little kids plumb wear me out."

Ben let her ramble on without comment since he had very little experience with children.

"Yes, indeed. My eight-year-old grandson swims like a fish, diving off the high board. Like to scare me to death just watching. And the three-year-old girl is never still a minute, nor is she ever quiet." Lucy sighed. "It'll take me a week to rest up from my vacation." She laughed at herself, then looked him over. "You look a little tired yourself, Ben. I guess you haven't caught the killer yet, since talk is that George was his latest victim. I couldn't make myself go over."

"No, we haven't caught him yet. I got a message that you'd called me before you left, but you said it wasn't urgent. Did you remember something?"

"Nothing specific. Just thought you might update me on what you've learned so far and maybe I can fill in the holes for you. I've lived in this town long enough to know just about everyone. This rampage has to be stopped. There's a maniac loose here. And you're no closer?"

"Well, I think I'm on to something, but I keep running into dead ends." Settling back, he told her all that he'd discovered so far during his visit to Marquette and Ishpeming, his whole frustrating search. "Do you recall that accident?"

"Oh, certainly. My first husband, John, had an avid interest in the law and so we followed the case closely, especially since his cousin was the court reporter at the hearing. Couldn't really call it a trial it was over so fast. I've always thought Henry Denton and Perry Fulton got their heads together and saw to it that those six boys got off scot free. They were good friends, you know, Henry and Perry. Grew up together in the South somewhere."

Ben wasn't surprised. "You think the boys caused the accident and not the driver of the other car, as they swore in their depositions?"

Lucy patted her white curls. "Well, I'm not one to go around pointing fingers, but let's just say that those six had a reputation from Marquette to Riverview and beyond for being a wild bunch. Certainly everyone in town knew that."

"What about the Thurmonds?"

"Terribly sad. Three of them died and that poor child was at death's door for weeks. They'd been visiting a relative in Ishpeming, as I recall, for the holiday and were on their way home. It was a rotten night, an unexpectedly heavy snowfall. Of course, anyone can veer off the road when conditions are bad. We heard that Mr. Thurmond was an auto mechanic who'd just lost his job and had no insurance, according to the aunt's testimony. Still, a family man's usually a careful driver, you know."

"You'd think so. The newspaper account I found said the sister's name was Mary, but no last name was listed. Do you remember if she was Mr. Thurmond's sister, or his wife's?"

"I believe the wife's because the last name was different. John's cousin told us she was a spinster and looked the part with this severe hairdo, tight-lipped, carried a Bible with her. What was her name? Let me think."

"It'd sure help if you could remember."

Lucy frowned thoughtfully, but finally shook her head. "It escapes me, truly. I'll try again later and maybe it'll come to me. It's a familiar name, I do remember that. Not foreign sounding or difficult. Mary wasn't a friendly person, we were told. She made no bones about hating to have to raise that poor child. She'd never held a real job, she told the judge. She was a seamstress, working out of the house she'd inherited from her parents. Oh, and she supplemented her income by raising bees and selling the honey. Even so, she said she didn't make enough to feed two mouths. Nevertheless, she didn't get a cent from the families of the boys no matter how she pleaded. It didn't seem right, but Perry Fulton dismissed the case, the old stuffed shirt. I never trusted that man."

"I guess I've got to drive back up to Marquette and see if I can find the case in the courthouse files. That's the only way I can think of to obtain the aunt's name. Without her, I'm having a terrible time tracing the kid."

"Well, of course the child's name was Lee Thurmond."

"Yes, but it's easy enough to get a name changed. Frankly, I think that Lee Thurmond's here in Riverview, using another name, and has been stalking these men and ultimately killing them one by one. At first, each death appeared accidental, but a shotgun blast to the face is seldom an accident."

"Oh, and I heard that poor Freddy was killed with his own knife while I was gone. Do you suppose his death's connected?"

"Yes, I do. It happened in the lot next to George's house, then the next thing you know, the killer returned and shot George. I tried to warn him, but he was so sure he could take care of himself."

"That old fool. Just as stubborn as my first husband. He died when a burglar broke into our home demanding our money. John stood up to him without a weapon and was shot on the spot. The young man got so frightened he ran off without a dime. Thank God, he didn't harm me or our two baby girls."

"You've been widowed a long time, haven't you?"

Lucy nodded. "That was the first time. Then five years later, I met Paul Hanover. A dearer man you'd never find. He married me and became a real father to my two girls. I was too young the first time, only sixteen. But Paul was my real love. He died four years ago, but I have wonderful memories. You know the kind I mean, I'm sure. I'd rather have spent ten minutes in Paul's company than ten weeks with any other man. When you find a person like that, you have to grab 'em up before they get away and you're left with only regrets."

She couldn't know about his strained relationship with Maggie, yet it seemed as if her words were meant for him alone. "What if you can't be everything that person deserves? What if they're better off without you?"

The old woman's shrewd blue eyes studied him a long moment. "I never met a woman yet who was better off without the man she loves, young man."

Ben decided he'd probably overstayed his welcome. Rising, he managed a smile. "Thanks for trying to help, Lucy."

She continued to take his measure through her glasses. "Don't let all this get you down, Ben. Life's too short to spend all your time worrying, and I think you're a worrier."

"You're probably right. I'll be seeing you." Ben strolled off toward the parking lot, his busy mind churning.

On a dusty dirt road filled with potholes on the outskirts of town, a dark sedan made its way bumping along, the driver scanning both sides of the deserted street. It wasn't long before the car slowed as skid marks became visible, wandering off the lane and zigzagging through the scrub grass. The sedan stopped opposite a skinny tree nearly bent in half by a vehicle that had rammed into it at an undoubtedly high speed.

The front end of the black Ford Bronco was smashed in and steam was pouring out from the crushed radiator. Slumped behind the wheel was Sheriff Grady Denton, a trickle of blood sliding down the side of his face.

The driver of the sedan smiled and spoke aloud into the si-

*lence of a hot summer day. "Almost. It's almost over. 'May
God have mercy on their miserable souls.'"*

*The sedan started moving forward, deftly avoiding the ruts
in the unpaved road.*

Chapter Seventeen

"He's out of danger," Dr. Alexander told Ben, "but he's weak from loss of blood." Standing at the nurses' station, he looked at the sheriff's deputy and the insurance investigator he'd just met. "I don't want you to stay too long or to get him agitated."

"Don't worry, Doc," J.C. assured him, "we won't."

"Opal and Carrie are in there with him. You'd best tell them to step out to the waiting room when you go in. Too many people crowding in at one time won't be good for the patient." Alexander ran a tight ship, bending the rules for no one, including the law.

"Right." J.C. walked down the hallway toward Room 210, his long strides leading the way.

"Has Carrie told you how Grady's taking this little setback?" Ben wanted to know. He'd rushed over to meet J.C. at the hospital after getting beeped while he was having lunch, but he hadn't had time to be briefed.

"Not good, as you can imagine, knowing Grady." J.C. paused before reaching the doorway. "You should see the Bronco. He's damn lucky to be alive."

"Where is it?"

"I had it picked up and taken to Sam's Garage. Sam's the best mechanic for miles around. We use him all the time. I told him to go over that sucker real careful like."

"You suspect tampering? When Grady left McCauley's yesterday afternoon, he was awfully mad. He could've just lost control."

J.C. sent him a dubious look. "You don't believe that and neither do I."

"The question is, will Grady believe someone messed with his Bronco?"

"I think this time he almost heard the angels sing. We might just see a changed man." Stepping forward, he gave a short knock on the door, then walked in. "Company, boss." J.C. walked immediately to Carrie's side, slipping an arm around her waist. "You okay, babe?" he asked her quietly.

Carrie nodded, smiling up at him. "I am now that I know my stubborn father's going to be around awhile longer to kick some butt. Right, Daddy?"

Grady's right ankle was in a cast and the side of his head had been shaved and was now covered with a large white bandage. An automatic pressure cuff was attached to one arm and a catheter tube trailed from under the sheet to a bag attached to the bed frame. He had a concussion and his head hurt still. He was pale beneath his tan and his chin no longer seemed to thrust out at a feisty angle. When he spoke, his voice was breathy. "I guess so."

"I *know* so," Opal said from her chair alongside the bed.

J.C. was about to request that the women leave for a few minutes as Dr. Alexander had instructed, when Grady spoke up. "Opal, why don't you and Carrie grab a cup of coffee? You been here since late last night. I need to talk to these two." His gaze slid to Ben.

So did Opal's as she remembered he'd been the one to set Grady off after George's funeral. Slowly, she got to her feet, bent to kiss Grady's unbandaged cheek, then turned to glare at Ben. "Don't you upset him or you'll answer to me, hot-shot."

"Yes, ma'am," Ben said with a straight face.

Carrie let go of J.C. and started past Ben, then stopped. "I heard you tried to warn him. I wish he'd have listened. My Dad and I, we're a stubborn lot, not real good at taking orders."

"I noticed."

"But thanks for trying." She touched his arm briefly, then followed her stepmother out the door.

Shoving his hands into the pockets of his khakis, Ben stepped closer to the bed and looked at Grady expectantly. He wasn't crass enough to put pressure on a man who'd just missed getting killed. But he did hope this close call might finally loosen Grady's tongue.

Grady swallowed, then ran a hand around his face once and again. "No man likes to admit he's been a horse's ass, Whalen, but I guess that's what I've been. Damn mule stubborn, as my granddaddy used to say."

"You'll get no argument from me on that one."

Grady hated the weakness that left him frail as a kitten, but he had to get this out. "I got a feeling someone tinkered with the Bronco, tried to kill me. Steering column for sure, probably brakes, too. I was going pretty fast, but I knew enough to slow down when I got to the dirt road. Brakes didn't hold and I couldn't control the wheel. Guess our killer finally got around to me."

Ben took the straight-back chair Opal had vacated, turned it around and straddled it, leaning his forearms on the back-rest. Grady had given him the opening he'd hoped for. "I want to know why, Grady. I never bought this hokey, aw-shucks country hick act. I know you're too smart not to have been suspicious from the start. Why'd you keep telling me and everyone else that the accidents were real?"

Grady glanced at J.C. standing at the foot of the bed, hating like hell to reveal his many flaws in front of both men. However, injured as he was, he needed their help, and he knew it. "For a long time, I thought, *I hoped*, that what I was thinking couldn't be true. There were only two people deeply affected by that accident, aside from the six of us. The aunt and the kid. When Dad died, I really thought it was an accident. He was seventy-five, getting on in years, not as quick as he used to be, and he had high blood pressure. Then there was Reed and I began to wonder. But when Jack was found, I knew. I just knew."

"You knew who was doing it and still did nothing?" Ben tried to keep the emotion from tinging his voice.

"I suspected, let's say. So I drove to Ishpeming, not once but twice. Found out that the aunt had died three or four years ago and the kid had moved away. So I decided I was wrong. Had to be accidents, I convinced myself, because I could think of no one else who might have had it in for Dad and Reed and Jack."

"What about when Kurt drowned and when Ed got locked in his own cooler?" Ben persisted. "Surely you didn't *really* believe those were accidents?"

Wearily, Grady shook his head. "Probably not, deep inside. But I wanted to." His eyes bore into Ben's, imploring him. "Honor and pride were everything to my dad. Only one thing did he regard more highly: family. So he abandoned his honor and integrity to save a member of his family thirty years ago. To save me and my friends. I owed him, damn it. I didn't want to dirty the good name he'd built up, to stain his memory by one false deed." It was time to be brutally honest. "And I got to admit, part of my denial was selfish, too. I'm an elected official, one who had the trust of the people of Riverview. How do you think they'll feel about me after learning I was involved in a cover-up where three people died?"

"I don't have the answer to that, Grady. Maybe if you make a clean breast of things, they'll understand. Your father and the judge were grown men who deliberately bent the law. You were young and . . ."

"Let's not pretty it up. I was twenty-one, just like the others. That's a man by any standards." He sighed heavily. "Anyhow, whatever happens, I'll face it when the time comes. For now, we need to find a killer before someone else dies."

Ben couldn't have agreed more. "This kid, he'd be about thirty-eight or forty now, right?"

"Yeah, around there. Forty, I think. Only you've got it wrong. The kid was a girl."

In the act of rising, Ben froze. "What did you say?"

Grady saw that J.C. was looking shocked as well. "I said the surviving kid was a girl. A ten-year-old girl named Lee Thurmond."

Stunned, Ben slowly sat back down. "A girl? You're sure."

"Hell, yes, I'm sure. It was in the newspaper."

"Not the one I found. It just said 'surviving child,' no gender stated." He shook his head, amazed. How could he have been so stupid? Of course, Lee could be a female name as well as male. "That's one I didn't even consider." But now that he knew, he shifted gears. "What do you know about this girl?"

Grady winced as he shrugged. "Not much. The aunt raised her, I believe. Some kind of religious nut, Dad told me later after seeing her in court. They had to drag her out after the disposition of the case. She kept screaming one thing over and over: those boys will pay." He shifted uncomfortably. "Seems she was right."

"Grady, it's highly probable that this Lee Thurmond lives here in Riverview or nearby, using another name. I understand the aunt was Mrs. Thurmond's sister, so her last name would be different. Do you remember what it was? Maybe the girl took the aunt's name."

Pursing his lips, Grady slowly shook his head. "I wish I did. You've got to realize, all I wanted to do was forget these people."

"Then how'd you hope to find them in Ishpeming?"

"Dad had an address for the aunt. I went there and found a new family living in the house. That's when the neighbor told me the former resident, an unmarried woman, had died and her niece left town. I'm not sure she ever mentioned a name." He looked sheepish, then disappointed in himself. "Pretty stupid for a lawman, I guess."

J.C. had a strong compassionate streak. "I can understand that. You wanted to know as little as possible about that family." Because they made him feel guilty. Like listening to Carrie talk about her disastrous marriage made J.C. feel angry.

Ben was pondering their next move when his beeper went off. He glanced at the number but didn't recognize it. "I've got to make a quick call. Be right back."

Down the hallway, he found a phone booth and dialed, waiting impatiently through three rings. Finally a low feminine voice answered. "This is Ben Whalen in Riverview. Did someone there call me?"

"Why, yes, Mr. Whalen. I did. My name's Martha Enright from Ishpeming. I believe you wanted to talk with me."

The schoolteacher who'd been vacationing in Hawaii. "Yes, ma'am. Thanks for calling back. I'm investigating a suspicious claim. We have reason to believe that one of the parties involved lived in Ishpeming about thirty years ago and attended the grade school where you taught. Doris Hodgkins tells me you have almost total recall when it comes to the children you worked with."

Martha chuckled softly. "I don't know about *total*, but I remember many of them. I taught so many sweet children."

"The one I'm seeking was ten or possibly a little older, a female, we think. She'd been in a bad auto accident and may have been physically scarred or perhaps behind a grade or two due to time spent in the hospital. Her parents died and she was raised by an aunt, one who took in sewing and raised bees. Does that description ring any bells with you?"

"You must mean Lee Thurmond, the poor child. She had such a rough go. Both arms were broken plus her collarbone, and she was badly scarred from burns. She had to have several operations and yes, she was behind a year. I tutored her for a while. She was bright and very determined to overcome her injuries. She was almost painfully shy and had few friends. She took up running to strengthen her legs." Martha paused the briefest moment. "There was something that bothered me about the child."

"What was that?"

"Her upbringing. Her aunt was so strict, a religious fanatic, I'd call her. She had that poor little thing reading scripture constantly, on her knees praying, quoting the Bible at every turn. That's very hard on an impressionable child. Mixes up their head, you know."

It surely did in this case. "Do you remember the aunt's name?"

"Certainly. Mary Bishop. Matter of fact, Mary felt strongly that Lee was a heathen name and so she had the child's name changed to Ruth. Like in the Bible."

Bishop. Ruth Bishop. Bells rang in Ben's head. The Green Thumb, the woman who'd bought the florist shop a few short years ago. The one who ran every morning. "Did she change the girl's last name from Thurmond to Bishop also?"

"Yes, she did, later when Lee was about twelve. That's when Mary adopted her. She wanted the child's social security benefits, you see, and likely thought it'd be easier if she was listed as the adoptive parent. Mary had initiated a lawsuit, but lost and she was very bitter. I got the feeling she highly resented having to raise Lee." Martha made a disapproving sound. "I never could get used to calling that child Ruth."

"So she graduated from school under the name Ruth Bishop?" No wonder they hadn't been able to find a trace of the name Thurmond.

"Yes, that's right. Mary died several years ago and Ruth sold that old house they'd lived in. Wasn't worth much. Then one day, she up and disappeared. None of us have ever heard from her in well over three years." Again, that slight hesitance. "I hope Lee's all right. I always felt sorry for her. In my message, you said something about a problem with an insurance claim. She's not involved in anything unlawful, is she?"

Oh, yes, that she is, Ben thought. "It's complicated. Listen, Ms. Enright, I very much appreciate your helping us on this."

"You're very welcome."

Ben hung up and raced back down the hall, earning a frown from the nurse behind the desk. He didn't care. He rushed into Grady's room where J.C. was chatting with the patient. "Grady, was the aunt's name Mary Bishop?"

His face brightened. "Yeah, that sounds right. Why? Did you locate her?"

"No, but I know where to find her." Barely containing his eagerness to be off, he looked at J.C. "I may need help."

"You got it." J.C. glanced at the sheriff. "We'll be back with a full report soon as we can."

"You two be careful, y'hear?" Grady warned, his voice weak. "If that's the gal who landed me in this bed, she means business."

"We will." J.C. walked out into the hallway where Ben was antsy to get going.

Neither of them noticed a shadowy figure not far from the bank of telephones during the commotion of a shift change.

Wearing her trademark green jogging suit, the florist set the plant on the nurses' counter and headed for the back stairs. She'd heard enough to make her palms sweat.

So they were on to her, were they? And that cocky sheriff had survived the crash. It was all that investigator's fault and Maggie for following him blindly.

Racing down the steps, Ruth Bishop knew just what she had to do.

Rushing off the elevator, Ben filled the deputy in on what he'd learned from the retired Ishpeming teacher.

J.C. was stunned. "Ruth Bishop? Hell, she was at all the funerals, delivering flowers from everyone. You sure?"

"Pretty sure. She had me fooled, too. She even sent flowers to Maggie and . . ." That thought had him swallowing hard. Red roses and one dead white rose. The description of the man who'd come in with cash and ordered them. All a lie. Why would Ruth send flowers to Maggie? A warning to back off? Was she also going to go after the children of the slain men?

On the first floor, they headed toward the double doors, passing through Emergency on their way out. "I got a funny feeling, J.C.," Ben continued. "Call it a hunch. How about we go together to the Green Thumb in your Bronco so I can use your phone to call Maggie. I need to make sure she's all right."

"I believe in hunches. I've had a few myself and . . ." J.C. moved aside as a gurney pushed by two ambulance attendants came through the double doors of the Emergency Room. Glancing at the patient's face, he stopped. "Hey, that's Judge Fulton."

Ben backtracked, running alongside the gurney, trying to get a good look. The man had a trach tube going down his throat, an IV in his arm, the blood pressure cuff already on. He'd know that thick gray hair anywhere. "What happened to him?" Ben asked the attendant as they wheeled him into one of the cubicles.

"Bee sting, apparently. Guy's having an allergic reaction."

Recalling the judge mentioning how allergic he was to bees, Ben stood in the doorway staring while the hospital staff took over. "Bees," he repeated to J.C. "Ruth Bishop's aunt raised bees." And hadn't he spotted jars of honey on the shelves at the Green Thumb?

"Yeah, Ruth raises them, too. Behind her shop. Sells the honey right there." J.C. caught the other ambulance attendant as he was leaving. "Is he going to make it?"

"Probably, if his heart holds up. His throat was nearly swollen shut by the time we got the epinephrine in him. You know the guy?"

Walking out with the attendants, Ben answered. "Yes. Do you know how he happened to get stung? He's a careful man."

"In his house. A friend came over to play chess and found him sitting in a chair, unable to talk, so he called 911. We saw half a dozen bees swarming around."

J.C.'s face was grim. "Everyone in town knows the judge is allergic to bees."

"Everyone including Ruth. Thanks, fellas." Ben tapped J.C.'s arm. "Let's go." At a dead run, the two men headed for J.C.'s Bronco.

"You're doing more cleaning in this house than I am these days, Maggie," Fiona scolded, her hands planted on her thin hips as she watched Maggie reorganize the bookcases in Jack's den. "You're putting me to shame."

Maggie blew at her bangs as she turned toward the doorway. "Now, Fiona, you know that's not so. It's just that some of these books have been here since Dad went to college. They're hopelessly outdated. I'm packing them up to donate to the library." Which was just one of the projects she'd thought up to tire herself enough so she could sleep. Just four or five hours would be a blessing, instead of lying in bed, staring at the four walls, reliving the past few weeks to see what she might have done differently to bring about a happier ending where she and Ben were concerned.

Ben. She missed him terribly.

"Have you heard if they've got a new librarian yet? Do you suppose Phoebe's really going to stay gone? No one's heard a peep out of Wilbur's wife." Fiona actually thought the woman was better off without the likes of Wilbur Oakley, but she held back from saying so.

Maggie bent to unpack the last shelf, wondering which question to answer first, when the ringing phone had her straightening to answer. She frowned, listening, not recognizing the woman's voice. "Who did you say this was, again?"

"Sylvia at Riverview Bank. In going through Mr. Becker's desk, we came across several papers needing your signature in connection with your father's estate. They should have been filed awhile ago, but in the commotion since the president's death, well, we're a bit behind. We need you to come over right away and sign these." Breathless, the woman ran out of steam.

"Right now?" Maggie looked down at her dusty clothes. "Can't it wait until morning?"

"I'm afraid not. We need to get these sent off right away." The woman sounded exasperated.

Maggie sighed. "All right. I'll be right over." Hanging up, she shoved a box of books aside on her way out of the den. "They need me at the bank, something about Dad's papers. I'll just clean up quickly and run over." She left the room with Fiona trailing after her.

"Who was it that called?" the housekeeper asked, curious.

"Woman named Sylvia. I guess things are in a mess over there since Mr. Becker died." She hurried on up the stairs.

Twenty minutes later, Maggie pulled into a parking spot on the bank's lot and noticed Ruth Bishop standing alongside her florist van a short distance over. Keys in hand, Maggie walked over. "How are you today?" The tall woman looked somewhat agitated, she thought.

"Not so good. I've got a problem with my van."

Maggie reached the open door of the van and gazed inside. There were metal shelves on both sides holding several flower arrangements and a few long boxes. Nothing looked amiss. "What kind of problem?"

Ruth let out a whoosh of air, sounding anxious as she glanced around the parking lot, thankfully empty of people at the moment. "Step in and let me show you."

Ducking her head, Maggie stepped up and inside, dropping her keys on the asphalt. As she turned to back up to pick them up, she realized Ruth was right up close behind her, holding a cloth in one hand. "What's going on?"

But before she could say another word, Ruth grabbed Maggie into a stranglehold with one arm and slapped a cloth soaked with chemicals onto her nose and mouth with the other. Lips clenched into a thin line, Ruth held on tightly.

Swallowing a muffled protest, Maggie kicked and squirmed, but the woman who held her down was much stronger. As she struggled, she ran out of oxygen and had to draw in a breath. In seconds, she slumped onto the floor, her eyes closing.

"Atta girl, Maggie." Ruth glanced out the open van door, relieved to find no one nearby. She slammed the door shut, grabbed a spool of florist cord from the second shelf, and tied Maggie's hands together behind her back. Testing, she slapped her hostage once, then twice and got no response. "Good. You just sleep now. We'll soon get where we're going and, in no time, your boyfriend will join us. Two birds with one stone." Giggling, the light of madness shining in her eyes, Ruth Bishop climbed into the driver's seat of the Green Thumb delivery van, and took off.

As J.C. drove from the hospital toward the Green Thumb, Ben used the police phone to call Maggie. Impatiently, he waited for her to answer, but it was Fiona's voice he recognized. "Fiona, it's Ben. I need to talk with Maggie."

Fiona wasn't feeling too friendly toward Ben these days. Just when she'd begun liking him, thinking he was good for Maggie, something had happened between the two of them. Something that had upset Maggie and put the sadness back in her eyes. "She isn't here."

Ben's face wore a worried frown. "Do you know where she is? This is important."

The urgency in his voice was contagious. "Is something wrong?"

"I don't have time to go into it now. Tell me where she is, Fiona."

"At the bank. She got a call a short time ago. They need her to sign some papers for Jack's estate."

Was it the real thing or a ploy? Ben remembered the white rose in the bottom of the florist box with its head twisted off. "Do you know who called her?" he asked Fiona.

"She said a woman named Sylvia. I don't recognize the name. Ben . . . is Maggie in danger?"

"I'm not sure. I'll call you later." He hung up and turned to J.C. "She was called to the bank by someone named Sylvia. Do you have their number anywhere?"

"Look in the glove box," J.C. told him.

It took several precious minutes to find the number for Riverview Bank, and about two minutes to ascertain that no one named Sylvia worked there, nor had anyone called Maggie Spencer today. "Damn!" Ben said, clicking off. "I've got a bad feeling about this."

J.C. took the corner on two wheels and whipped into the bank's parking lot. "There's Maggie's Explorer."

Ben was out and hurrying over as J.C. stopped. The Explorer was unlocked and deserted, none of her things inside. Puzzled and growing more concerned, he walked back to the Bronco. "Where in hell is she?" he asked no one in particular.

"Hey, Ben, look over there! Some keys in that vacant space next to the blue Lincoln." He eased the Bronco toward the spot as Ben rushed over and picked them up. "Are they Maggie's?"

"They sure are." Ben climbed back in. "See the Brass *M* on the ring." His eyes skimmed the parking lot. "Wonder if anybody saw anything." But except for a mother stuffing a toddler into a car seat on the next aisle, the lot was deserted.

"Let's go to Ruth's shop and see what we can find. Maybe Maggie dropped her keys and went walking down Main Street on some errand." J.C. didn't believe his own words, but he hoped Ben did.

His mind racing, Ben considered possibilities as J.C. did a U-turn and pulled up in front of the Green Thumb. "Bring your gun," he said, getting out.

But the shop was locked up. However, there was a handwritten note taped to the door. Ben yanked it down and read aloud as J.C. looked over his shoulder. "Ben: Meet me at Freddy's cabin and I'll explain everything. Maggie. P.S. Come alone!"

The hair on the back of Ben's neck rose. He'd seen Maggie's handwriting on the notes they'd scribbled at the courthouse during their search, and it looked nothing like this.

J.C. was already rushing back to the Bronco. "Get in."

"No sirens, okay?"

"Right." J.C. pulled out into light traffic. "We'll find them, don't worry."

Ben was sure they'd find them. But would they be in time?

First there was the darkness, then the nausea. Maggie came to slowly, her stomach rolling and the room spinning when she opened her eyes. She blinked, trying to orient herself. It was dim and dusty, smelling stale. A small, crowded place, one big room, odd-lot furniture, none too clean, birds twittering just outside the open door, trees visible through the window.

"You guessed it," Ruth said watching her from across the narrow room where she sat, a large hunting knife resting on her lap. "We're tucked away deep in the woods."

Feeling groggy, Maggie licked her dry lips and tried to reach up to brush her hair from her face when she realized her hands were bound behind her back. "What . . . what are we doing here? Why am I tied up, Ruth?" She remembered the call from the bank, then climbing into Ruth's van. "Someone named Sylvia called and . . ."

"There is no Sylvia. That was me on the phone. I had to find a way to get you into my van."

"But why? I don't understand."

"No," Ruth sneered, "your kind never understands people like me. You have everything, always have had. A lovely home, parents who loved you, the best schools, money, beauty. You even have that handsome stud warming your bed, now, don't you?"

Maggie drew in deep breaths, trying to rid her body of whatever drug the woman had given her, for whatever reason, trying to clear her head. "When did I ever hurt you?"

Ruth snorted. "Not you, but your kind. Yeah, they hurt me plenty. In school, they made fun because I was slow since I lost so much time being in the hospital. They laughed at my scars." With that, she rose and walked over, pulling up her pant legs. "See these scars?" Next she shoved up her long sleeves past her elbows to reveal old scars faded to white, the skin puckered and bulging in places. "And these? I got 'em on my back, too, my chest. Everywhere. Doctors said there was hardly a square inch on me that hadn't been cut or burned from the hot metal of the car part I landed next to in the accident. You ever wonder why I always cover up, even in summer?"

The accident. It was beginning to dawn on Maggie. "*You're* the Thurmond child, Lee, the one who survived the auto crash? We thought you were a man." Of course, the name fooled them.

"Did you, now?" Ruth asked, sitting back down.

Dear God, she'd been living right here in their midst in Riverview. What was it, over three years? Biding her time, making her plans for revenge, stalking her victims. "You're the one who killed my father."

The smile was cunning and tinged with madness. "Yeah, honey, and I'd do it again in a heartbeat. Every one of them deserved to die a horrible death, like my parents and my baby sister did. They needed to suffer for leaving me like this, so scarred no one could ever want me." She stumbled on a choked sob.

"It was an accident, Ruth. No one person was to blame."

"Oh, yeah? My aunt told me afterward how the sheriff and the judge schemed to get all six of those college boys off. She came to Riverview later and heard those boys bragging about how they'd gotten away with murder."

"No!" Maggie cried out, knowing instinctively that the aunt had to have lied. "That couldn't be so. They wouldn't have done that. Maybe their car did hit your car, but it was snowing and dark. To suggest they laughed it off is to not know the truth. I won't let you slander my father's name."

Again the slow, menacing smile. "Too late, honey. He's paid, gone to his eternal reward and I sent him there." She leaned forward, her eyes shining. "Don't you think it's clever how I waited until they all trusted me? I smiled and flattered your father, asked if he'd please let me go up with him to look at the house he was inspecting. He hemmed and hawed, said he rarely let anyone up, but he finally agreed because he knew I was a runner, strong and surefooted. It was pathetically easy. He even helped me climb up."

She had to keep Ruth's venomous words from affecting her, had to keep her talking, had to believe that someone would come looking for her. Maybe Fiona would call the bank when she failed to return home and learn she'd never been there, then call J.C. or Ben.

With shaky fingers, Maggie tried to loosen the cord tied around her wrists while she searched her foggy mind for something to keep the madwoman speaking. She could see empty birdcages hanging from the porch ceiling outside. Then it dawned on her exactly where they were. "How did you get a key to Freddy's place?" The awful truth slammed into her drowsy brain. "No! Oh, God, not Freddy, too."

"Figuring it all out, are you?"

"Why Freddy? He never hurt anyone."

"The stupid jerk. He didn't trust men, but he trusted me. He got in my way, that's why. I'd have had George that night, but the fool showed up with one of his birds, jabbering away. I couldn't afford to let someone hear us. So I put him out of his misery. His life was even worse than mine. I did him a favor."

Oh, God, how could this crazy woman think killing someone would be doing them a favor? Maggie wondered as she tugged at the stubborn knot in the cord. "And that man buried near where Dad fell? Harper something. Did you do him in, too?"

"Another fool. He came snooping around because someone told him Jack was out at the house. Only by the time he showed up, I'd already shoved Jack off and I was bending over him, checking to make sure he was dead, when the creep came up and asked me what I was doing. What choice did I have? I grabbed the nearest thick board and let him have it. He should have stayed out of it and he'd still be alive. But, from what I heard afterward, he wasn't worth saving."

"But you buried him and not my father. Why?"

"I didn't want to distract the others from that fool's meaningless death. I wanted those remaining to start worrying, to begin figuring it all out, to sweat and wonder and worry which one of them would be next."

Suddenly Ruth jumped to her feet, agile as only a practiced runner can be, brandishing the huge knife. "None of them were worth saving. 'Behold a pale horse and his name is death.' That's what the Bible says."

Maggie ordered herself not to panic. "The Bible also says something about vengeance is mine saith the Lord and forgiveness is divine." Maggie's heart was pounding as she prayed someone would arrive before Ruth used that big knife on her. Was the cord giving way a little or was she imagining it?

"Forgiveness is for the weak," Ruth went on as she moved to the table. "Hate is my shield against the world, against the pain. Do you know that the accident left me in constant pain, that I have to take a handful of pills daily just to be able to get around? That's why I run, why I push myself. I refuse to let this defeat me. Aunt Mary told me on her deathbed to seek vengeance on those who hurt us, to kill all the sinners." Removing the top from a large red can, she turned to face her hostage. "Don't you see, it's my mission?"

Maggie searched for something to say, anything to delay her. "When did your aunt die?"

"About three years ago. I sold that dump we lived in and came here. I never lived in Chicago like I told you. The Green Thumb being put up for sale was perfect for my plans." She flashed a grin. "Ingenious, eh?"

"But all that happened thirty years ago. Why didn't you use that money from the house sale to make a new life for yourself? Why, after all this time, start massacring people?"

"*Because!* Because the guilty must pay!"

"Ruth, please, stop this. You're going to have to live with so many regrets."

"You're wrong. I have no regrets. None. I know what I have to do to make the sinners pay." She started through the cabin, splashing the contents of the can onto the floor, a dilapidated lounge chair and footstool, several rickety tables.

Gasoline. The fumes reached Maggie's nostrils. My God, she was pouring gasoline! "What are you doing?" Maggie asked as she worked furiously at the cord. The woman was insane. She had to hurry, had to get loose, and somehow make it to the door.

"Setting the scene, my dear." Ruth placed the empty can on the table and uncapped a second one, liberally sprinkling its contents around the rest of the cabin, thoroughly soaking the area around Maggie's chair.

Her heartbeat was thundering in her ears as Maggie realized that Ruth was going to toss a match onto the gasoline-soaked floor and send her up in flames.

Satisfied with her work, Ruth sat back down, once more holding the large hunting knife. "Soon now, our hero will arrive to rescue his fair maiden." A giggle she couldn't suppress burst from her. "Only he's in for the surprise of his life."

"Our hero?" Maggie asked, totally confused and trying to tamp down her fear so her hands wouldn't tremble as she worked.

"Ben Whalen, my nemesis, the one who thinks he's going to catch me. Only he's going to be outwitted this time. I left him a note so he'd come after you."

Maggie was having trouble avoiding breathing in the fumes that enveloped her. That Ben would know where to find her was good news. Even though they'd parted badly the last time, she knew he'd come after her if he discovered she was missing. That this madwoman had set him up, removing the element of surprise, was bad news. What were another couple of killings to someone who'd already murdered so many?

"Ben's strong. You won't be able to . . ."

"Sure I will. I'm strong, too. I've been working out, preparing, planning for this for years." Her face moved into a smirk as if she couldn't resist the urge to brag. "I've got it all worked out. He's going to come charging in here and I'll be behind that door, waiting. He'll rush to you and I'll stab him with this." She waved the knife, swishing it through the air once, twice. "Then I'll leave you two in here to have a hot time together." Again, the maniacal laugh. "He deserves to die, too. I broke into his room and read his insurance reports. At first, I didn't think he was smart enough to figure it out. But I was wrong and now he has to pay."

"If you throw a match down, you won't be able to get out before the cabin blows up. You won't get away with this."

"Sure I will. See this?" she asked, pointing to a kerosene lamp on the table next to her chair, its long wick burning in oil tinted red. "I don't need a match. I won't even be here. Won't be long now and the flame will ignite the fumes. Then boom! An explosion. By then, I'll be far from here, over by the back road where I parked my van." She smiled at her victim. "Smart, eh?"

"It won't work. You wait and see." The knot was loosening. Maggie could feel it. If she just had a few more minutes.

"You shut up." Setting the knife aside, Ruth took a scarf from her pocket and moved toward Maggie. "We'll see how chatty you are with this gag on. Wouldn't want you to warn our hero." She wound it around Maggie's head twice, then tied it tightly in back. "There, now let's just sit back and wait."

Maggie's fingers clawed at the bindings frantically as she sent up every prayer she could remember.

Ruth cocked her head and listened. "What's that? Is it a car? Never mind. He'll be here soon." She beamed another mad smile at Maggie. "And then, it'll be showtime."

Chapter Eighteen

"Can't this thing go any faster?" Ben asked J.C. They were hurtling along the main road leading to the new housing development being built by Spencer Construction and beyond that, the woods. The woods where Freddy's cabin was located. But it was rush hour and commuters who worked north of Riverview and some who had jobs toward the south were on their way home, making speed next to impossible. Intellectually, Ben knew that. But emotionally, he needed to vent his anxiety.

J.C. understood, but he couldn't fly over the tops of cars in front of them, and there were no shortcuts up this way with much of the land undeveloped. "Hang on, Ben. We'll get there in time." He hoped.

In time for what? Ben asked himself. In time to see Maggie dead like all the others and the madwoman who'd plagued Riverview standing over her, relishing still another murder? In time to find an empty cabin maybe, and another note urging him to yet another location, making a game of the killing and the chase that gets the adrenaline pumping?

The way the deaths had occurred, most set up to appear accidental, all indicated that Ruth Bishop considered this one big game of revenge. But she'd gotten hasty and careless recently.

In time. The question was, would they get there in time to save Maggie, the least guilty victim of all? She had no blood thirst for revenge and, even now, she was probably pleading with her assailant to give herself up, sure that Ruth was sick rather than a maniacal killer who'd carefully plotted all these killings. No, Maggie didn't deserve to die.

And she didn't deserve what he'd done to her. Especially since it had all been a lie. He'd run from her love when inside, he loved her far more than his own life. He loved her gentleness, her kindness, her passion. She'd changed his life, given it meaning once more. He'd been afraid to burden her with a troubled man who suffered dark moods. Yet when he'd finally told her that, she'd said she'd help him get past the fear.

And what had he given her in return? Pain and shame. He'd hurt her and humiliated her by refusing to accept the love she offered with an open heart. He'd turned his back on the one good thing that had happened to him in years. He'd been arrogant and selfish, so sure he was saving her from more pain when, in fact, he was afraid she'd leave him and he'd be the one hurting.

Time to grow up, Ben reminded himself. He swerved toward the window as J.C. bounced the Bronco off the main road onto a dirt path. Time to stop running, to face life. Time to admit he was a mortal man like so many others, one who not only needed love but was quietly withering up without it. Maggie had brought sunshine into his life, and he'd chosen to stand outside alone in the dark, clutching his grief and loneliness and fear to his shattered heart.

No more. He wasn't a praying man, but he prayed now as they circled the housing development and the woods came in sight up ahead. If God would grant him one more chance, if only they'd find Maggie alive and unhurt, he'd get down on his knees and do everything in his power to make her happy, to keep her smiling. She couldn't die without knowing how much he loved her.

When you find a person exactly right for you, you have to grab 'em up before they get away and you're left with only regrets, Lucy had told him. How right she was. He had so much to make up to Maggie, if only he'd be in time.

He'd see to it, he vowed, if only she'd have him.

J.C. pulled the Bronco close to the edge of the woods where a narrow trail was barely visible. Ben jumped out before the engine was off and started running. With his long legs, J.C. caught up with him in moments. "Hold on. Let's talk about what we're going to do before we get there."

Ben knew J.C. was right, knew he was facing a critical situation here. He was once more involved emotionally and not thinking with his head, but with his heart. It took no small effort to stop and face J.C. At least he knew that the deputy understood the situation he faced as well as any man could.

"Let's think this through," J.C. said, calmly, carefully. He knew he was talking to a powder keg with a short fuse right now. "If Ruth's got Maggie, she's either drugged her and tied her up, or she's got a weapon aimed at her. Am I right so far?"

"Yeah, I guess."

"I know that cabin. I've been here to check on Freddy with any number of complaints. There's a front door but none in back. However, there's a fairly large shuttered window in back in the bathroom and it's kept closed with a hook-type latch. I thought of a plan if you're willing to listen."

Tension flowed through Ben in his anxiety to get to the cabin, to get to Maggie. "What is it?"

"I think you should go to the front door, because the note

warned you to come alone. We don't want to set Ruth off and cause her to do something rash. Meanwhile, I'll circle around the back and sneak in that window. I've got my weapon and I should be able to surprise her, take her from behind maybe, while you distract her."

Ben realized that J.C.'s plan made sense. However . . . "You remember what you said to me when we were going after Wayne? When we get there, he's mine, you said. Well, in this situation, you remember that when we get in, Ruth's mine. And if she's hurt Maggie . . ."

"*You* remember that you kept me from killing that bastard. Now know this. I won't let you kill her, no matter what. For *your* sake, not hers. Understand?"

"Yeah, okay." Easy to promise. Much harder to do.

"Give me a minute or so head start," J.C. said, "so I can circle around back without drawing her attention. Then you move in, but be careful. We don't know what she's capable of. She's done it all." With that, he took off, working his way through the trees, as silent as any human could be.

Ben counted to ten and took off, his patience strained to the limit. He heard the birds chirping noisily before he caught sight of the cabin. They hadn't seen Ruth's van, but that didn't mean it wasn't around somewhere. Cautiously, he moved closer.

The front door was closed, the window slightly raised, but there was no sign of life except the twittering birds. Still his sixth sense told him Maggie was in there. Stepping on the porch, he thought of and discarded several options. Finally, he braced himself and with one swift kick, he booted in the door.

He saw Maggie immediately sitting in a wooden chair, hands pulled behind her back, a gag in her mouth. At the same moment, a smell registered. Gasoline! Ruth must plan to torch the place with them in it. Had she taken off, or was she laying in wait for him?

He took a cautious step forward onto the threshold, his eyes scanning every which way, but he could see no movement. He looked again at Maggie and saw her frown of frustration as she shook her head from side to side. A warning not to enter? But he had to free her. He took another step in and heard Maggie's muffled yelp.

Swiveling about, he caught a glancing blow on the shoulder from a heavy object as his arm reached up to block it. He wheeled backward and saw the upraised knife Ruth was holding. Dodging, he knocked it from her grip with a karate chop to her forearm, the force causing her to stumble forward. With his other hand, he landed a left hook to the woman's chin, catching it dead center, lifting her up off the floor, right before she dropped with a thud. Ben kicked the knife across the room before turning back to Maggie.

Moving swiftly, he fumbled in his pocket for his Swiss Army knife and cut through the gag on her mouth, then bent to her hands.

"Ben," she shouted, "the kerosene lamp! It's going to explode from the fumes. We've got to get out of here."

He glanced at the lamp, then to the back toward the only closed door. "J.C.? Are you in?" He didn't hear an answer and the damn cord was so tightly twined about Maggie's wrist that he couldn't get the blade in without cutting her. "Hold on," he said, and picked her up, chair and all.

He was almost to the door when he heard a sound behind him. Thinking it might be J.C., he stopped and turned.

"Last laugh, you two," came the screeching voice of Ruth Bishop as she reached out for the kerosene lamp from where she'd dragged herself to a kneeling position on the floor. One-handed, she raised the lamp high, aiming it toward the door. But her hand was slippery, the lamp too heavy. Suddenly, it was falling, falling toward the gasoline-soaked floor and the woman who lost her balance and dropped facedown.

Ben watched the scene as if in slow motion. Just as the

lamp started downward, he gripped the chair and sprinted through the open door, running for all he was worth down the porch steps and on into the woods. He dove toward the ground with Maggie and her imprisoning chair still in his arms just as the first explosion ripped through the cabin. Was that an earth-shattering scream he heard, muffled by the blast? Shuddering, he sheltered Maggie with his body, as flames burst skyward, the smoke turning black and swirling up to blot out the sun.

He wasn't sure how long they stayed like that, until finally, Ben eased himself up and checked Maggie. "Are you hurt? Maggie, talk to me."

She drew in a shaky breath and opened her eyes. "I'm okay. Are you?"

"Yes." He angled the chair with its broken legs around, and using the knife he'd held in his fist, finally managed to cut her free. Then he pulled her into his arms, needing to feel her heart beat against his, needing to assure himself she was alive and unhurt.

Maggie clung to him, tears rolling down her sooty cheeks. "Oh, God, Ben. I thought she was going to kill us both. I couldn't get the ropes undone and she ranted on and then you were there and I thought she was going to bury that knife in you and . . ."

"Shh." He stroked her hair, her back, holding her gently now. "It's all right. It's over now."

"Thank God you came."

But suddenly Ben let her go. "J.C. He was going to climb in the back window. I've got to go find him. Stay here." Hurrying, he circled the blaze and went around back. Flames engulfed the entire back of the house, too. "Oh, no. J.C. Not you, too." He inched closer to the inferno, trying to locate where the bathroom might have been, trying not to breathe too deeply of the acrid air, when he heard a sound behind him.

Turning, Ben saw J.C. lying on the ground about twenty feet out into the backyard. Relief flooded him as he ran over. "What happened?" he asked, checking him over.

Slowly, J.C. sat up, with Ben's help. "I got in, but the damn door to the main room was locked from the other side and I couldn't get it open." His fingers probed a bump on his head. "I didn't want to tip Ruth off that I was there, so I started to climb back out. That's when all hell broke loose and I guess the force of the blast sent me flying out here." He rubbed his rump as he gingerly got to his feet, favoring his left ankle. "Man, did I land hard."

"Are you okay?"

"Yeah. Maybe a sprained ankle. What happened? Where's Maggie?"

"She's safe. Come on, I'll brief you on the way. We need to call this in from the Bronco and get the fire department out here before these trees catch."

With Ben supporting one side, J.C. made his way around the cabin. "What about Ruth?"

"Ruth's never going to hurt anyone again," Ben said quietly.

"She was a she-devil, she was," Fiona stated emphatically. Placing the tea tray on the coffee table in Jack's den, she straightened. "She deceived us all."

Seated on the leather couch with her feet tucked under her, Maggie shook her head. "She wasn't a devil, Fiona. She was very, very sick. Underneath the rage that ate at her, was grief. Grief for her lost parents and baby sister, her lost childhood, her empty future. She endured so much pain that it probably affected her mind. Then there was that batty aunt who raised her and filled her head full of revenge chants, all in the name of religion. Who wouldn't wind up criminally insane with all that?"

From the far end of the couch, Ben studied her. Her color

was much improved after a bath, but he noticed that her hands still weren't steady. All in all, she'd handled things awfully well.

They'd stayed until the fire department had doused the small cabin thoroughly, then let J.C. drive them to Maggie's. The deputy had left them there to go to his office to take care of the paperwork. Ben had said he'd notify Grady.

So, while Maggie cleaned up, he'd stopped by the hospital and found that the formerly uncooperative sheriff had humbled even more. He'd gotten a call from Sam's Garage and learned his brake line had been cut and the steering column fluid drained, just as he'd suspected.

Finally, after relaying all that had happened at Freddy's cabin, Ben thought it was time to lay all the cards on the table. "You were driving that night, weren't you, Grady?" he'd asked. Looking much older than he had a few days ago, Grady stared at his shaky hands.

"I told myself it didn't matter, that we all shared in the guilt, the shame." Finally, he'd looked up and his brown eyes were suspiciously bright. "Only it did matter and still does."

Ben decided he wouldn't add to the man's misery so he'd checked on the judge and learned that he was going to make it. However, Ben was more than ever convinced that before he'd retired, the judge had taken the Thurmond file and made sure no one would ever find it. That last act had almost cost him his life.

Finally, he'd called Pete Williams to update him before driving back to Maggie's. She hadn't felt like eating nor had he, but they were on their second pot of tea. She was one tough lady, Ben thought. By looking at her, you'd never guess all she'd been through. Except for the haunted look in her eyes, which he knew would take much longer to disappear. "You'd forgive the woman who killed your father that easily?" he asked quietly.

"Yes, Maggie, think of that," Fiona added, pouring tea for them.

"It's just that I think vengeance is wrong," Maggie said. "That's what brought Ruth to this terrible end. Anger yes, but hate, no. Hate destroys the one doing the hating, does them more harm than the object of that hate." She turned toward Ben. "I hate what she did, not only murdering Dad, but all the others. But I also feel sorry for her, for the life she had to live that made her that way."

He had no answer that would top that one.

"Ben," Maggie said, her voice not quite steady, "Grady's the only one left who knows who was driving that night. Do you think he'll tell me?"

Ben let out a rush of air. "Maggie, what good will it do you to know? Let it go, please."

Fiona nodded. "I say amen to that."

He knew how difficult it was for her to put the question out of her mind. He reached over and trailed his fingers lightly along her arm, letting her know he understood.

Fiona knew when three was a crowd. "Well, if you won't be needing anything more tonight, I'll go on up to my room."

In unison, they turned to bid her goodnight.

"Maggie," the older woman said, pausing at the door, her plain face softening, "I'm so very glad you're home safe." Her eyes went to Ben. "Thank you for bringing her back."

"My pleasure." He watched her leave and discreetly close the door. "Looks like I'm back in her good graces." He shifted closer to Maggie. "But then, she's an easier sell than you, isn't she?"

"Possibly." She'd felt so vulnerable tied up at the cabin and was grateful to Ben for rescuing her. But she knew there was much that needed to be said between them. Still, she owed him her life. "Ben, I never want to feel that scared again." She was afraid to close her eyes, afraid of the nightmares to come.

"Me, either." He'd rather fight a pit bull than get into this discussion, but there was no getting out of this, not if he wanted Maggie. And God, how he wanted her. "This whole thing has taught me a great deal," he began uneasily.

"Oh?"

"Maggie, I'll put it to you as straight as I know how. I thought ˈ could protect myself from ever being in pain again by staying away from you. If I didn't care, then if you walked away, I wouldn't hurt. But something happened today when I realized I might lose you before I told you how much I cared. It hit me that I hurt more by not having you in my life than I ever could if you left me later."

Her eyes stayed on his. "Quite a long speech from someone who hates talking about his feelings. What must I do to make you believe that I have no intention of leaving you?"

"I suppose marrying me would go a long way in convincing me."

Eyes wide, Maggie sat up and faced him. "Is that a proposal?"

"Pretty half-assed, right?"

"It could use some improvement."

"Want me to get down on my knees?" He remembered on the frenzied drive to Freddy's cabin that he'd been ready to.

"No, that's not what I want." And she waited.

He squirmed a little. Words were always so hard to come by. He knew what she wanted to hear, but he still felt he faced an uncertain future with much unresolved. The thing was, could he face it without her? "I come with a lot of baggage, Maggie. But it's occurred to me that all of us have to go through certain experiences to become the people we wind up being. If we didn't have those experiences and survive them, we'd be two very different people. You've had some and so have I. I can certainly live with your past. Can you live with mine?"

"I'll do my damndest."

"The night sweats, the black moods, the lost hours?"

"They'll one day disappear altogether. I'm sure of it." She scooted closer and kissed him lightly. "I'm sure enough for both of us."

The right thing. How did she always know the right thing to say, when he so seldom did? "In that case, I think I should tell you that I love you. I've probably loved you ever since I saw you standing on that windy hill out there, looking so sad at your father's funeral, yet so beautiful. Then you took off your sunglasses and gave me that frosty go-to-hell look. Right then and there, I should have known I'd met my match."

Maggie snuggled into his arms, but tipped her head back to look into his eyes. "You're sure now, absolutely certain?"

"If you'll have me."

Then came the Cheshire grin. "Just try to get away." And she pressed her mouth to his.

Prologue

On the winding walkway of the Public Gardens on Charles Street across from the Boston Common, Briana Morgan snapped pictures of her seven-year-old son tossing chunks of bread to the sassy ducks in the pond. In the morning sunlight, the child's blond hair shimmered with golden highlights as he watched an elegant swan regard him disdainfully before swimming off. A baby duck upended himself in the blue water, shaking his little tail, and Bobby giggled.

Briana smiled as she lowered her camera, then checked her watch. "It's time to go. We don't want to keep Dad waiting." Every other Saturday since the divorce, her ex-husband picked up their son for the weekend. The arrangement was amicable.

Bobby tossed the rest of the bread at the ducks, then skipped along the walk, his mother following. They hadn't gone far when he spotted a green balloon caught up in the branches of a tree. Without waiting for permission, he started climbing.

It wasn't far up, Briana decided, so she let him go. He was a spontaneous child who loved life, and she hated to squelch him in any way. So instead, she took more pictures of her son reaching out to the green balloon, finally freeing it, then carefully scampering back down and looping the string around his wrist. He sent her a triumphant glance, his blue eyes shining, then continued hopping and jumping because merely walking was boring.

They reached the street and Briana looked up and down the block, finally spotting her ex-husband at the corner of Beacon and Charles. He was in an animated conversation with a man whose back was to her. There was quite a lot of foot traffic always along the Common, people blocking her view and making recognition of Robert's companion impossible. So she busied herself snapping more pictures of Bobby studying a caterpillar and passersby hurrying to complete weekend chores and tourists enjoying a warm and lovely April morning.

When next she looked up, Robert Morgan was walking toward them with long, angry strides, his face wearing a dark frown. But when he saw his son running toward him, Robert's smile was genuine and welcoming. Briana snapped father and son sharing a warm hug. She decided not to ask Robert why he'd seemed angry since he'd apparently put aside whatever had upset him. Instead, she bent down and kissed her son good-bye.

"I love you, Mom," Bobby said, as he always did.

"I love you, too." She watched him reach for his father's hand as they crossed the street together on their way to visit the zoo. "Be careful," she called after them, as she always did.

She'd planned to drive over to Chinatown to take more pictures for a book in the works, but she could find no better subject anywhere than her son. For the moment, she stood next to a lamp post and kept shooting frames, tilting this way and that for better angles. She switched from wide lens to zoom, capturing each small gesture, each nuance and smile, as Bobby chattered away to his father, the green balloon weaving along on a mild breeze.

4

She shot around a city bus, a yellow cab changing lanes and a gray sedan barreling up the street in a rush of speed, nearly colliding with a blue van overflowing with children. Then she shifted her attention to a forsythia in full bloom, its golden blossoms a welcome sign that summer was near.

The crackling sounds didn't register at first. Briana didn't even pause in her picture taking, thinking the noise was a car back-firing. It wasn't until she heard people screaming that she lowered her camera. Peering with ever increasing horror through the Charles Street traffic, she could see several people on the ground directly across from her, others scurrying for cover and a few shouting for help.

No! It couldn't be.

Dodging cars, Briana raced across the street, not for a moment considering her own safety as a convertible swerved and a Volkswagen screeched to a halt, narrowly missing her. People were gathered around two still on the ground, while others got warily to their feet, fear in their eyes. Shoving, she broke through the crowd, looked down, then screamed as she fell to her knees.

Robert was on his side not moving, one leg twisted under his body, a horrible gaping hole in his cheek. And next to him, lying very still, was her son, his denim jacket soaked through with bright red blood. The green balloon, its string still tied around his wrist, flipped and flopped in a macabre dance.

She gathered Bobby to her and held him close, a keening cry bubbling forth from deep inside. A voice behind her yelled for someone to call for an ambulance, quick.

But Briana Morgan knew it was already too late.

Chapter One

Four months later . . .

It was half a mile from Gramp's house to Brant Point Lighthouse on Nantucket Island, a walk Briana Morgan had taken countless times. There were fewer tourists up that way, the sand not quite so pure with clumps of grass growing sporadically along the slight incline. The lighthouse itself sported a new coat of white paint and the walkway leading to the front door looked recently renovated.

Leisurely strolling along the beach, Briana lifted her face to the warmth of the August sun. She'd flown over from Boston via Hyannis, arriving bag and baggage a mere hour ago, glad to have left behind a chilly three-day rain. It seemed to Briana that she'd been cold a very long time.

Her eyes skimmed the horizon, then drifted to the weathered rocks carelessly stacked at the water's edge just this side of the lighthouse only a short distance away now. She could see a man sitting on one of the higher boulders where she'd daydreamed away many an hour as a teenager. It was one of her favorite spots.

She noticed that the man was barefoot, wearing jeans and an unbuttoned blue shirt, its open flaps blowing about. His black hair shifted in a playful breeze as he stared out to sea, seemingly lost in his thoughts. Over the years, Briana had come to know almost all the permanent residents, by sight if not personally. She didn't recognize the man, who was likely a summer visitor.

Slowing her steps, she kept watching him, wishing he'd chosen to sit elsewhere. She'd have liked to climb up the steep rocks, carefully avoiding the green moss clinging to the sides, and spent an hour emptying her mind as she gazed at the ever changing sea. But someone had beaten her to it.

As she neared, the man started to rise, then teetered on the slippery rocks for several nervous seconds and finally toppled backwards. He lay very still exactly where he'd fallen. He might have hit his head, Briana decided as she rushed over, both curious and concerned. Carefully, she climbed up the familiar formation and reached his side.

He was on his back wedged into a crevice in a semi-seated position, eyes closed. Leaning forward, she pressed two fingers to the pulse point of his neck and felt a strong heartbeat. She slipped her hand to the back of his head, searching for a bump or a cut, but found nothing. Easing back, she stared down into his face. He had at least two days' worth of dark beard shadowing his square jaw. Ruggedly handsome, most people would call him, with thick eyelashes and a small, interesting scar just above his left brow giving his face a dangerous slant. Unaware of her, he sighed heavily and began to snore lightly. Not injured but sound asleep. An odd place for a nap, in broad daylight on a pile of uncomfortable rocks decorated with seaweed alongside a fairly remote lighthouse.

The wind shifted, making her aware of an unmistakable smell. Eyes searching the area, she spotted a brown paper bag alongside his hip. Checking, she found that it contained half a dozen empty beer cans. Not merely asleep, Briana realized, straightening. Passed out drunk.

The sun was most decidedly not over the yardarm, yet here he was, an able-bodied man somewhere in his mid-thirties, drunk as a skunk at the edge of a public beach. What a waste.

She was about to turn away, when something made her glance back at him. Even in a deep sleep, his forehead seemed drawn into a frown. There were tiny lines near the corners of his eyes, lines that seemed to her to have been put there more by worry than laughter. There was no relaxation in the way he held his mouth; rather there was tension evident even in his alcoholic slumber.

Briana sighed. Who was she to judge this stranger? Perhaps he carried burdens as heavy as hers. If she'd thought she could find an answer in alcohol, she might have tried it herself. She had a feeling that, whoever he was, he was going to discover soon that drinking only made things worse. And he was going to have a whopping headache when he finally woke up.

Not her problem, Briana thought, scrambling down. Studying him from the ground up, she decided he was firmly entrenched in his crevice and out of harm's way, with no likelihood of falling off. Even the tide rolling in wouldn't reach him. It wouldn't be dark for another couple of hours, and he'd probably awaken before then. Later, after she'd unpacked and returned from getting her supplies, she'd check on him again. Just to be sure.

However, she felt certain that God looked after fools and drunks with equal ease.

She'd almost reached Gramp's house when a high-flying beach ball came out of nowhere and whacked her on the shoulder. Turning, she caught it on the bounce and swung around. A towhead around seven or eight with two front teeth missing stood several yards from her, grinning his apology. For a long moment, Briana just stared at him, at the beautiful young boy gazing up at her, so full of life.

"Hey, lady," he finally called out impatiently. "I'm sorry. Can I have my ball back?"

With trembling hands, Briana tossed him the ball, then turned and hurried into her grandfather's yard and up the stairs. Inside, she leaned against the door, breathing hard. Tears trailed down her cheeks as she swallowed a sob and waited out yet another storm.

Who'd have believed that old wooden porch shutters would be so heavy? Briana thought the next morning as she struggled to remove the third one. Taking several steps backward to keep from toppling over from the shutter's weight, she finally managed to place it alongside the other two. Blowing her bangs out of her eyes, she paused a moment to catch her breath.

Much as she hated to admit it, there were times when a strong man really would come in handy. However, finding a handyman was easier said than done. So she'd learned to manage on her own.

Briana took a long swallow of her bottled water, then glanced over at the house next door. Gramp's neighbor, Jeremy Slade, had lived there as long as she could remember. Somewhere in his sixties now, Jeremy was one of her favorite people, an artist whose work hung in many a Nantucket home as well as being extremely popular with tourists. Watercolors, mostly seascapes, predominantly pastels.

Yet, although Jeremy's white Ford pickup was in his drive, she hadn't seen him around. There'd been no lights on in his house last night, so she'd assumed he'd gone to the mainland on one of his infrequent trips. Then this morning, just as she'd removed the first shutter, she'd seen a man step out onto Jeremy's porch. He'd knocked over Jeremy's rocker, then cursed the chair, the bright sunshine and the fates in general. Moving closer to the screen for a better look, she'd recognized the man she'd seen on the rocks by the lighthouse yesterday.

Last evening, concerned for his safety, she'd strolled along the boardwalk to check on him after her grocery run, and found him curled up and still sleeping it off. She'd even felt sorry for him, thinking he'd be stiff as a board and really hung over this morning. That is until she'd seen him come out onto the porch, pop the tab on a can of beer and drink half down without stopping. A little hair of the dog that bit you, apparently. Some people never learn.

Reaching up to unhook the fourth and last shutter, Briana wondered who the drinking fool making himself at home in Jeremy's house was. She'd never heard Jeremy speak of family or even mainland friends and found it difficult to connect the drunken stranger to the gentle man she knew.

None of her business, Briana decided as she freed one hook. Steadying that side, she worked on the other hook, trying to dislodge it so the shutter would release. But the metal was slightly rusty and being stubborn. One-handed, she pushed and poked at it, growing ever more frustrated as she balanced the heavy shutter with her other hand.

Annoyed, she gave the hook a mighty punch and it slipped free. But she lost her balance at the sudden shift of weight and the shutter slipped from her grasp. "Oh!" she yelled as she slammed onto the painted boards of the porch floor, quickly rolling sideways to keep from being hit by the unwieldy window covering as it fell with a loud clatter.

Seated on the open porch next door nursing a small glass of Maalox, Slade couldn't help hearing what sounded like a cry for help followed by a loud crash. He felt shaky and decidedly unneighborly; still his training was too deeply embedded to allow him to ignore the possibility of someone in distress. Sipping the chalky antacid, he slowly made his way over and entered the enclosed porch.

The woman rubbing her hip looked more embarrassed than hurt, Slade thought as he set his glass on a corner table before picking up the fallen shutter and setting it out of the way. "You all right?" he asked, offering her a hand up.

"I think so." His hand was big, calloused and strong, Briana thought as he helped her up. She found herself looking into eyes deep blue and noticeably bloodshot. "Thanks. I managed the first three, but this one got away from me."

Face to face with her, Slade did a double take. The resemblance was remarkable and quite startling. She was small and quite slender, but so were millions of women. But this one had the same honey-colored shoulder-length hair and her face was oval shaped just like the one that haunted his dreams. Yet it was the eyes that bore the most resemblance. They were a rich brown, flecked with gold, filled with pain and brimming over with sadness. Intellectually, Slade knew he was looking at a stranger, yet he felt an emotional jolt nonetheless.

Uncomfortable under his intense scrutiny, Briana frowned. "Is something wrong?"

"You remind me of someone." With no small effort, he

11

turned aside. "These are too heavy for a woman as small as you." He began stacking all four of the shutters near the door.

"Yes, well, my grandfather always took them down in early spring and put them back up in late fall. I arrived yesterday and decided to air out the place. The house has been closed up since he moved to Boston."

Just what his pounding head needed, a chatterbox neighbor. "I'm sure he appreciates you taking care of his place." He swung around, unable to resist studying her again. Of all the luck, flying three thousand miles and running into someone who's the spitting image of the woman he couldn't seem to forget.

"Actually he's in a nursing home now and . . ." Briana's voice trailed off as she remembered her last visit here in the spring. Gramp had already been slipping, having memory lapses, but he'd so enjoyed fishing with Bobby and strolling on the beach after dinner.

A sick grandfather was undoubtedly the reason there was such a sorrowful look about her, Slade decided. "Where do you want these?"

"I can manage from here, really." She hated being thought a helpless, hapless female.

"Where do these go?" he asked again, his patience straining.

Far be it from her to interfere with his macho image, Briana decided. "In the garage, if you don't mind." She held the porch door open for him as he picked up two shutters, then led the way around back, yanking up the garage door. "Over there will be fine," she told him, indicating a space in front of Gramp's blue Buick Riviera.

Briana stood aside as he walked past her with his heavy load, then waited while he went back for the others. She

12

was about to pull down the door after he finished, but he reached past her and yanked it shut himself. Apparently he thought her not only clumsy but totally inept to boot. "Thanks, I appreciate the help."

"No problem." Slade started back toward her porch, the pain in his stomach a sharp reminder. "I left my glass in there."

Following him, she glanced at the solid brick house next door. "Where's Jeremy? I haven't seen him around."

Slade paused at the porch steps. "Jeremy died about a month ago. He left his house and everything in it to me." Hearing himself say the words out loud still shocked him. He stepped onto her porch and picked up his glass, came back out.

"Died? I'm truly sorry to hear that." Briana remembered the last time she'd seen Jeremy on Easter week. He'd been teaching Bobby to play chess on his porch, their two heads bent over the board, one gray haired, the other so very blond. "How'd it happen? Had he been ill?"

"Heart attack, so they tell me. His lawyer phoned with the news." Uncomfortable with the conversation and with being here, he shifted his weight to the other foot. He wanted to go inside and lie down, try to get rid of his headache. But he found it difficult to turn his back on her stricken look. "Did you know him well?"

"Since I was a little girl. He was a real gentleman, unfailingly kind and very talented."

Everything he wasn't, Slade thought without rancor. Maybe if Jeremy Slade had stuck around and helped raise his son, things would have turned out a lot different. *He* would be different.

"Forgive me for prying, but we never heard Jeremy

13

mention anyone other than his Nantucket friends. You must have known him in another life."

So his father hadn't told his closest neighbor about him, not in all those years. Slade wished the knowledge didn't hurt so damn much. "You could say that. I'm his son, though I haven't seen him since I was ten."

Ten. There had to be a story there, Briana thought, but it was none of her affair. A private person who disliked personal questions from near strangers, she decided to drop the whole thing. If Jeremy's son wanted her to know more, he'd tell her himself. Instead, she glanced at the glass he held, the inside stained with some thick white liquid. "I see you've switched drinks."

About to walk away, Slade turned back. "How's that?"

"From beer. I ran across you yesterday while I was walking on the beach by the lighthouse. You were . . . napping on some rocks."

Terrific. She was even tracking his movements. "Yeah, I went there to be alone, to think. Guess it didn't work since you found me."

Chagrined, she nodded. "Point taken. I'll butt out."

"Good idea." Angrier than the incident called for, Slade marched up onto his father's porch and went inside, closing the door with a resounding thud.

So much for neighborliness, Briana thought as she walked to the front yard. From outward appearances, Jeremy's son had inherited none of the older man's gentle ways. Or good manners. However, she hadn't come here to make new friends.

She was here instead to let this tranquil island heal her, Briana reminded herself. As she looked around the familiar yard, memories washed over her. There was the picket fence she'd painted the summer she'd turned fourteen.

14

That had been half her lifetime ago, back when her grandmother had still been alive. How Briana had loved spending her school vacations on Nantucket. Even as a college student, she'd come often; then later as a new bride, she'd brought her husband to meet the grandparents she adored. Only Robert had been too restless to enjoy the peaceful island. After that first visit, she'd left him home and come with Bobby.

But now her grandmother was gone, and they'd finally had to put Gramp in a nursing home last month as Alzheimer's robbed him of his precious memories along with his dignity. And Robert and Bobby were gone, too.

So much sadness, Briana thought as she gazed at the drooping daffodils that her grandmother had taken such pride in. The porch steps were wobbly, the door didn't close quite right and the lovely gray paint was peeling off the wood shingles, the white off the shutters. Inside, there was a shabby, neglected feel to the house that had once been a proud and happy place. It seemed as if with the loss of its occupants, the heart had gone out of the home.

Briana knew just how that felt.

She let the sea breeze ruffle her hair and breathed in the clean, salty air. Her eyes were shadowed, her heart heavy and her smiles still infrequent. But yes, she'd made the right decision in coming here to the house her grandfather had built so long ago. The house where she'd always felt safe.

Lord only knew she hadn't been doing well lately in her Boston townhouse. Most days, she paced the rooms, restless and fidgety, unable to concentrate on her photography. Nights she pounded the pillows, fighting sleep, afraid her dreams would replay her worst nightmares. Dad had suggested a change of scenery, knowing how Briana loved

Nantucket, and she'd reluctantly agreed. Perhaps here, she'd find peace again. Perhaps here, she could come to terms with all that had happened, if that even was possible.

Maybe a walk into town would be good, past Brant Point Lighthouse to South Beach and on to Main Street. She'd clean up and change clothes, take a leisurely stroll, stopping in to reacquaint herself with some of the shopkeepers she'd visited often over the years. Perhaps she'd pop in for lunch at that charming little inn overlooking the ocean, the one that served tiny tea sandwiches and scones with clotted cream.

And, please God, perhaps the people and places along the way would distract her from the pain in her heart that was a living, breathing thing.